Praise for

EVERY OTHER WEEKEND

"A kaleidoscopic story about the complexities of modern love and the possibilities of starting anew. *Every Other Weekend* is a fast-paced, vividly imagined, and utterly absorbing novel."

—JASMIN DARZNIK,
New York Times best-selling author of *The Bohemians*

"It's hard to believe this is attorney-in-real-life Margaret Klaw's first novel. *Every Other Weekend* is written with the arms-flung-wide confidence of someone who has been paying very close attention to the always messy, sometimes funny, and never boring world of divorce. This delicious dissection of a good-on-paper family torn asunder will keep you happily reading well past your bedtime."

—CELIA RIVENBARK, *New York Times* best-selling author
of *Stop Dressing Your Six-Year-Old Like a Skank*

"So many things about *Every Other Weekend* blew me away. As I was reading, the characters' dilemmas followed me everywhere—into the shower, into my dreams, busting into my train of thought when I was supposed to be working. Few books have had that effect on me. *Anna Karenina* comes to mind, and the scope and depth of Klaw's novel is indeed Tolstoy-esque. *Every Other Weekend* smacks of intensely observed reality, made spellbinding and poignant by a very talented author. The ending will have you begging for more."

—CATHRYN JAKOBSON RAMIN,
New York Times best-selling author of *Carved in Sand*

"Margaret Klaw's debut novel, *Every Other Weekend*, achieves the very difficult, which is to offer a deliciously readable, rollicking tale that nevertheless explores the deeply tangled threads of domestic life. In her wry stew, made up of over-the-hill hipsters, gossiping yoginis, polyamorous millennials, aging dogs, and scared-of-the-dark kiddos, Klaw raises deep questions about love, loyalty, and justice in a world where there are no pure heroes and villains."

—LISE FUNDERBURG,
author of *Pig Candy* and *Black, White, Other*

"Margaret Klaw's debut novel, *Every Other Weekend*, is a clever, page-turning master class in blurred lines, moral ambiguity, and the complicated aftermath of divorce. Written from the perspective of an experienced family law attorney, *Every Other Weekend* tells the same story through the lens of the attorneys, friends, parties, witnesses, and children involved with staggering results, begging the question: when relationships break apart, how can we ever get to the whole truth and nothing but?"

—AMY IMPELLIZZERI,
author of *In Her Defense* and *I Know How This Ends*

"Incisive, smart, and page-turning, *Every Other Weekend* is much more than the story of a dissolving marriage. Klaw's keen observations, spot-on turns of phrase, and astute social commentary pepper this tale of an entangled community, half-truths, and outright lies. Perfect for fans of Liane Moriarty!"

—ANDREA J. STEIN, author of *Typecast*

"Jake Naudain, an aging wanna-be hipster in the tight-knit enclave of Greenwood, is at his wit's end: his wife wants a divorce, and the novel takes off on a face-paced, wildly entertaining romp that pokes fun at dog owners, yoga moms, and vegans, while digging deeper into the musings of a feminist lawyer who represents a self-absorbed, male privileged client. A refreshing read!"

—DEDE CUMMINGS, author of *The Meeting Place*

"A satiric, insightful, and thoroughly enjoyable look at the evolution and dissolution of an American family and the lies and truths we tell others and ourselves, from a powerful writer with a deep understanding of the chaos of modern life."

—JON MCGORAN, author of *Spliced* and *Drift*

———

Praise for

KEEPING IT CIVIL:

The Case of the Pre-Nup and the Porsche & Other True
Accounts from the Files of a Family Lawyer

"This book shows how today's cultural conflicts are played out in the lives of ordinary families in true-life cases that involve love, money, sex, betrayal, and power. Margaret Klaw's keen observations about the law and human nature are eye-opening and jaw dropping. A must-read!"

—LISA SCOTTOLINE,
New York Times best-selling author of *Come Home*

"A prominent family lawyer shines a light on the tumultuous and complex world of domestic relations law in the optimistic yet cautionary expose. Substantive yet accessible. . . this book accomplishes an admirable goal: to foreground the humanity in the halls of justice."

—*PUBLISHERS WEEKLY*, starred review

"Conversational, entertaining. . . informative and smart. . . an accessible description of an intricate field of law, examined in an open-hearted style."

—*KIRKUS REVIEWS*

"With a lawyer's mind and a writer's heart, Klaw brings a deeper understanding of the way cultural attitudes about sex, money, women and relationships influence the law—and vice versa."

—*PHILADELPHIA TRIBUNE*

Every

Other

Weekend

EVERY OTHER WEEKEND

A Novel

MARGARET KLAW

SHE WRITES PRESS

Published 2023
Printed in the United States of America
Print ISBN: 978-1-64742-479-4
E-ISBN: 978-1-64742-480-0
Library of Congress Control Number: 2022916244

For information, address:
She Writes Press
1569 Solano Ave #546
Berkeley, CA 94707

Book Design by Stacey Aaronson

She Writes Press is a division of SparkPoint Studio, LLC.

For Zoe and Robin, my "Greenwood" girls

TABLE OF CONTENTS

1

Judge Jones: *Naudain v. Naudain,*
October Term, 9:30 a.m.

"Your Honor, *Naudain v. Naudain,* number two on your list,
expedited custody trial," Melinda says, head swinging in the
direction of the court reporter as she leads the parties and counsel
into the well-ordered courtroom of the Honorable Andretta A.
Jones.

"Petitioner on this side," the judge's clerk continues, gesturing to Attorney Stephen Boyle.

Dear God, not him again, the judge thinks, reminded once
more how the vision she had crafted during the long, difficult
months of her campaign—the vision of a wise jurist presiding
over important and complex civil litigation, listening to well-
crafted arguments presented by seasoned attorneys—had been
quickly and utterly eclipsed by the grim reality of her assignment to family court. The building is dingy and crowded. Her
courtroom has fluorescent lighting and no windows. And so
many of the lawyers who appear before her are that scattered
type of solo practitioner who operate on the fly, wearing rumpled suits, and chewing gum while they negotiate deals in the
hallways. Stephen Boyle is a perfect example—loud and aggressive, with an annoying and disrespectful habit of wearing

cowboy boots in her courtroom. As Sheriff Bob had said to her court reporter after a previous Boyle appearance, "Out West, dude could get away with that. Guess he forgot he's in Philly."

Attorney Boyle and his client, a pretty blonde woman in a black dress, take their spots at counsel table on the left side of her courtroom. Attorney Ellen Ackerman, who is new to the judge's courtroom, is close behind with her client, a stylish young man wearing a slim dark suit and looking much like a lawyer himself—and a considerably more put-together one than Mr. Boyle, the judge notes. They must have made a handsome couple. Too bad.

After the Naudains promise to tell the truth, the whole truth, and nothing but the truth, so help them God, and counsel identify themselves for the record, Judge Jones looks over her glasses at Stephen Boyle. "Mr. Boyle, this is your petition, and you asked for an expedited hearing. I see that you've made allegations of a very serious nature against Ms. Ackerman's client about an incident involving one of the parties' children, and I expect that you'll be able to prove these allegations, or you wouldn't have made them. Please call your first witness."

"Absolutely, Your Honor," Attorney Boyle replies. "Lisa Naudain."

As Ms. Naudain takes the stand, the judge learns that the attractive witness is her neighbor, living only a few blocks from her in Greenwood. She does look familiar; perhaps their paths have crossed. At the nail salon? Or the dry cleaners? She can't quite place it. The Naudains are divorced. They have two daughters, twelve and eight years old, Elizabeth and Charlotte, who go back and forth between them on alternating weeks as does, apparently, the family dog. Ms. Naudain is a professional, a nurse practitioner working in women's health care. *A laudable field*, thinks the judge, wondering exactly what the scope of her responsibility is, when the action picks up in the courtroom as Attorney Boyle asks Ms. Naudain why she and her husband separated, causing Ellen Ackerman to jump to her feet.

"Objection," Attorney Ackerman says. "What possible relevance does this have to the allegations in Mr. Boyle's petition?"

"Counsel?" says the judge, turning toward Attorney Boyle. She put aside for later her thoughts about whether nurse practitioners actually deliver babies, and if they do, are they called midwives, and if so, does that require a different professional degree?

"Your Honor," Boyle says, "the sexual acts committed by Mr. Naudain in the presence of the child—"

"Counsel," interrupts Judge Jones, "any activity, sexual or otherwise, is merely alleged in your petition at this point. And tell me why questioning your client about the reasons she and her ex-husband separated has anything to do with that allegation? I am not holding a hearing on the demise of these parties' marriage. I don't care about that. I care about their children."

"Your Honor," Boyle responds, "I understand. However, it's important for the Court to consider a little of the background here, the issues which led my client to want to end her marriage to Mr. Naudain. They're directly relevant to the extremely poor parenting decisions alleged in our petition."

Jake Naudain, face flushed, leans forward and opens his mouth as if to speak. Judge Jones watches his lawyer quickly restrain him with a firm hand on his arm and whisper something into his ear. He slumps back down into his seat and glares at his ex-wife. Despite her mild pique in curiosity, the judge knows that her list of cases is too long to indulge it. On a different day, with a lighter list, she might allow that testimony. But this is not the day.

"Objection sustained," the judge says. "And remember, I'm going to need time to interview the children. They're here, right?"

"They're outside with their grandmother, Judge," says Boyle.

"Very well," says the judge. "Move on, Mr. Boyle."

"Ms. Naudain, let's move forward to this past September. Did something occur during one of Mr. Naudain's custodial weeks that caused you particular concern?"

"Yes. When they came home on Sunday night from their dad's, Charlie started telling me about—"

Attorney Ackerman jumps up again. "Objection, hearsay."

"Sustained," says the judge.

"But, Your Honor," pleads Boyle, "this is a custody case. I'm asking for some latitude here."

The judge sees Melinda look up from her desk on the side of the judge's bench, clearly knowing that Boyle's plea will result in one of her boss's favorite admonishments. Which, as if on cue, the judge proceeds to dispatch with gusto.

"Mr. Boyle, if by 'latitude' you mean ignoring the rules of evidence, the answer is no. The rules apply in this proceeding, just like every other proceeding in the Court of Common Pleas. The objection is sustained."

"And, ma'am," the judge says, turning toward Lisa Naudain, who looks confused and upset, "you can't tell us what your daughter said to you. Only what you yourself heard or saw."

Directing her gaze back to Attorney Boyle and adopting an appropriately stricter tone, the judge says, "Mr. Boyle, can you please move along to the allegations involving sexual acts in the presence of Charlotte, which are, I believe, the only reason we're here. You filed a petition with this Court making very serious allegations about Father's conduct, and that's why this case was scheduled on an expedited basis. That's why it was moved to the front of the line, so to speak, jumping ahead of many, many other parents who are waiting patiently for their cases to be heard. So please, get to the point right now, or I'm going to reschedule this as a regular modification hearing, which are being listed about six months out. And at that hearing, you will be free to present evidence about Father's alleged poor parenting or anything else you want. And who knows? After I hear all that testimony, I may in fact decide to change the custody schedule. But, Mr. Boyle," the judge says, intentionally raising her voice and leaning forward over the bench, "*that is not what we're here for today. Do I make myself clear?*"

"Yes, Your Honor," replies the plainly unrepentant Boyle. "No further questions for Ms. Naudain."

Stephen Boyle needs to be handled this way, thinks the judge. *He needs to be reined in. He's one of those attorneys who is used to running the show.* But not in her courtroom! Despite her disappointment at being relegated to the hinterlands of the judicial system, it is still a wonderful feeling to wear the robe and call the shots. How many Black women ever get to do that? And at age sixty-three, no less—to be in charge, to rule with a firm and fair hand?

And really, it isn't that bad. Once she had come to terms with her assignment, after she prayed on it and realized there was certainly God's work to be done in family court, the judge had rolled up her sleeves and set about doing it in as classy a way as possible. She had the dirty walls of her chambers painted a soothing shade of green. Every week, she has Melinda bring fresh flowers into her chambers—at the judge's expense, of course, not on the taxpayer's dime! And in her courtroom, she does her best to maintain high standards. She may not be able to stop Stephen Boyle from wearing cowboy boots, but she can and will refuse to tolerate legal laziness.

"Cross-examination," the judge says, nodding in Ms. Naudain's direction and settling back into her seat.

Ellen Ackerman looks up from her legal pad, smiles reassuringly at her client, and turns toward his ex-wife. "Ms. Naudain," she says, "it was your decision to end your marriage to my client, wasn't it?"

"Objection!" shouts Stephen Boyle. "Your Honor ruled that this testimony wasn't relevant!"

"Overruled," says the judge. "This is cross-examination. And please, lower your voice. You may answer the question, Ms. Naudain."

Under cross-examination, the judge hears Ms. Naudain acknowledge that she initiated the parties' divorce, that she and Mr. Naudain agreed not to put the children in the middle of their conflict, that Mr. Naudain willingly moved out of the marital residence, and that they never considered anything other than the joint custody schedule they currently have. Then Attorney Ackerman, whose calm and methodical approach really is quite impressive, the judge notes, starts to ramp it up a bit.

"Ms. Naudain, you were upset that Mr. Naudain didn't tell you before he introduced the children to his girlfriend, right?"

"Yes, because I think that's a major decision, and he should have talked to me about it."

"Would you agree with me, Ms. Naudain, that reasonable parents might disagree over the best way to handle that situation?"

"Not really. He should have talked to me."

"It's a hard adjustment when your ex-spouse gets involved in a new relationship, isn't it?"

"Not really."

"It can be painful, can't it?"

"Objection," says Attorney Boyle. "Calls for speculation. How would Ms. Naudain know what other people experience? And it's beyond the scope of direct examination."

"I agree," says Judge Jones, although she was, truth be told, curious to hear Ms. Naudain's answer. "Objection sustained. Ms. Ackerman, you've made your point. Can you please wrap this up? I'd like to interview the children before the lunch break."

"Understood, Your Honor. Just a few more questions and I'm done. Ms. Naudain, you just testified that you and Mr. Naudain should discuss important issues involving the children, right?"

"Yes."

"But you didn't call him after your seven-year-old daughter supposedly told you she . . . let me find the exact language in the petition you filed, Ms. Naudain . . . here it is. When Charlotte allegedly told you that she was in bed with Mr. Naudain and his—now I'm quoting directly—'naked paramour' and she allegedly saw them engaged in, quoting again, 'multiple acts of sexual conduct'?"

"No. Because I knew he would lie."

"You knew that without even speaking to him?"

"Yes."

"You were so sure of what a seven-year-old told you, that you filed this petition against her dad, looking to take all meaningful custody time away from him, without even talking to him?"

"Yes."

"You didn't want to hear his side of the story, did you?"

"I didn't need to."

"No further questions, Your Honor."

2

~

Jake: Marriage, One Year Ago

It was a Saturday night, and Lisa and I were getting ready to go to this dinner party at Tom and Aly's house with two of the docs she worked with at the hospital. For some reason, she was really jazzed up about this event, like instead of just bringing a bottle of wine, which is all Aly asked us to bring, she insisted on bringing a dessert. And then, instead of picking up some Häagen-Dazs and strawberries or something, like we usually did, she spent the whole afternoon making these elaborate cannoli-like things, which was unusual for her. And when it was almost time to go, she was still upstairs taking forever deciding what to wear. Which somehow caused her to conclude that it was critically important that we, meaning me because she was still trying on outfits, clean up the living room before the babysitter showed up. Which made no sense, but whatever. She was right about it being a mess—the girls' shit was all over the place, and I did almost trip over Charlie's backpack, which had been lying on the floor in front of the couch. So I did as I was told.

Actually, I've always loved my girls' backpacks. I loved the pink, grimy surface of Charlie's, with the klatch of Disney princesses all sitting together in their frilly prom-dress garb. And inside, the window into her little life: the second-grade homework folders covered in drawings of cats, the pencil case shedding its pink glitter, the fraying hair scrunchies she wore for gymnastics, and the empty bag of Fritos she got from some kid in the cafeteria whose parents packed him that junk for lunch. I loved Elizabeth's too, although this was around the time she started not wanting me to open it because she was beginning to have those secrets that I guess middle school girls have with their friends—about what, I really had no clue. Teasing other girls? Or boys, maybe? It was weird, but I felt a faint, tiny ping of pride about her being so pretty and thinking about boys being attracted to her. I know dads are not supposed to feel that way; at least, all the dads I hung out with made jokes about locking their daughters up when they got to be teenagers. Not literally of course— they're not Neanderthals or anything—but it's, like, a guy thing to say you can't stand the idea of your daughter being with a guy. Because you are a guy, and you know what you were like, and it's disgusting when you imagine some other guy thinking about your daughter that way.

That's how it's supposed to be anyway, and I said the same thing when the subject came up with other dads at the Greenwood soccer league or whatever. But if I were being honest with myself, it really wasn't quite that way for me. I mean, yes, I lusted after girls starting around age twelve, but I was also terrified of them and sort of worshipped them from afar. They seemed to have so much power. They could bestow a look or a nod, and I was just like this helpless, tongue-tied idiot. So when I think of those early relationships, if you can even call them that, with girls, I think of the girl having all the power. And that's how I saw Elizabeth. She's always had all the power.

She changed Lisa's and my world completely, and she pretty much dictated how our lives were lived the second she was born. Lisa and I used to joke about feeling like servants, catering to her needs. Like, I remember recently helping Elizabeth with her math homework in the dining room, and she was complaining to me about something Lisa was making for dinner. Lisa overheard it and yelled from the kitchen, "Sorry, the staff didn't get the request in time." This made me laugh but of course totally infuriated Elizabeth, who honed right in on the fact that we were making fun of her and stomped off to her room. Anyway, it seemed natural to me that she would continue to wield the power vis-à-vis some poor seventh grade boy who played clarinet in the concert band with her, or whatever.

Lisa called down to me, again asking if I had picked everything up, and I thought how, in some ways, nothing had changed that much for me since I was twelve. I was a little scared of Lisa, and I did sort of worship her. I knew she had plenty of flaws—she could be bossy and impatient with me when I didn't feel like doing something she wanted to do. She had a terrible sense of direction and this annoying habit of constantly getting lost, and things like that. But still, when I would see her in public, from a distance, and she would come walking toward me with that rolling gait she has and her pretty smile and that streaky blonde hair swinging around her face, I couldn't believe my good fortune that this beautiful woman was my wife. It sounds really corny when I say it, but that is how I felt. And it wasn't just that she was beautiful; she was so fucking competent. That was the scary part. She took care of all these women and teenage girls at the clinic, she was an amazing cook, and she's got a beautiful voice —she sings killer harmony. And she was constantly volunteering for things, like working at the community garden, or being on the board of this breastfeeding advocacy group, or going on the girls' trips at school. And back then, she was chair of some nurse practitioner group that seemed to meet constantly. Sometimes I felt like a total deadbeat by comparison, because I was happy if I could make it to band practice.

My bandmates, Petie and Earl, liked to bitch about their wives nagging them to fix things around the house and all that, and I would join in sometimes. But really, I didn't mind that much when Lisa bugged me to do something, because she was usually right about it, although I still did not get why we had to clean up the living room for the teenage babysitter. No question—married life had its up and downs. Sometimes we did fight about things, like when she had her friend Kate from college, who I can't stand, stay with us for three weeks while she looked for an apartment; how much time I spent at band practice; and what we spent money on. But really, when it came down to it, I was basically a very happy guy.

I was kicking Pinky's dog bed into the corner of the living room when Lisa finally came downstairs, wearing this sexy, black, peasanty sort of shirt. *Wow*, I thought for the gazillionth time. "Ready to go?" she asked.

3

Lisa: Marriage, One Year Ago

When Aly first invited Jake and me to her and Tom's house for dinner, I thought it was just going to be the four of us. I figured it would be fun, because we'd gotten together as couples before. I knew that Jake would be able to talk to Tom about music, and I wouldn't need to worry about him checking out or being irritated by an evening of shoptalk about women's health care. But that Thursday at work, Aly told me that Andrew and Brad and their wives were coming as well. I saw those docs on our clinic days at the hospital, but we'd never socialized outside of work. Brad I've known for a while—we went through the pandemic together—but Andrew had just started a couple of months before, and he and I had really connected. He had set up this mobile pediatric clinic in Haiti. He got the grants for it and everything, and he took these regular trips down there to volunteer—so impressive. But the minute I heard they were coming, I started to worry about Jake. Or, to be more accurate, not really "worry" about Jake but about how I would feel about Jake in that context. How would Jake appear to them? What would doctors who worked so hard, who had successfully pushed through long, grueling years of medical school and residency, who were ambitious and smart and energetic, think of Jake?

This was not a new feeling, just a different iteration of one that had become distressingly common over the previous year or so. If I was being brutally honest with myself—which should be a no-brainer, but it's not always easy—on a fundamental level, I was disappointed by who Jake had become, or not become.

And it wasn't just about his job. I mean, he had finally left the bike shop and started working at his friend Jim's business, and I tried to be supportive and put a good face on that. But I knew whenever I said, "Jake's in IT with this start-up," or however I described it to other people, I'd consciously try to make it sound like a bigger deal than it was. Because basically, it was pretty low-level. He didn't supervise anyone or really have much responsibility, as far as I could tell. And I was pretty sure that he only got that job because Jim was his buddy from college, and they used to get stoned together and cruise around the club scene in Boston. And because—no doubt about this—Jake was an asset to Jim's office culture in terms of the cool factor. He has that hipster vibe, he can talk to anyone, he plays in a band, he wears great shoes. That's the stuff Jake is good at, but it wasn't enough for me anymore. That's what was keeping me up at night: Jake was going nowhere. All the energy to move things forward for us and the girls, as well as most of the money, had to come from me. Heading into middle age, it was increasingly clear that I was the driver, and Jake was just along for the ride.

When I went upstairs to get dressed for the dinner party, the anxiety about Jake was swirling around in my head to the point of major distraction. I had to get myself together, so I employed a strategy I'd recently found to deal with negative thoughts about Jake: I took myself back to the first time I saw him. All these years later, it was a memory that still had the power to excite me. It still made me catch my breath and squeeze my thighs together. Familiar and shopworn as it might have been, it delivered instant relief, like an epidural. At least briefly.

I'm twenty, sitting in my statistics section, 8:30 in the morning, with a group of bewildered psychology majors. It's one of those still-hot September days in Boston, and I'm wearing an olive-green halter top that makes my breasts look perfect. I wish they still looked like that, and I wish I could still wear that top. The door opens, and in walks this guy wearing a beat-up Jimi Hendrix T-shirt and carrying a guitar case. Everyone turns to look at him, because he's late and because most people don't bring musical instruments to early-morning statistics class. I would have been embarrassed to make such a conspicuous entrance, and I would have worried that the TA would be annoyed. But Jake did not appear to have any such concerns. He just smiled at everyone, slipped into the empty seat next to me, tucked the guitar case underneath, and gave me this conspiratorial look like, "We all know this is bullshit, right?" I didn't think it was bullshit. I actually liked statistics. And I generally disapproved of people showing up late. But Jake had this casual, drapey elegance about him, this air of confidence, and this head of beautiful thick, dark, shaggy hair. So at the end of class, when he asked me if we could study together for the exam ("Please," I could still hear him say, "I'm fucked otherwise"), I said of course. But all I could think about was his hands on my bare skin, taking off my green halter top and dropping it on the floor.

And that was it. I helped him with statistics, we started sleeping together, he passed the exam. He was like no one I'd dated before. He was sexy and strong, very male but not in a macho way. He was a psychology major. He told me he wanted to work with kids. He had zero interest in sports, a welcome contrast to every male member of my family and every boy in my high school. He lived in an apartment instead of a dorm. He knew how to cook. He made me coq au vin and spaghetti carbonara.

I could have gone on and on with this catalogue, flipping forward through our early days and years, but I didn't need to. The statistics-class snapshot was enough to settle me down, to put Jake back into a frame where I could desire him. I took a deep breath, went over to the full-length mirror on the door of our bedroom closet, tried on three pairs of jeans, and picked the tightest ones. I put on bronze eyeshadow and my flowy black top with the perfect neckline. When you've only spent time with people while wearing scrubs, you have some catching up to do.

At the party, I chatted with the wives a bit but ended up talking mostly to the docs. I already knew about Andrew's Haiti project, but I learned a lot more details about how he started it, about the Haitian doctor and nurses he worked with, about the little town way up in the country outside of Port-au-Prince where they did a massive number of vaccinations, and about how the church up there opened its sanctuary to him and his team so they could sleep in the pews. And Brad, it turned out, was this serious athlete who'd done five Ironmans. I couldn't even begin to imagine how he found the time to train for them. And he also coached his fourth-grader's baseball team.

While absorbing these interesting facts about my colleagues, what I was really thinking about was what it would be like to be married to one of them, or any other guy like them. They gave off this sense of being in command of the world around them. The point wasn't the specifics of what either one did; it was that, in their lives, they make things happen, which was such an aphrodisiac. They, of course, make a lot more money than Jake, which would certainly make my life easier. But it wasn't just that, either. It was the totality of what they represented, how they made me feel about the choices I've made in my life, that was churning me up.

When I looked over at Jake, who was flirting outrageously with Andrew's overly made-up wife, Angela—that is something he definitely is good at—I was struck by a vision of my life going forward in perpetuity with this man who had no ambition, who made no decisions, who would never surprise or thrill or impress me. And right there, at that moment, sitting in Aly's dining room, as the predictable social dance of a Saturday night dinner party swirled around us, all the anxiety and unhappiness that had been bubbling away deep within my psyche shot up to the surface of my consciousness and exploded in my brain in a silent blast of terrifying, liberating clarity.

4

Jake: Hit by a Truck

So we went to the dinner party, and the docs both seemed like nice guys—crazy type A people, of course. One of them was this serious triathlon dude. The other ran some clinic in Haiti and went down there every other month in addition to his full-time gig at the hospital and having three kids, and so on and so on. But they were fine. I chatted with Mr. Ironman about what music he listens to when he trains. Mr. Haiti's pretty wife, Angela, works in IT, so she and I were trading working-with-software-nerd stories. I remember feeling kind of wry and charming. Angela was laughing at my jokes, and we were flirting a little in that incredibly mild and safe way you can do when happily married couples are socializing—no risk of anything happening. Just a little sexual heat to juice up your evening, and then you go home and have hot sex with your wife, or in her case, with Mr. Haiti.

But that could not be further from what ended up happening. Instead, I got back from driving the babysitter home, and when I walked into the kitchen, Lisa was stomping around, pulling containers of leftovers out of the refrigerator and throwing them into the sink. I asked her what was wrong, and she wouldn't answer me or even look at me; she just kept on stomping and throwing. Her vibe was so hostile that even Pinky seemed to sense it, because he jumped off his spot on the sunporch sofa and ran upstairs. I asked her again what was going on, and then it happened. This diatribe came pouring out—gushing, actually, like a flood. It seemed like it had been memorized and rehearsed weeks, or maybe months, earlier. It was like she had figured it all out and tucked it away, waiting for a time and place to release it on its unsuspecting target—me.

This is what Lisa said: she was unhappy with our marriage, and she had been for a year. We had been "growing apart" and had "different goals." When I asked her what she meant by that, she told me that she wanted to do new things and take on new challenges and move forward, and that I didn't seem to care about that, that I was content just to work at my not-that-exciting job and play the same songs with the same guys in the same band. She made me sound like such a loser. And she didn't come out and say this, but obviously, I was being compared to Mr. Ironman and Mr. Haiti. Obviously, the apparently excruciating experience she had just undergone, of seeing her underachieving husband displayed in stark contrast to the overachieving doctors, had something to do with this. So I asked her—how could I not?—if she was having an affair with one of them, or with someone else. She took great offense at that question. She said of course she wasn't, she wouldn't do that, and it wasn't anyone else —it was me. I was the problem, which is probably worse. I don't know, but I think it is.

I asked her if this had anything to do with the financial issues we'd disagreed about in the past, basically our different attitudes about borrowing and spending, which I thought we had put behind us a long time ago. She said no, it was much deeper than that. She told me she'd been thinking and thinking about this, and she just didn't see how our marriage was going to work, because of our "different values." And then I said I had no idea she'd been feeling this way for a year. In the previous twelve months, we'd been raising our kids, and working on our house. We'd been lying in bed late at night, in the dark, talking about our days, and having sex early on Sunday mornings before the girls woke up. I said that I had no clue whatsoever that she was plotting this mutiny. She accused me of being unobservant and so into my own head that I hadn't noticed that she'd been unhappy. She said I hadn't noticed that she was spending more time with her girlfriends, and that I hadn't noticed that we'd been doing things separately with Elizabeth and Charlie more and more often. Basically, she chastised me for not noticing that she had been going through a deep existential crisis about our marriage. But how the fuck was I supposed to know, when she hadn't even bothered to talk to me about it?

And then, as I sat there in the living room, feeling like I was watching a movie of someone else's life, she started talking about the logistics of divorce. I couldn't believe it. She expected me to absorb the flood and then respond when she switched into this sort of practical mode, like we were having a discussion about whether to refinance the mortgage or something. She said she was thinking that she would move out, that I could stay in the house, that she'd get a place really close by, and that, of course, we'd have joint custody of the girls. Because after all, I was a great dad, and she wouldn't want to do anything to keep me from seeing them—as though that were even an option. And then that was it. Just like that, fourteen years of marriage tied up in a package and thrown away like some obsolete product we could no longer use, like a VCR, or the girls' old bunk beds.

It was during the aftermath of this flood that it really started to hit me that my marriage had just ended, right then and there. She didn't ask for counseling, or a trial separation, or anything like that. She had been planning this for a year, she'd figured out what she wanted, and she already had one foot out the door. Lisa had decided our fate, and I had no choice in the matter. At the time, all I could offer up was the pathetic statement that I was going to bed and that she wasn't welcome in the bedroom.

"Fine," she said. "We'll talk more about this tomorrow." Then she got up, went into the guest room, and closed the door.

When I woke up on Sunday morning, the first thing I was aware of was that Lisa wasn't in bed with me, and for a nanosecond, I thought she must have gotten up early to go for a run. And then the previous night came crashing down on me. My mother always uses the expression "I feel like I've been hit by a truck" when she feels bad, like when she's sick or when something upsetting has happened. It's always bothered me, because it's such a cliché and also usually totally out of proportion to whatever she's complaining about. But that's the image that popped right into my head and stayed there as I put the pillow over my face and made a ridiculous attempt to go back to sleep: the your-marriage-is-over truck just ran me down on I-95, and I was lying there, flat on the pavement, like a cartoon character.

The flattened-on-I-95 me was simultaneously thinking about the end of my world and how I was going to act when I got myself up and out of the bedroom and encountered my wife. She had said we would talk more about it the next day, but how could we? The girls were home, and we were going to have to pretend like everything was normal. Lisa usually made pancakes or something special for breakfast on Sunday mornings, and we would all sit down together, the one morning that breakfast was actually a family meal. And afterward, sometimes she and I would walk down the street to the Green Life Café, grab coffee, and gossip with our neighbors.

What was I going to find on the other side of the wall? Would she be ladling pancake batter onto the skillet and chatting with our pajamaed daughters, who would likely be zoned out in front of various screens, only halfway listening—a scene so ordinary, I had never thought about it twice and that all of a sudden seemed just heartbreaking? I actually felt an ache in my chest. How could she do this to them? How could she drop this bomb on innocent civilians? Why should her midlife crisis be allowed to wreak havoc on three other people, all of whom she was responsible for? I mean, she wasn't responsible for me, but she was responsible for making the decision to marry me, back before she decided we had "different values." And she was definitely responsible for our children.

When I finally dragged myself out of bed, it was just like I imagined. Lisa was making waffles, and the girls were watching TV. She actually said good morning to me—as if she hadn't rendered that completely impossible. I knew it was childish, but I didn't answer her. I instantly realized I could not face sitting down to a meal with her and the girls right then—I just didn't think I could hold it together. And we certainly weren't going to be strolling down to the café afterward—like, never again, in fact. And to make it all even worse, it was a beautiful October day. The leaves were turning; the sun was shining. It was that sort of weekend where everyone was happily enjoying time with their families. The whole scene was just surreal. Pinky was hovering around me, so I went for the quickest excuse I could think of. "I'm taking Pinky to the park for a run," I said and started gathering up some old tennis balls. Lisa didn't argue with me, didn't try to convince me to stay for waffles. I'm sure she was relieved. Charlie was way off in TV land, and Elizabeth had switched over to Lisa's iPad. Nobody noticed, nobody cared, so I put the bouncing Pinky on his leash and took off for the Greenwood dog park.

My band, Man With a Dog, rehearses on Sunday afternoons at four at Petie's house. Petie is the drummer, and he has a house with a basement that used to be a speakeasy during Prohibition and later on got switched over to an after-hours club. It still has the old bar in the corner and a couple of booths and this fading, red, flocked wallpaper. And it's soundproofed. We all agree that it's the perfect man cave and rehearsal space; there could not be a better spot. I leave one of my electric guitars and an amp there during the week. I looked forward to band practice, especially at that time when we were just starting to play out, which made our rehearsals way more focused—and because Petie and Lee, who plays bass, are really my closest friends in Greenwood. The three of us met when our kids were all at the same preschool. Moonbeam prides itself on diversity of every type—racial, ethnic, sexual orientation, gender nonconforming, whatever—but you'd be crucified for letting your three-year-old anywhere near a screen of any type, or sticking a piece of candy in her lunch box. Which was exactly why Lisa was so into it—she totally bought into all those rules, and I just kind of went along with it.

After our kids all left Moonbeam, they ended up at the same school. Our rhythm guitarist, Earl, lives in North Philly and used to play professionally. We were able to nab him because he stopped playing altogether for a while—not sure what the deal was there—and wanted to get back into gigging, even though the pay for the ones we'd booked at that point barely covered our parking. You can tell Earl's a pro. He can pick anything up really fast, and he also sings decent harmony. I play lead, most of the time anyway. It's really working out. We all get along, and we have lots of synergy, musically.

So the point is, these guys were and are my refuge, not that I ever thought I'd need a refuge. But that day, the day after I was hit by the your-marriage-is-over truck, and after I got back from throwing the ball for Pinky at the dog park and dropping Elizabeth off at the bowling alley for her friend's birthday party, I just wanted to be with them. I didn't plan to say anything about what happened. But when I got there, Petie said, "Hey, man, what's goin' on?"

My intention was to say, "Not much," or whatever, but it just didn't come out that way. I said, "Things aren't great," or something like that.

Lee, who's divorced and was in the thick of the dating scene, said, "How could anything be wrong, Jakie, with a hot wife like yours?"

And I just kind of lost it. I didn't go into detail about the "different values" or anything else she said, but I told them the important thing. I told them, "Last night, Lisa said she wants a divorce. And she's been thinking about it for a year."

They were pretty stunned, because I was, like, Mr. Happily Married in that group. They just said they were sorry and stuff, but they also totally closed ranks around me, which I really appreciated. They gave me a beer, and Petie gave me a big hug, and the three of them were shaking their heads and going, "Man, that's rough." And then I told them that she already started talking about how it was going to work, like it's a done deal, and how "of course" we'll have joint custody of the girls. I was just saying it to show how cold she was, that she would go there right away, but Lee jumped right in on that topic.

"That's good," he said. "Good that she won't fight you on custody. And if she makes more than you, she'll have to pay you child support too."

I couldn't believe that less than twenty-four hours after I learned my marriage was over, I was engaging in a conversation about child support, but that's exactly what was happening.

Petie said, "Is that right? Even if they have the kids fifty-fifty?"

And Lee said, "Yeah, it is. And you should get yourself a lawyer."

5

Ellen: Initial Consultation

The morning routine at the law firm was already well underway when Ellen Ackerman finally found her keys in the bottom of her bag and let herself in the office door. Keeping the front door locked was always a bit of an annoyance but necessary. Ellen and her partners had decided this after a particularly creepy in-person visit from the disgruntled ex-spouse of one of their clients. He had walked into the office ranting about his ex-wife stealing money out of the mouths of their children and refused to leave until they called building security. And just recently, another creepy guy had called demanding to speak to Ellen's partner. When the receptionist asked the caller's name, the man screamed, "Just put that fucking bitch on the phone!" Which, of course, the receptionist did not. But she did identify him by a reverse lookup of the number he had called from, which turned out to be his dog-walking business in Manhattan.

It always amazed Ellen, who spent so many of her waking hours dealing with the dark, emotional underside of people's lives, that most of the time, those same people were presenting a completely different face to the world: a mild, quotidian one, the personality equivalent of the dominatrix's day job. They chatted with coworkers over morning coffee; they picked up their dry cleaning; they went to Back to School Night. And no one saw the stuff she knew about. No one knew that they went home and stayed up into the wee hours watching porn on their laptops with a compulsion they felt powerless to control, or that on their lunch break they would drive down to the badlands of Kensington to score heroin, or that they had a fetish about leather bustiers, or that during office hours at the university they were having sex with their students in the hallway closet. But such is the lot of the family lawyer, Ellen had come to know: they see the messy stuff.

After greeting her paralegal and dropping her bag in her office, Ellen made straight for the coffee. She was tired, the result of a late and stressful night editing her daughter's college essays, an activity problematic on so many levels, such as the possible inappropriateness of doing so at all. There was also the embarrassing fear that if she didn't, Marni would have no chance of getting into Wesleyan or Swarthmore or any of her top choices. She would be relegated to State School, an idea that bumped up against the rational recognition that there was nothing wrong with State School—think of the money she and Dan would save!

All these thoughts jumbled up in a ball, but the psychic heft of this ball was significantly outweighed by the pleasure of the fantasy that had played out repeatedly in her head last night. In this fantasy, she was waiting for yoga class to start at the gym, or standing in line at the Greenwood food co-op, and she casually dropped into the conversation, "Got to take Marni back to school this weekend—hate that drive to Middletown!" And in this fantasy—which happened to be marked by a high degree of social acumen, as far as Greenwood is concerned—no fellow yogi or co-operator would think that Ellen was bragging, because she hadn't even mentioned the name of the school. And because on its face, the expression of displeasure at the prospect of a long drive up the New Jersey Turnpike to anywhere was a reliable topic over which to bond with fellow Philadelphians.

And yet, the task was still accomplished, stealthily. The reference point was given to those in the know, those other parents of students at independent high schools whose children hadn't yet run the college admissions gamut; those parents of former students at independent high schools whose children had run that gamut and came in below (because of course, most of them would, given how hard it is to get into Wesleyan); and those few other parents whose children attended schools of similar desirability. All those parents would get the reference. They would catalogue it, they would be impressed (or would be reminded of how impressive their own children were), and they would think admiringly of Ellen and Dan and Marni. They would quietly, maybe even unconsciously, move the Ackerman family up, or welcome them into, that particular social status box reserved for families with successful children.

Coffee mug in hand, Ellen opened up her computer and surveyed the day's calendar. It was light. She had a phone conference with Marjorie Levy at eleven to discuss changes she wanted to make to the draft Ellen wrote of her divorce settlement (which would take a long time, because Marjorie never understood what Ellen told her without having it explained three times). There was a lunch meeting with her partners to discuss their new website, which had become a stubbornly elusive project to complete. And at 3:00 p.m., there was a consultation with a new client, which appeared to be a Philadelphia County divorce case, referred to her by a Greenwood neighbor.

In the firm, there was envious joking among her partners that Ellen got all the cases they'd dubbed "Greenwood divorces." This was shorthand for that certain type of contemporary twenty-first-century uncoupling in which both parties were highly motivated to approach divorce collaboratively, aspired to work out their own agreements, assumed that they will have joint custody of their kids, and realized that they needed to have a working relationship with one another in the future. Ellen loved these cases. First of all, the clients were her peers and often became her friends. Second of all, these highly evolved aspiring ex-spouses—who might be public interest lawyers or academics or playwrights, and usually did actually hail from the progressive living rooms of Greenwood—tended to want to use Ellen's skills and expertise in more of an advisory role rather than as command and control, so the cases were usually characterized by a low level of conflict.

All of these attributes made for cases that were good for Ellen's mental health, as opposed to those that threatened to destabilize it. Ellen could do conflict as well as the next divorce lawyer. She actually loved the inside of a courtroom, and she used to frequently find herself full of righteous indignation at the parade of horribles inflicted upon her clients by their exes. But at this point in her life, after doing this type of work for over twenty years, that spark had become way slower to ignite. She had grown weary of listening to the complaints of her clients about things she could not fix, and, increasingly, she found herself getting irritated with them, especially when it came to conflicts over custody. *Grow up*, she found herself thinking more and more. *Be the parent, suck it up, and shield your child from all this.* So another Greenwood divorce case was always welcome, and the consultation with the new client appeared as a pleasant event on the horizon of her workday.

Angst about the college-admissions process fading, Ellen retrieved Marjorie Levy's file and reacquainted herself with the settlement agreement she had previously drafted. She tried to figure out a new and more effective way to answer Marjorie's inevitable question, asked every time they'd met or spoken, about why she is not getting more money as compensation for

her husband's numerous—and, Ellen had to agree, very icky—
marital infidelities.

It was 2:45 p.m., and Ellen had not eaten lunch. She had envi-
sioned a pleasant, manageable workday. There would be a gentle
stroll through the billable hours, speaking with clients she liked,
dispensing sound advice that would be appreciated, absorbed,
and paid for. This would be followed by a mildly interesting but
ultimately low-stakes debate with her partners about the merits
of including a testimonials page on their new website—tacky, or
good contemporary business practice?—over salads in the conference room. The day had taken a drastically wrong turn around
noon, when she received a call from opposing counsel in one of
her custody cases. Stephen Boyle was a lawyer Ellen particularly
disliked, as he seemed constitutionally incapable of not treating
everything his client told him as the gospel truth. Boyle was calling to tell her that he was standing in the family court clerk's
office filing an emergency custody petition in the Patel case. He
was asking the court to prevent Ellen's client from taking the
parties' ten-year-old son to California for her sister's wedding,
alleging that there was no wedding and that it was all a ruse to
move the kid permanently to California.

"You better get down here," he said. "I'm emailing you our
petition right now. They just took it upstairs to the emergency-
motions judge."

This was a classic Boyle move. If there was an issue about a
trip to California for a family wedding—which Ellen knew nothing about, and why would she?—why didn't he call her to discuss it? Why spend his client's money drafting and filing an
emergency petition when maybe this could have been worked
out with a phone call?

So Ellen had to call her client, the lovely Asha Patel. She, of course, had no plans to move to California and was indeed taking the parties' son to her sister's wedding in Los Angeles over the weekend. Ellen had to now hoof it over to court, sit in the emergency judge's crowded courtroom for over an hour until the case was called, get Asha on the phone to testify, and have a mini-hearing before Judge Ramsey. The judge promptly denied the petition and scolded Stephen Boyle for wasting the court's time when he could have avoided the whole proceeding, had he done a minimal amount of investigation into the veracity of his client's story.

Ellen, furious about what she considered to be a total abuse of the judicial process and encouraged that Judge Ramsey seemed to be on her side, made an oral motion on the spot for sanctions against both Dr. Patel and Attorney Boyle in the form of a fine paid to the court and payment of her fees. But Judge Ramsey refused to grant the motion, leaving Ellen only with the satisfaction of hearing the judge scold her opponent. She felt put-upon and irritated because really, in the end, Dr. Patel got what he wanted. He was able to harass his ex-wife by making her think their son might end up missing her sister's wedding and by forcing her to pay her lawyer to defend a petition he must have known to be false. Whatever the price Dr. Patel had to pay Stephen Boyle, Ellen was pretty sure he considered it money well spent.

By the time she got back from court, hungry and cranky, Ellen had fifteen minutes before the referral from her neighbor was scheduled to come in for an initial consultation. She grabbed a handful of mini chocolate bars from the perpetually full candy jar perched so invitingly on her office manager's desk, washed them down with cold coffee, and applied lipstick. She removed all the piles of documents from her desk, hiding them behind her chair on the floor. The illusion of spaciousness and calm was instantly created, an open blonde expanse of Ikea desktop, her office an empty vessel waiting to be filled with a new client's story, waiting to hum with the connection she would create with him, with the relationship that would evolve between them over the next hour or two and might carry forward for a year, or two years, or ten.

Walking into the reception area after she was told that her new client, Jake Naudain, had arrived, Ellen saw a man she knew —not the man himself, but the type. Greenwood was teeming with Jake Naudains, only not all of them were so good-looking, Ellen realized, as she closed in for the handshake. He was a fortyish hipster dad, with dark hair tousled but well-cut, designer or possibly designer-knockoff glasses, and a messenger bag that undoubtedly contained multiple Apple products. He wore black jeans and suede wingtips, that slightly ironic take on businessman shoes that Ellen was always wishing Dan would wear. Meeting new clients was just like speed dating, which of course Ellen had never tried, given the longevity of her one and only marriage, but which she knew for a fact she would if she ever found herself single again. Because don't you have a pretty good sense, with a remarkable degree of accuracy, as to whether you like someone (or at least don't like someone) within thirty seconds? So far, Jake was in the "like" category, and Ellen had every expectation he'd remain there.

When the office door was closed and the preliminary chit-chat concluded, some clients wanted to tell Ellen all the reasons they were getting, or were thinking about getting, divorced, and some did not. While a lengthy blow-by-blow account of the history of marital strife was not helpful in the no-fault Commonwealth of Pennsylvania—and could be a real time suck, especially if she was hungry or tired or overbooked—certain information about this topic was necessary. For example, who was pushing the divorce, and who was resisting? The resister holds the leverage in settlement negotiations, and the pusher may be willing to pay a premium to get it all over with. And in a case where children are involved, all skeletons in both parents' closets need to be taken out, dusted off, and examined. Alcoholism, drug use, criminal history, mental health diagnoses—Ellen needed to sift through this stew of human frailty, quickly identifying and discarding the irrelevant bits and taking note of items that might be important. She needed an inventory of those facts she might want to offer up, appropriately honed, in negotiations between counsel or to the judge at trial (mom drives the kids when she's drunk), or those about her client that needed to be protected from view if possible, minimized, and explained away (dad's treatment for sex addiction).

With Jake, there was no chitchat. He came in, sat down in Ellen's mid-century modern client chair across the calming blonde Ikea sea, took his laptop out of the messenger bag and opened it, and looked up. Before Ellen could even ask for his address, he declared, "I love my wife. I don't want any of this to happen. But it seems like she's made up her mind, and nothing I've said to her is going to stop it." Ellen made a mental one-eighty, going right to the issue of strategy. This would usually be a topic for discussion later in the consultation, after she knew the children's names and ages and where they went to school, after she knew the value of the 401(k) and the amount of the mortgage, and after she understood more about who the person was sitting in that chair. Was he happy at the prospect of being liberated from the tyranny of a bad marriage, guilty but consumed by the sexual passion of a new relationship, devastated about losing the love of his life, tearful, indifferent, nervous, calm, focused, scattered? Take your pick.

"Well, you're right," Ellen told him. "If she wants to get divorced, you can't stop it. All you can do is slow down the process and make her wait longer, but it's going to happen sooner or later. And even though I don't know any of the particulars about your case yet, as a general rule, you're better off if it happens sooner, because she's probably feeling badly right now about ending the marriage, which means she's likely to be more generous financially and more accommodating in terms of the kids. If you drag it out, you take the risk that those feelings will dissipate over time. Or that something will happen that could allow her to feel like you're the bad guy, to be angry at you. And you really do not want that. I can imagine that you're sad and hurt, and you may be thinking, 'Why should I make this easy for her when I don't want it?'"

Jake nodded.

She continued. "But you really need to be strategic about this, and in my experience, being cooperative is going to make it more likely that you'll come out of this with what you want."

Jake nodded again. "Well, I don't want any of it," he said, "but I hear you. And that's why I'm sitting here."

Changing direction, Ellen went back to the beginning. She learned that Jake and Lisa were still living together; that they owned their house, but it was mortgaged to the max; that they'd had some issues with debt in the past, which were now cleared up; and that Lisa earned more than Jake. She learned that even though initially Lisa told Jake he could stay in the house and she'd move out, realistically he couldn't afford it on his own. And their other property consisted of bank accounts with little in them, a couple of modest retirement accounts, an eight-year-old Toyota, and what Jake said Lisa referred to as his "toys"—several guitars and a very expensive custom-made bicycle that was his primary mode of transportation. *But of course*, Ellen thought.

"All I care about is Elizabeth and Charlie. She can have the house if she wants. I just want my girls," Jake said.

"Have you talked about what type of custody arrangement you think would work best?" Ellen asked.

"Not specifically, but Lisa would never try to take the girls away from me. She knows I'm a great dad, and she knows how bonded they are to me. And she's a really good mother too. So I'm sure we'll just split everything equally, you know, fifty-fifty. I don't think we're going to disagree about that. And I don't want any child support from her. I heard I could get it, because she makes more than me—is that true?"

"Yes," Ellen replied. "If you have them equal amounts of time."

Jake shook his head. "Yeah, that's what I heard. But I don't want that. I don't want her money. I just want the girls half the time. That's realistic, right?"

Ellen assured Jake that it was very realistic, after he told her about how involved he'd always been in caring for them and the flexibility of his work schedule. She also went through the skeletons-in-the-closet line of questioning, and there weren't any, unless you count recreational marijuana use, which Ellen absolutely did not. Parenting sins rise and fall with the culture, and at this particular moment in history, unless her client was smoking weed with his sixth grader or dealing large quantities of it out of the living room, Ellen did not expect it to factor into her cases. Certainly not in Philadelphia, anyway; maybe out in some of the more parochial counties where she ventured periodically, but not here, not on their home turf.

And so, a plan of action was formed, a plan Jake would propose to Lisa. Jake would move out but stay in Greenwood, preferably within walking distance of his current house. Lisa would keep the house and take over the mortgage. They would divide their accounts, continue to share the Toyota for now, and the girls would spend alternate weeks with each parent. And there was also a dog, Ellen learned, that the whole family was very attached to. Ellen suggested that the dog follow the kids, that he go back and forth between Lisa and Jake's households on the same schedule as the girls.

"That's perfect," Jake said. "We'll have joint custody of Pinky too. And if Lisa and I can work out the details of all this ourselves, you can just write it up, right?"

"Right," Ellen told him, "or Lisa's lawyer, if she has one."

"She doesn't," Jake said, "but I told her I was coming to see you, and she's fine with whatever you think is fair."

Ellen refrained from commenting on that. She did not want to rock that boat. She knew how delicate a balance this was. One side was motivated by guilt and not wanting to hurt the other any more than she already had, bending over backward to make him feel like he had control of the situation, even though of course he didn't. The other side was devastated but trying to do the right thing, trying to recognize the good in his wife even though she inexplicably didn't want to be married to him anymore. Both of them were trying, trying, hoping for the best. It had all the makings of a perfect Greenwood divorce, and if that balance held, Jake would be fine, and she would have very little work to do.

6

Jake: The Negotiation

It was so surreal, being in that lawyer's office, sitting across the desk from her, talking in this calm way about who was going to get the car and which nights the girls were going to spend with me. I couldn't believe it was really happening. I know it sounds like such an incredible cliché, but I really did keep waking up in the morning and thinking, for a second, that everything was normal and I must have dreamt the whole thing. But then I would see that Lisa wasn't next to me. She'd been sleeping on the futon in our study—which doubles as a music room, junk room, and guest room—ever since she dropped the bomb on me. The sickening reality would creep up from my toes and kind of settle in my stomach with a thud. Actually, the whole thing was a cliché, really; it felt so common and tawdry and so not what I thought Lisa and I were all about.

I had been smug about us. We are both good-looking people. When we were dressed up for a party, or both in sports clothes running errands, or in bathing suits and T-shirts headed to the beach in our expensive Ray-Bans with our two gorgeous daughters in tow, we give off—I should say, gave off—a whiff of glamour. We seemed successful and fun and fashionable. That may sound shallow, but it's there, and I ate it up, that feeling of being admired. But after Lisa unilaterally obliterated our marriage, in addition to my personal misery, there was an annoying public side of it, which is that I was embarrassed. By having our perfect marriage and family thing unravel, people who used to admire us were now going to pity us. Now they'd be the ones going home and having those conversations like Lisa and I used to have about other couples who got divorced, where we'd be all secure and cozy in our own happily married skins while we exchanged the gossip or whatever and speculated about why or who caused it or how it was going to affect their kids. Now it would be other couples, in kitchens and bedrooms all over Greenwood, who'd be having that conversation. One would say, as he takes off his clothes to get ready for bed or puts place mats on the table for dinner, "Hey, did you hear about the Naudains?" And the wife would say, "No, what?"

And the husband would reply, "They're splitting up."

And then the wife would turn around and face the husband, with a concerned look on her face, and say, "No! I never would have guessed. What happened?"

And the husband would answer, "I heard Lisa initiated it. Dunno what's going on there; maybe she's involved with somebody else?"

And the wife would mentally check the status of her own happy marriage for a second, just enough to distance herself from the marriage-incompetent Naudains, and respond, "Oh, poor Jake."

I know none of this should have mattered to me, but it did. It embarrassed me, and I felt embarrassed that it embarrassed me. The whole thing just completely sucked.

So when are we going to talk? That's the text I got from Lisa when I was at work, the day after I met with Ellen. When we were in the house, playing out this bizarre charade in front of Elizabeth and Charlie, she talked to me about normal kid stuff, like who was going to take Charlie to gymnastics, and how Elizabeth needed poster board for her science fair project, so would I pick it up at CVS? But the minute we ended up in a different room than the kids, her face would go into screen saver mode, like I had no access to any content, and she wouldn't talk to me. If she had anything to say about what was really going on, anything related to the topic of how she blew apart our marriage, that is, she texted.

She was right that we had to have that conversation, though, because I was not going to keep living like that. And I thought Ellen was smart, which she better be, at $450 an hour, when she told me that I had the advantage while Lisa felt guilty, which she should—that I was in a better position to get what I wanted right away than I might be later when Lisa had somehow managed to rewrite history to such an extent that she'd convinced herself I was an asshole. So I texted Lisa back that we could talk on Thursday night, after the girls were asleep, which gave me two days to mentally prepare, somehow. She said okay. Which in itself showed how guilty she must have felt, because normally if I suggested a time to do something, she had a reason why it wouldn't work and why it needed to happen a different time. And, annoyingly, she was usually right, because she remembered all the kids' activities, and I could never seem to keep that stuff straight, even though I strove to be the perfect dad who was involved in every aspect of his children's lives. I realized I would need to up my game in that department, given the joint custody plan. I couldn't give her any reason to try to mess with that.

Thursday at work, I was staring out the window at the industrial Philadelphia roof scape that spreads out to the north, ignoring the emails that were flowing into my inbox like so many determined salmon, and feeling like I was getting ready for my annual performance review with Jim and Mario. It was that same sense of dread, of being afraid of what was going to be said. And like a review, I was going over talking points in my head, organizing them, figuring out how to make my case. The difference was that my "case" here was all about what a great father and reasonable soon-to-be ex-husband I was, as opposed to what a good job I had done with Barry's account and how I had brought the KLC project in under budget. I know it seems ridiculous to equate the two, but the internal vibe felt the same, the not-being-in-control-of-your-fate vibe.

I got home first. I fed and walked Pinky. The girls did their homework while I made dinner. I cooked pasta with butter and parmesan just the way they liked it, super buttery, with pesto on the side for Lisa and me. I made a salad. I set the table. I was watching myself do all this and making sure when Lisa walked through the front door that everything looked right and under control, and she'd be reminded of what a competent father I was.

She came home, the four of us sat down to eat, and we talked about whether Elizabeth was going to try out for the middle school musical, which was *Peter Pan*. She was sure she wouldn't get the Wendy part, because Nora had the best voice in the whole school but hadn't gotten Adelaide or Sarah Brown when they did *Guys and Dolls* last year, and so she'd *definitely* get Wendy. They were going to cast a boy whose voice hadn't changed as Peter, instead of a girl, so she'd just end up as a Lost Boy, and there were so many rehearsals, and she wouldn't be able to do swim team. But the musical was really fun, even though Teacher Linda was directing it this year and she was really mean.

I remember Elizabeth was treating this topic as one calling for a running monologue rather than a discussion, and she kept tucking the same strand of beautiful streaky brown hair behind her left ear as she talked because it was constantly falling in her face and getting in the way of the pasta she was shoveling into her mouth with abandon. Elizabeth loves to eat. I was trying to really pay attention to the monologue, in case I was called to weigh in on the decision, which seemed unlikely. But I was mesmerized by the sweet familiarity of her hair-tucking gesture and the unabashed pleasure she was taking in her pasta—the pasta I had made for her, just the way I knew she loved it—and the unselfconscious way she held court at the table. She was still a little girl, even though her adolescent self was straining to break through and was actually starting to come out, more and more. But back then, at that precise moment in time, before she knew her parents were getting divorced, and before she crossed that line where her world would involve sex and drugs and lying and insecurity, she radiated confidence and happiness. And the thought of not living in the same house with her every day, of not being privy to the daily middle school report for a whole week at a time, made me sick. And yet I ate, and listened, and looked at the clock on the stove, and realized that Lisa and I would be having "the conversation" in less than two hours.

It was nine thirty, and both girls were upstairs in their bedrooms with the lights out. I sat down on the living room couch, wishing Pinky were lying at my feet, but I knew he was in Elizabeth's room. I felt cold. Lisa sat down in the green armchair across from me—wonder who'd get that chair?—and said, "Well?"

I had my prepared talking points, but looking at her sitting there, in her black yoga pants and her old Penn sweatshirt, looking tired but sexy, looking like Lisa, I just lost the script. "Are you absolutely sure you want to do this?" I asked.

"Oh, come on, Jake, I thought we were past that," Lisa answered, sounding impatient.

"Well, you may be, but I'm not. I still don't understand why you want to totally fuck up our kids."

"Jake, we've been over this a bunch of times, and I'm really sorry, but it's just not good for us to stay married. We've grown apart. And it won't fuck up our kids if we do this the right way, because we'll both be happier—"

"Maybe you will. But I won't. Don't act like there's some benefit for me in your midlife crisis. This is all about what you want. Just like it always is."

I knew I sounded pathetic and whiny. I really wanted to carry this off in a dignified way, even though her self-serving narrative about how this would be better for both of us was beyond offensive.

I took a deep breath. "Okay. Sorry. Let's move on. So I spoke to the lawyer, and here's what she said. She said that since you make more than I do, you're in a better position to afford to keep the house than I am, but since we owe almost as much on the mortgage as the house is worth, you don't need to buy me out, you just need to refinance the mortgage to get my name off it, and I'll sign the house over to you. Or we could sell it if you want, but I'd rather see you stay here, so the girls don't have to get used to two new houses. I'll find a place to rent that I can afford, hopefully three bedrooms but maybe two, because the girls could share, right?"

"Yeah, that'd be fine."

"As close as possible to here, ideally within walking distance. And we would have joint custody, which we could do lots of different ways, but I'm thinking just alternating weeks, and they go between us on Sunday afternoons so they have time to get ready for the school week, is best." Lisa was nodding. "And then that's really it. We can divide up what's in the bank accounts, which is like nothing anyway, we each keep our 401(k)s, and if you want, if I can find a place really close by, we can still share the Toyota."

Lisa kept nodding and looked incredibly relieved.

"Oh, and I think Pinky should go back and forth with the girls. So he'll be like a constant for them."

The screen saver opened up. Lisa smiled at me.

"That all sounds good, Jake. I agree with you about keeping the house—I'd like to try to hang onto it. And I really appreciate you being willing to move. It really does seem like the only way, because I don't see how you could handle the mortgage on your own."

"Well, if I got child support from you, I probably could, and since we're doing fifty-fifty, I'm entitled to it if I want it, but I'm not going to go there."

Lisa's eyes narrowed, and she stopped smiling. I guess she really hadn't talked to a lawyer, because this was clearly news to her. "But we're going to each have the kids half the time. So why are you talking about child support?"

"Well, according to my lawyer—"

"'My' lawyer?" Lisa said, sitting up straighter and glaring at me. "I thought you were just consulting her so we'd have the information to work this out ourselves. Now it's 'according to my lawyer'?"

"Don't get angry—I'm just telling you what she told me. She said that there are guidelines for child support, and even if the parents have equal custody time, if one earns more than the other, that parent still has to pay child support. Well, not 'has to,' I mean, that's what the law is, like if we went to court, that's what it would be. But I don't need your money, and I don't want it. So we're not doing that. I'm just saying, that would be a way I could stay in the house. If I wanted to. But I don't."

"Oh. Okay." Her body relaxed, slightly. But she was still glaring.

The child support thing didn't go over the way I had expected. I was looking to get psychic credit for being magnanimous. (When Ellen did the calculation, she said all I'd get was like $250 per month anyway, because when it's joint custody, it's less, but I didn't plan to tell Lisa that.) However, she seemed pissed off that I even mentioned it. I mean, what did she expect? I went to a lawyer like we discussed, and the lawyer told me what the law is, and I was being incredibly nice and undemanding about this whole fucked-up situation. She didn't realize how good she had it.

But I remembered what Ellen said about the girls, that if Lisa wanted to fight me about joint custody, she probably wouldn't win, but it could be a long, nasty, destructive process—not to mention totally unaffordable. And I would do anything to avoid that. So I needed to keep Lisa calm so she'd go along with the custody plan. I really didn't care about anything else. And I meant it when I told her I didn't want money from her. That would have made me feel like a total pussy.

"So, do we have a plan?" I asked.

"Sure," Lisa said, as she stood up, our meeting apparently over. "And we can talk later about what we're going to tell the girls. And when." She was back to looking relieved. The flash of anger had passed. "So you'll tell *your* lawyer"—she gave me a half-smile as she said this, already making a joke of the one-minute-old conflict—"to write it up, right? And she'll do the paperwork? And we can just pay for it out of the savings account."

"Right. That's what I was assuming. And if you get a lawyer too, we can pay for that out of there."

"I don't need a lawyer," she said. "See you in the morning."

And with that, she turned around and went upstairs, ponytail swinging behind her, leaving me alone in the living room, her living room, I guess, and all I wanted was Pinky.

7

Elizabeth: Family Meeting

Elizabeth's dad was yelling from downstairs that they had to leave *now* or they'd be late. Elizabeth could not find her favorite lip gloss, the one that was just a little orange and went so well with her skin, as Becky had said, and Becky always looked awesome. Mom had a no-makeup rule, which seemed ridiculous now that Elizabeth was in sixth grade, and anyway, she wasn't even sure where lip gloss fell on the continuum between medicine and make-up. Like, the clear lip balm from Burt's Bees that her mom bought her from the co-op was acceptable because it wasn't tinted. But this lip gloss from Urban Decay, called Dreamcatcher—Billie had shoplifted it from Sephora last time they were at the mall—was mostly just like that, except with *way* better packaging and that hint of orange that made her look more grown up, more put together. So what was the big deal?

Always a good multitasker, Elizabeth was conducting a very thorough search and rescue mission for Dreamcatcher at the same time as she was parsing the nuance of different lip products and how they related to the Rule of Mom. Locating Dreamcatcher on her bedside table under her science folder, she dropped it into her backpack and ran downstairs. Application of the contraband product would be done right after her father dropped her off in front of school. He probably wouldn't have noticed anyway, but she wasn't taking any chances. He told Mom everything, it seemed like.

Charlie and Dad were waiting by the front door. Instead of saying something about her being late again, her father just held the door for her and beeped open the car. Elizabeth claimed her rightful place in the front passenger seat and turned her attention to her new iPhone, relegating an uncomplaining Charlie to the dog-hair-covered back seat, the lot of one who had the distinct misfortune of being born second. Deep down a TikTok rabbit hole, Elizabeth didn't even notice when they pulled up in front of Mariposa, the small independent school both girls had attended since kindergarten. ("Just when did private schools start being called 'independent'?" Elizabeth had heard her dad say to her mom on more than one occasion. "Who's the marketing genius who thought of that?") As Elizabeth was swinging her backpack over one shoulder on her way out of the car, her dad said, "Remember, girls, we're going to have a family meeting tonight." Charlie paid no attention and ran into the schoolyard without even saying goodbye.

"Remember?" Elizabeth asked. "Did you tell us that before? What about?"

"Yes, I did, and it's just about some stuff we all need to talk about."

Elizabeth looked at her father for a second, thinking this was weird and uncharacteristically vague, thinking maybe it was about getting a kitten, which she had been dying for and kept getting told no, or maybe it was about that kid they were sponsoring in Honduras—maybe she was coming to visit? *Whatever*, she thought. "Bye, Dad," she said, turning toward the schoolyard and simultaneously reaching down to the bottom of her backpack for Dreamcatcher, which was waiting there patiently, right where she had left it.

Elizabeth stayed after school for her first *Peter Pan* rehearsal. Being a Lost Boy was actually fine, even though she wasn't going to get to sing very much. It was fine because Leo Turrell was a Lost Boy too, and he was really cute with his cowlick and that slightly bowed upper lip, and it seemed like he liked her too, even though Billie had said that all the boys who tried out for the musical were gay. *Well, they weren't,* Elizabeth thought. *That's stupid.* But she didn't say anything to Billie, because Billie was so definite about her opinions, and Elizabeth didn't really know how to challenge anything she said. Or actually, she had decided that she would only argue with Billie about something if it were really important—like if Billie said that Charlie had Asperger's or something like that, which she hadn't said. But Elizabeth knew that she wouldn't be able to let that kind of thing pass, so she'd save up any challenge to Billie's statements for a time when it was truly necessary. And it definitely was not in the case of her comment about Leo Turrell, since that wasn't really even about him directly, but about all the Lost Boys who were actually boys. It was just dumb, because Marco was a Lost Boy too, and he had been going out with Tasha all year, and everybody knew it.

Rehearsal was over at 5:00 p.m., and their mom was picking up Charlie and her. Charlie had stayed for the after-school program, and Elizabeth went downstairs to get her, because they were supposed to wait in the lobby. Charlie had done some sort of art project involving, very apparently, purple paint, which had somehow gotten into her hair. She ran up to Elizabeth, purple-flecked brown curls bouncing behind her, and almost knocked her over. "What happened to your hair?" Elizabeth asked, looking Charlie up and down with that older sister how-could-you-be-so-childish expression she had recently perfected. She actually thought Charlie looked cute with the purple-dotted hair, but she was conscious of the fact that Mira and Ashleigh from her class were down in the after-school room too. Neither of them had younger siblings, and she wanted them to understand her level of maturity. Unlike them, she had a job to do, she had a younger sister to pick up, and she wanted to make sure she came across as appropriately parental with just the right amount of cool detachment.

"We did self-portraits," said Charlie, "and I painted mine in purple." While this wasn't a direct explanation as to how the paint got into her hair, Elizabeth didn't really care or think it was a problem; she only brought it up in case Mira or Ashleigh were listening.

"Well, Mom isn't going to be happy about that," she said, causing an instant flicker of panic to cross Charlie's face, a face that always made Elizabeth think of a kitten's: small, sort of heart-shaped, coming to a pointy little chin. *All she needs is whiskers*, Elizabeth thought. She did feel a little guilty, given that their mom wasn't really going to care at all and that Elizabeth was actually planning to ask her about getting purple streaks in her hair next time she had it cut, but also proud of her ability to manipulate her little sister so perfectly, especially in front of her sibling-less peers. They may have the benefit of never having to share their stuff, sure, but they would never know (and must secretly envy) the rush that results from wielding power over someone who hangs onto your every word and wants nothing more than to be with you—just like Pinky.

Charlie grabbed her coat and backpack, and the girls ran upstairs to the Mariposa lobby, a space the size of a small living room. It was plastered with children's artwork and overflowing bulletin boards: "Third-grade parents! Helpers still needed for

Thanksgiving potluck and December 10 trip to the Academy of Natural Sciences—see Teacher Sonya right away if you can help out with either/both!" and "Mariposa family looking for after-school babysitter for our three boys ages 6, 8, and 11. Driver's license, good organizational skills, and sense of humor a must!" A few worn, gray upholstered chairs, occupied by children in various states of relaxation, were clustered around a table on one side of the room. The admissions office was on the opposite side, by the entrance, a sign on its closed door proclaiming MARIPOSA: EMERGE FROM THE CHRYSALIS! and featuring the school logo, a brilliant blue butterfly perched on a twig. Mom was already there, standing near the chairs and chatting with Leo Turrell's mother, much to Elizabeth's horror.

"Mommy, I'm sorry about the paint in my hair," said Charlie, going for the preemptive strike.

"What paint?" Mom asked, as Charlie approached her for a hug and then, upon closer inspection, "Love the purple! Don't worry, it'll come out. We'll just need to wash your hair tonight. Okay, Karen, nice talking to you. Girls, we need to get going." Charlie shot Elizabeth a look of triumph, which Elizabeth ignored, eyes turning back to her phone.

"Okay," said Mom as she stood up from the dinner table, even though Charlie was still working on two baby carrots, which it did not appear would ever be eaten. Her approach was to take a carrot, dip it into ranch dressing that she kept adding to her plate, suck off the dressing, redip, and repeat. "Time for a family meeting."

Elizabeth looked up at her mom, who was not smiling, and asked, for the second time that day, "What about?"

"Let's go sit in the living room," Dad said. "And Charlie,

enough with the dressing. Eat the carrot, and come on." This was not usual. A spike of concern, like the faintest hint of a chill, worked its way up Elizabeth's spine. Other times their parents had called for family meetings, it was about decisions they needed to make together, like, "Here's three places we could go on vacation this summer—what do you girls think?" Although there was one family meeting, she just remembered, when she was in fourth grade, when their parents told them that Marianne, Henry's mom who lived across the street, was very sick with cancer and that she might die. They said that Henry and his dad were really sad, and they should make an extra effort to play with Henry, and they shouldn't be afraid to talk to him about his mom, because when someone is scared about something, it's a good thing to talk about it, not a bad thing. Thinking about *that* family meeting, the chill hit Elizabeth full-on, like a blast.

Elizabeth's parents sat down on the couch. Charlie was already on the floor next to Pinky, who, as usual, was sleeping. Elizabeth sat in the green armchair, sinking down into the familiar pillowy seat.

"So girls, your dad and I have made a decision," Mom said. "And this decision has nothing to do with you. It has to do with us. We love the two of you more than anything, and we always will. Nothing will ever change that. And we will always be a family." *Oh my God*, Elizabeth thought, *they're getting a divorce.* This is exactly what Anya had said her parents had told her, this whole speech about how everybody loved everybody, and then her dad was gone, like, the next day. Tears welled up behind her eyes. "And Daddy and I love each other too, but right now it's not good for us to live together, so we're going to try living in different houses."

"What?" said Elizabeth. "Are you serious?" She could feel

herself starting to cry, which she really didn't want to. "Are you getting divorced—is that what you're trying to say?"

Charlie was silent, looking down at Pinky, who picked up his head, groaned slightly, turned it to the other side, and went back to sleep.

"How is that even possible? How can you just sit there and act like this is some meeting about a vacation or a pet or something?" Elizabeth was now full-on crying and yelling at the same time.

"You're getting divorced?" asked Charlie.

"No, girls, we're not getting divorced, not now. Your mom and I just need to spend some time apart to figure out some things," said Dad.

"Like what things? And where are we going to live?" Elizabeth's voice was rising in pitch. Mom got up from the couch and knelt down in front of the green chair, taking Elizabeth's hands in one of hers and stroking her cheek with the other. "Sweetie, you'll live with your dad and with me, just like now. But it'll be in two places. I'm going to stay in this house, and Daddy's going to move to a place—"

"What place?" wailed Elizabeth. "What do you mean, a *place*? Where is Daddy going to live?"

Leaning toward her, speaking softly, Dad said, "Elizabeth, I don't know yet, but I'm going to rent a house or an apartment, and it will be close by, somewhere in Greenwood. It'll be nice. And you and Charlie," turning toward the littlest member of the family, who now had her head buried in Pinky's back, "will change houses every Sunday afternoon. So you'll be here with your mom for a week, then with me for a week, then back here. Like that."

"But I don't *want* to do that!" Elizabeth yelled. "I like it here. And, Daddy, I don't want you to move to a different house. And what about Pinky?"

"Pinky will go with you girls," said Mom. "It'll be the three of you, like a pack." Elizabeth looked down at her mom, who was still kneeling in front of her chair. She could see that her mom was crying too, and she started to wail again.

"But I don't want to do this! And what about Charlie? She doesn't want this, either—do you, Charlie?" The back of Charlie's head moved back and forth, a silent no. "You're *ruining* our lives. We don't *want* this!"

"Girls," said Dad, "we know you don't want this. But sometimes adults have to do things kids don't want. We need to do this. And nothing will change, really, except that you'll have two bedrooms. And if you want to see Mom when you're at my house, or you want to see me when you're here, you'll just call Mom or me, and we'll work something out. We'll work this out together."

"But why do we have to work anything out?" Elizabeth said, blowing her nose. "What needs to be worked out?"

Mom let go of Elizabeth's hands and cheek, stood up, and went around the coffee table to the Charlie-and-Pinky pile on the floor. She sat down and drew Charlie up and into her lap. "Girls. We'll always be a family. That will never change."

Pinky awoke, slowly got up, went over to the couch, and put his head in her dad's lap. Elizabeth finished blowing her nose and looked across the coffee table at her dad. He was crying.

CHORUS #1

The Moms

Hi, Karen. Hey, Petra, said Miriam, scooching her way around the coffee line at the Green Life Café to join her girlfriends at the little corner table in the back. Several sets of eyes followed her, sweeping over the TABLES HAPPEN! sign by the cash register. People were surveying the territory, assessing which tables—all of them full—were about to "happen" anytime soon. Aware of the looks, Miriam felt the faint, irrational pleasure of being in the know, of belonging, of not having to worry about getting a table because her seat didn't have to "happen"—her seat was secured by her girlfriends, awaiting her arrival.

The women settled in, moving handbags and cell phones to accommodate their third. Tidbits of news about husbands, kids, and jobs were handed to the group—examined with more or less attention depending on the level of mutual interest invoked—consumed, and digested. Men and their exasperating behavior topped the morning's topics. Petra's husband had been away at a conference for four days. She realized how much easier it was with him gone, which you wouldn't think. But really, he could be so oblivious to what was going on with the kids and the house, that sometimes it was just easier to do everything herself, you know?

Miriam and Karen definitely did know, for sure, because even though you missed them when they were away (maybe), all that negotiating about what to do and who was going to do it just disappeared— poof!—and you realized how much time it saved when you could just make all the decisions yourself. And then you could fall into bed right after the kids went to sleep, and read or look at Instagram and watch whatever TV show you wanted, and you didn't have to talk to anyone. Or, Miriam added, be made to feel guilty because you didn't feel like having sex, because really, who wants to on a weeknight, anyway?

Although, Karen said, leaning in and lowering her voice, while it's great for a while, let's not kid ourselves. Being a single parent long-term would be rough. Like Lisa Naudain is about to be—she told me last weekend that she and Jake are splitting up. And FYI, this is totally confidential. I promised Lisa I wouldn't tell anyone. So you two are sworn to secrecy.

Wow, said Petra, of course we won't say anything. But that is really surprising, because I always thought Lisa and Jake seemed like the perfect couple. I guess it just goes to show, you never know what's going on in anyone else's marriage, right?

Right, Karen said, and actually, Lisa had opened up to her when they were cochairing the Mariposa silent auction. Apparently, Jake has a real Peter Pan complex—all he wants to do is play with this band he's in. He works in a dead-end job and doesn't seem to care that he's going nowhere professionally, and he is totally irresponsible about the kids— he loves them, of course, and he's good at playing the fun dad, but Lisa said she couldn't count on him for anything. She had to take care of it all—the household and the kids, and she also earns most of the money. It had come to a place where all they had in common were the girls, and Lisa said she'd done lots of soul-searching, and she just wasn't willing to spend the rest of her life with someone she had nothing left in common with. And who she had to take care of.

And despite all that, Miriam said, you know he'll be single for like five minutes. He'll take up with some thirty-year-old with no kids, am I right?

Absolutely, the other women agreed. I mean, Miriam said in a conspiratorial whisper, he is easy on the eyes. I'd date him.

Hmm, said Petra, raising two perfectly shaped eyebrows. Can't say I disagree with your assessment, but let's be real here. Not sure "date" is really what you're referring to. Which left the group giggling as they stood up for refills, re-caffeinating for the dive into the topic of standardized testing in middle school. It was an issue of great significance for their kids' futures but one which would have to be treated with tact and delicacy, as they all knew Petra's older daughter, poor thing, would not do well on the tests.

8

Elizabeth: *Naudain v. Naudain*,
October Term, 11:30 a.m.

Grandma is trying to act like this is a normal visit, which is ridiculous because there is nothing normal about it. Elizabeth and Charlie didn't go to school this morning, which usually would have been a good thing, but not in this case—because their parents are fighting over custody of them, and they need to come to court to speak to the judge. That wasn't exactly the way their mom had explained it—she said she and daddy needed "help" from the judge—but Elizabeth knows that isn't really it. Really, it's about Samara. She knows that because she heard her mom talking to Charlie about something that happened when they were at their dad's house. She was asking Charlie about Samara sleeping with Dad, and Charlie being in bed with him and Samara, which was kind of gross. And which Charlie probably was, because lots of times when Elizabeth wakes up in the morning at Dad's, Charlie isn't in their room. Charlie is afraid of everything and has this habit of waking up in the middle of the night when they are at Dad's and going into his room to sleep.

Samara is pretty and fun and has the cool tattoos and all, but Elizabeth doesn't really like her sleeping at Dad's so much. It's weird and gross to think about Samara having sex with her dad, which obviously is the reason she's sleeping there. And also, obviously, it would be super weird if Charlie were sleeping in bed with them, but whatever, it probably wasn't weird to Charlie, because she's all huggy kissy with Samara anyway. But the point is that, for whatever reason, her mom is mad at her dad, and she actually asked Elizabeth if she would prefer to live with her instead of switching weeks like they had been doing since her dad moved out. Elizabeth told her mom no, that wouldn't be fair to Dad, because he would really miss her and Charlie. Although really, she wouldn't mind staying at her mom's all the time, because it's a pain to go back and forth and have to have clothes at both houses, and all that stuff. But lots of her friends do it, and really, that's just what happens when your parents get divorced. It sucks for kids, but they don't ask their kids—they just do it.

Anyway, Grandma came down last night and stayed over and then brought them into Center City to court this morning after their mom had already left. The court is not what Elizabeth thought it was going to be. She had imagined it as a big white building with lots of steps leading up to it, sort of like a church. But this court is just an office building, a big tall one, where you go through metal detectors in the lobby and then take the elevator to a floor with lots of chairs in rows, where people are sitting, looking at their phones, and waiting for their names to be called. Grandma is acting all cheerful in this fake way, asking Elizabeth the same questions about school and her friends she had asked her in the car on the way here, which Elizabeth already answered. Charlie is basically clueless—she and Grandma are playing checkers on Grandma's iPhone. She keeps talking about what she is going to get for lunch, because Grandma promised to take them out to lunch after court at this dumpling place in Chinatown that Elizabeth and Charlie love.

A door opens into the waiting area, and a man in a dark blue uniform who looks like a police officer comes out. "Elizabeth Naudain," he says. "Judge will see you now."

Elizabeth's palms feel sweaty, and her stomach hurts. She doesn't move.

"Stand up, honey," says Grandma, "and follow the gentleman." Like the walking dead, Elizabeth stands and goes over to the police guy.

"Follow me," he says, and she does, through another door, down a corridor, and into a small office, where he deposits her and leaves.

"You must be Elizabeth," says a woman who is obviously the judge, since she is kind of old and wearing a black robe. "So nice to meet you. I'm Judge Jones. Have a seat here," she says, sitting down at a glass-topped table and motioning Elizabeth toward a green chair directly facing her on the other side of the table. "Let me introduce you to Ms. Yvonne, my court reporter. She's going to take down what you say on her machine, all right?"

This doesn't seem like a real question, as in it doesn't seem like the judge is really asking her opinion, but Elizabeth nods anyway. "And behind you"—Elizabeth turns around—"are Mom and Dad's attorneys, Ms. Ackerman and Mr. Boyle. They are just here to listen to our conversation, not to talk. Okay?" It was another not-real question. Elizabeth nods again.

"All right, then," says the judge. "Let's start by swearing you in. How old are you, Elizabeth?"

"I'm twelve."

"So you're almost a teenager. You are a lovely young lady. And I know you know the difference between telling the truth and telling a lie, don't you?"

"Yes."

"Can you describe it to me?"

"Well, a lie is something that's not true. Like, that didn't happen. And the truth is what really did happen."

"What happens if you tell a lie?"

"You get in trouble. Like at school, if you cheat on a test, you have to go to a meeting with the head of school, and your parents have to come in and stuff."

"Exactly. So, Elizabeth, I'm going to ask you a few questions, and I need you to answer them truthfully. All right?"

"All right." Elizabeth waits while the judge takes one of those lined pads out of her desk and sets it up in front of her, pen in hand, ready to take notes. Elizabeth thinks that's weird, because the judge had said the woman with that machine she was typing on would record whatever Elizabeth said. So why does the judge need to write stuff down too? But whatever. The judge smiles and leans toward her.

"So, I understand from your parents that you and your sister spend a week at your dad's house, then a week at your mom's, then a week at your dad's, and so on. Is that right?

"Yes."

"What is your dad's house like?"

"He lives in an apartment."

"How many bedrooms does it have?"

"Two. He has one, and Charlie and I share the other. And Pinky," Elizabeth says, thinking that really there are three of them sharing that bedroom, which is kind of funny—two human roommates and one dog one.

"Who's Pinky?"

"Pinky's our dog. He comes with us when we go to Dad's. And he always sleeps on my bed, at home and at my dad's."

"I see. Now do either you or your sister ever sleep in your dad's room?"

"Charlie does. She wakes up at night a lot and goes into

Dad's room—well, I don't really see her go into his room, because I'm sleeping—but I know she does because she's not in our
room in the morning sometimes."

"Now, Elizabeth, does anyone else ever sleep at your father's
apartment when you and Charlie are there?"

Oh great, here we go, thinks Elizabeth. *This whole thing is so
lame.* "Yes, Samara does. Well, she has. A few times."

"And who is Samara?"

"She's my dad's girlfriend."

"Have you spent time with Samara?"

"Yeah, a little bit."

"And do you get along with her?"

"Yeah, she's pretty nice."

"Now, Elizabeth, I'm going to ask you a question, and I want
you to think very carefully before you answer. And if you don't
know the answer, that's fine too, you can just say that."

I know what the question is, Elizabeth thinks. *Let's get this
over with.* "Okay," she says.

"Do you know if Charlie ever slept in your dad's bed on any
of the nights that Samara was there?"

"No. I mean, I don't know. I don't remember."

The judge puts down her pen and looks at Elizabeth, waiting. "Are you sure about that?"

"Yes," says Elizabeth. "I'm sure. I don't remember. But anyway, it's no big deal if she did. She gets scared at night sometimes, and she wants to be with Dad. So if it did happen, it was
just because of that. But I don't remember if it happened when
Samara was there or not."

The judge leans back in her chair.

"Elizabeth, thank you very much. I appreciate your candor,
and I can tell you that both Mom and Dad love you very much,
and they both want what's best for you and your sister. Some-

times they just don't agree, and that's where I might need to step in and make some decisions. But it sounds like most of the time they are able to agree on things, and you and your sister are very lucky to have two such loving parents. You know that, right?"

"Yes."

"I see many children who don't have that, so I want you to know how fortunate you are. Okay?"

"Okay."

"All right. Now I'm going to call Sheriff Henry to come and take you back to the waiting room, and then it will be your sister's turn to talk to me. It's been a pleasure to meet you. You are a very mature young lady. Come, shake my hand before you leave," says the judge, getting up in her long black robe—*like the ladies in the choir at Grandma's church*, Elizabeth thinks—and extending her hand to Elizabeth, who stands and shakes it. Sheriff Henry is already there waiting, so she turns around to leave. Her mom and dad's lawyers are still sitting there, and both of them smile at her as she follows him out the door. *So weird*, she thinks. *This whole thing is so weird. I never want to come back here.* She follows Sheriff Henry back to the waiting room, where Charlie is still playing checkers with Grandma.

"Charlie, get up," she says. "Your turn." Charlie stands up, pulling at the hem of the turquoise shirt with the flower on it that she loves so much, and, walks, hesitantly, across the waiting room behind Sheriff Henry, disappearing as the door into the hallway closes behind her.

"Is everything okay, sweetheart?" asks Grandma.

Elizabeth nods and reaches across Grandma for her backpack. "Fine," she says.

9

Ellen: A Walk in the Park,
Eight Months Ago

Ellen was sitting at her dining room table, having just polished off the Sunday *New York Times Magazine*, Style section, and Book Review. She was now working her way through Travel, idly imagining the sunny pleasures of a Caribbean jaunt, when Marni clomped down the stairs. She was wearing tiger-striped pajama bottoms, a faded blue tank top featuring a picture of an open box of Chinese take-out food with the words "Chop Suey" written across it in kitschy bamboo-like letters, and a decidedly grumpy expression on her face.

"Aren't you cold, honey?" asked Ellen, surprised at her daughter's bare arms. After all, it was February, there was snow on the ground outside, Dan refused to turn the heat above sixty-eight, and she could actually feel the wind blowing in around the dining room windows from her seat at the dining room table.

"Yes," said Marni. "It's fucking freezing down here."

"Marni! Stop swearing. It's so unappealing. And it's rude." This was a recent battle. For some reason, Marni seemed to be cultivating a love of cursing. Or, to be more precise, a love of the casual use of the word "fuck" in everyday conversation, for emphasis. They'd actually had an argument about this earlier in the week, in which Marni accused Ellen and Dan of being hopelessly out of touch with contemporary English usage.

"Language constantly *evolves*," she had told them, "and I understand that to you guys 'fucking' is a bad word, but *my* generation uses it differently. It's part of the contemporary vernacular. Now it's more like the way Daddy uses 'damn.' Like he would say 'that's so damn expensive.' That's all it is. So don't be so *uptight* about it."

Oh, the pain of being lectured to by your arrogant seventeen-year-old, Ellen had thought at the time. That pain was tempered somewhat by an involuntary welling of parental pride at her offspring's ability to formulate and deliver an articulate argument. This was an ability rooted, no doubt, in the DNA she had received from two lawyers as well as the massive amounts of cash those same two lawyers had shelled out for her education at a school whose mission is to "create the women leaders of tomorrow." The upshot of the argument was an agreement to disagree about this topic, with a directive from Ellen and Dan that Marni was not to use the term in casual conversation around them, because they found it offensive regardless of how she meant it. And so would, they pointed out, any teacher, potential employer or—perhaps most significantly at this point in her life—college interviewer.

"Sorry," said Marni, sounding anything but. "I forgot." She opened the coat closet, took out Dan's "You have the right to remain silent: USE IT" sweatshirt—one of many tattered mementos from a career spent at the public defender's office—pulled it over her head, and headed into the kitchen.

"What're your plans?" Ellen called from her seat at the dining room table, hoping that maybe she and Marni could do something together today. Marni's impending flight from the nest had been weighing heavily. Ellen couldn't believe that in six months, she and Marni would be prowling the aisles of Target, shopping for sheets and towels for Marni's dorm room, an unknown room, with an unknown roommate or roommates, at a location yet to be determined. The future was so uncertain in its particulars and yet so brutally certain in the salient fact that her only child would be moving out and moving on, bringing to an abrupt end the parenthood phase of Ellen's life. Rationally, she knew it wasn't quite that way. She knew that kids in college come home on vacations, that some of them move home afterward, as many of their friends had been complaining about (for real, or whether they were posturing, she was never sure), and that from what she could see with her friends who had daughters, she would probably be talking and texting with Marni every day, if not several times every day.

But still—that anchor to her life, that reason to leave the office by 5:30 and shut out her clients' problems with their families, that school play, that track meet, that group of teenagers tromping through her house, most of whom she'd known since they were in preschool—that would all be over. And it would just be her and Dan with only Chester to take care of, Chester who was old himself and smelled and would probably die soon. Chester, who had come to them as the result of Marni begging and begging to get a dog; them caving in, even though Dan didn't like dogs; and Marni keeping her promise to take care of Chester for about a year, maybe two. And now? He was Ellen's responsibility. She was the default caregiver, as was just about every woman she knew, so she had gotten stuck with a now-geriatric dog she really didn't want in the first place.

"Dunno," Marni replied from the kitchen.

"I was thinking of taking Chester to the park to throw the ball for him. He hasn't been getting any exercise lately, and I really think he needs it. Want to come?" Ellen asked.

"Not really. And you do realize it might kill him, right?"

"Oh, come on. It will not. And you're the one who's supposed to take care of him, anyway. So the least you can do is keep me company. Plus I need some quality mother–daughter time."

"Right." Ellen could picture Marni's eyes rolling as she responded. "Okay, I'll come if it's not going to take too long. Because I have stuff to do. And because it's so fucking—oops, sorry, what should I say instead? *Freaking? Flipping?* C'mon Mom, you know those sound lame. Even *you* wouldn't use those words."

Half an hour later, Ellen and Marni were standing in a large, open public park in the heart of Greenwood called Daffodil Field, mysteriously named given that for the past fifteen or so years that Ellen had been going there, she had never seen even one lone daffodil. What she did usually see, though—and this day was no exception, despite the weather—were lots and lots of dogs. And their down-jacketed, tennis-ball-toting owners, some of whom—a group Ellen had seen, and smelled, on a number of prior occasions—were smoking weed, and some of whom were just standing around in an apparently weed-free group, chatting.

Dog-related socializing was really not Ellen's cup of tea, but she had grudgingly accepted, since taking charge of poor Chester's care, that a modicum of it was unavoidable. You went to the park, you threw your ball, and someone else's dog intercepted it. Then that dog's owner (or "human," which wasn't too objectionable, or "parent," which was just ridiculous) would approach you and apologize, her dog running around yours, and you'd have to say something. You'd have to say, at a minimum, "No problem! Wow, she/he's adorable/handsome/beautiful! What is he/she?" And the owner/human/parent would so often answer with the dog's heritage being preceded by the term "rescue" and a humble apology for not knowing the exact lineage, but hey, you never really could know with a rescue, could you? Oh, how Ellen longed for the days when people just adopted dogs from shelters rather than rescued them. It all seemed so overly dramatic. Happily, this time, since Marni was there with her, she felt some level of protection against the random social encounter with a rescuer. She and Marni took turns throwing the tennis ball for Chester, who obediently trotted his aging cocker spaniel, poodle, and something-else body after it and brought it right back to them just like he was supposed to. Ellen found this slightly touching, as he really didn't seem that excited about it, not like when he was younger. It seemed almost like he was doing it for her, like this was her recreational activity, rather than the other way around.

It dawned on Ellen, with grim amusement, that both Marni and Chester were similarly humoring her by accompanying her on this freezing cold expedition. Therefore, they might as well go home, because she would prefer to sit in her living room and finish the Travel section anyway. Just then, a large black dog on the other side of the field ran toward the ball Marni had just tossed. Triumphantly beating the long-suffering Chester to the ball, he scooped it up and ran back to his owner, a guy in a leather jacket standing by the baseball field with two young girls. Ellen saw the guy talking to the bigger girl and gesturing toward Ellen and Marni. The girl yelled something authoritative at the dog, who immediately dropped the ball. She picked it up and ran over to Ellen and Marni, the dog following close behind her.

"Hi. Sorry about that," she said. "This is yours, right?" The girl, looking to be about eleven or twelve and strikingly pretty, smiled at Ellen and Marni from inside the cocoon of her faux-fur-lined hood.

"Yes," said Ellen, taking the muddy, slobber-covered tennis

ball. "Thanks so much, honey." The dog, whom Ellen had sized up as a black Lab, pit bull mix (the practiced eye of a dog park attender at work), ran up to Marni, who crouched down and started making various cooing sounds. Leather-jacket dad and the younger girl were walking toward them. As they approached, Ellen realized he looked familiar.

"Ellen?" he said. It was her client, Jake Naudain. Thank God she remembered. Sometimes people greeted her, and Ellen had no idea how she might know them, and her biggest fear was that they were clients whose faces she had forgotten. How badly would that make them feel? Their own lawyer, to whom they had entrusted their most intimate secrets, didn't recognize them? But it was understandable, really, because many of Ellen's clients only met her face-to-face once, that first time they came to her office—or Zoomed with her, during COVID, in which case she was even less likely to recognize them in person. After that, if their cases could be successfully negotiated, Ellen communicated with them by phone and email, so instead of hours spent in court together—which would indelibly burn a client's image in her mind—Ellen would be familiar only with their voices and their writing styles. Not a problem with Jake, though. His handsome, tousled, more-fashionably-dressed-than-the-Greenwood-average-man came back to her in a flash.

"Hi! This is my daughter, Marni."

It was always awkward, this situation, when she didn't want to use the person's name so as to protect client confidentiality, but it was such an artificial way to greet someone. In fact, Dan and Marni instantly noticed, any time they ran into a person whom Ellen knew but neither of them did, when she failed to introduce that person by name or association. After the encounter, they'd look at each other and say, simultaneously, "Client."

But Jake apparently didn't care, and that was, of course, his call. "Nice to meet you Marni, I'm Jake," he said. "And this"—gesturing toward the older girl, who was engaging in what appeared to be a tribal-like ritual in which she and Marni were both crouched low to the ground, mutually cooing over each other's dogs—"is Elizabeth. And this," he said, motioning toward his younger daughter, also pretty and also cocooned inside a faux-fur hood, "is Charlie. Girls, this is Ms. Ackerman, and her daughter, Marni."

Ellen greeted both girls warmly, told them to please call her Ellen, and began mentally attaching to them pieces of information Jake had given her, while at the same time acting as if she had never heard of them. She knew they both attended Mariposa, which was a bit too self-consciously earnest for her taste. Her friends Roger and Donna sent their kids there, and the school was always hosting these endless parent potlucks where you had to put a label on your dish that listed all the ingredients, lest someone unsuspectingly take a bite of gluten. She knew that Jake and his wife had had "the talk" with the girls, and Elizabeth seemed to take it harder than Charlie—not surprising, in her experience, given their ages. She also knew that he was in the process of finding a new place to live and was debating whether the girls should share a room or not. She had even heard about this dog, because Jake told her to put into the custody agreement she needed to draft this coming week that their dog—Pinky, she thought his name was—would go back and forth with the girls between his and his wife's homes. And she needed to draft the divorce complaint too; she had forgotten about that.

"Your dog is beautiful," Ellen said, looking at Charlie. "What's his name?"

"Pinky!" the little girl said. "Daddy, can we go? I'm cold."

"Sure," said Jake, "just one minute. Ellen, I'll give you a call this week, okay?"

"Great," said Ellen. "Goodbye, girls. So nice to meet you!"

"You too," said Elizabeth, patting Chester one last time, standing up, and going over to her father. As they walked away, Ellen heard her say to Jake, "How do you know that lady? What are you calling her for?"

Marni put Chester back on the leash and turned toward her mother. "Client," Marni said. "Let's go. And by the way, he's hot."

10

~

Jake: House Hunting

I had to find a place to live. Ellen had already written up the agreement, and Lisa was after me on what seemed like a daily basis. She was trying to act sympathetic, so she would say, "How's it going? Have you found something yet?" instead of what she clearly wanted to say, which was, "When are you moving out, and why is it taking you so fucking long?"

It was taking me so fucking long because I found the process unbelievably depressing. First of all, there was very little available in our immediate neighborhood, which is where I wanted to stay, so that I'd be close to Mariposa and Daffodil Field and all that, and so that the back and forth with the girls would be easy. And second of all, the places that were available—and allowed dogs, which narrowed the field even more—were complete dumps.

The first apartment I looked at was a three-bedroom, four blocks from our house. The description on Craigslist sounded promising, and the rent was okay. I met the landlord out front, and the minute he opened the door, I knew I could never live there. It was dark and kind of dingy, and the kitchen had stained acoustical tiling in the ceiling and a shit brown electric stove, like from 1964. I just couldn't. Not that our house was so perfect, but it was nice. I liked having people over, because Lisa and I had good taste in furniture, and we'd painted the walls interesting colors, which people always remarked on, and it felt comfortable. And why, again, was I the one who had to leave it? Because I couldn't afford it by myself, and my wife was going through a midlife crisis. It was so fucking unfair, but there was nothing I could do about it except fight it, which was a lost cause—how can you make someone want to be with you?—or suck it up. Which is what I was obviously doing, but I had to preserve my dignity somehow. I just could not live in the kind of apartment I shared with Carly and Tom in Boston when we all moved there after college. Which had, come to think of it, the same shit brown electric stove as the Craigslist place.

I also looked at a house, which I would have preferred, but which was really too far, in a kind of fringe neighborhood outside of Greenwood. It had a rough vibe, trash on the streets, and projects a few blocks away. Again, a strong whiff of postcollege days—not doing it. So at band practice, I talked to Petie, because his sister is a realtor in Northwest Philly. He said he'd talk to her and see if she knew about any rentals. Later, he called me and said she did handle rentals and could show me an apartment in East Greenwood—not ideal—that was in a nice building, pets okay, high ceilings, wood floors, new appliances, all that good stuff, but only had two bedrooms. At that point, I realized I couldn't be too picky, because I was afraid that if I didn't move soon, Lisa would start getting hostile. Then I'd be furious, and then we'd end up fighting in front of the girls. Which I did not want to do.

Ellen had told me about what she sees with her clients and also what she'd read. She was like this font of divorce knowledge—helpful to me, but what a weird thing to focus your professional life on. I wonder what her marriage is like? She said that the most stressful time in a divorce, and the worst time for kids, is when people have decided to get divorced but are still living in the same house. And I totally got that, because I was living it. Seeing the woman I used to be able to touch and kiss whenever I felt like it, whose body was my personal territory, now off-limits—as just another adult person I know, whom I happened to share a kitchen and bathroom and a bunch of bills with, some random roommate—was heartbreaking. And so unfair, because I didn't do anything to deserve it. I didn't do anything but love her. I went to work every day, I brought home a paycheck, I didn't fuck anyone else, I didn't go out with the guys all the time, nothing. I felt like Pinky. Like I was just a dumb loyal dog who was being kicked out of the house but was still wagging his tail and licking his master's hand. It was humiliating, but I just didn't have an alternative. Because when I thought about the girls—and how Elizabeth wailed that night we had "the talk" and how Charlie buried her head in Pinky's back like she wanted to sink inside his body and shut out the bad news— when I thought about them, I felt sick. I felt like they were all I had left at this point, and I had to be as good a father as I could. And that meant protecting them from seeing me mad or unhappy.

I was really trying to take it like a man, as stupid as that sounds, but that's what I kept thinking about. Like, I kept remembering that Jordanian pilot who was captured and burned alive by the terrorists, and they made a video of him in this cage they stuck him in, waiting to die. And you looked at that guy, and he was standing there, straight up—not crying, not pleading—silent and defiant to the last minute. The video was horrifying, but I couldn't help myself from watching it, and I couldn't get that image out of my head. I realize it is ridiculous to compare getting divorced to getting murdered by terrorists, but that was the image that kept coming to me, and I respected that poor guy so much. If he could be that stoic in the worst situation anyone could ever be in, I could keep it together through a divorce. I wanted to be my own version of him, in my own little first-world personal crisis.

Petie said he'd take me to meet his sister at the East Greenwood apartment on a Sunday before band practice. I protested, but not too much, and he insisted. He really had my back through this mess. He came by to pick me up in his white Beamer, a 3-series from the early 90s that he treated like a baby, and we drove over there. It was about a fifteen-minute drive from my house—not too bad. The neighborhood was similar to ours but scaled down —mostly row houses rather than twins, mostly brick instead of stone, but fine. The apartment turned out to be on the top floor of a large house that had been converted to three units. Millie, Petie's sister, who was all decked out in realtor business-casual wear, was bubbling enthusiastically about the apartment. "Sorry to hear about you and Lisa," she said.

"Yeah, me too," I replied, which had become my stock answer. I mean, what else could I say?

"I think this place could be perfect for you and your girls. Petie told me you've been looking for a three-bedroom, but that's a little tough in your price range," Millie said, raising her eyebrows and leaning toward me to emphasize the importance of this humiliating fact, "and the bedrooms are really good sizes. And the landlord's fine with pets—he just wants an extra deposit with your security, you know, in case they have to do extra cleaning, but otherwise, pets are not a problem. And it's available right away. I could get you in here March fifteenth, if you want. Want to go inside?"

Two flights up, the front door opens, and Millie was right. Perfect, no, but even in my depressed I-don't-want-to-do-any-of-this mindset, I had to admit to myself it was nice. Lots of sun-light, large living room with a bay window, two huge bedrooms that were bigger than the ones in our house, and a kitchen that looked like it had just been redone with stainless steel appliances and granite—well, probably fake granite, but it looked fine—countertops. Kind of generic and bland, but way, way nicer than the other places.

"Hey, man," Petie said, "nice crib." I agreed but told Millie I had to think about it a little more, because it only had two bed-rooms. She said she understood, but I should get back to her ASAP.

"Because," she said, lowering her voice to a conspiratorial whisper, "at this price, it will go soon."

"Okay," I told her. "Tomorrow. I'll tell you tomorrow."

But on the way home with Petie, we already decided I should take it. And it wasn't like a permanent thing, just a one-year lease, because eventually I would buy my own place. Or that's what he said. I couldn't figure out how I would ever do that again, but I just said, "Right. Just temporary. Anything might happen."

11

Charlie: First Night at Dad's

"Girls, let's go!" Charlie's dad was standing in the living room, putting the leash on Pinky. Charlie was excited to have a sleepover at Dad's. He had taken her and Elizabeth to Ikea and let them pick out new beds for their room. Hers was white, and the part that goes behind your head had hearts carved out above where the pillows go. It looked so pretty in the big room where all the beds were, and it had a puffy pink-and-white quilt on it that she really wanted too, and Dad had said okay and bought it for her. Elizabeth's new bed was white also, but the back part was just plain and didn't have the hearts. Charlie had asked Elizabeth why she didn't want to get the heart one too, so they would match, and Elizabeth had said the heart bed was for little girls but not for girls in middle school. And even though their dad tried to make Charlie feel better by saying that he liked the hearts, and maybe he would get a bed like that too—which Charlie knew was a joke because it was a small bed, not the kind grown-ups sleep in, and it was definitely only for girls—she was embarrassed that she had acted so excited about the hearts. And she was mad at Elizabeth, who always said things like that to her, which was so unfair. But she still liked her new bed, and Dad said today they could decorate their bedroom.

There were two doors to their dad's new house. Downstairs,

there was a dark blue door Dad had to open with a key, then you walked up lots of stairs to a white door, which also had to be opened with a key, and then you were inside the house. It was actually called an apartment, because other people lived in the same building. Charlie's dad carried her purple duffel bag and another large suitcase as he climbed the stairs in front of her. Elizabeth was behind him with her green duffel bag, and Charlie was last, clutching Pinky's leash.

Charlie had seen the apartment once before, but it had been empty then. She had run around with Pinky chasing her, going from room to room, while Elizabeth helped Dad measure their bedroom so that Dad would know what furniture to buy. Charlie had heard Elizabeth complaining to their dad about how she didn't want to share a bedroom with Charlie, because Charlie would mess up her stuff and use her clothes, and she wouldn't ever be able to have friends over because they wouldn't have any privacy. Dad had said that he always shared a bedroom with his brother when he was a kid and that this was a really big room, and it would actually be fun to set it up together—it would be like a special girls' club.

"Oh, right," Elizabeth had said, "really special, Dad. It's not fair. Why don't I just stay at Mom's when Charlie sleeps over here? That way we'll always have our own rooms." Then Dad had closed the door, and Charlie heard them talking but couldn't hear what they said. For the rest of the day, Elizabeth had acted all sulky and wouldn't talk to her.

But now, Elizabeth seemed excited about setting up their room. Charlie's heart bed was against one wall, and Elizabeth's plain bed was against the wall across from it. They had a new rug with black-and-white zebra stripes on it in between their beds. Dad had helped them put up posters they brought from home, including, over Charlie's bed, her favorite one, which was a picture of three kittens in a basket between balls of yarn. Elizabeth said that poster was corny, but Charlie didn't care, because those kittens were so cute. She didn't have a kitten, but she at least had three that she could look at before she went to sleep and pretend they would be there in the room snuggled up on her bed, after the lights were turned off.

Charlie woke up. It was dark, and at first she didn't know where she was. Then she looked at the opposite wall and saw Elizabeth, quilt pulled over her head as she always slept, Pinky curled up at the bottom of her bed. He was snoring. Then she remembered. There were no curtains on the windows, and the night outside was black and deep. Except for Panda, the stuffed animals she usually slept with weren't on her bed, and the closet door was a little, scary bit open. She missed her mom so much. She wished she was in her bedroom, the real one, with her own old, brown wood bed covered with stickers and her lamp shaped like a star on the little green table by her bed.

Afraid of the dark, afraid to get up and look for her dad, she called him. "Daddy," she said, not very loud, not wanting to wake Elizabeth. He didn't come. "Daddy!" This time, she yelled but still no response.

She realized she was going to have to get up, but it was so dark. Holding Panda to her chest, Charlie got out of bed and went into the hallway. The door to her dad's room was right there, she knew, but it was closed. Suppose he wasn't in that room? Suppose this wasn't really Dad's house? Suppose they were alone? Charlie started to cry.

"Charlie?" Dad called from inside the room. Charlie opened the door and ran in just as her dad was sitting up. "Baby, what's the matter?" he said, reaching out for her. Charlie rushed into his arms, pink nightgown twisting around her, hot tears on her cheeks.

"Daddy," she said. "Daddy." Dad took her into his arms and rocked her back and forth, back and forth, just like he used to do when she was a baby.

"Charlie, it's okay. Everything's okay. There's nothing to be afraid of. I'm right here," he said. Gradually, Charlie stopped crying, but kept her face buried in his chest, breathing the familiar smell.

"Daddy, can I sleep with you?" she asked.

"Sure, baby," he said, as he moved over to make room and picked up the covers, pulling Charlie underneath with him.

Charlie snuggled in, her breath calming, her grip on him loosening. "Daddy, I miss Mommy."

"I'm sorry, baby, but I'm here, and I love you, and I'll take care of you."

"But I miss Mommy."

"Okay, baby. We can call her in the morning, okay?"

"Okay," she said, and then, silence. Daddy lay still, and Charlie felt the soothing rise and fall of his chest underneath her face until she too fell back asleep.

12

Jake: Brooklyn

Sometimes I felt like I was back in Boston, after college, before Lisa and I moved in together. When I signed the lease on my new place, I realized that the only time I had lived on my own, without her, was those two years when I was sharing the apartment with Carly and Tom and a rotating group of other recent BU graduates and guys in my bands. That was almost twenty years ago. Of course, that was totally different. I had roommates, and the apartment was messy, and I slept on a mattress I had trash-picked in Back Bay, in those pre-bedbug days when you could still do that. But I was alone, in the sense that I made all my own decisions about what to do and where to go. Once Lisa and I moved in together, it was different. When I'd go to the grocery store, I'd ask her what she wanted me to pick up; when I felt like doing something on a Saturday night, I'd ask her what she wanted to do; and when I was getting home later than I thought I would, I'd call to let her know.

But in this new phase of my life, I had become acutely aware that I was essentially alone on the planet. Which I had been all along, of course—we all are. But when I would wake up in the morning, a morning when the girls weren't with me, I would sort of vibrate with autonomy. I could stay in bed and watch porn. I could smoke weed and make a hamburger for breakfast. I could call in sick and drive down to my uncle's place in Avalon and spend the day on the beach. And no one would care. In my darker moments, that feeling could devastate me, because I liked living an intertwined life. I liked waking up in a shared bed, wrapped around each other; then separating out into the world during the day but still touching base, lightly, just enough to keep Lisa in my consciousness; and then reconnecting at the end of the day, sharing the tidbits I'd subconsciously put in the "I gotta tell Lisa this" file: the small successes, the common failures, the gossip. I basked in that familiar ritual. But increasingly, I started liking the alone vibration. There was a sense of possibility, of spontaneity, I hadn't felt since those Boston days.

Even though I had moved to East Greenwood, West Greenwood was still my center of operations. That's where Lisa's house—my house too, technically—was, where Mariposa was, and, carrying what I realize is a ridiculous amount of importance in my life, it's where the Green Life Café was. Green Life is ground zero for West Greenwood. It only opened about five years ago, but it's hard to remember what the neighborhood was like before it was there. It's the place where you go to meet up with your friends on the weekend. It's the place where the tattooed young mamas come with infants swaddled to their chests to drink herbal tea and swap stories about, I don't know, essential oils or whatever. It's the place where teenagers come with their friends to chase away their hangovers after late nights partying, and it's the place local realtors meet with potential buyers to impress them with the vibrancy of life in the neighborhood. It is always full of chatty, highly educated progressives—who do things like take Brazilian drumming classes, or represent people on death row, or run adult-literacy programs—all of whom are drinking excellent and extremely expensive fair-trade coffee.

For the last year or so before the split, Lisa and I had this ritual on Sunday mornings, when we would leave the girls home alone watching a movie and walk down the street to Green Life to get coffee. We'd always see people we knew, and it was just like a nice, low-key way to hang out with friends. It made me realize why people join country clubs—you just show up, and people you like are there. So Green Life was like my country club —no membership fee, just overpriced coffee.

But it had become a bit rough to navigate. Even though I tried really hard to maintain all the friendships we had as a couple after Lisa dumped me, with some people, it was difficult. It became instantly clear when someone's primary allegiance was to Lisa, because all of a sudden this person, who had been at my kid's birthday parties, or told me intimate stories about her crazy family one drunken evening when we were all out at a bar, started treating me more like an acquaintance than a real friend—superficial. So I still went to Green Life—I actually went there a lot, because I really craved that country club feeling now that half the time I was home alone—but I did not want to run into any of Lisa's close girlfriends there. When I did, they would treat me with exaggerated politeness, but I could tell they wanted to get away from me, fast. I don't know if it was because Lisa told them horrible things about me, or because they thought divorce was contagious and they might be next. Or maybe they just felt awkward, like when you find out a friend was diagnosed with cancer but he hasn't said anything directly to you, and you don't know what to say, so it's easier just to avoid him.

It was a beautiful Saturday in early May, one of those first really warm days of spring, and I didn't have the girls with me. I woke up feeling kind of "re-birthy," like the winter of my discontent might finally be over. I actually liked my apartment: the way the sunshine came blasting into the living room, the way I had my guitars set up on stands next to the red couch, acoustic and electric, side-by-side like cousins from opposite sides of the family. And I liked the way Charlie had started jumping in bed with me sometimes when she woke up at night, and I could comfort her back to sleep—she was looking for me, not Lisa— her curly head snuggled into my chest, her mouth open, that faint warm wetness on my skin. It's not what I ever wanted, but we were all adjusting, it was working itself out, and that morning I was feeling the vibration. I put on my Mariposa T-shirt with the chrysalis on the back and the bright blue butterfly on the front, hopped on my bike, and headed over to the café to get a coffee, survey the territory, and see where the day would take me.

Green Life, not surprisingly, was buzzing. Petie was sitting outside at one of the café tables with Dylan, who still looked like a little boy, even though he was Elizabeth's age. "My man!" Petie said, jumping up and giving me the big guy hug.

"Hey, fellas. A little father–son outing here?" I said, smiling at Dylan and suddenly missing Elizabeth so much, missing her physical presence, missing her running commentary, missing her as a beautiful companion, missing just being a dad out on a Saturday morning with his kid.

"Yup, just us guys this morning. We're watching the ladies, right, Dylan?" Petie said. Dylan looked up at me, rolled his eyes, and turned his attention back to his iced macchiato or whatever he was drinking. I went inside to get in the drink line.

I was standing there, thinking that I needed to stop moping about not being with my kids and decide whether I wanted a double or triple shot. A small woman with long dark hair walked in the door, looked around, and joined me at the back of the line. "Hi," she said. "Wow, this place is popular. Must be good."

"It is," I said. "The best." I turned and looked at her full on, and she smiled, a big, wide, kind of mirthful smile. She was wearing a miniskirt, leggings, and converse sneakers. She looked late twenties, if that. She was petite and delicate but kind of tomboyish. She was adorable.

"Hi." she said. "I'm Samara. I just moved here last week. And I'm a total coffee junkie. So happy to find this place."

"Hi, I'm Jake. Nice to meet you. Where'd you move from?"

"Brooklyn," she said. "I'm starting grad school at Temple this summer. Wow, nice shirt—love the butterfly."

"Thanks. Yeah, it's a favorite of mine." First, that sounded dumb, and second, I couldn't believe I didn't tell her it's where my kids go to school, which would be the obvious thing to say about the shirt. I was just looking at her breasts, which were the smallish, perfect kind, like models have, and at the gold cross she was wearing around her neck on a tiny, fine little chain. I ordered my coffee. I thought about the fact that I hadn't had sex for six months. And before that, I hadn't had sex with anyone but Lisa for, like, twenty years.

Samara ordered. I chatted up one of the owners, John, who was working the counter. As Samara was paying for her coffee, I noticed that she had some kind of abstract swirly tattoo on the inside of her tiny wrist. A drummer I knew from a band I used to play with came in, and I joked with him. I was hyperaware of being a man in charge of the situation, a guy people know, a guy people respect. I could feel Samara watching me. Samara. What is that? Indian? Or did she just have hippie parents, like Lisa's friend Mandala?

"So, Jake, what are your favorite things to do in Greenwood?" Samara asked, turning toward me after she got her coffee.

"Big topic," I said, trying to figure out what I could do to prolong the conversation, while simultaneously realizing that this was a total invite from her to do just that—maybe even to sit down at a table together. She didn't seem to be in a rush to go anywhere, she was just standing there, smiling at me, holding her cup in one hand, and twirling a lock of her hair with the other, chipped purple nail polish shining at me, reminding me suddenly of Elizabeth. That was disgusting, of course, so I immediately banished Elizabeth from my mind and thought instead about pulling Samara's black shirt over her head and licking that little hollow in her neck where the gold cross had come to rest.

"Want to sit down for a minute?" I asked.

"Sure," she said, setting her coffee down on an empty table and pulling out the chair.

"Hi, Jake," I heard a woman call from behind me in the coffee line. I turned around and saw Karen, a doctor who worked with Lisa and whose kids also went to Mariposa.

"Hi, Karen," I said, "how's it going?" and turned back to Samara, hoping that she wouldn't really answer that question, hoping that she wouldn't say anything to me about the kids, or Lisa, or some boring parental topic like student-teacher conferences.

"Fine," Karen said, making her way toward me and Samara. Karen had to be older than Lisa and me, but not by that much. Maybe she was forty-five. But she looked frumpy and totally middle-age-mom-like. Her hair was mostly gray and short, and she was wearing glasses on a cord around her neck and the kind of jeans that are sort of baggy around the butt. *Lisa wouldn't be caught dead in that getup*, I thought. A pang of longing for my blonde, swishy, sexy almost-ex-wife passed swiftly through my body, exiting quickly as I looked at the lovely Samara, waifish and mischievous, smiling up at me as she sipped her whatever-it-was with almond milk.

"Oh, sorry, I didn't realize you had company," Karen said, smiling at Samara, which struck me as kind of an odd description because it wasn't my house, after all—can you have company in a restaurant?—but then I realized I needed to respond.

"This is Samara," I said. "She just moved to Greenwood from New York, and she's interviewing me about all the wildly hip and exciting things there are to do here."

"Hi, Samara, welcome to our little slice of heaven," said Karen, smiling in a vaguely maternal manner. "Jake, I'm running. Great to see you. You'll be at Mariposa for the fundraiser next weekend?"

I replied that I would, and Karen left. Lisa was going to hear about this. I knew it. At work tomorrow, Karen would say, "Hey, I ran into Jake in the Green Life Café, and he was with a young woman—looked like he was on a date."

And Lisa would be jealous. I knew she would be—I don't care how much she didn't want to be married to me anymore. "How young?" she'd probably ask.

And Karen would say, "Twenties, I guess," and Lisa would feel something in her chest or her stomach or her crotch or her knees. And I hoped that something she felt was pain. She deserved that pain. What'd she expect? She threw me away. I was forty-one, good-looking, and a nice guy. And women responded to me. And I realized, for the first time since the day I got the bad news from Lisa, that I fully intended to capitalize on those features.

I pulled out the chair opposite Samara and sat down. "So, Samara, what are you going to grad school for?" I said, leaning toward her just a little, close enough to see that the swirly tattoo on the inside of her wrist was actually a group of little stars, connected to form a circular shape by a fine green line, and close enough to catch a sweet musky scent emanating from the little hollow in her neck as she leaned forward, dark hair falling around her face.

13

Ellen: Divorce Papers

Connecticut College wasn't Wesleyan, and it wasn't Swarthmore, but it was a perfectly good school, a respectable school, Ellen thought, and Marni seemed happy. Ellen was still reeling from the fact that, just like that, it was all over. The whole overblown, obsessive-making college admissions process, kicked off by that first parents' meeting at the beginning of tenth grade and ending with the signing of that deposit check now rolling its way north to New London at this very moment. And what an anticlimax. All those SAT prep sessions and practice tests, all the time and money and vacation days spent on college visits. All the elaborate postmortems in the car after each one, with Marni dissecting everything the student tour leader said—and wore—and Ellen and Dan reminiscing about this or that out-of-date bit of information or anecdote they had heard about the college just visited, things they knew to be too old to be relevant but yet couldn't help themselves from recounting. Couldn't help themselves, because the process they were going through with their daughter took them hurtling back to their own late adolescence, to a rosy remembrance of what it felt like to be on that brink, about to cross that glittering, transformative bridge to the rest of their lives.

But all that was done, and it all boiled down to this, to the simple fact that their daughter would be attending a not particu-larly distinguished, but nonetheless very expensive, small liberal arts college. A college ranked number fifty-five in *U.S. News & World Report*, lower than Lafayette, and Franklin & Marshall! It was shocking to Ellen, really, since she was positive Marni could have gotten into either of those schools had she bothered to apply, and she would have been closer to home. Nonetheless, she didn't, and she won't, but she would still be less than five hours away, and Connecticut College was really nothing to be embarrassed about.

As this post-admission reverie was taking place internally, Ellen was trying hard to wrap up a phone call with one of her more annoying clients, a very successful sculptor named William. William always managed to irritate her by implying that while she was just a boring worker bee, he saw the world differently, because he was an artist, and therefore he could think of "creative solutions" in a way he just couldn't expect poor old bean counter Ellen to understand.

William was in the middle of telling her that he had read her email about how he could expect to see his and his wife's assets divided by the court if he rejected his wife's current settlement offer, but it couldn't be right. He just couldn't see how a judge could award his wife half the value of his sculptures. He was sure that he would be able to explain to the judge that art is not like a house or a bank account, because his soul had gone into it, because it was the tangible embodiment of his artistic expression. *Right*, thought Ellen, *that testimony will get you far*. In other words, the things his labor had created during the marriage—enormous bronze abstractions that sell for upward of $50,000—should not be considered assets, but more like appendages. Not going to fly. After reiterating for the fourth time that she heard his concerns, but her advice about accepting the

—very reasonable—offer hadn't changed, Ellen told William to sleep on it and managed to extract herself from the call.

Feeling cranky from a combination of low-level angst about the mediocrity of Connecticut College, letdown from the completion of her last official job as mother of a high school student, and stress from holding her tongue while being condescended to by the arrogant William, Ellen looked around her desk for something mindless and calming to do. At the top of one of several piles was the Naudain divorce agreement. She had written a draft and printed it for editing the day before but forgotten about it. Perfect, she thought. Iced coffee in hand, sandals kicked off beneath her desk, Ellen read through the contract, clauses she had written hundreds of times before soothing her with their familiar content and pleasing clarity of language. Simple, this contract was, as Jake and his wife didn't really own anything. All they had to do was transfer title to the house to his wife; everything else could stay where it was.

As she finished editing the agreement, Ellen pictured Jake when she ran into him that day with his daughters, and she wondered why his wife wanted this divorce so suddenly. Jake was handsome and sociable, he had a decent job, he seemed like an involved father. Another relationship would explain it, but Jake had told Ellen definitively that neither he nor Lisa were involved with anyone else. Of course, maybe someone was lying about that. But maybe not. *If anyone should know that appearances can be deceiving, I should,* Ellen thought. Maybe Jake was actually cruel or stupid or had some weird sexual fetish. Images of Jake in chains wielding a whip flashed through Ellen's mind as she dialed his number.

"Hi, Ellen," he said, causing Ellen's brain to instantly reject those images and replace them with the smiling dad at the dog park.

"Hi, Jake," she said. "The agreement is done, so I'm going to email it to you to look over, and if it's okay, you can go ahead and send it to Lisa. She still doesn't have a lawyer, right?"

"Nope," Jake responded. "She doesn't need one. Because she knows everything."

That would be an accurate description of many of the unrepresented spouses in her current caseload, Ellen thought. "Well," she said, "makes it easier for us. If Lisa's on board as well, you can just take it to a notary and sign it. But if she wants any changes, we'll need to discuss."

"Okay, got it. I still can't believe this is really happening. But, whatever, it is. And, Ellen, you'll be glad to know, I'm starting to move on. I even have a date."

Of course he does, she thought. "Jake, that's great. Glad to hear it. I know some lucky woman will snatch you right up."

"Thanks, but I don't think I want to be snatched up anytime soon. I am so burned still."

"I know," Ellen murmured sympathetically. "I get that, but I predict remarriage in your near future. Just my gut."

"All right," Jake said. "You're the expert. Hey, I want to ask you something, which might be a little weird. If you think it is, just tell me. Your daughter, the one I met a few months ago at the dog park—does she ever babysit?"

"Marni. Yeah, she does. Not as much as she used to, now that she turned eighteen and considers it the job she used to have back in the long gone era of her youth, but she still does. She loves kids."

Jake continued. "Would it be okay with you if I contacted her to see if she could babysit for my girls? If this is crossing some line because you're my lawyer, I would totally understand. It's just that I know we live in the same neighborhood. And I'm sure your daughter's responsible, because she's your kid, and I really don't want to ask Lisa for the contact info for the babysitters we used to use. She handled all that stuff when we were together, and I want to deal with this myself. Plus, I don't want to have to tell her where I'm going or why I need a sitter."

Ellen thought for a second about whether this was problematic. Her quick conclusion was no, not at all. Jake's divorce was over, for all practical purposes, and she had zero expectation of any future custody issues, because he and Lisa had that all worked out from the get-go. This was a file she was going to close very shortly and never see again. And Marni was only going to be in Philly for the next three months, so there was no possibility it could turn into an ongoing babysitting job. Anyway, Marni probably wouldn't want to do it. Her peak babysitting days had pretty much come and gone by junior year.

"Jake, I think it's fine. Not weird at all. Your girls seemed lovely, and I'm sure Marni would be happy to babysit for them. Only thing is that she's very tied up with end-of-senior-year stuff, so she might not be available. I'll send you her cell and let her know you might be contacting her. Text is best."

"Great. I'll give her a try. Really appreciate it. And I'll look over the agreement and let you know if I have any questions. Hopefully not, and Lisa and I can just sign it. I'm ready to get this done. Thanks again, Ellen. You're the best."

Wishing all her clients were so easygoing and appreciative, Ellen hung up the phone and emailed Jake her daughter's cell phone number. Babysitting already seemed like an earlier era. Now she was the mom of a college student. Now she was going to be an empty nester. She'd always disliked that phrase, because she thought it was vaguely pitiful. It was one of those names manufactured specifically to sanitize, to make a sad or depressing thing sound happy and upbeat, like "senior citizen." Whatever happened to just being an old person? Ellen felt nothing upbeat whatsoever about having an empty nest. She felt old and used up, that's all, and like her life was about to become way less interesting. And she wouldn't be able to do any of those supposedly fun empty nester things, like take swing-dancing lessons or pottery classes, because she'd be working longer hours than ever so they could pay the ridiculous tuition bills for Marni's second-rate college education.

Now cranky in the extreme, Ellen turned off her computer, put on her sandals, and headed home, where she could either pick a fight with Dan over something stupid or drink too much wine or, more likely, do both.

14

Jake: Dinner Date

Frighteningly, like I'd been doing this for years, I knew just what to wear—my new jeans, the skinnier black ones that Elizabeth helped me pick out, and my John Coltrane T-shirt. I didn't know if Samara was into jazz, and I'm not really that into it myself. But jazz is cool, John Coltrane is a cool dude whose name she would definitely know, and the shirt was soft and kind of tight.

When she said, "Hey, come by for dinner on Friday, some friends will be visiting from Brooklyn, and I think you'll like them," I kept it very casual.

I said, "Sure, I'd love to—will try to make it."

But I'd been thinking about it all week. I had no idea if Samara was going to act like I was her date, or like I was some random person she met at a café and took pity on because he was going through a divorce. So I was going in blind. And everyone would probably be fifteen years younger than me. But she was really hot, and I couldn't stop thinking about her, so at some level, I didn't care what the context was. I was definitely in pursuit mode.

Samara's address turned out to be a rambling old Victorian house—multiple porches, peeling paint, overgrown yard—broken up into apartments. Her last name was Bard. I found the doorbell for the third-floor apartment. Next to it was a label which said Bard/Butterfield. I was guessing Butterfield was her roommate. I could hear the buzz of a party, electronica getting louder as I climbed the stairs. The door was open. I walked in. Not your typical Greenwood crowd, or maybe it was if you were twenty-eight and didn't have kids, but I didn't know about it. Not the Mariposa parent scene, I guess is what I mean—lots of black clothing, tattoos, and big beards. And hats—of the porkpie variety, not the baseball cap variety. Samara was standing in the corner with a beer in her hand, barefoot, wearing a very short flowery dress. She turned around just as I started to make my way over to her. "Jake!" she said, giving me a greeting-anyone type of hug. "You made it! Welcome to our house. Owen, come meet Jake."

A guy with long hair in a checked shirt appeared, holding out his hand. "Welcome, man," he said, "I'm Samara's husband. She told me all about you. Really glad you stopped by."

I felt like I just got punched. How could this be? Could I have totally misread her that day at the café? Am I that out of touch? And why wasn't she wearing a wedding ring? I'd checked that out right when I first saw her; I'm not that stupid. But apparently I was. Like, here I was, all big and bad about the fact that this captivating younger woman was attracted to me and invited me to her house, when she probably just felt sorry for me. Oh God, how pathetic.

"Great to meet you too," I said, looking over at Samara as I shook his hand. She was just standing there, smiling, like this was all perfectly normal. As Owen released my hand, I noticed that he had the same group of little stars tattooed on the inside of his wrist as Samara did. Ugh. So now I was stuck at this party that I really had no interest in. I mean, I like parties, but I was there because I thought I had a date with Samara. The happily married but non-ring-wearing Samara. It would have been rude to just walk out, but the weight of my new understanding was crushing. I had zero interest in making chitchat with a bunch of overgrown teenagers. I should have stayed home with my girls. I could have taken them to the movies, or we could have gone out for gnocchi at the Italian place Charlie loves so much because the chef's wife always fusses over her and gives her those sour yellow candies from the bowl by the cash register, despite my staged protestations. It's a game we'd been playing since she was three, and it never ceased to amuse and delight her. So what was I doing? In addition to being a chump, I was also falling down in the dad department.

"So, Jake," Samara said to me as the annoyingly handsome Owen retreated to the kitchen, "sorry there's such a crowd here. I didn't expect this, it just kind of happened, you know?" I didn't, really, but I nodded. "I was hoping we could get to know each other a little better, and I wanted you and Owen to hang out too."

"Samara, why didn't you tell me you were married?" I said, without planning to. So much for maintaining my cool.

"Because it doesn't matter to me. Does it to you?" she said, moving closer, putting her little hand on my arm. I quivered.

"Of course it does. What do you mean?"

"Because you believe in monogamy?" she asked. Wow, I didn't expect that. This girl got right to the point.

"Well, yes," I said. "I mean, if you're married, yes."

"Well, we don't," she said, leaning closer, talking just above a whisper. "Owen and I are polyamorous. We don't buy into the whole just-one-partner-for-life thing. We're open to having relationships with other people, so long as we talk about it and agree. And I told him about you. I told him I really liked you, and I've never been involved with anyone older before. I think it's hot."

I was staring at her, transfixed.

"I think you're sexy," she said, moving even closer and putting her hand on the middle of my chest, lightly, right over John Coltrane's face, causing a major blood rush to my face and my penis. "And I thought Owen would like you too."

"What do you mean?" I asked. "Because he has to, like, approve?"

This was getting pretty far out there, pretty far from the tame married world I'd been inhabiting. But hey, she was coming on to me, and she was talking about having sex with me, and she clearly was not looking for a husband. This was all awesome. My evaluation of the evening took a radical swing back toward the positive.

"Well, yeah, because we need to be open. But also because I thought he might be attracted to you, too. Sometimes we have three-way relationships with other people. We're both bisexual, so the possibilities are pretty cool."

Now we were moving into territory that made me flinch. Let me be your pool boy, or actually your suave older lover, I was thinking, and let that be okay with your husband so we don't have to sneak around, but I was not going to fuck him too. I just looked at her, speechless, my body rigid.

"I realize that may not be your thing," she said. "And it's not like it's some sort of requirement for you and me to get together. But it can be really transformative if you're open to it. And I do think you're Owen's type too."

Transformative? And I really did not want to be Owen's type, although I had certainly noticed that he was good-looking in a skinny, slightly androgynous sort of way. But wow, I was so not gay, or bi.

"That's really not my thing," I said, "but you definitely are." There didn't seem to be any point in being indirect.

"Well, good," she said, rising up on her tiptoes and kissing me softly on the cheek. "We'll need to make a plan to get together soon, then. Obviously, with not so many people around. We may be polyamorous, but we don't generally host orgies," she said, smiling. "At least, not too often."

I stayed for the minimum amount of time I could without seeming rude. Had a beer, made small talk with some of the Brooklyn guys who turned out to be musicians, said goodbye to Samara and Owen (got another hug you'd give to anyone, from Samara), and took off. I didn't really feel like going home, since I had gone to the trouble of hiring a sitter, and I was still buzzing from the polyamory revelation. Obviously, I'd heard about it. There was a small group of parents at Mariposa who were close friends and rumored to have some type of complicated but consensual, mutual open marriage thing going on. It was kind of titillating to think about, but I didn't know the details. When Lisa and I learned about that group, we kept trying to figure out how it worked, like if wife A wanted to have sex with husband B, would she just do it and tell husband A afterward, or would they talk about it in advance, or what? We thought the whole thing was weird, and we sort of laughed about it. But I think we, or at least I, also envied them a little because they were being sexually adventurous and unconventional, and our lives had fallen into such a by-the-book, conventional rhythm. We followed the template, and they, apparently, were creating their own, and it made them seem sort of sparkly and daring.

I decided to call Petie, on the likely chance that he would be hanging out at his favorite neighborhood bar, called, coincidentally, "Pete's." He was that type of guy who goes out on Saturday night without his wife to watch sports at the bar and drink with his bar buddies. I was never that kind of guy. Lisa wouldn't have put up with it, but also I wasn't really interested when she and I were together. I wanted to go out with her, or put the kids to bed and stay home with her—drinking wine and talking in the dark, quiet living room, having sex. I used to cherish that Saturday night time when we were both out of our workweek heads and we didn't have to go anywhere the next day, even if one of us did have to get up early with the kids. Didn't she feel that way too?

That's what I couldn't figure out. I couldn't understand how she could have just faked the whole love and marriage thing toward the end. I wish I knew when—when did she stop really loving me, when was I being played, when did I become the pathetic husband who blindly loved his wife while she was plotting to get rid of him? What a bitch. I knew I had to get along with her for the sake of the girls and all that, but I could not come close to forgiving her for just discarding me for no reason.

Petie answered his phone. I heard, in the background, the cacophony of a Saturday night at the bar. "Jakie," he said. "Come join, man."

I had told Marni I would be back by midnight, so after two more beers and a conversation about everything but the fact that I had been propositioned earlier in the evening by a beautiful poly-amorous twenty-eight-year-old—which I kept in my pocket like a found treasure to be examined later, alone, when I got home—I left Petie engaged in a drunken debate with a neighborhood ward leader about the upcoming City Council race, and drove to my apartment. When I opened the door, Marni was lying on my couch with Pinky, doing something with her phone.

"Everything go okay?" I asked, already knowing the answer, knowing that my girls must have loved spending the evening with her, so pretty and nice and so cool in her confident teenage-girl self.

"Everything was fine. They were great. The only thing was that Charlie really didn't want to go to bed at nine, so I let her stay up a little later, and then she wanted me to read to her, so she didn't end up going to sleep until closer to ten. I hope that's okay."

I told her it was fine, of course. She got up from the couch and reached her arms over her head in a slow stretch, which made her shirt rise up, showing her perfect, flat teenage stomach. She held that position for just a couple of seconds longer than necessary to get the benefit of the stretch, while I stood there, staring at her. For a minute I was lost. Then I snapped back, reached for my wallet, and handed her three twenties.

"Thanks," she said. "Hey, I saw your guitars. The girls told me you play in a band. That's cool."

"Yeah," I said. "Man With a Dog."

"Cool name." Marni was just standing there, not getting ready to leave.

"Yeah. Well, thanks, Marni."

"You're welcome. Any time. Until I leave for college, that is." She was still standing there.

"I'll walk you downstairs and make sure you get into your car okay," I said.

"Okay, thanks."

I opened the front door, and she went through it, brushing against me. It seemed like not quite by accident, and she started down the stairs ahead of me. She turned around. "You coming?"

I followed her downstairs, and then we were sort of stuck in the vestibule, because I needed to get around her to unlock the front door. I put my hand on the small of her back just to move around her so I could get to the door, and then I'm not sure what happened. I guess she turned around to face me, I'm not really sure, but what matters is, we ended up kissing—the deep, slow kind. And then it's like I came to, and I broke away and said something like, "Hey, I'm sorry."

And she said, "Don't be," and she went out the door, got into her car, and left. And I thought *shit, she's my lawyer's daughter, and she's eighteen years old.* This was a major fuckup. But I also thought: *no harm—I just won't have her babysit for me again. She's not a minor, it's not like I'm her teacher or anything, she was definitely flirting with me, and it was just a kiss. Who cares? Why am I worrying about this? This is my new life. Women flirt with me, and I can act on it. I don't have to be on someone's leash. I'm a free agent.*

And then I proceeded to take my mildly drunken and very aroused self back upstairs, lie down on the couch with Pinky, and google polyamory.

15

Elizabeth: Tattoo

This was the first summer Elizabeth was going to a real sleep-away camp. She had been to two-week sessions of Girl Scout camp with Billie the last two summers, and she had liked it pretty well, but that was really for little girls, not for her anymore. She was twelve, and she was going to be a seventh grader in September. She was not going to go to a camp where you have to pack a separate outfit in a separate plastic bag for each day you're there because there's no way to do laundry, and sleep in a moldy tent, and go on muddy hikes in the rain. And where there are no boys. No, for four weeks this summer, she was going to Willow Dell, a performing arts camp in Massachusetts where the campers are ages ten to sixteen. There were different tracks you could pick, and she was going to do the musical theater one, where she'd be in both a showcase and a full musical during her session. She didn't know yet what the musical would be—she'd find out the first day of camp and then audition for whatever roles she thought would be good for her. But Elizabeth knew they'd pick a show with lots of parts, like *Peter Pan* had. Maybe they'd do *West Side Story*, which would be amazing.

She hadn't visited the camp, but she and her mom had gone to an information session in January where they met counselors and other prospective campers, and they watched a video. The bunks looked really nice—no more disgusting tents—and they also had a rock band track, which appeared from the video to be what all the cute boys were in.

Elizabeth was leaving in a week, and this was her last weekend with her dad because next week she would be at her mom's, and her mom was going to drive her up there. She had a list of stuff she needed to get for camp, like a plastic caddy to take her shampoo to the bathhouse and bug spray and that kind of thing, and her dad said he would take her to Target to buy it. This was way preferable to her mom taking her. She could probably get her dad to buy other stuff she wanted too, like new sunglasses and, more importantly, a hair straightener, which her mom definitely would say no to. And Charlie was at a birthday party, which meant they would be able to spend longer at Target, since Charlie wouldn't be there trying to get their dad to buy her things too.

Elizabeth was happy about the upcoming trip to Target and very happy about going to camp. She'd been feeling like she really needed to get away from home. She needed a break from the joint custody thing. It was working out fine, really. Her parents didn't fight or say mean things about each other to her and Charlie, or anything like that—not like Anya's parents did all the time. Anya had told Elizabeth that her parents got into an argument one time when her dad was dropping her off, and he started yelling and called her mom a stupid cunt. And then Anya's mom said she was going to call the police, which she didn't, but when she took Anya inside she said her dad had "issues," but she wouldn't tell Anya what the issues were.

Obviously, her parents weren't crazy like that. It was just that things weren't the same. She didn't like having two houses and two bedrooms and having to move all her clothes and books and electronics every Sunday. She always forgot stuff, and then if she couldn't find something, she wouldn't know if she should keep looking for it because it was just lost in the house where she was or if there was no point because she'd left it at the other house.

So all of that was aggravating, but really it was her parents that were bumming her out. They both seemed kind of distracted and like they were not really listening to her. It was not what she would have expected, because with only one adult around, you'd think they'd focus more on the kids than when there were two of them together having their own conversations. And still, no one had told her why they were getting divorced. The only thing she was pretty sure of, not that they had ever come out and actually said it, but she'd figured it out from some comments her dad had made, is that it was her mom's idea, not his.

When she first talked to her girlfriends about it, they asked her if her dad was cheating on her mom, and Elizabeth said no, he couldn't be. But now she wonders if maybe he had been, because why else would her mom want to divorce him? She had asked both of them more than once why they split, and they just gave her this obviously rehearsed response about growing apart. She was sure they had read books about how to act with your kids when you're getting divorced, and the books had told them what to say. She felt like she was being lied to, and there was this fake cheerfulness they both had sometimes when they tried to act like everything was the same as it had been when, of course, it wasn't at all. Not that she would want to hear her dad calling her mom a stupid cunt like Anya's horrible dad, but she needed some information. She was twelve years old, and they were treating her the same as Charlie.

So camp would be a good break. And then there was the camp boyfriend thing—she was determined to have one.

After she and her dad got in the car—the new, cute orange

car he just bought, which was still clean inside—and were heading toward Target, Elizabeth asked if they could stop at the Green Life Café so she could get a latte. This was a new thing for her, coffee. She liked having a to-go coffee cup with her to sip on when she went to a store or walked down the street; it was a sophisticated look. Her dad agreed—he was like a coffee addict—so they pulled up outside the café and went in to order. As they walked toward the coffee line, a really pretty girl with long dark hair and hot-pink lipstick walked up to her dad and gave him a hug.

"Hi, Samara," Elizabeth's dad said, kind of awkwardly and not really hugging her back. "This is my daughter, Elizabeth."

"Hi, Elizabeth," the Samara girl said. "Nice to meet you. Where are you two headed?"

"Target," Elizabeth said, trying to figure out how her dad knew this girl, who wasn't old enough to be anyone's mom that she knew. "I'm going to camp next week, and I need to buy some stuff."

"Oh, right, I remember that," said Samara. "Like, you need new toothpaste and flip-flops and towels and stuff, right?"

"Right," said Elizabeth.

"Well, I'm sure your dad will get whatever you ask him to, right, Jake?"

"That's the plan," said Elizabeth.

"Not really," said Jake, "but I do have a list."

"Like I said," Samara smiled right at Elizabeth, "I think he'll do what you want."

Back in the car, seatbelt fastened and latte in hand, Elizabeth asked, "Dad, who's Samara? How do you know her?"

"She's just someone I met at Green Life a couple of months ago," Jake said. "She moved to Philly this year to go to film school, and she was looking to meet people in the neighborhood. Remember how I went to a party a few weeks ago when Marni babysat for you guys? That was her and her husband's party. I went to their house. His name is Owen."

At the mention of a husband, Elizabeth felt her body relax. "Oh," she said. "She's nice. And I love that tattoo she has on her wrist. Did you see it? I want one like that."

"I didn't notice," her dad said. "And you can't get one until you're eighteen."

CHORUS #2

The Girls

The thing about the Green Life Café, Emma thought, as she put down her hair straightener, took one last approving look in the mirror, and skipped out the door, flat, glossy locks streaming behind her, is that it's cool even though your parents go there too. Because it's not just your parents, it's people in their twenties, who sit with their laptops and write or study, and drink lots of coffee, and talk with their friends about books and art and stuff. It's almost like Brooklyn, where her older sister lives. Well, maybe not almost, but closer than any other place in Greenwood that she knew. Plus, her parents kept a card there, so she could just tell the barista to charge whatever she got on their card, so she didn't have to spend her babysitting money, which was another good feature.

Her girls were already there when Emma walked in, six long legs sprawled out around a window table. Three shiny heads were together, whispering.

Sit down, Alice said. You're not going to believe this. See that guy over there, in the coffee line, the one with the dark hair and the Wayfarers? Marni, tell Emma what he did, it's soooo creepy.

So, Marni said, motioning to Emma to lean in, that guy is named Jake Naudain, and he's divorced, and my mom was his lawyer. I met him one time when I was with my mom at the dog park, and he was there with his kids. So after that, he asked my mom if I babysat—and you know how much I fucking love babysitting—but anyway, he texted me and asked if I could sit for him, and it was some night I didn't have any plans, so I said sure, because I really needed the money. And he's got two girls, who are really cute, and I figured it would be easy. Which it was.

Get to the point, says Alice.

I'm giving Emma the context, said Marni. Okay, bossy? I'm setting the scene. So, like I was saying, he comes home late, and he's maybe a little drunk, whatever. And I'm asleep on the couch, and when I get up, he's looking at me in this kinda creepy way, and I'm like, woah, perv alert. And then he walks me downstairs to the front door—he lives in an apartment—and we're in this small hallway kinda place, and he like grabs me and starts kissing me and shoving his tongue in my mouth and pushing against my boobs and putting his hands on my ass. And I, like, break away and run out the door to my car and get the hell outta there. This is the first time I've seen him since then, and I totally want to avoid him, which is why I'm trying to hide behind Alice. Alice, can you please move your chair over?

Oh my God, said Emma, that's gross. So you told your mom, right? And what did she do, like, fire him? Can a lawyer fire a client?

That's the thing, Alice interjected. She didn't tell her mom. And that's what Laura and I were just telling her, when you came in—that she needs to. Right?

Totally needs to, said Emma. Don't you think she should know that about her own client?

Well, what's the point? said Marni. It's not like I'm afraid of him or anything. I'm never going to sit for him again, obviously, and I'm going to college in like two months, and what does it have to do with anything? What's my mom going to do with that information? He's not a child molester or anything, he's just a creeper.

Well, maybe he sort of is a child molester, said Laura. That's the point.

I'm eighteen, said Marni.

But Marn, said Alice, he's got daughters, and when they're teenagers, they'll have friends around. Ewww. And suppose this would be important in his divorce case, and your mom doesn't know it, and you do?

I dunno, said Marni. I just think it was more like a one-time thing. And my mom will flip out, and who needs that? Just one more reason not to babysit, is all. And remember: don't get in small spaces with older drunk guys.

Well, it's your call, said Emma. But if someone's forty-year-old dad hit on me like that, and I didn't tell my mom, and she found out later, she'd kill me for not telling her. And then she'd kill him. Collective laughter.

Okay, said Marni. Thanks for the advice, crew. Which I'm not going to follow.

16

Jake: *Naudain v. Naudain,*
October Term, 1:30 p.m.

Watching my girls, first Elizabeth, then Charlie—especially Charlie, biting her lower lip and twisting the corner of her shirt the way she always does when she's nervous—follow that sheriff back into the judge's chambers is sickening. How did Lisa become a person who would do this to me? Or, more importantly, do this to them? Was she always like this, and I just never saw it? Was I blinded by her golden-girl looks and the rush of knowing that other people thought of us as this perfect family, to such an extent that I didn't really see her for what she is? She's vindictive, in a major way, and harsh, and dismissive—so sure she's right. Or has she changed drastically since we split up? I really don't know.

Ellen says the morning went really well. She says that the judge didn't hear anything from Lisa that would make her change the custody schedule, that Elizabeth didn't remember whether Charlie had ever gotten in bed with me and Samara, and that Charlie wouldn't talk at all. Apparently, Judge Jones chatted her up and gave her candy and stuff, but she was nervous, and the judge really couldn't get her to say anything other than to talk about Pinky. Also, Ellen says, it was clear that she was annoyed with Lisa's asshole—she didn't say that, but he is—

lawyer for filing a petition without clear allegations about what I supposedly did. I get what she's saying, and that's all good, but I really don't understand how any of this is Lisa's business in the first place, so why should I have to defend myself about my personal life anyway? But I do, and I'm glad I have Ellen in my corner, even if it costs a fortune. She seems like she knows what she's doing, and the judge seems to think so too, so hopefully that will translate to how the judge feels about me.

It's so uncomfortable sitting in the waiting area. Lisa brought the girls, because it's her week, and she brought her mom to sit with them while we're in the courtroom. That's fine; I wouldn't really want them sitting out here alone, although the place is crawling with sheriffs, but it's like I'm persona non grata. I mean, I don't think either Lisa or my mother-in-law would explicitly tell the girls not to talk to me, but you can see their confusion. Like when I arrived, they were already here, sitting with Lisa and her mom. Instead of coming right over to me and giving me a hug, like they would normally do when we haven't seen each other for a few days, they were all hesitant and looking at Lisa like they needed permission. I guess she told them it was okay, because then they did run over to the part of the waiting area where I was standing talking to Ellen, and I introduced them—they didn't remember her from the dog park that day, but they remembered Marni—and they were kind of shy and awkward, even Elizabeth. So we had this sort of stilted conversation, I gave them a quick hug, and they scurried back to Grandma, like they had done something wrong by hanging out with me.

Judge Jones had told us to be back in court at one thirty, so here we are. Ellen asked her to dismiss the case without even hearing my side, because the judge had told Boyle she might do that if the girls didn't tell her about the "sexual conduct" that supposedly happened. But the judge has shot that down. Which makes me nervous, like the girls must have said something, even though Ellen told me they didn't. But I can't obsess over that, because it's my turn to testify. If this wasn't so serious, it would be funny, because being in a courtroom and having a trial is one of those scenarios that you've seen so many times on TV and in movies. The things people say—"call your next witness" or "objection sustained"—sound like a script, like a parody of reality. Obviously it's not a parody at all, but I find my mind sort of wandering between being in the moment—watching the court reporter refill her odd, old-fashioned machine with a roll of odd, old-fashioned paper, hearing the faint rustle of pages being turned as the sheriff in the back of the courtroom tries to read the newspaper without the judge noticing—to moving outside my body. I imagine the whole scene from an aerial view: me and my lawyer on one side of the room, Lisa and her lawyer on the other, the judge in the center, sitting up high so she looks down at us. It's so graphic. A picture of the playing out of conflict according to ancient theatrical rules. It's like a dance, a dance Lisa and I don't know, but everyone else in the room does.

I'm jolted back to reality and down from my imaginary drone by the sound of Ellen calling my name. I walk up to the witness stand. The judge reminds me I am still under oath and tells Ellen to begin. Ellen stands up and smiles at me.

"Mr. Naudain, how long have you and Ms. Naudain been living in separate homes?"

"Since March. Close to eight months."

"Now, you heard Ms. Naudain testify that you and she share custody of your daughters on an alternating-week basis, correct?"

"Yes."

"Whose idea was that?

"Both of ours. We never discussed any other possibility."

"When did you first receive a copy of the Petition to Modify Custody, filed by Mr. Boyle?"

"When you sent it to me—I think it was two weeks ago."

"So about October first?"

"That sounds right."

"Since March, when you moved into your current home, up until the day you received a copy of the Petition to Modify Custody filed by Mr. Boyle, did Ms. Naudain ever mention that she wanted to change the schedule?"

"No."

"For that same time period—March through the day you saw the petition—did Ms. Naudain ever express concern to you about your parenting of the children?"

"Only one time."

"When was that?"

"I think it was in July."

"What were the circumstances?"

"It was just like she said this morning. She called me up and said that Elizabeth told her Samara had stayed over at my place one of the nights they were with me. And she was really mad about it."

"Did you discuss that with her?"

"Yes. I told her it was true, that I was dating Samara, and that the girls had both met her several times, and that she stayed over that one night. And then Lisa started asking me questions about my relationship with Samara, and it turned into an argument, because I didn't think I needed to answer those questions, I didn't think they were any of her business, and I didn't think I needed her permission to introduce my kids to my girlfriend. I'm aware that it's a sensitive issue." Ellen and I had rehearsed this part. "But I'm a very hands-on kind of parent, I know what's going on with my kids, and I wouldn't do anything, ever, that I thought was bad for them. So Lisa and I disagree about this. But that is literally the first disagreement about the kids that we've had since I moved out."

"Now turning to the night of September seventeenth, which is the subject of Ms. Naudain's petition, did Ms. Bard—that's Samara's last name, correct?"

"Yes"

"Did Ms. Bard sleep at your house?"

"Yes."

"Where did she sleep?"

"She slept in my bedroom—with me."

"That night, did Charlie wake up?"

"Yes."

"Is that a common occurrence?"

"It was. When I first moved into my new place, she would often wake up in the middle of the night and say she was scared. The first few times it happened, I let her sleep in bed with me, which is what she was used to because Lisa and I had let her sleep with us if she woke up. She's always had trouble sleeping through the night. But I didn't want to get her in the habit of doing it with me at the new place, so after a few times, when she would wake up, I started going into the girls' room and putting her back in her bed and sitting with her. I rub her back until she goes back to sleep."

"What happened on this particular night?"

"What I just described. I heard her crying, and I got up and went out in the hallway, and she was standing there, crying. So I picked her up and carried her back into her room, put her back in her bed, and sat on the bed with her until she fell asleep."

"Are you sure you did not take her into your bedroom?"

"Yes. I wouldn't have done that because Samara was there."

"Why wouldn't you have done it because Ms. Bard was there?"

The answer to this question was a major topic I covered with Ellen. When she asked me about this at her office, my initial answer was that I wouldn't have done it because I didn't want Lisa to find out, which was way closer to the actual truth of the matter, but obviously not the thing to say to the judge. So we worked out a response. I wonder how much of the time witnesses have rehearsed their answers like I did for this one.

"Because I think it would be confusing for Charlie. I mean, it's one thing for them to know Samara occasionally sleeps over, which I'm fine with because they're fine with it, and a totally different thing to have Charlie in bed with me and her. I mean, I just don't think it's appropriate at this stage of my relationship with Samara—and maybe it's never appropriate, now that Charlie's getting older—but anyway, I didn't do it."

"Mr. Naudain, you realize you're under oath, right?"

"Yes."

"No further questions."

Judge Jones looks at me and then looks at Lisa's lawyer. "Cross-examination, Mr. Boyle."

Stephen Boyle stands up with a legal pad in his hand. I feel a bead of sweat trickle down my chest, stop right in that hollow over my sternum, and land on my stomach. "Good afternoon, Mr. Naudain," he begins, smiling, which is so unnerving, like we're business colleagues meeting at a conference or something, instead of hunter and prey, which is what is really happening here. I'm definitely prey. And the thing is, I have to play along and sound friendly, which is sort of humiliating. But if I don't, the judge will think I'm an asshole, which obviously I can't afford to have her think. So I have to swallow my self-respect and reply, "Good afternoon." Now that he's established dominance, he moves on.

"Mr. Naudain, am I correct in understanding that you just moved out of the marital residence this past March?"

"Yes, that's right."

"So you've been in your apartment for about seven months?"

"That's about right—closer to eight, I think."

"And you would agree with me, would you not, that it was a big transition for your daughters when you moved out?"

"Yes, sure. It was a big transition for all of us."

"They each have their own rooms at home, don't they?"

"At Lisa's house, our old house, yes, they each have their own bedroom."

"But in your apartment, they have to share a room, correct?"

"They like it."

"Mr. Naudain, that's not what I asked you. Please answer my question: do they have to share a room in your apartment?"

Ellen sighs and stands up. "Objection, Your Honor. Argumentative. If Mr. Boyle wants to establish that the Naudain children share a room at their father's home—and I don't know why he would, given that it was already established on direct and is not in dispute—he can ask that question and skip the 'do they have to' characterization."

The judge looks irritated. "Ms. Ackerman, this is cross-examination. But Mr. Boyle, could we please move on? If you think this Court is going to look negatively upon Mr. Naudain because his daughters share a bedroom, I can tell you right now that you're wasting your time. Next question."

"I understand, Your Honor," says the hunter. "Mr. Naudain, would you agree with me that it's important for you and Ms. Naudain to communicate well about the children?"

"Yes."

"And if one of you has to make an important decision about something that could have a big impact on the children, you should talk about it with the other before making the decision, shouldn't you?"

"Well, I'm not sure what you mean by an important decision, but sure, we have to decide things together, like about their school, and after-school activities, and their health, stuff like that."

"Would mental health be included in that list?"

"Again, I'm not sure what you mean, but yes, their mental health, like if we wanted to send one of them to a therapist, sure."

"Don't you think the decision to have a new girlfriend sleep over, in your bed, when your daughters are present, just a few short months after you moved out of the marital home, could have negative mental health consequences for your children?"

"No."

"And don't you think this is just the sort of major decision that you should have discussed with their mother before you did it?"

"No. Like I said before, I think it's personal."

"Now, Mr. Naudain, you testified on direct that you frequently sleep with your eight-year-old daughter, correct?"

"No, that's not correct."

"Okay, so let's break it down, then. Your daughter, Charlotte, is eight, correct?"

"Yes. She just turned eight. Her birthday was last week."

"And you testified that she wakes up in the middle of the night, correct?"

"Yes, sometimes. Not every night."

"And you testified that when she does, you take her into bed with you to sleep, correct?"

"Yes, at first I did."

"When you say 'first,' does that mean for the first month after you moved?"

"Longer than that."

"The first two months?"

"Maybe more like the first three months. I can't really say. But like I said before, I stopped a while back because I didn't want her to get in the habit."

"And you didn't want her to get in the habit, because you know it's not appropriate for a seven- or eight-year-old girl to be sleeping with her father, correct?"

Ellen stood up. "Objection."

Judge Jones looked at her. "Basis?"

"Argumentative. Mr. Boyle is badgering my client."

"Overruled. This is cross-examination. Mr. Naudain, you may answer the question."

"Well, I didn't want her to get in the habit of sleeping with me for a lot of reasons, mostly because I want her to be independent, and I don't want to do something that might encourage her to keep waking up in the middle of the night. But if by 'inappropriate,' you mean something sexual, that's ridiculous."

"At a certain age, you'd agree with me it would be inappropriate, wouldn't it?"

Ellen stands up again and objects. "Your Honor, we are not here to discuss Mr. Boyle's views on co-sleeping. This is beyond the scope of direct."

"Sustained," says the judge. "Mr. Boyle, how much more do you have? This petition was on my morning list for expedited cases, and I held it over to the afternoon just so we could finish it up. This is not a trial list. And I have parties waiting patiently outside in another matter that was listed for one thirty. So unless you can wrap up in the next ten minutes, I'm going to have to give you a date to come back and finish."

"Your Honor, I won't be able to complete my case in ten minutes. This is a very serious matter, and there are more issues I need to explore on cross-examination. And I will probably need to put my client back on for rebuttal. So unfortunately, I think we'll need a new date to finish it up."

Ellen looks at me and rolls her eyes.

Boyle continues. "In the meantime, Your Honor, as we wait for the new date, I'd ask that the Court enter a temporary order restricting Mr. Naudain from having any girlfriends sleep at his home and directing him to refrain from sleeping with the children."

Ellen hasn't even gotten to her feet when the judge starts talking.

"Counsel, your request is denied. I have no basis at this time for changing the parties' current custody order. The hearing is concluded for now. Parties and counsel, please wait outside, and Melinda will bring you notice of the date for the continuation of today's hearing as soon as we can find a time slot."

Ellen is already packing up the file, my file, my life, which was spread out on the table. She's done, I can see that. She's already shifted gears; she's looking at her phone and checking her email, on to the next case. And here I am, in limbo with these accusations—which Lisa, apparently, has no way to prove. But I have to be subjected to more torture by Boyle and pay thousands of dollars more to Ellen. And I did nothing to endanger my kids, and I never would.

17

Jake: New Horizons,
Three Months Ago

Elizabeth was at camp, Charlie was spending the week with Lisa's parents, and Samara was in my bed. It was two o'clock on a hot summer Saturday, and she'd actually been with me since Friday night. It was kind of a blur: lots of red wine and weed and candles, and clothes peeling off and floating down to the floor. I was ravenous for her, for sex, for losing myself in the newness of another woman's body. I felt like the world telescoped down to this tiny tunnel, where all I could experience was the sensation of pleasure. And I didn't think about Lisa at all. But now we were naked and exhausted and sweaty, and she started talking about Owen, who I really didn't want to hear about.

She was telling me how there is this other couple they're in a relationship with, and specifically how the guy, Grady, had never had a sexual relationship with a man before Owen and had been really hesitant about it. At first, it was just that she was involved with Grady and his girlfriend, Kara, which she called a "triad." But now Grady and Owen had gotten together, and Grady was into it, and sometimes the four of them spent the night together.

"Hey, let's not talk about your husband right now, okay?" I asked her.

"All right, old man," she said, giving me a kiss on the cheek as she pulled away, got up out of bed, and started walking toward the kitchen, stark naked, treading lightly, daintily, like a little tattooed panther.

"What do you mean, 'old man'?" I said. "I'm only forty-one. I can't help it if you're still a baby."

"I just think"—Samara turned around, facing me, smiling her merry smile, standing proud in her perfect little feline body —"you're from, like, a different generation, almost. You're in a different headspace. Like you buy into this idea that marriage has to be two heterosexual people—"

"Wait a second," I protested. "I totally supported marriage equality and all that. I am not homophobic. That's not fair."

"Okay, sorry," she said, "two *people*, who agree to have this sexually exclusive relationship for the rest of their lives, and then when that doesn't work out—which you obviously know about, since you just got divorced—they feel like they failed at something, but of course they did, because it was completely unrealistic in the first place. Human beings live for a long time. The idea that one person, who you meet when you're twenty or whatever, is supposed to fulfill every need you have, is supposed to be your best friend and your roommate and your lover and the parent of your children and the moon and the stars—it's really bullshit. I know they're some couples who are like that, and that's great for them. But it's not for everyone, and why should it be? Why should we all have to fit in that box? Why can't you want to live with one person but have sexual relationships with two others? Or have a baby with one guy who is a really great dad but only live with him part of the time and live with the guy you love to have sex with the rest of the time? And don't you think sexuality is fluid? Why aren't you willing to try sleeping with another man? Or maybe just kissing him and seeing how that feels? I just think, Jake, that you're locked down, and you're not open to new experiences. What's holding you back?"

I found myself simultaneously annoyed by being lectured about life by someone who was just being born when I was starting high school—afraid that she was right and I am boring, conventional, and out of touch—and captivated by watching this beautiful naked girl-woman deliver an impassioned speech about sexual freedom in the middle of my bachelor pad bedroom. A lot had changed in the last few months, that's for sure.

"Baby, come back to bed." The minute I said this, I regretted it. It sounded insulting and dismissive, like a line from a bad rom-com, and it certainly wouldn't make her want to jump back in bed and fuck me again. Stupid.

"No way! Unless"—she smiled. Apparently I dodged that bullet—"you promise to really think about this and be open. That's all I ask, old man. That you're open."

"Okay. I got it, and I'll think about it," I said, opening my arms. "You're living a really different life than I have been. I don't think it's wrong, I actually think it's really cool. But I just don't see myself as a part of it. But I promise to think more about that. Now could you please come here?"

Samara smiled, padded back across the room, and hopped into my arms.

"Great," she said. "Maybe we'll have you over with Grady and Kara, and all of us can work on loosening you up."

"Maybe," I said. "I mean, great!" Samara laughed and dove under the covers. A surge of lust washed over me. Really, I would do anything she wanted, so long as we could keep doing this.

18

Charlie: The Fair Thing

Charlie's door was closed. She knew she was supposed to be asleep, but she was busy trying to get Pinky settled down at the bottom of her bed. He always slept on Elizabeth's bed, which didn't seem fair, because he belonged to both of them and their parents too, so why did Elizabeth get to have him on her bed all the time? Even though Elizabeth was at sleepaway camp now, Pinky still wanted to sleep in her room. When Charlie went over to Dad's house, it wasn't as bad, because she and Elizabeth slept in the same room there, so Pinky was with both of them. But still, he would jump on Elizabeth's bed and curl up at the bottom, even when she wasn't there. It wasn't fair. So tonight, Charlie had decided to bring Pinky into her room, close the door so he couldn't get out, and talk to him the way Elizabeth did so he would sleep with her. If it worked, maybe when Elizabeth was back, they could start taking turns with Pinky on their beds, which would be the fair thing. Even though Elizabeth wouldn't like it, it would still be the fair thing.

So far, it was working pretty well. Charlie had gone into Elizabeth's room and taken the old pink bear with the eyes missing from the bottom of the bed, and also the little quilt Grandma had made for Elizabeth when she was a baby that was pink and green with a frog on it, carried them into her room, and put them both at the end of her bed. The baby quilt Grandma had made for her, which was pink and purple and had the moon and stars on it, was already at the bottom of her bed, and it was prettier than Elizabeth's. But Pinky was used to Elizabeth's quilt, so that's why she did it. Then she sat on the bed and said, "Come on, Pinky. Come on, good boy," the way her mom always called him, and patted her hand on the frog quilt so he would jump up on it. He did jump up on it, and he did curl into a ball just like on Elizabeth's bed, but he wasn't exactly going to sleep. He kept moving around, like he couldn't get comfortable, so Charlie whispered to him, "Good night Pinky-poo, I love you," which is what Elizabeth said to him every night, and kissed the top of his head, just like Elizabeth did. But he still kept moving around and scrunching up the frog quilt, and Charlie was afraid that he would do something to it, and then Elizabeth would know Charlie had taken the quilt off her bed and be mad.

Charlie decided she needed to get more stuffed animals from Elizabeth's bed so Pinky would stop moving around. She slipped off the bed, went over to the door, and opened it a crack. She could hear her mom in the living room, talking on the phone and walking around like she might be coming upstairs. "Sorry, I can't make it because I have the girls that night. No, there's no point in asking Jake, because he never takes them extra. Right, too busy with the young girlfriend. What, you know her? She's your teaching assistant?"

Charlie's mom didn't seem to hear her, so Charlie tiptoed across the landing to Elizabeth's room. Her mom was still talking, and Charlie could tell it was to her friend Tilly, who always gave Charlie colored pencils and pads and smelled like the lavender soap Elizabeth had, which Charlie wanted because it was purple, and purple was her favorite color. It seemed like her mom and Tilly were talking about Samara, because that was

Dad's girlfriend, but she wasn't sure. "She's into *what*? And she's making a film about it? You've got to be kidding. What else do you know about her?"

Charlie opened the door to Elizabeth's room slowly so it wouldn't make any noise, went in, and grabbed the yellow bunny and the other shaggy blue animal that was either a turtle or some kind of fish, and tiptoed quickly back to her room. When she opened the door, Pinky hopped off her bed, pushed his way past her, trotted across the landing into Elizabeth's room, and jumped up on Elizabeth's bed. Charlie felt like she might cry. Elizabeth wasn't even there. It just wasn't the fair thing.

19

Lisa: Joint Custody

I'd read the co-parenting literature. I knew that I wasn't supposed to grill the girls when they came back from Jake's about everything that happened there. But it was really hard not to. I used to know about every detail of their lives, and I found it so unsettling not to know what they ate for dinner, or what color the sheets were on their beds. I realized these things weren't that important, or really important at all, but it's not what I was used to. I was used to being able to summon up a picture in my head of what each girl was doing at any given time. When I had that free moment at work, in between patients and charts and meetings—that moment when I could sit down, take a breath, and look at my phone—I routinely did a quick mental check-in with them. If it was three fifteen, I could see Charlie running down the stairs to the after-school room, her little feet in their purple sneakers a blur as she flew by. I could see Elizabeth, two floors up, chattering away with Billie and Anya as she crammed her lunch bag into her already overstuffed backpack and zipped up the top. These check-ins comforted me. They grounded me in my workday. They instantly transported me back to the center around which my life revolved, my daughters.

I couldn't always do that anymore. There were long blackout periods. I'd never been in Jake's apartment. I didn't know how the light came through their bedroom window in the morning. I didn't know what plates they ate breakfast off of. I didn't really know if they even ate breakfast. And Jake had made it very clear that he was not interested in sharing information—anything I asked him about just made him defensive. He loved to throw it in my face that I initiated the divorce, that this is what I wanted, so now I needed to live with it. He smugly claimed the moral high ground, even though it was his bad conduct that was responsible for the end of our marriage. I was just the one who pulled the trigger. Like everything else in our relationship, I was the default adult. I had to take care of it.

So the policy I developed for myself with the girls was that I wouldn't question them first, but anything they brought up, I would take as an opening. I'm not sure if this really comported with all the divorce experts who kept reminding you not to put your children in the middle, but I did it anyway. That Sunday night in July, after I picked the girls up from Jake's, Charlie was sitting on the living room floor with Pinky, holding his face between her hands. She was cooing at him, "Pinky, we're back at Mommy's. Mommy's so happy to see you. Mommy's going to walk you tonight" or something adorable to that effect, which I was only half listening to. Then she said, "But we have fun at Daddy's too, right, Pinky? And Samara loves you so much too."

That was a first. I knew who Samara was. I knew that she was the age-inappropriate girl Jake was dating. I knew she was Tilly's teaching assistant. I knew she was married, I knew she was into polyamory, and I knew she was making a film about it. What I didn't know was that she'd been spending time with my kids. So I asked, trying to sound nonchalant, "Honey, was Samara visiting at Daddy's last week?"

Charlie, still looking deep into Pinky's eyes, nodded. "And she loves Pinky, Mom," she said, turning toward me. "This

morning she got up before Daddy and took him for a walk herself."

Up before Daddy. Heat shot up my body. I could not believe
Jake had the audacity to have this girlfriend, or whatever she was
to him, that he'd had for like ten minutes, sleep over when my
kids were there. Was he so overwhelmed by lust that he couldn't
wait twenty-four hours until the girls were back with me? How
many times had this happened before? Had there been other
people too? And wasn't the decision to start having a girlfriend
spend the night in his bed while our kids were there something
we should have discussed and decided together?

"Did Samara sleep over, honey?" I asked, already knowing
the answer.

"Mm-hmm," Charlie said. "She had a sleepover."

"Where did she sleep?" I asked, aware that I might be making Charlie worried about something that she clearly wasn't but
not able to stop myself in the quest for information.

"In Daddy's room," she said, not seeming concerned at all. I
almost asked her if Samara had slept in Jake's bed, but I managed to restrain myself from posing that completely unnecessary
question.

"Has Samara done that before?" I asked, trying to sound
casual. "Had a sleepover at Daddy's, I mean?

"I don't know," said Charlie. "But she loves Pinky."

"You don't know, or you don't remember?" I asked. I really
did not like cross-examining my child, but what was I supposed
to do? I had no confidence that I'd get the truth out of Jake.

"I don't know," Charlie said again. "Mommy, do we have any
ice cream? Daddy said we would have ice cream for dessert before you picked us up, but I think he forgot."

I did, in fact, have mint chocolate chip ice cream, Charlie's
favorite, in the freezer. There didn't seem to be any point in

questioning her further, and I saw no reason to bring Elizabeth into this, who was already upstairs in her room with her headphones on. This was between Jake and me. And he was going to hear about it. "I do," I said. "Let me grab you a bowl, and then we need to get you ready for bed."

I worried the whole next day at work about confronting Jake. I hadn't called him the previous night, because by the time I had gotten both girls to bed, I was exhausted and had to get ready for the week, and I just couldn't deal with it. But the conversation needed to happen, so I texted him the next morning saying I wanted to talk to him that night. Of course he asked what about, and I said an issue with the girls—what else would it be about?—and he said okay and that he could talk after eight. Once I had wrangled both girls into bed, or at least into their rooms, I made the call.

"Lisa. So what's up?" he answered.

"Hi, Jake," I said. "Charlie told me last night that Samara—that's the name of your new friend, right?—slept over on Saturday night. As in, slept with you, in your bedroom."

"Yes, her name is Samara," he said. "She is my girlfriend, and yes, she did sleep over."

I paused for a beat and launched into the speech I had prepared. "Jake, we've only been living separately less than five months, and you just met this girl, right? Don't you think that's way too early to be moving her into your bedroom when Elizabeth and Charlie are there? And isn't this something we should've talked about first?"

"First," Jake said, "I'm not 'moving her into my bedroom.' And second, no, I do not need to discuss what happens in my house with you. You didn't want to be married to me anymore, remember? You got what you wanted, and now we have separate lives and separate places, and we don't need to make decisions together. Except about the girls, like what school they go to. I'm their father. I know how to take care of them when they're with me, and you know that."

I could have written this script. He was so predictable. Any fantasy that he might actually have apologized, or shown humility, or even, God forbid, agreed that he probably should've discussed this with me first, vanished completely.

"Jake," I said, against my better judgment, since I already knew it was futile, "this issue of when to introduce the girls to new partners is absolutely something we should discuss. That's, like, Co-Parenting 101. Assuming you are in a serious relationship with Samara, and she's going to be part of the girls' lives on an ongoing basis, yes, you should introduce them to her but slowly. And having her sleep with you when they're there would be like the final phase of that, and you and I should discuss the timetable. It's an awful lot for them to adjust to so quickly."

Silence. So I continued. "And, if this isn't that type of relationship—which I really wonder about since you can't have known her very long, and I understand she's a lot younger than you and still married to someone else—then you have no business introducing her to the girls at all. Jake, you only have them half the time. You have seven nights out of every fourteen to have anyone you want sleep over. You do not need to have Samara or anyone else there when you're supposed to be spending time with our daughters."

This time, a slow exhale. "Lisa. I don't owe you any information about my relationship with Samara, who is separated from her husband, by the way. And my sex life, now that I actually have one again, is none of your fucking business. None."

"When you don't have the girls," I said, "I don't care what

you do. When they're with me, if you want to spend all your time sleeping with twenty-somethings you just met, I couldn't care less. But when the girls are with you, then your sex life does become my business if you're flaunting it in front of them."

"Man, Lisa, that's brutal," he said. "But I am really not going to go there. About Samara, the girls like her, I am not flaunting anything, and I reject your idea that I have to discuss any of this with you. However, I will tell you that Saturday night was the only time she has ever slept over when they were with me, it wasn't something we planned in advance, and I don't have plans to make it a regular thing. Okay, are we done now?"

I knew what he meant by not planning in advance. I know Jake. I knew that meant they were in his bed having sex after the girls went to sleep. God, I hope the girls were asleep. They were probably having that long, luxurious type of sex Jake loved and I used to love too, late at night, coming more than once, whispering in the dark in between. I did miss that. But really, fuck him, because who cared if they fell asleep afterward. It was his job to make sure she wasn't there in the morning. Since the beginning of time, two people have been having sex at night at one of their houses, and the person who doesn't live there has been leaving in the middle of the night so someone else who does live in the house doesn't see them there in the morning. That takes such a minimal amount of awareness, it's astonishing. But I could not even get into that with him. I had grown weary of the conversation but unable, somehow, to stop it.

"Knowing you didn't plan it is worse, as far as I'm concerned, not better," I said. "But it happened, so there's nothing we can do about it now. How can I trust you that this was the only time and that you're not going to do it again?"

"I didn't say I would never do it again, just that I have no current plans to. And you can trust me that this was the only time, because I'm telling you it was—me, the father of your children, the guy you were married to for fourteen years. Doesn't that count for anything? What do you want me to do—take a lie detector test? Jesus, Lisa. Relax a little, why don't you?"

I didn't want to take his bait, but I couldn't help it because he was so infuriating. "Jake," I said, trying hard to slow down my words as an alternative to yelling, "you know exactly why I have problems trusting you. And please do not, ever again, tell me to relax. Remember when you told me to 'just relax and chill out' when I was on maternity leave with Charlie, and you bought that ridiculously fancy bike that you claimed your boss gave you as a bonus, but he didn't, and you finally fessed up that it cost three grand?"

"Lisa, God, we went over that like a million times, and I apologized. Weak moment. I'm not perfect like you."

I couldn't stop. "And remember that you had borrowed that three grand from your boss, and he was taking the money out of your paycheck every month to get reimbursed, and that was why we had no money? And that was part of the reason I had to go back to work early from my leave? Remember that? And remember my going back early meant I had to wean Charlie earlier than I had been planning to? Your baby daughter. Remember? And you wanted me to relax about that too. And then, after that, when you were *still* paying off the bike, and we *still* had no money, remember when you brought home a new guitar, I think it was your fifth one, and I was upset about it, and you told me you bought it on Craigslist from some guy in West Philly for, quote, 'next to nothing,' unquote? And I'm pretty sure I was supposed to relax about that too. Remember that, Jake? And it wasn't until later that I found out you had paid eighteen hundred dollars for it? Remember? So do not *ever* tell me to relax."

"I can't believe you want to revisit that, Lisa. You beat that guitar issue to death at the time, which is like six years ago now. And as I know I explained to you at the time, I did get it in West Philly from a guy on Craigslist, and I did get a really good deal on it, which is exactly what I had told you, which was accurate, because it was worth like ten times what I paid for it."

"Okay, right, and that was really helpful for me to know when I was at work crying in the break room because I missed Charlie so much. All I really want to say, Jake, is that if you continue to make bad decisions like this that negatively affect the emotional well-being of our daughters, that are potentially traumatizing to them, in fact, you will be forcing me to take action to protect them. So do not put me in that position."

"Traumatizing? Taking action? You are really going off the deep end, Lisa. Do not fuck with my relationship with my kids. We are definitely done here," Jake said and hung up.

My eyes were tearing, and my heart was racing. I didn't understand why he was being such an asshole about this, but I was not surprised. I really didn't want to fight with him. But how could I have stood by silently when he pulled a stunt like that? I had to think of the girls first, always. My phone vibrated in my hand, one short, urgent shudder. Was it possible Jake regretted how harsh he sounded, and he was going to apologize? Or maybe I had made him nervous, and he was going to try to walk this back somehow? I turned the phone over. It wasn't Jake.

My face got hot. I sat down and opened the text:

Hey beautiful, missed you over the weekend and got stuck at the hospital all day today. Thinking so much about our convo last week. I'm ready when you are. Pls come on the next Haiti trip with me. We'll be a world away. See you tomorrow morning.

20

Ellen: Storm Clouds

"Jake Naudain for you," the receptionist said as Ellen walked in the door. "You want to take it or call him back?"

"I'll take it," Ellen said, dumping her bag filled with files for court that afternoon on the couch in the waiting area. Files she had lugged home the night before in the throes of that late-in-the-day optimism, when the evening stretched ahead, fat with the promise of big, clean blocks of unscheduled time beckoning so invitingly, singing that seductive siren song, "Go home, go home, there's a whole evening ahead of you to get this done." A song that, every time, deceives. That vista of wide-open opportunity for productivity faded even during the commute home. By the time the dog was walked, the mail was checked, and she was in jeans, pulling food out of the fridge to start cooking dinner, the immediacy of those files, the need to review them *that day*, to get a leg up on tomorrow, had already softened to a vague sense of duty. Their importance was downgraded to one task on a to-do list composed of many tasks that would also not get done that night. And later, when Dan had handed her a glass of sauvignon blanc, and they were chatting about their days and gossiping about the neighbors while chicken breasts were simmering on the stove, and she was blanching broccoli rabe and wondering what she did before she discovered this miraculous vegetable, the window had closed completely.

All of which meant she wasn't prepared for court and probably shouldn't have taken any calls. But she liked Jake, and now she had a personal connection to him since he had hired Marni to babysit, which made it harder to put him off. So she went into her office and picked up the phone.

"Ellen, thanks for taking my call," Jake said. "I need your advice. I'm concerned I screwed something up. I got this call from Lisa last night, and she was really pissed off at me because she found out that this woman I'm dating slept over one night when the girls were there. And she's married. And she's younger than me. Which I have no idea how Lisa knows. I mean, she is married, but she's separated from her husband, and so what if she's younger, and I don't know what business this is of Lisa's, anyway. She told me I should have talked to her about it before introducing a new girlfriend to the girls and all this crap. Really? Do I need to do that? She left me, and now she wants to approve the people I date?"

Ellen listened while she turned on her computer and skimmed through new emails. Category assigned to Jake's call: textbook problem. Level of urgency: low to medium. Solution: reassurance that this is not strictly a legal problem, tempered with cautionary word about having new girlfriend sleep over.

"No, of course she doesn't get to approve your new girl-friend, Jake. Sounds to me like she's just upset. And that's pretty common, in my experience, when new boyfriends and girl-friends show up on the scene. But I would tread cautiously. I actually don't think it's a great idea to have her sleeping over on the nights you have the girls until you're comfortable that it's a serious, committed type of relationship. You don't want to be introducing them to every woman you go out on a date with. It can be confusing to your kids, and Lisa could use that against you if she decided she wanted to modify the custody arrangement."

"Right, of course, I get that. And this woman, Samara, she only slept over once when they were with me. It wasn't planned, just sort of happened."

Thinking ahead to the worst scenario, that leap over all the more likely outcomes that lawyers are trained to make and paid to anticipate, "just sort of happened" would be a weak explanation on direct examination and a disaster on cross. *He needs to take this more seriously*, Ellen thought.

"Okay, got it. And what do you mean by 'younger,' by the way?"

"She's twenty-eight."

"All right, no red flags there. Just wanted to make sure she wasn't a college student or something. Anyway, given that this is a new relationship—right?"

"Yes."

"Then my advice is, don't let it happen again until it's serious and the girls know her, until you've included her in activities so they get to spend time with her, and then let them know in advance that she'll be sleeping over. Talk to them about it. But for right now, since you have them half the time, seems easy enough to limit the sleepovers to the nights they're with their mom, and just focus on them when they're with you, okay?"

"Okay, that's my plan anyway. So I didn't screw up, and Lisa's out of line, is what you're saying?"

"She's out of line to think she has control over this, because legally she has none. But I think her concerns are valid, and I bet you'd feel the same way if you heard from your girls that Mommy had a friend sleep over in bed with her."

"Not really. I don't care what she does, Ellen. I really have moved on. This is what she wanted, and I went along with it. And this is the consequence."

Bravado, Ellen thought. *He's kidding himself.* "Well, even if you wouldn't feel that way, Jake, my advice, which you're paying a lot of money for, is don't do it. You do not want to end up in court, and we could pull a judge who takes a very dim view of this type of thing. So don't push the envelope."

"I totally get it. And you know my girls are the most important thing in my life. No more sleepovers."

"For now. Not forever. Just hold off a bit."

All these World's Best Dad types, Ellen thought as she billed Jake for the call, rounding up for the aggravation of having to explain an obvious parenting issue. One young girlfriend, and it's all out the window.

21

Jake: Polyamory

Lee's ex-wife Rosa had organized a fundraiser for the food pantry she ran out of a church in East Greenwood, and she asked if Man With a Dog would play at it. Which of course we said yes to, not just because it's Rosa's thing and we all loved Rosa (including Lee, despite their divorce), but it was also great for us—she said there'd be a really big crowd, and knowing Rosa, I totally believed it. I admired Rosa for the work she did at the pantry. You wouldn't believe how long the lines are, she told me once when we were waiting outside Moonbeam for our kids to come back from a field trip or something. And some people are ashamed, she said. They made a point of saying they'd never been there before, even though she knew they had.

I liked my job fine, but I rarely thought about it after hours. My focus was on my girls; my friends; at that point, a lot on Samara; the band; my bike; music I like to listen to; and stuff like that. Which felt so unimportant compared to what Rosa did. I mean, what could be more basic than feeding people who are hungry? As opposed to working on software that made it easier for some business to track their inventory of crappy sneakers made by people working under terrible conditions in China. Every once in a while, especially if I had a bad day at work, or Jim and Mario were on my case about something, I think, *fuck it, I should quit this job and go to work for a nonprofit that does something meaningful.* But then I would think about the pay cut I would have to take, and our nice workspace with the couches and the coffee bar and the ping-pong table, and how much harder I'd probably have to work, and I just didn't think I could do it.

The fundraiser was on a steamy Saturday night in August, and I was sweating as I hauled our amps out of Petie's van and lugged them into this huge warehouse in the industrial part of East Greenwood. But I felt light; I had that pre-gig excitement, not really nerves, more like a buzzy kind of tension running through my body. I was feeling the vibe. It was gonna be a great night. In this neighborhood, no one was away at their shore houses or sailing off the coast of Maine. They were home in their hot apartments, looking for summer fun. White hipsters, Black community activists, people from the church—it was an audience made for us. We were going to rock the hipsters with our excellent cover of "Tainted Love," and pull in the Black, churchgoing, older group with that killer arrangement Lee had worked out of "Ain't No Sunshine When She's Gone."

I had invited Samara. She was all excited about seeing my band perform, which was a total turn-on for me, of course—who doesn't want to be the cool guitarist that all the girls want? She asked if it was okay to bring Owen and their friends Kara and Grady. The orgy friends, as I think of them. What was I going to say? I couldn't really say no, don't bring your husband, since she made it completely clear to me that Owen was her "primary" relationship and that he was cool with her sleeping with me, which I still didn't get. I mean, I got that they sincerely felt that way, or at least she did—I didn't really know about Owen, except that he knew when she was with me, and he'd been nothing but friendly the few times I'd seen him—but I cannot feel it myself. I still can't even think about Lisa with another man, tucking her hands inside the waistband of his jeans, stroking his face with her beautiful fingers, rubbing her breasts against his chest. My head just gets flooded with those kinds of images, and I literally feel pain, that weird kind that feels like it should be physical, except there's no one particular place it hurts; it just envelops you and temporarily immobilizes you. So sure, I told her, bring Owen and the orgy friends, why not? More money for Rosa's food pantry.

We really crushed it. As I predicted, Earl brought down the house with "Sunshine"—he had everyone on their feet. And the church ladies went wild when he sang that great line, "I know, I know, I know, I know"—so great because you never do know when it's going to end. I was playing my red Strat, which is really my favorite. I bought it on a total whim a long time ago for what seemed like a fortune. I couldn't even admit it to Lisa at the time —told her I got it cheap on Craigslist—but it was so worth it. That night, I was wailing on it. I kind of blew one solo, but I'm sure no one noticed but the guys. My solo in "Soul Finger" came off really well, and I included lots of Guitar Hero–type moves on stage. I could see Samara and her friends dancing and cheering, and she was yelling out, "Go, Jaaake!" at the end of the solo.

After we finished playing, I got a beer and went over to see them, dripping wet from the stage, savoring that great feeling when you're talking to people who just minutes ago were watching you perform and are then telling you how great you were. Elizabeth and I are alike that way. She loves being the center of attention, never has stage fright. Other kids mumble or forget their lines or look terrified, but she never does. She always seems thrilled to be up there, and then, when it's over, she sweeps down among her adoring masses to bestow kisses and hugs all around—a total diva.

Owen gave me a hug, the straight-man kind, and complimented me on my guitar playing. Samara came rushing over, dark hair flying, red high heels clicking on the polished cement floor, threw her arms around me, and kissed me on the lips, short but hard.

"You guys were amazing," she said, "especially you." I couldn't believe she was standing there, arms around my neck, lips inches from mine, in front of her husband. Like, how could he possibly deal with that? I realized I had not been tutored in polyamory etiquette. Or at least Samara and Owen's etiquette, because Samara had told me there was no one way to be polyamorous.

"Thanks," I said, and awkwardly disengaged from her embrace. But that encounter did turn me on a little, I had to admit, having him watch me kiss his wife. Then the orgy friends came over and told me how great the band sounded, how much they enjoyed it, blah blah blah, and invited me to come back to their place with Owen and Samara and some other friends.

"Gotta come to the after-party, Jake," Grady said. "You'll be the guest of honor."

Really, what I wanted to do was go back to my place with Samara, light some candles, and watch her take everything off but the red high heels, but it didn't seem like that was a possibility, so I said, "Sure, I'll stop by for a bit."

Turns out that Kara and Grady live near Samara and Owen, in the same kind of run-down neighborhood with beautiful but dilapidated houses, yards overgrown with tangles of weeds, lush in the height of summer. Hip-hop and the smell of barbecue waft out to the street from late-night backyard parties. This is the neighborhood all the white people in West Greenwood moved out of when they had kids, because there was too much crime, and they weren't "comfortable" with the local public schools, which is code for the fact that most of the students were Black and poor. The Jamaicans and the Haitians and the lifelong working-class Philadelphians, whose families had owned their houses for generations, weren't there to provide character to some white liberal's urban-pioneering experience he could tell his kids about twenty years after he moved away, across the metaphorical tracks to the tidier, safer, better-schooled West Greenwood. They were there for good. This was their community.

I was thinking about all this during the drive to Kara and Grady's house, because it made me so aware of the age gap between Samara and her friends and me. They weren't looking long-term; they were focused on finishing grad school or working as baristas or bartenders while they pursued their painting careers or acting careers or whatever. It wasn't the stuff that Lisa and I thought about: mortgages and real estate values, and public versus private school, and after-school sports. Maybe I am an old man, like Samara said. But here's the thing: a divorce does kind of liberate you, even if you didn't want to be liberated in the first place. It forces you to try new things, like living alone when your kids aren't with you, and being a single parent when they are. And like being open to new relationships. Why was I constantly comparing my relationship with Samara to what Lisa and I had? It wasn't comparable, in any way. But it was exciting. And the whole polyamory thing, it was also exciting, just to rub up against it, so to speak, just to have a window into another way of life, even if it wasn't the way I chose.

Hours later, I was jolted into consciousness, sunlight hitting me right in the face, startling at the memory of Owen's body pressed against Samara. It was quite a night. It started out like just another party, sitting around Kara and Grady's living room drinking tequila and smoking weed—really strong weed, I realized later. Not sure whose playlist it was, but we were listening to reggae and R&B, laid-back, good-time, late-summer music. Samara was snuggled up on the couch with Owen, which should have bothered me, but I remember just feeling loose and sort of disconnected from it, like I was watching someone else's life, which in a way, I guess I was. I got up to go into the kitchen, and Samara reached up toward me and pulled me down on the other side of her, close, and started kissing me. I looked over her head at Owen, and he just smiled and reached his hand over Samara and put it on my thigh. That's the last really clear image I have, seeing this large, masculine hand a couple of inches away from my crotch, and then I closed my eyes and things just went from there.

Owen, Samara, and I ended up in a bed together. I know he and I both had sex with Samara. I remember watching him go down on her while I was kissing her neck, and we were all sweating and breathing together like some slow-moving, multi-limbed creature. I know Owen and I kissed at one point, and I remember that it was really surprising because his mouth was just like a woman's mouth; it didn't feel different, it was soft and fleshy and wet. I also touched him, I think just his back, which was so totally different, so hard and muscled. But I'm really not sure what else I did. I'm pretty sure it didn't go further than that with Owen, but maybe it did. I just don't know, and at some level, I don't want to know.

And then there was Kara. After the whole ménage à trois scene in the bedroom with Samara and Owen, I somehow ended up back in the living room with Kara, who told me how sexy she thought I was when I played guitar. I couldn't remember exactly what happened after that—of course I would remember the guitar-player remark—but I know we ended up having sex on the couch. It was quick, hot, high school–type sex, with her dress still on, just pulled up to her waist and my jeans—why had I put them back on?—pushed down but not off. And I think Owen went into their bedroom with Grady, and I don't know where Samara was. And then I guess everyone sort of passed out for a while. I woke up in the very early morning, naked, back on the bed with Samara and Owen, who were both asleep. I got up and put my clothes on and drove home and crashed. I don't remember if I said goodbye, or thanks—which would be a weird thing to say, but what would you say?—or anything. At that point, I couldn't have been drunk or high anymore, but I think I was sort of in a state of shock.

As I was lying in my bed mulling all this over and trying to retrieve memories that must have been in there somewhere, working hard to fill in the blank spots, especially about the Owen part, I remembered I was supposed to be somewhere. I was supposed to be at Charlie's end-of-ballet-camp recital. It started at noon. I grabbed my phone, which I must have put on silent last night. It was almost one. I had three texts and a missed call from Lisa. The first text, from early that morning: don't for-get Charlie's recital today at noon.

The second one, sent at 12:10 p.m.: where are you?

And the third text, sent at 12:20 p.m., lets me have it: i can't believe you're missing your daughter's recital, guess you had a late night with the new girlfriend.

I felt nauseous, the combined effect of a hangover and the forgotten recital. But really, it all led back to Lisa. Because ultimately, none of this would have happened if she hadn't decided to break up our family. Because I knew this: if she hadn't unilaterally decided to divorce me, for no good reason whatsoever, Lisa and I would be there, sitting in those uncomfortable chairs at the ballet studio, side by side, or maybe with Elizabeth between us. We'd be bonded by parental pride, a little nervous for Charlie, complaining to each other about how long these recitals go but not really minding it. And once the show started, I would be fiddling with my phone to set up the best angle for getting an action shot of Charlie, and Lisa would be checking the little printed program and whispering commentary into my ear about the other dancers. I can almost hear it: *That's Leah, she's the one the teacher recommended try out for* The Nutcracker *at the Academy . . . that's Madeline, her moms didn't want her to take ballet because they thought it was too gender stereotyped, and all she really wanted was to wear the tutu, and as far as they were concerned, the whole thing was just another manifestation of her Disney princess obsession, but Madeline begged them, and look how good she is at it . . . guess they've changed their tune.* And all the while, we'd be shifting in our seats, straining to see the curtain at stage right, because that's where Charlie would come from. And when she did, our faces would light up, and Lisa would take my hand and squeeze it.

All of which did nothing to help me deal with the situation at hand, in which I was totally fucked. Because it was, like, a twenty-five minute drive to the studio, and even though those recitals seemed endless when you were there, they were not actually that long. I had missed it; that was all there was to it.

I picked up my phone and saw a text from Elizabeth: mom's mad u better have a good excuse lol. This gave me pause, because I was so far from having a good excuse. I replied first to Lisa: Sorry left phone at party after gig last night just got it back didn't remember about recital till I saw your text. Give Charlie kiss for me I'll get her flowers & bring them when I pick girls up tonite. To Elizabeth: Really sorry bet Charlie was great see you tonite love you.

22

Charlie: Like a Dream

Charlie liked sharing a bedroom with Elizabeth at their dad's house. One thing she liked about it was that she knew Elizabeth hid makeup, like lipstick and the pencil you use in your eyes, in a gray felt pouch she kept in the top drawer of their dresser. It was one of Elizabeth's drawers—Charlie's drawers were the bottom two—but Charlie looked in it all the time anyway, even though Elizabeth had told her not to. Elizabeth wasn't allowed to wear makeup at their mom's, but their dad didn't notice. Elizabeth had told her if she ever said anything about it, she would tell Billie and Anya how Charlie was such a baby that she still made their mom check her bedroom closet to make sure there was no monster in there before she turned out Charlie's light. Which was true, and Charlie was embarrassed about it because she really knew there was no monster, but she still wanted her mom to look, and her mom didn't mind, so who cared? At Dad's house, it was different. Charlie wasn't afraid of a monster in the closet, because Elizabeth and Pinky were in the room with her.

But even so, Charlie still woke up crying sometimes at Dad's. She didn't really know why, but it felt different there, different and sort of lonely. Nothing was the same as at home, and her mom wasn't across the hall if she needed her. When she woke up, Elizabeth never heard her, so Charlie would usually get up and go out into the hallway and call for her dad. He would come out of his room, pick her up, bring her into his room, and let her sleep with him in his bed. Then in the morning when she woke up, she'd be back in her own bed. Elizabeth would still be asleep with the quilt over her head, and Dad would tell her he brought her back, but she wouldn't really remember it. Actually, sometimes she wasn't sure whether she had woken up at all the night before, because it was all mixed up, like a dream. And then sometimes, later in the day, all of a sudden, she would remember it for a moment. Like, she would remember how the sheets on her dad's bed felt cool when she lay down on them or how Elizabeth rolled over in her sleep when Daddy brought her back into their room. She'd remember just for a moment, and then it would be gone again.

On Sunday morning, which was the day they went back to their mom's, before she opened her eyes, Charlie thought she was in her dad's bed. Then she heard the thump Pinky always makes when he jumps down off Elizabeth's bed, so she knew she wasn't. But she couldn't remember sleeping in her bed. She remembered crying, and she remembered her arms around her dad's neck. She remembered they were in the hallway, and Dad wasn't taking her into his room, even though she kept asking him to. Then she heard Samara's voice. And then Dad carried her into his room and laid her down in his bed like she wanted, but Samara was in there too. And then Dad got in the bed on the other side of her, and then she had those funny dreams where everything ran together, like Mom and Dad and Samara and Pinky and Elizabeth and three kittens climbing all over Dad and her and Samara. But they were really the kittens from the poster above her bed, which are just on paper, but they were meowing and meowing, and they were so cute. And then she was back in her own bed. How did she get there? *Later,* Charlie thought, opening her eyes, *later I'll remember.*

23

Ellen: The Bomb

The mail arrived late in Ellen's office. Often she was just seeing it as she was closing out the day, making the remaining phone calls on her list from the morning—or the day before, or the day before that—and answering the emails she had put off because they were complicated, or she didn't like the client, or opposing counsel was a bitch, or some other reason to defer action. The 4:00 p.m. mail delivery used to feel like more of a problem than it did now, given that mostly everything important had already been emailed to her. The mail on this particular Thursday in September looked typical in that regard: notices from the bar association about continuing education programs ("Ahoy There, Mateys! Maritime Law for Beginners"), office supply catalogues, overdue discovery responses in a complex divorce case that opposing counsel had already told her were on their way. At the bottom of the slim pile, though, was something unexpected. A letter from none other than her least-favorite opponent, Stephen Boyle, announcing that he had been retained by Lisa Naudain to represent her in custody proceedings, and enclosing (she should please find) a time-stamped copy of his Petition to Modify Custody which had been filed with the court three days earlier. "Based on the serious nature of the allegations at issue," the letter stated, "we will be seeking an expedited listing of this matter for trial."

Ellen's first response was surprise that Lisa Naudain, whom she had never met but of whom she had a clear image nonetheless, would have chosen Steve Boyle to represent her. He was the last lawyer she would think of as being compatible with the Greenwood divorce, with people like Jake and, she had gathered, Lisa, who believed in working things out themselves and had both the intellectual and emotional tools to do so. These were people who sent their children to Mariposa, people who played in bands that did benefit concerts for food pantries (or at least those who had married those people—Ellen had seen a flyer about Jake's concert at the Green Life Café), people who shopped at the food co-op. People, in other words, like her and Dan, only younger. And not lawyers. Stephen Boyle? *Lisa Naudain must have made a mistake*, Ellen thought. Remembering the call from Jake about his girlfriend sleeping over once, and Boyle's propensity to blow everything wildly out of proportion, case in point being the Patel wedding fiasco, she figured this would be more of the same: expensive, annoying to untangle, damaging to the parents' working relationship going forward, but ultimately not something to worry about.

Turning to the petition, Ellen saw first Boyle's proposed order, which, if signed by a judge, would have reduced Jake's time with his daughters to every other weekend, daytime visits only, and no overnights at all. *Ridiculous*, Ellen thought. *Boyle has really outdone himself now.*

Flipping forward to the petition itself, she started to read the allegations. She skimmed through the preliminaries, zeroing in on the mother lode. "On or about September 17," Boyle had written, "Father brought the parties' minor daughter, Charlotte, into bed with him and his naked paramour, whereupon Father and said paramour engaged in multiple acts of sexual conduct, which were witnessed by Charlotte."

Wow, Ellen thought, *Jake couldn't possibly be that stupid.* What did Charlie tell her mom that she saw? It couldn't have been anything specific, or Boyle would have put it in the petition. Whatever it was that led her mother to conclude that Charlie had seen multiple acts of "sexual conduct," whatever that meant, would Charlie repeat it when interviewed by a judge? *She's only seven, or maybe eight now,* Ellen recalled, *but that's easily old enough to be declared competent as a witness.* If she wouldn't talk, would the judge overrule Ellen's hearsay objection and let Lisa testify about what Charlie told her? That, of course, would depend on what judge the case got listed before. If he or she was in the "this is family court, where we ignore the rules of evidence" camp, Jake could be really screwed.

Ellen felt immediate and crushing weariness. She saw the case stretching out in front of her, a road she had travelled many times before, leading to a place she had no desire to ever visit again. A place where she would simultaneously be worried and anxious that her client might lose custody of his kids based on false accusations of the most insidious kind, and worried and anxious that she might be helping a parent who was damaging his kid. The pressure on her would be tremendous; Jake would be completely dependent on her skill and judgment, and the weight of the outcome would rest on her shoulders. Because no matter what a great job she might do, if the judge ruled against him based on factors completely beyond her control, she would get the blame. She knew, from brutal experience, that clients really don't care about the great defense you put up if they end up going to jail or losing their kids. And then there was the issue of having to deal with Steve Boyle, whose annoying presence and inflammatory rhetoric would be with her every step of the way down that road. Channeling her daughter, Ellen concluded that everything about this was totally fucked up. She put the petition facedown on her desk, picked up her purse, told the receptionist something came up and she had to leave early, and went across the street to the nail salon to get a manicure.

The next day, fortified by a good night's sleep and shiny new orange nails, Ellen called Jake and read him the relevant portions of the petition.

"No way!" he said. "That's total bullshit! Lisa's pissed because she knows I have a girlfriend. I already told you about the night she slept over and Lisa found out. I can't believe she's doing this."

"Do you know what incident she could be referring to? Did your girlfriend—what's her name?"

"Samara."

"Samara. Is the night you called me about the only time Samara slept over when the girls were there, or did it happen again?"

"Just one other time since then. I know you told me not to, but Samara was at my house, and I didn't expect to have the girls that night—it's a long story—but anyway, she did sleep there again. It's no big deal—the girls really like her. And the stuff that lawyer is saying about me taking her into bed and us being naked and having sex with her there—that is ridiculous. It's a total lie. Charlie did wake up in the middle of the night. She does that at my place a lot. And I do sometimes let her come in bed with me until she falls back asleep, and then I carry her back to her bed. But that night, because Samara was there, I heard Charlie, and I got up and went into the girls' room before she came into mine. I sat on her bed and rubbed her back, which she likes me to do, until she went back to sleep. And I wasn't naked. I can't believe this shit."

"Did Charlie say anything to you about Samara that night? Or the next morning? Did she ask you any questions? I'm trying to figure out what she might have said to Lisa that got twisted into this. And what about Elizabeth? Did she wake up when you came into the room and were rubbing Charlie's back?"

"No, Elizabeth sleeps through anything. She wouldn't have woken up if we had been screaming at each other two feet from her head. And no, I don't remember Charlie saying anything about Samara. I'm telling you, this is just a complete fabrication. I didn't think Lisa was capable of something like this. Isn't this perjury?"

"Possibly, but she's not getting prosecuted for it, so let's not spend time on that issue. My guess is that Charlie said something to Lisa that Lisa misunderstood or took out of context. Because as I said, if she said something specific like, 'I saw Daddy kissing Samara's vagina'—"

"Ellen, Jesus."

"Well, that's the kind of thing this could be referencing, right? Sexual conduct? But instead, the petition is totally vague. My point is that if Charlie had actually said something like that to Lisa, she would have reported it to Boyle, and I guarantee you, Boyle would have included it in the petition. Underlined and bolded. So she said something else, and the 'multiple acts of sexual conduct' is Lisa's interpretation. But Jake, I need to ask you this again: are you sure she didn't get in bed with you both? That seems like something a seven-year-old would accurately report."

"Yes, I'm sure. No, she didn't."

"Okay. Well, there are some serious evidentiary issues here. I found out who our judge is. It's Judge Jones, and the good news for us is that she's not likely to let Lisa testify to what Charlie told her. That would be hearsay, but some judges allow it in custody cases, depending on the age of the child and some other factors. But based on what I've heard about Judge Jones, which is limited because she just came on the bench this year, I don't think she will. Which means that Charlie will be interviewed in chambers by the judge, and if she doesn't describe being in bed with you and Samara while the two of you had sex, then they have no way to prove their case. So that's good for us. Downside of Judge Jones, for you, is that I hear she's a bit of a Bible-thumper, and she trends conservative on parenting issues. If they successfully paint a picture of a younger, still-married, naked girlfriend frolicking around your apartment when you have the kids, she may think that's detrimental to them even without the sex allegations. But I can't imagine she'd make any drastic alteration in the schedule because of that; she'd probably just give you a stern lecture."

"Okay, good. Because it didn't happen, and my ex-wife is now officially crazy. Ellen, I'm counting on you to get me out of this."

I know, thought Ellen. *But maybe I can't.*

"Got it. You seem like a great dad, Jake, and this really did come out of the blue. I'm going to transfer you to the receptionist, and she'll set you up with a time to come in to prep for the hearing."

CHORUS #3

The Dads

The autumn sun had finally risen, and light was seeping through the dirty gym windows when Nat plopped down on the bench with a sigh, took a towel out of his bag, wiped the sweat from his face, and bent down to loosen the laces in his sneakers. Boy, he said to Wink, who was sitting next to him, massaging his right shoulder with his left hand and wincing, my knee is killing me. How's your rotator cuff doing?

Shitty, said Wink. I've been going to physical therapy three times a week, and it's still not better.

Sometimes I wonder, Nat said. We've been playing in this game for what, fifteen, sixteen years? Maybe it's time to pack it in. It's getting to the point where every Tuesday morning, when that alarm goes off at five thirty, and I drag myself out of bed, instead of thinking about my brilliant layups and how I'm going to crush you all, I'm wondering if my knee is gonna hold up and hoping I don't tear my calf muscle again. And look at you—you're like our fourth rotator cuff injury, right?

Yeah, said Wink. Basketball is definitely not an old guy's game. But I'm not ready to quit. And neither are you. So don't even talk about it.

I hear you, Nat said, but you gotta admit that now that the Legal Services guys dropped out, we need some younger blood. We need some guys who won't be moaning about their injuries the way we do.

Good idea, said Wink, unscrewing the top of his water bottle, lifting it up to the opening in his massive beard where Nat knew his lips were, even though he could barely see them, and swigging it down. Got anyone in mind?

Let me think about it, said Nat, looking over at another basketball club regular who was still on the court, practicing his jump shot. Hey, Tito! he yelled. Know any younger guys who might want to join us? Wink and I decided it's time to bring the average age here below fifty.

The sound of the ball hitting the floor echoed through the gym as Tito dribbled it over to the bench. You guys know Jake Naudain? Tito asked. He might be down for something like this.

Nat shook his head. Wink nodded. Yeah, I know him, sort of. He lives on Lapham Street, right around the corner from me.

Not anymore he doesn't, said Tito. Did you know he got divorced?

No, said Wink, but I can tell you that was a bad move. Ever see his wife? I mean ex-wife, I guess. Lisa. That guy must be crazy.

Wasn't up to him, said Tito. What I heard is, she threw him out. And now he's gotten himself into some trouble.

What kind? asked Wink.

Woman-related, Tito said. He's got this young girlfriend who's married, and she and her husband are swingers, and Jake is mixing it up with both of them and their swinging friends. And Lisa found out. And she's seriously pissed.

Man, Tito, how do you know all this? Wink asked. I thought you just locked yourself in that studio all day, being an artist and shit. Guess not.

Grapevine, said Tito, smiling. There's some serious grapevine going on over at Mariposa. Suzanna's in the same grade as the Naudains' older daughter.

Nat looked up at Tito, who was now tossing the ball from hand to hand. Why's the ex-wife mad? I thought you said she dumped him.

Well, yeah, she did, Tito said. He tossed the ball, left, right, left, right. But I guess she didn't expect him to become, you know, like swinger of the year. The tossing stopped. But here's the real thing— she's so mad, she's trying to take custody of the kids away from him. In court.

Wow, said Wink. That's harsh. Not to sound like a total sexist or anything, but—woman scorned?

Yeah, I guess that's about right, said Tito. So I was thinking maybe he needs to find some other forms of entertainment.

Wink smiled. Like basketball at six in the morning with a bunch of old dudes talking about their rotator cuffs?

Yeah, exactly like that, said Tito, putting down the ball and joining them on the bench. Might be just the thing.

Okay, said Nat. Fine with me. Maybe he'll spice up our boring lives by telling us about his sex adventures.

Fine with me too, Wink agreed. Go ahead and ask him. And while you're at it, ask him what he did to make that gorgeous wife unhappy.

Great idea, said Tito. I'll be sure to do that. You guys are so sensitive.

Yup, that's just what Cathy always tells me, Nat said, standing up and hoisting his gym bag over his shoulder. Go back to your jump shots. I gotta go to work.

24

Elizabeth: Mom Sucks,
One Week After

No one is really telling her anything, but she knows what's going on anyway. It's so obvious. Her mom is mad at her dad because of Samara. Not that she's crazy about Samara being at Dad's house so much, but really, what's the big deal? It isn't like her dad is cheating on her mom or anything. They're divorced! So what does her mom expect? Everyone's divorced parents that she knows have boyfriends and girlfriends, and that's just part of the deal. And some of them decided they were gay, so the moms have girlfriends, not boyfriends. But whatever. And it isn't like Samara is trying to act like their new mom or anything. She's more like a babysitter or an older cousin or something. And really, she isn't around that much; it isn't like she comes to their school or has met their friends or any of that stepmom type of thing. She and her dad are dating. And yes, that means they're having sex. Of course. And so what? That is totally normal. Mom is just acting like a bitch about it and filing for custody and making them go to court and talk to that old judge. And Grandma was all weird about her and Charlie going to sit with Dad when they were in court last week, like he was some kind of enemy, which was just so totally fucked up, she couldn't believe it.

She had asked her mom, the night before they had to go to court, why she was doing this to Dad, and her mom told her she just wanted to make sure she and Charlie were "safe." Safe? With Daddy? Like, okay, he is sometimes late getting them to school, and he isn't super organized about making sure their homework is done. Like last Tuesday night, when he didn't have the poster board for her science project, and CVS was already closed, but so what? Who cares? And when she asked Mom what she meant, Mom wouldn't tell her. She said it was a "grown-up thing" and it wasn't "appropriate" to discuss with Elizabeth, which is stupid and fucked up. This is her father, she's practically a teenager, and this is her life her mother is talking about!

And then when she got to court, she had to go back and talk to that judge about whether Charlie got into Daddy's bed when Samara was there. So maybe that happened, she doesn't really know, but it could have. But it's not like her dad was sexually abusing Charlie or something, and Samara's a girl, like them, so why is it such a big deal? And when her parents were married, Charlie used to get in bed with them all the time. And Elizabeth did too, when she was little. So really, her mother is so out of line here, it's just crazy.

When she told Anya about it, Anya said Elizabeth's mom is probably just jealous because she doesn't have a boyfriend. Maybe. It just sucks so bad that her mom gets to do all this and maybe take her and Charlie away from Dad, and she can't do anything to stop it. And when she talked to her dad about it after court, he was just like, "Don't worry; everything will be fine." Which she does not believe, not for a second.

25

Owen: Service of Process

Owen Butterfield is tired of eating dinner alone. It seems like Samara is never home any more. She has evening classes two nights a week, and some other nights she has meetings at school with her film crew. He had a long day; his new gig as assistant in the urban farming program run out of Merriweather Middle School is exhausting. The combination of motivating seventh graders to take an interest in growing hydroponic microgreens, and trying to extract a miniscule level of financial support from the school district for a program they had committed to host, and happily taken credit for in the press, is, to put it nicely, challenging. But still, he's happy working there. He's happy to have finally left the string of postcollege server jobs that had become something of an embarrassment at the age of thirty, when all the friends he started with in the restaurant business had either dropped out or embraced that world as a career, moving up to become managers, or chefs, or sommeliers, or reps for craft bourbon companies, or something he didn't understand that had to do with food distribution. At last, he had landed a job his parents are proud to tell their friends about. Well, maybe not proud exactly, but certainly not ashamed of. Especially their friends from church, who would definitely be impressed that the Butterfields' son, the older one who married that pretty girl and moved to Philadelphia, is teaching underserved children to grow organic vegetables.

Owen opens a beer and rummages around in the refrigerator, looking for ingredients to make a pasta sauce, with a microgreens salad on the side—and the beauty of hydroponics: they don't need to be washed!—when the doorbell rings. Given that he's not expecting anyone, that it is eight o'clock, and that their neighborhood is a little sketchy, he goes down the two flights of stairs, beer in hand, to see who is there rather than buzzing the person in. Looking through the window to the right of the front door, he sees an overweight, middle-aged, white guy wearing an Eagles jersey and a baseball cap. Owen opens the door.

"Is Samara Bard here?" asks the guy.

"No," says Owen. "I'm her husband. Can I help you?"

"Does she live here?"

"Yeah," Owen replies. The guy reaches into his back pocket, retrieves a rumpled envelope, and holds it out. "What is it?" Owen asks.

"Papers for your wife," the guy says. "What's your name?"

"Owen. Owen Butterfield. What do you mean, 'papers'?" Owen asks, as he takes the envelope.

"Subpoena," says the guy, writing something down on a piece of paper. "Make sure you give it to her." He turns around to leave, looks back over his shoulder at Owen, winks, and says, "Have a good evening."

The sauce—onion, garlic, tomatoes, and zucchini—is bubbling on the stove when Samara walks in the front door. "Smells great," she says. "I'm starving."

"Yeah, me too," says Owen, who is sitting on the couch next

to an empty beer bottle and a stack of *Modern Farmer* magazines. "But we need to talk first."

Samara tugs her black sweater up over her head and dumps
it on the kitchen table along with her backpack, shakes out her
hair, and sits down next to him. "Okay," she says. "What's up?"

Owen hands her the envelope, already opened. "A guy came
to the door looking for you, like an hour ago. Since you weren't
here, he gave me this."

"What is it?" Samara asks, taking a sheet of paper out of the
envelope. Owen doesn't answer. Samara looks at the paper. "Oh,
shit," she says. "I'm supposed to go to court? To testify in Jake's
custody thing? Fuck."

"Exactly," says Owen. "Like, why are you involved in this?
How did you get in the middle of this bullshit? A custody trial?
People fighting over their children like they're property? It's disgusting. This has nothing to do with us. You're not going to go,
right?"

Samara looks down at the paper again and then up at Owen.
"I don't think I have a choice," she says. "It's from the court. It
says I'm ordered to appear. I need to call Jake about it."

"Well, that's bullshit," says Owen, standing up and starting
to pace around the living room. "What's going to happen if you
don't? And don't call Jake about it. Samara, you can't get involved in this. What do you have to do with Jake's fighting with
his ex-wife about their kids? Zero. Nothing."

Samara is silent.

"Right?" says Owen, leaning down toward her, the volume
of his voice amping up a notch.

"I mean, you're right, in a way," Samara says, slowly folding
the subpoena and putting it back in the envelope, "but the thing
is, he's a really good dad. And she's a bitch. She's trying to take
custody away from him."

Owen jerks upright and jumps back from the couch. This is confirming, in a big way, the misgivings he's been starting to have about Samara's relationship with Jake. It's different than their other secondary relationships have been. It's more private. Aside from the one night they were all together with Kara and Grady, he's only seen Jake a couple of times in passing, and from the little bit Samara has told him—and now that he thinks about it, it really is just a little, little bit—it doesn't seem like Jake has any real interest in polyamory. Jake is just some straight guy having a midlife crisis who is into dating a younger woman. And that's a problem. That's not the kind of relationship he and Samara agreed to have. It isn't that all their secondary partners have to be polyamorous themselves, but they have to accept the lifestyle—they have to buy in and understand how it works.

This relationship, Owen thinks, is too closed. Samara never discusses Jake with him the way they discuss Owen's relationships with Kara and Grady, or the way they talked about Olivia when he was sleeping with her. He would tell Samara about what he and Olivia did, not the details of the sex, but just like stuff she said to him, or funny anecdotes, like about running into her mom, and Olivia struggling to figure out how to introduce him —things like that. They kept it above board. But Samara never volunteers any information about Jake other than that she is going to stay over at his house on a certain night, which seems to be happening more and more frequently. When he asks her anything about Jake or what they've done together, she only gives the most minimal answer and then changes the subject. This is the first time he's heard about this custody case, which sounds like a pretty big deal.

It's particularly disturbing, because up until now Owen thought they had it all figured out. He and Samara were polyamorous before they got married, and Owen had definitely not wanted to buy into the mainstream dominator culture where relationships are ranked in a hierarchy. But they did decide to get married and to live together just the two of them; they made a decision that their relationship would be primary, and other ones they developed would be secondary. It wasn't like an actual ranking of the other partners, not at all—just more of a description of how different relationships would fit into their lives. And they realized, and had talked about, how not everyone in the polyamory community was comfortable with any hierarchy of relationships at all, about how honesty and mutual respect were so essential to the polyamory model. So they agreed that they needed to be completely up front with other partners that the level of involvement either of them could have would always be less, in terms of time and intensity, than their relationship with each other.

But this thing with Jake doesn't seem to fit what they'd agreed to, and it's pissing him off. Not that he is jealous, really—more like angry that she's broken their agreement. Of course, if he tried to talk about this to anyone in the monogamy culture, they'd just say he was jealous, and they'd act all "I told you so" about it. Owen knows that feelings of jealousy are natural, but he also knows he can work through them. People in the straight world are so focused on jealousy, that's all they talk about when you try to explain polyamory. And that's ridiculous. When you're a kid, you learn to share things you love. That's the entire focus of preschool. And yes, you feel jealous of your friend who has more toys or plays basketball better or gets into a better college. But growing up means learning to move past that, learning to be happy for your friend. And to share what you have with others.

Like, if you were to punch your friend in the face because he has a nicer car than you that you wished you could afford, everyone would think you were a loser. But if you punched your friend in the face because he had sex with your girlfriend, everyone would think it was justifiable. Why? Why, in the context of love and sex, do we accept that? Owen has never understood the rationale, but he knows it's all part of the monogamy culture. Straight society condones out-of-control jealousy in this one context; it even glorifies it. And it just doesn't make any sense. To Owen, it seems obvious that people should try to act like grown-ups, not four-year-olds. But anyway, this latest development with Jake, this putting Samara in the middle of his court case with his ex-wife—this is unacceptable.

"You knew about this whole thing?" Owen asks. "And you never said anything to me about this? This is just so not cool. This is not what we agreed to, Samara."

Samara looks up at him, startled. "Are you jealous?" she asks. "Owen, you have nothing to worry about."

"Jealous? Me?" says Owen, volume going up another notch. "No. I am not jealous of that guy with his divorce and his corporate job and his private school tuition and all that shit. No. I'm just worried that he's dragging you into it; he's dragging you somewhere you don't belong. Where we don't belong. I think you need to cut it off with him. End it. And don't go to this court thing, either."

Samara is quiet.

Suddenly famished, Owen just wants to eat dinner and forget about Jake Naudain. "So let's eat," he says, holding his hand out to help Samara off the couch.

"Wow," she says, finally, not taking his hand. "It's actually not okay for you to tell me what to do. But I heard what you said. I'll think about it. And just so you know, I have no interest in being involved in Jake's custody case. None. But you realize this subpoena is from his wife. His ex-wife, I mean. Well, actually from her lawyer. Jake probably doesn't even know about it."

"And he doesn't ever need to, because you're not going. Right?"

Samara takes Owen's proffered hand, her tattooed stars aligning with his, wrist to wrist, and stands up. "Let's eat," she says. "I'll dress the salad."

26

Marni: PowerPoint

Sitting cross-legged on her unmade, extra-long twin bed next to a massive pile of dirty laundry she plans to take home for winter break, Marni is on her laptop, scrolling through the requirements for her next Intro to Sociology paper.

"I can't believe I have to work on this over break," she says to her roommate, Paris, who is standing in front of their closet, naked except for a towel wrapped around her small and elegant head, surveying the chaotic scene inside.

"That sucks," says Paris. "Have you seen my gray plaid pajama bottoms? Those ones Amy left here?"

"No," says Marni, "sorry. You can borrow my red ones if you want."

"That's okay, but thanks anyway. I really need to find mine. I want to pack them," says Paris, stepping into a pair of black leggings, unwrapping the towel from her curly wet hair, and slipping a Questlove sweatshirt over her head. "What is it you have to do over break?"

"I have to do field research for Intro to Soc," says Marni. "It has to be about a quote, 'contemporary social movement in your community which is effecting social change,' unquote."

"So what social movement are you picking?" asks Paris, as she drags a dusty black leather duffel bag out of the closet.

"I don't know yet," Marni says. "I've got to think of something that's going on in Philly, preferably in my neighborhood, so I can find people to interview. Something interesting."

"God, that would be hopeless in my neighborhood," says Paris, pulling multiple items of high-end black clothing out of the closet and dumping them into the bag. "Trust me, there is nothing happening in Darien, Connecticut, that is effecting social change. Or that is interesting. I'd end up having to interview a bunch of hedge fund managers."

Marni smiles, stands up, and starts stuffing her dirty clothes into a pink laundry bag on the floor next to her bed. "I know I've told you what Greenwood is like, right?"

"Yup. Very crunchy."

"Oh yeah. I could interview people about veganism. Or recycling. Yawn."

"Does being vegan qualify as a social movement?" asks Paris. "Doesn't seem like it would."

"I'm not sure. Maybe it doesn't," says Marni. "But even if it did, I wouldn't pick it, because I'm so sick of hearing people talk about what they eat. And recycling is very important, obviously, but it's totally boring. So I'm not doing those. Any ideas? I'm like brain-dead from my bio exam."

Paris turns around, her now-full duffel in her hand. "How about polyamory?" she suggests. "That's definitely not boring. And it would be considered a contemporary social movement, wouldn't it? I mean, I'm sure it's been going on forever to some extent, but now all these people are talking about it. There's, like, polyamory Meetup groups and stuff. I just read an article about it in *Slate*. And my cousin told me about the polyamory scene in Barcelona, which was really big when she was there for the semester. I'm sure she'd be cool with talking to you about it, but that wouldn't exactly satisfy the 'in your community' part."

"Yes!" says Marni. "Love you, girl. That's perfect. They're probably having those Meetups literally down the street from my house at our local coffee shop. They're probably sitting right next to the knitting group."

Paris giggles. "Let me know what you find out. Maybe it's even happening in Darien."

"Oh yeah, for sure it's happening in Darien," says Marni. "You may not have any vegans or knitters. But I'm pretty sure there are polyamorous-ers. Or whatever they call themselves."

"I guess you'll find out what they call themselves," says Paris. "And lots of other good stuff. Maybe I'll even read your paper."

"That will not be necessary," says Marni. "But I can give you the highlights. Maybe I'll prepare our own little private Power-Point."

"I'll look forward to it," says Paris. "Okay, I'm going to sleep now. My mom is coming to pick me up ridiculously early tomorrow. Like at eight. I have no idea why."

"Don't complain. You're lucky," says Marni. "I have to take the train. With my laundry."

"Ewww, that is bad. Sorry. At least you don't live in boring Darien, though."

Marni smiles. She knows she is so lucky to have landed this nice, funny, no-drama roommate. Really, she doesn't know what she would have done if she had ended up living with a crazy person, like her friend Sarah did. That girl is always drunk or high, and she's always bringing guys home from parties and locking Sarah out, and then when Sarah finally gets into the room the next morning, it's completely trashed, like used-condoms-on-the-floor trashed. So, so gross. Paris is like a saint, by comparison.

"I'll probably still be asleep when you leave, so have a great break, and I'll see you in January," Marni says, leaning over and giving her a hug.

Paris hugs her back, jumps into bed, wet hair and all, and pulls her dove-gray linen duvet cover up to her chin. Everything Paris owns is tasteful and expensive. Her mother must have taken her dorm shopping at Nordstrom, instead of Target, like Marni's mom. Oh well. She really isn't stuck-up about being rich, so Marni can't even justify being annoyed with her about it.

"See you then," Paris says, as she snuggles down into her quilt. "Merry Christmas and all that. And don't forget the polyamory PowerPoint."

27

Judge Jones: *Naudain v. Naudain,*
December Term, 1:30 p.m.

The Naudain custody case is back. Judge Jones had ordered the notes of testimony transcribed so she could review them before the next hearing date. Given that more than two months have now passed, during which time she has been assigned custody lists exclusively, and thus subjected to the intimate details of upward of two hundred unhappy families, she had no clear memory of the matter prior to picking up the slim, bound volume during her lunch break. Fortunately, since she is due on the bench to hear the remainder of the *Naudain* case in forty-five minutes, it comes back to her right away as she skims through the pages.

Greenwood family, two girls, allegations that younger child witnessed some unspecified sexual shenanigans between Dad and girlfriend. Mom possibly overreacting to Dad having a new girlfriend, or possibly not. Mom's lawyer, the arrogant Mr. Boyle, had tried to offer hearsay testimony of the younger girl's statements through his direct of Mom. But opposing counsel had objected, and she had sustained, as usual, and the child had been unresponsive to her questions in chambers. She had denied a motion for directed verdict at the close of Dad's case—which apparently she herself had invited Dad's counsel to make—but now cannot remember why. It seems from the transcript that she made a mistake. There was no evidence offered by Attorney Boyle to substantiate the claims in the petition. Was she just curious to hear Mr. Naudain's side? Or had she had some kind of gut feeling that there might be more to this? Whatever her reasoning at the time, she can't remember it.

Nonetheless, it appears that all that remains is for Attorney Boyle to finish his cross-examination of Mr. Naudain and perhaps put on some rebuttal testimony from his client, and they will be done. And then, absent some big surprise, she can dismiss the petition. She only has two other cases on her afternoon list —one just being a bench warrant and the other a holdover from the morning that the attorneys were outside in the waiting room, trying to settle—so it looks like she might actually be able to leave early for a change. There are only ten shopping days left until Christmas, and she is woefully behind. If all goes as anticipated, she could be at Macy's and maybe over to Nordstrom Rack—terrific buys!—by four thirty. She is determined to send off the packages to her sister and her nephews and their families, all of whom live in Atlanta, by Saturday at the latest.

"Melinda," she calls to her clerk, who is eating lunch at her desk in the anteroom, which opens into chambers, "Could you see if parties and counsel are all here on *Naudain*? I want to take them right at one thirty." Before Melinda can answer, Sherriff Bob, who is apparently in the anteroom as well, calls back.

"Judge, they're all out there. And no cowboy boots today. Maybe he's waiting for Santa to send him a new pair."

"Thank you, Bob," says the judge, ignoring the cowboy remark because she thinks it better to keep a little distance from the court staff, to maintain just the right degree of separation and a certain level of decorum—like what a good parent does with their children.

"I'll go out and let them know we're starting in five. And judge," says Melinda, ever the mind reader, "do you want my 25 percent off coupon for Macy's? Storewide, just for today."

The conclusion of Attorney Boyle's cross-examination of Jake Naudain is uneventful. *Really,* the judge thinks, *he could have taken care of this in the ten minutes I gave him two months ago and saved us all from having to bring the case back.* He questioned Mr. Naudain about a missed ballet recital and an incident in which he took the children to his band practice and failed to bring lunch for them. Attorney Ackerman objected on the basis that these topics were beyond the scope of her direct, which they were, and because the testimony was not relevant to the allegations of sexual conduct, which it was not. But the judge had overruled her, and at the same time admonished Boyle to finish up. When he asks his last question, Judge Jones nods approvingly.

"Counsel," she says, looking at Attorney Ackerman, "you don't have any redirect, do you?"

"No," the lawyer answers, smiling in acknowledgement of the not-so-subtle hint from the judge that she doesn't want to hear any more and is ready to rule.

"Mr. Boyle, do you rest?"

"No, Your Honor. We have a rebuttal witness, Samara Bard."

Ellen Ackerman springs up, talking as she rises. "Your Honor, we had no knowledge of this witness. And I want an offer of proof regarding her testimony." From her survey of the tableau rapidly unfolding before her, the judge can see that Mr. Naudain looks terrified, and Ms. Naudain looks quite satisfied. And Ms. Ackerman is trying to buy time.

"Well, Counsel, there is no requirement that you be given advance notice of a rebuttal witness or any fact witness, for that

matter, in a custody proceeding, as you well know. As for your request for an offer of proof, I'm happy to ask Attorney Boyle for it, but given that the witness is your client's girlfriend, and she's being called to rebut his testimony, I'm thinking it's probably relevant. Don't you agree?"

As the judge is speaking, Attorney Ackerman bends down toward her client, who is whispering furiously in her ear. She puts her hand on his arm, straightens up, and says, "Your Honor, I don't. This is trial by ambush. Mr. Boyle clearly hid this witness from us. She was not in the waiting room, so he must have had her stay downstairs in the courthouse. He did not mention her to me when we spoke outside the courtroom just prior to the start of this hearing. My client did not know she had been subpoenaed. We're concerned that she was perhaps threatened or coerced into appearing today. Had I known she was subpoenaed, I would have interviewed her."

"Attorney Boyle, what's your offer of proof?" asks the judge.

"Your Honor, I honestly cannot tell you exactly what this witness will say, because she declined to be interviewed by me. However, she responded to the subpoena, she was present, obviously, during the events at issue in this case, and we have reason to believe she will rebut Mr. Naudain's version of those events."

Attorney Ackerman is back on her feet. "What Mr. Boyle *believes* a witness he has not even spoken to *may* testify about is not a valid offer of proof, Your Honor. Subpoenaing this witness, my client's girlfriend, was obviously done for the purpose of harassing and embarrassing my client, not to present meaningful evidence to this court. Without a specific offer of proof as to relevant testimony, we object to the Court hearing from this witness at all."

Good try, thinks the judge, *but really, this young woman could resolve the whole issue, either way.* However, it is odd that Boyle subpoenaed her: an uncooperative girlfriend would appear so unlikely to produce any helpful evidence, from his perspective. But perhaps he is willing to take a flyer on her because he has nothing else at this point, and he knows his petition is very likely to be dismissed. If the girlfriend confirms Mr. Naudain's story, they haven't lost anything. Still, a bold move, to put on a witness you haven't interviewed—very risky. And why wouldn't the witness have contacted Mr. Naudain, who is, according to his testimony, her boyfriend, when she received the subpoena? Is it possible she was in fact coerced in some way? All very strange, but absolutely not grounds for precluding the witness's testimony.

The judge sighs, seeing her productive shopping trip fade away. "Ms. Ackerman, I understand your position, and I do think it's unfortunate that you had no advance notice, but that really falls into the category of lack of professional courtesy," she says, turning and focusing a disapproving look on a very unrepentant-looking Attorney Boyle, "not admissibility of the testimony. So I will allow Ms. Bard to testify on rebuttal. Which I remind you, Mr. Boyle, means that your questions must be strictly limited to topics addressed by Mr. Naudain during his direct and cross-examinations. I will not allow this to become a free-for-all. Understood?"

"Understood, Your Honor. Absolutely. Thank you."

Sheriff Bob leaves the courtroom and reappears with a small, dark-haired young woman wearing leggings, boots, and what looks to the judge like some kind of smock garment with beads attached to it. *Like a college student*, the judge thinks. Sheriff Bob does the handoff to Melinda, who walks Ms. Bard up to the witness stand and administers the oath. As the witness turns away from the bench while she affirms, rather than swears, to tell the truth, Judge Jones notices that she studiously avoids looking at either of the Naudains.

"You may be seated, Ms. Bard," says the judge. "Attorney Boyle, your witness."

"Ms. Bard, where do you live?"

"Nine twenty-two Camden Street, apartment three, Philadelphia.

"With whom do you live?"

"My husband, Owen Butterfield."

The judge sees Ellen Ackerman's eyebrows rise and fall, a quick, inadvertent facial shrug of surprise.

"Your husband," Attorney Boyle repeats slowly. "Okay. And what do you do for a living?"

"I'm a student right now. I'm getting my master's in film at Temple. And I work as a teaching assistant in the undergraduate film and media arts department."

"And are you currently making a film as well?"

Ellen Ackerman stands and objects. "Your Honor, this is completely irrelevant. And not proper rebuttal testimony, either."

"Agreed," says Judge Jones. "Attorney Boyle, remember our discussion before you called this witness? I permitted you to call her without an offer of proof, over Ms. Ackerman's objection, but I reminded you that you are strictly limited to rebuttal of Mr. Naudain's testimony. And I do not recall Mr. Naudain testifying about a film being made by Ms. Bard. Nor do I think this topic has any relevance to the issue raised in your petition, which is the reason we're all here, Mr. Boyle. Objection sustained. Move on."

"Very well, Your Honor. Perhaps the Court will permit me to revisit that question later, when I might be able to lay a better foundation for the question."

Dear Lord, thinks the judge, *we'll be here until dinner.* "Doubtful," she says. "Continue."

"Ms. Bard, how do you know Jake Naudain?"

"I met him last May."

"And after you met him, did you subsequently enter into an intimate relationship with him?"

"Yes."

"May I presume that you were, at the time, separated from your husband?"

"Objection. Leading and irrelevant," says Attorney Ackerman.

"No, I wasn't," says the witness, before the judge can respond to the objection.

"Ms. Bard," says the judge, "when you hear an objection from counsel, don't answer the question until I rule. If I sustain the objection, that means you can't answer it. If I overrule the objection, you go ahead with the answer. Okay?"

"Yes, Your Honor, sorry. I didn't understand."

"I realize that, Ms. Bard, and you don't have a lawyer here representing you who would have explained this to you, so I'm just letting you know how this works. Mr. Boyle," says the judge, turning away from the witness stand and over toward counsel table, "the objection is sustained. This is my second warning. Get to the rebuttal testimony. If you continue to ignore my instructions, I'm going to dismiss this witness."

"I apologize, Your Honor. However, I do think it's relevant that this witness, whom Mr. Naudain has represented to be his girlfriend and with whom he's sleeping in the presence of the parties' children, is married and apparently not even separated— much less divorced—from her husband."

Ellen Ackerman is, once again, on her feet. "Your Honor, the particulars of the relationship between this witness and her husband have absolutely nothing to do with the unsubstantiated allegations about sexual conduct being made by Mr. Boyle and his client. This is a hearing about the Naudain children. Ms. Bard's personal life is not relevant."

"I see your point, Ms. Ackerman, but it is curious to me, as well as being proper rebuttal testimony, since Mr. Naudain did identify this witness as his girlfriend, that she is apparently saying she is not, which would contradict his testimony. Overruled. Actually, I believe the witness already answered the question. You may continue, Counsel."

Attorney Boyle looks at his notes, whispers something to his client, takes off his glasses, and looks back at the witness. "Ms. Bard, how would you describe your relationship with Mr. Naudain?"

Judge Jones turns toward the witness stand. She has to admit to herself that this is getting somewhat interesting, which is only fair, given that but for this unexpected witness she'd be on the first floor of Macy's happily trying on new shoes right about now. Ms. Bard is looking down at her hands, which are fidgeting with one of the beads on her blouse.

"I would say he's my boyfriend," she says.

"But you are married, correct?"

"Yes."

"And you and your husband are not separated, correct?"

"Yes. That's right, we're not."

"So would it be fair to say you and Mr. Naudain are having an affair?"

"No. That's not how we describe it."

"Who do you mean by 'we'?"

The judge can see a look of resignation on Ellen Ackerman's face, as her client squirms beside her. She clearly had made a call, based on the judge's last ruling, to just get this over with as quickly as possible, whatever it was going to be, rather than to continue to object to the questions and drag it out further.

"I mean me and my husband, Owen. We don't use the word 'affair' to describe our other relationships. Because they're not secret."

Sherriff Bob, seated at the desk in the back of the courtroom, looks up from the sports page and slowly turns his gaze toward Jake Naudain.

"Your other relationships," Attorney Boyle repeats slowly, drawing out each word. "How many do you have?"

That question apparently exceeded the limits of what Ellen Ackerman had resigned herself to, and she stands up again. "Objection! Your Honor, this is way beyond the scope of Mr. Naudain's testimony, and it's not relevant to the allegations in his petition. And it's badgering the witness."

"Overruled."

"But Your Honor, you gave Attorney Boyle strict parameters for this witness's testimony. And he's completely ignoring them."

"Counsel, I've ruled. This may in fact be relevant to the sexual conduct allegations. Ms. Bard, you may answer that question."

Samara shifts in her seat. Ellen Ackerman sits down and sighs. Lisa Naudain leans forward, looking intently at Samara. Sheriff Bob continues to stare at Jake Naudain. "My primary relationship is with my husband. But we each have other boyfriends and girlfriends. We're polyamorous. Right now, I have a relationship with Jake, and there's a couple that Owen and I have a relationship with together."

Having heard many details of intimate human relationships spill forth in her courtroom, Judge Jones is not easily surprised. But she was only vaguely aware of the term "polyamorous." Although of course she understands it—anyone with the most rudimentary knowledge of Latin would get its meaning—it had not made its way into her courtroom yet. Or probably it had, but it had not been disclosed and explained in such a matter-of-fact way as it had by this little waif of a girl. She looks barely old enough to be out of high school, much less married and involved in this complicated structure of sexual relations with other people, who, if the judge understands correctly, are women as well as men. *Really, it is probably something her husband convinced her to do because he wanted multiple women,* the judge thinks. He wanted to be polygamous, like those Mormons with all the wives who live in a compound together, but it's the twenty-first century in Philadelphia and he can't do that, so he convinced her that they would do this polyamory thing.

"Polyamorous," says Boyle. "Okay. Are the other people you and your husband have these relationships with also polyamorous?"

Samara Bard doesn't speak right away. Then she says, "I'm not sure how to answer that."

"Try," says Boyle. Ms. Ackerman is sitting very still, staring at the witness.

"Well, I guess I'd say yes. They might not necessarily be committed to polyamory themselves, but anyone either of us has a relationship with knows that we are married and that we have multiple intimate relationships. So they accept that. And sometimes they also have other relationships."

"Does Jake Naudain also have other intimate relationships, to your knowledge?"

"Objection!" *Appropriate,* thinks Judge Jones, *but I'm going to overrule it because this just might lead somewhere significant.* And it's got Sheriff Bob's attention—he hasn't looked at his newspaper once since Ms. Bard started talking about her "other relationships"—which, she has learned, is a fairly accurate barometer of when some really significant testimony might be on the way. So why not give Boyle a bit more leeway?

"Overruled."

"Your Honor," Ms. Ackerman responds, "this is way outside the scope of my client's testimony on direct. And it's irrelevant to the allegations."

"Counsel, I'll note your continuing objection. But I'm allowing it. Ms. Bard, you may answer the question."

"Okay. About Jake's other relationships, I don't know. What do you mean by a 'relationship'?"

"I mean a relationship of a sexual nature."

"Well, I don't know. I only know about one night when he joined Owen and me when we got together with the couple we're in a relationship with."

"What do you mean by 'got together'?"

"I mean we all spent the night together."

"And Mr. Naudain was there?"

"Yes."

"What took place?"

"We had, like, a little party. And Jake and Owen and I stayed over at our friends' house."

"And what exactly happened at this little party?"

"We hung out, we listened to music, and we all spent the night together."

"Ms. Bard, when you say you all spent the night together, do you mean you all had sexual relations together?"

"Well, not all together, but in different combinations during the night."

"And was Mr. Naudain a participant in these different combinations?"

"Yes."

"And just to clarify, Ms. Bard, since you began your relationship with Mr. Naudain, has he known that you were married and living with your husband?"

"Yes, definitely. He's always known that. He met Owen before he and I started our relationship."

"So if Mr. Naudain told my client that you were separated from your husband, that would not be true, right?"

"Right."

"In fact, he would be lying, because you never told him that, right?"

"Objection," says Ellen Ackerman. "Leading. This is direct, not cross."

"I agree," said Judge Jones. "Sustained."

"I'll withdraw the question, Your Honor," says Boyle. *Of course he will*, thinks the judge. *He's more than made his point.*

"Ms. Bard, have you ever spent the night at Mr. Naudain's house?"

"Yes."

"And have you done so when his children are there?"

"Yes."

"How many times?"

"I really don't know. Quite a few times."

"Do you recall a time, during one of those nights, when Mr. Naudain's daughter Charlotte woke up crying?"

"Yes."

"What happened?"

"She was crying, and Jake got up to calm her down, but she kept crying. At that point, I was awake too, so I told him to just bring her into the bedroom with us so she wouldn't wake Elizabeth. That's her sister. They share a room."

"What did Mr. Naudain do?"

"He carried her into the bedroom and put her in the bed between us and stroked her hair and told her everything was okay, you know, like, to calm her down. I guess she wakes up at night scared, but it's not like she's really awake, she's still sort of asleep, so he just has to calm her down, and she goes right back to sleep."

"You say she was between you and Mr. Naudain in the bed?"

"Yes."

"Ms. Bard, what were you wearing?"

"What was I wearing? What do you mean? I was in bed."

"I mean, were you wearing pajamas of any sort?"

"Pajamas? No."

"Were you wearing anything?"

"No."

"So you were naked?"

"Yes. I always sleep naked."

"Was Mr. Naudain wearing anything?"

"You mean, like pajamas?"

"Yes."

"No. He doesn't wear pajamas, either. He might have had boxers on. But maybe not. I don't remember."

"Okay, so you, Mr. Naudain, and little Charlotte are all in Mr. Naudain's bed together."

"Right."

"And you're naked, and Mr. Naudain is either naked or just wearing boxers."

"Yes."

"And Charlotte is lying between you."

"Right. She was between us, but Jake was sort of snuggling her."

"What do you mean by 'snuggling'?"

"Like, he had his arms around her or something. I don't remember exactly."

"Were you touching Charlotte as well?"

"Probably. I don't remember that exactly either, but I know she was lying next to me, and I probably patted her or hugged her at some point—to comfort her, you know."

"What parts of your bodies were touching?"

"I really don't remember."

"Were you at all concerned, Ms. Bard, about being naked in bed with Mr. Naudain's child?"

"No. No, I wasn't. I think human bodies are beautiful." Sheriff Bob and the court reporter exchange a quick glance. *No doubt this pronouncement will be bouncing around chambers for the next week*, thinks the judge.

"Did you have any concerns about Mr. Naudain being in bed with his daughter, naked?"

"I said, I don't remember if he was naked or if he had boxers on. But either way, no. He's her dad. I don't believe in parents hiding their bodies from their children. I think nudity is healthy."

Surveying the territory otherwise known as counsel table, Judge Jones sees Lisa Naudain, who had been sitting rigidly at attention, let out a sigh and roll her eyes. Jake Naudain is doing his best to contain the growing look of horror on his face. Attorney Ackerman is furiously taking notes. And Attorney Boyle looks, as the judge's mother used to say, like the cat who ate the canary.

"Ms. Bard, did Charlotte stay in bed with you and Mr. Naudain for the rest of the night?"

"No, Jake took her back to her room at some point. I'm not sure when. I fell back asleep."

"At any point, between the time Mr. Naudain brought Charlotte in bed with you until she went back into her own bedroom, did you and Mr. Naudain have sexual relations?"

"No. Of course not."

"Did you have any sexual contact?"

"I don't really remember. I mean we might have kissed or something like that."

"What would 'something like that' include?"

"Like touched each other. I mean, we were in bed together. It's not a king size bed or anything, just a regular bed—a queen. But it would be hard to avoid touching. I think we were both kind of curled around Charlie from opposite sides, facing each other, so I'm sure our legs were touching. But we were not having sex with Charlie in the bed."

"Thank you, Ms. Bard. No further questions, Your Honor."

Ellen Ackerman's cross is brief. She asks the witness a couple of questions to emphasize that there had been no sexual activity between her and Mr. Naudain, and that was it. She asks for time to confer with her client, presumably, the judge thinks, to decide whether she should put him back on the stand for surrebuttal. Apparently the decision is not to, and Attorney Boyle rests his case. Given that it is already four forty-five, and the court staff is becoming increasingly grumpy as it is looking inevitable that they will be kept past five, the judge dispenses with any closing statements and dismisses counsel and the parties to the waiting room while she writes her order.

Really, she just needs some time to collect her thoughts. On credibility, she has little doubt that Ms. Bard's version of the events on the night in question is more accurate than Mr. Naudain's. And apparently Mr. Naudain had not been truthful with his ex-wife about other matters besides the particulars of that evening. If she were to believe Ms. Bard, Mr. Naudain downplayed how often she slept over at his house. And it appeared, from Attorney Boyle's questioning of the witness, that Mr. Naudain had also lied to Ms. Naudain about the fact that Ms. Bard was separated from her husband, when he knew that was not the case. This second point is of no consequence, really—what man *would* tell his ex-wife that his new girlfriend was part of some sort of swingers group and was having sex with this one and that one?—but the first point is significant to the judge. Not being truthful about how often Ms. Bard slept over would be consistent, she thinks, with being similarly untruthful about taking Charlotte into bed with him and Ms. Bard. Mr. Naudain certainly had a motive to minimize the extent of contact the young Ms.

Bard had with the parties' daughters so as to not to upset his ex-wife.

The thing that puzzles the judge most is how Ms. Bard's appearance could have been a surprise to Mr. Naudain, which it clearly was. When she was subpoenaed, why didn't she tell him? Why didn't she talk to him? Why didn't she find out what he was planning to say? Why didn't they conform their testimony to create a consistent story? That's what everyone else does, the judge well knows, which is why one always has to apply an extra level of scrutiny to the testimony of witnesses who are family members or close friends of the litigants. And that's why, she has noticed, some of the lawyers who appear before her frequently don't even bother to cross-examine such witnesses in custody cases. Instead, they prefer a quick and dismissive, "No questions," to send a clear message to the Court that the testimony of those people is so obviously and inherently biased that it is not even worth dignifying with cross-examination. Because really, what mother would say something bad about her child?

But back to Ms. Bard. For whatever reason, she had not wanted to protect Mr. Naudain, and she had been very forthcoming about her beliefs and unconventional lifestyle. So in terms of a factual finding, Judge Jones concludes she would find that Mr. Naudain did, as alleged by Ms. Naudain, take the younger child into bed with him and his girlfriend and let her sleep there with them. And Mr. Naudain lied about that, under oath.

But where does that get her? Although Ms. Bard admitted that she was naked and Mr. Naudain was either naked as well or close to it, she emphatically denied that she and Mr. Naudain had sex while the child was in bed with them. So really, the judge cannot find that "multiple acts of sexual conduct" took place.

Or maybe she can? If they were both naked and touching

the child and each other in any manner, that really does disturb her. Her job, her sacred mission in fact, is to determine the best interest of the Naudain girls, regardless of whether or not the specifics of Ms. Naudain's petition can be proven. And this type of conduct, in her book, is not. At best, it would have been confusing to the little girl. At worst, it was inappropriately exposing her to adult sexuality and nudity, which could be considered a form of abuse. And there is another issue lurking about whether the older child actually knew what happened and was covering up for her father, which is also of concern, if she felt she had to protect him or, worse, if he asked her to do so.

"Melinda," Judge Jones calls, turning her head toward the office outside her chambers, "can you come here a minute, please?" Melinda scurries into chambers on her shiny black and very high heels, legal pad in well-manicured hand. "What do you think I should do?"

Melinda sits down and looks across the desk at her boss. "I think that guy's a creep," she says. "If I found out that Christina's dad was rolling around naked in bed with her and his poly-whatever girlfriend, he would never see her again. And also, my father would kill him." Melinda, a single mother who had worked her way through law school while raising her twelve-year-old daughter, could always be counted on for a strong opinion. Her thinking tended to be unencumbered by either subtlety or nuance, the judge had found, but it was often useful to get her reaction, more as a mother, perhaps, than a lawyer.

"But Christina is twelve," the judge says. "This child was only seven when this happened. Does that make a difference to you?"

"No, Judge, it doesn't. She shouldn't be exposed to that, period. She's a little girl. What was he thinking? I mean, he can have sex with whoever he wants, but do it on his own time. They have a week-on, week-off schedule. Why can't he just pay attention to his daughters on his custodial week and do all his polyamory business on Mom's custodial week? I mean, why does he need her to sleep over while his kids are there?"

From the office, the voice of Sheriff Bob answers: "Because the human body is beautiful. And he wants to see it. A lot."

"But, Melinda," says the judge, "Mom alleged that the child witnessed multiple acts of sexual conduct. I'm not convinced we have any direct evidence of even one such act. On what basis would I take all overnights away from the father?"

"Judge, who knows what they did or didn't do in that bed? But really, what does it matter? To me, that whole thing is sexual conduct. I mean, the naked girlfriend curled up around that poor child 'comforting' her? And maybe—but she can't quite remember—her naked self was kissing the kid's dad? Come on, Your Honor. And I don't think you need to take away all his overnights. I just think he shouldn't have shared custody. Look, he lied on the stand, and he has no boundaries with those children. And the mom's very responsible, she's a nurse, and she's not doing crazy shit like this—excuse me, Your Honor—so why not have them live with her? Judge, if I were you, I'd grant the petition and reduce his time to every other weekend. And give him a dinner visit on Wednesday night. That should be fine. I'm sure he can refrain from polyamory-ing every other weekend."

Judge Jones thanks her law clerk and starts writing her order by hand. "Sheriff Bob," she calls out, "could you please bring the parties and counsel back into the courtroom? I'm going to make my ruling, and then we can all pack up and go home."

28

~

Jake: The Loves of My Life

I am so angry at Samara, I can't breathe. She must have high-tailed it out of the building after she finished testifying, be-cause while we're waiting for the judge to call us back, I text her multiple times, and she doesn't respond. What the fuck is wrong with her? She totally screwed me, and I have no idea why. Why didn't she tell me she got a subpoena from Lisa's dick of a lawyer? Did Lisa threaten her or something? I really have no idea, but my heart is pounding, and I'm gulping down air like I can't get enough of it. How can she fuck up my life like this? She knows my girls are everything to me. If I lose custody of them because of her getting up on that witness stand and going on about polyamory and the beauty of the naked body, I don't know what I'll do. Actually, I do know what I'll do, which is even worse, because the answer is nothing. I mean, what would my options be? Even if I was the violent type, which I'm not, I wouldn't beat her up and make things even worse by ending up in jail. I am completely powerless here. And I don't know who I hate more right now, Lisa or Samara.

Ellen is sitting next to me, checking email on her phone. She does not look happy, obviously. But she's not saying anything. I ask her if she thinks the judge believed Samara, and she just looks at me, no smile, and says yes, then goes back to her phone.

I want to ask her if the fact that Samara denied that we had sex in the bed with Charlie was enough to save me. But she doesn't seem receptive to a discussion right now, and really, what's the point? There's nothing we can do about any of it.

A skinny kid in a Homer Simpson T-shirt walks past us and disappears into another courtroom with his lawyer. I think about the nice court clothes I'm wearing, my navy-blue suit to impress the judge, and how it doesn't matter anymore. It won't protect me from Samara's testimony. I might as well be in sweats and a hoodie. The TV high up on the wall is tuned to CNN, closed caption. Silent images of massive wildfires in Australia are raging across a parched landscape. Time is dripping slowly by. Very few people are left in the waiting room. A couple of lawyers talk softly in the corner, gossiping about something some judge did that they both seemed to find amusing. It is all so mundane, and here I am, waiting to see if I'm going to lose custody of my girls, the loves of my life—more than Lisa ever was.

The courtroom door opens, and the sheriff comes out. "Counsel and parties on Naudain," he says, and we all stand up and walk back into the courtroom.

The judge is on the bench, looking over her glasses. "Everybody may be seated," she says. The court reporter straightens up and puts her hands up over the roll of paper inserted in her machine, poised ready to attack it, ready to record whatever terrible thing the judge is going to say. The small young woman in very high heels, who's dressed like a lawyer and was in the courtroom when Samara testified, comes back in through a door behind the judge's bench and sits down at the desk to the right of the judge, stage left, and the play begins.

"Counsel, thank you for your presentation of this case. Mom and Dad, I want you to know that you both have excellent attorneys, and your interests have been well represented. I have carefully considered all the evidence. Mom, I cannot find that multiple acts of sexual conduct were proven, as there was no evidence of any specific sexual acts occurring in the presence of the child, and, in fact, the one thing that Mr. Naudain and Ms. Bard did agree upon was that there were not.

"However, my job, as I'm sure both your counsel have explained to you, is different in a custody case than in any other type of case. In a custody case, my job is to determine what is in the best interests of your children when the two of you are unable to agree, regardless of the specific allegations contained in the pleadings either of you file with this court. And I am deeply disturbed, Dad, by the testimony of Ms. Bard—whom I found to be a very credible witness—regarding your willingness to place your seven-year-old daughter into a situation involving adult intimacy and nudity, especially in the context of what is apparently a rather casual relationship between you and Ms. Bard. I find it highly inappropriate, and I find your actions to be irresponsible. And I further find that your testimony about the events in question was not credible. I do not believe that you were truthful, despite being under oath, when you testified back in October, and that further concerns me. Because with a shared custody arrangement such as you have had with Ms. Naudain, you both need to be able to trust one another to relay accurate information about the children, information that the other parent can rely on. That's the bedrock, if you will, of successful shared custody. And I find you have violated that trust. So I find that it is in the best interests of the children to grant the petition.

"However, Mr. Boyle, I do not find your request to restrict Mr. Naudain to daytime visits only to be reasonable. But I do find that Mom is the more stable and reliable parent, and therefore I am entering an order modifying the physical custody schedule. Effective today, Mom will have primary physical custody, with Dad to have partial physical custody every other weekend, Friday pickup from school, through Monday morning return to school, and every Wednesday, pickup from school through 8:00 p.m., return to Mom's residence. Legal custody will remain shared. Holidays, vacation schedule, and all other provisions of the parties' previous order to stand. Counsel, if you and your clients will wait outside, you'll receive copies of the order. Mr. and Ms. Naudain, good luck to you both."

That's it. It's over, just like that. Lisa totally fucked me, or Samara did, or both of them. If I heard that judge say "the best interests of the children" one more time, I think I would have lost it. These are my children, not hers. I kissed their heads and changed their diapers and carried them on my chest and on my back and in my arms. I made them meals and put them to sleep and cleaned up their vomit and took them to day care and preschool and school and camp and ballet and art class and music lessons. They are mine. No one loves them more than me. How is it even possible that a judge can take them away from me, just like that, based on what my very part-time and obviously kooky girlfriend has to say about sleeping nude? What business is it of the judge's how we sleep and whether Charlie comes into bed with us? Lisa and I always had the kids in bed with us, just like every other family in Greenwood, I bet. This is so Big Brother, so overreaching, so totally, utterly fucked up.

Ellen walks out with me and takes me to the back of the now-empty waiting area, so we can get away from Lisa and Boyle. I know she's mad at me because she thinks I didn't tell her the truth, but I can tell she also feels sorry for me.

"How can the judge do this?" I ask. "Can we appeal? We need to appeal."

Ellen makes me sit down and tells me we can talk about an appeal later, we have thirty days, but that right now, I just need to calm down. I guess I look crazed or like I'm going to deck someone, because she says that twice.

"I know you're upset, Jake," she says, "and even though you apparently did take Charlie in bed with you and Samara, there was no evidence whatsoever that anything explicitly sexual happened. I think Judge Jones is being prudish, and I think she's substituting her religious or moral code for yours, which I don't think is appropriate. But it doesn't help that you lied. You did lie, right?" She doesn't wait for an answer. "You lied to me, so I couldn't prep you effectively. Had I known what actually did happen, I could have figured out how best to explain it so as to minimize the negative effect. Jake, that's my job. That's what you pay me for. I can't represent you well if you don't tell me the truth."

I tell Ellen I'm sorry—of course I am—but ask her to please lay off because I feel like I'm going to cry, and there is no point in her rubbing salt in the wounds. I mean, I really do get how I just participated in my own demise here. And I really, really need to get out of this building and away from Lisa and that asshole lawyer who is undoubtedly celebrating his big victory, at the expense of my children.

Ellen tells me she understands, I should call her tomorrow, and she will wait for a copy of the order so I can leave. Which I do, and find myself somehow out on the street, heading toward the parking lot, wearing my new pathetic-loser mantle of every-other-weekend dad.

29

Ellen: The Real Story

She had planned to sleep in on Saturday, but Ellen wakes up early, with a start, to the pink streaks of a predawn sky brightening the branches of the oak tree in front of her bedroom window. A bad feeling about the *Naudain* case rushes in to replace the deep void of unconsciousness where she had happily floated just a minute before. No matter how long she's practiced law, no matter how clear it is, from an objective analysis, that a bad outcome has not been caused by anything she did or didn't do, she feels responsible. And it is such a familiar feeling. Time had certainly dulled and contained it; she knows, intellectually, that it will be gone by the end of the weekend, maybe even by the second cup of coffee. But lying there in her bed, Dan snoring lightly into the pillow over his head, and the day stretching out before her, she keeps flashing on Jake Naudain's face. Of course he screwed up by lying to her, and being blindsided by the girlfriend's testimony put her in an uncomfortable position. But still, he really does love those girls, and Judge Jones really was out of line.

This is the problem with custody cases, Ellen thinks, for the hundredth or maybe the thousandth time. They are so subjective. Judges base their best-interest determinations on their own experiences, through the filter of their age, their culture, their religion—it all plays a part. How many times has she heard a judge say in chambers, and sometimes even on the record in open court, things like, "*My* daughter was babysitting by that age" or, "*My* father spanked all of us." So this judge—who she knows is unmarried and has no children, and is probably somewhere in her mid-sixties—this judge's frame of reference has to be her own childhood. Which, Ellen is pretty sure, involved strict parents and lots of church. And no children sleeping with naked parents or, God forbid, parent plus naked, polyamorous, married girlfriend.

But while it's certainly understandable that a person's own childhood indelibly informs her outlook on child-rearing, it should be a judge's job to transcend that, to take the wider view, to understand changes in the culture and allow for legitimate differences in parenting. Homeschooling, co-sleeping, the age children should stop breastfeeding or can be left alone, screen time limits or lack thereof—the list goes on and on. There are no right answers; it's all contextual. And there is just no evidence here that, despite the somewhat unconventional, maybe best described as bohemian, nature of Jake's relationship with Samara, and the questionable choice to expose Charlie to their intimacy, that the Naudain girls would be better off by drastically reducing the time spent with their father, whom they obviously adore. And so what if he lied to his lawyer and lied under oath? Not a great thing, but he certainly isn't the first parent to do so. Why punish the children for this relatively minor moral failing by taking away their time with him when really, on a day-to-day basis, he is a responsible parent?

Dan rolls over, takes the pillow off of his head, and asks Ellen why she is awake so early. "I don't know," Ellen says, "just woke up worrying about that case I told you about where Judge Jones took away my client's shared custody."

"Oh, you mean polyamory guy?" he asks.

"Yes," says Ellen. "Polyamory guy. And don't ask me again if you know him, because I'm not telling."

"Okay," says Dan, putting the pillow back over his blonde-turning-gray buzz cut. "I'm going back to sleep. I'm going to do some polyamory dreaming."

Ellen lifts the pillow, kisses her husband on the ear, and gets out of bed. She can feel a box closing around her morose musings about the *Naudain* case, and she is anxious to lock it up entirely and put it away for the weekend. In order to do so, she plans to avail herself of a popular Greenwood remedy: yoga, followed by coffee at the Green Life Café. She puts on her most flattering yoga capris, guaranteed to lift her spirits due to the extraordinary effect of spandex on her thighs, and grabs her keys and phone. She leaves the house and her slumbering family, one dreaming about polyamory, and the other happily back in the nest after her first semester, probably dreaming about some aspect of college life, or sex—or maybe that is one and the same dream—and heads to the yoga studio.

Marni is sitting on the living room couch immersed in her laptop when Ellen walks in, pleasantly invigorated by twenty sun salutations and a triple grande latte. "Did you bring me a latte?" Marni asks, without looking up.

"No," Ellen says, "I thought about it, but I figured you wouldn't be up yet."

"Great. Thanks."

"Sorry, sweetie. What're you doing? I feel like I haven't seen you forever."

"I'm studying for my stupid psych exam. I can't believe it got postponed until after the break. That is so cruel. You?"

"Just recovering from a rough week at work. Yoga definitely helped."

"Yeah, and maybe those two entire bottles of wine you and Dad drank last night. Just remember that next time you lecture me about the effects of alcohol. What happened at work?"

"We did not drink two entire bottles of wine. And nothing terrible at work, just was a really hectic week, and on Friday I finished up this custody trial where my client ended up losing custody of his kids. It was all very messy, because he lied to me about some important facts, so I didn't know the full story, and then the other lawyer subpoenaed my client's girlfriend, who came in and contradicted his testimony. And the judge believed the girlfriend, not my client, and she was not happy, to say the least, that my client lied under oath. She ended up reducing his time with his kids from joint custody to every other weekend. So I feel bad about it, even though there was nothing I could have done. Under the circumstances."

"Bummer. What was he lying about?"

"None of your business. I've already said too much. Forget I told you about this."

"Mom, that is so ridiculous. You didn't tell me anything. It's not like I know who your client is. I mean, I know you represent Paula Meyer's dad, but he doesn't have a girlfriend because he's such a loser, and she would have told me if her parents were in court, and anyway, she's in tenth grade now. Oh, and I know Jake Naudain, that guy I babysat for with the two cute daughters. It's not him, is it?"

Ellen looks at her daughter. How could she have been so stupid as to forget that Marni knew Jake? "No," she says.

"Mom. I don't believe you. You have that look. It was Jake, right? Well, fine, don't answer, but I'm not surprised he would lie to you and to the judge. Because he's creepy."

"What do you mean?" asks Ellen. "Why would you say that?"

"Well," says Marni, closing her laptop and looking up at Ellen, "I wasn't going to tell you this, because it's not a big deal, and I totally handled it, but that night I babysat for him, he hit on me."

"What? What do you mean by 'hit on'? What did he do? Why didn't you say something?"

"Mom, calm down. It's okay. I'm eighteen, okay? He was just acting weird with me when he came home, and then when I went to leave, he sort of cornered me and was kissing me and stuff."

"Stuff! What stuff? What else did he do? I can't believe you didn't tell me this!"

"Really, nothing happened, Mom. He was just touching me when he was trying to kiss me. But I pushed him away and told him to back off, and I got in the car and left. That's all. It's not like he tried to chase me or wouldn't let me leave or anything. He was just acting like a drunk dude."

Ellen's mind is racing. She cannot understand how Jake could be so stupid, so out of control, as to sexually assault her daughter! Or maybe sexual assault was an exaggeration, but make a pass at her! Who cares if she's eighteen? She's still a child, he's a grown man, and she was his babysitter, not to mention his lawyer's daughter! It's all so unbelievably pathetic and tacky. How could he possibly think that wouldn't get back to Ellen? And how could he sit there in her office, prepping for a trial, knowing that he had tried to have sex with her daughter?

Ellen sits down on the couch next to Marni. "You're sure he didn't hurt you, honey? Are you telling me everything?"

"Yes, Mom," Marni says, in an exasperated tone, "I'm telling you everything. No, he did not hurt me. He just grossed me out. He's like *forty* or whatever. And it was especially weird because he's your client. But that's all that happened. I swear. It's not like I was raped or something. I totally would have told you that! I just got kissed by a groper. And, you might have noticed, he never asked me to babysit again. And I never would, either. So that's the guy in your trial who lied. I didn't know he had a girlfriend, but that's a good thing. Now maybe he'll stop hitting on the babysitters."

"Marni, this is not a joke. I am furious with him. And I'm very disappointed that you didn't tell me about this when it happened."

"Mom, look, I didn't think it was that big a deal. I'm not a little girl. I'm eighteen. Men do shit. You know that. I can take care of myself."

"But Marni, he's my client. Didn't you think—let's just say, I might possibly be representing him in a custody case, and he's got two daughters—didn't you think I might want to know that he attacks teenage girls? That he's a predator?"

"Mom, oh my God, don't be so dramatic! He is not a predator. And anyway, don't be mad at me. He's the creeper."

"You're right about that. And I'm going to talk to him about this first thing next week. Or maybe I'll call him right now."

"Mom, really, do you have to? That makes me so uncomfortable, to think that you'd be talking to him about me. It really wasn't that big a deal. To have you talk to him about it makes me seem like a baby."

"You've got to be kidding. It is a big deal, and you're not a baby. I cannot continue to represent him and pretend I don't know about this. The whole thing has implications way beyond his appalling conduct with you."

"Mom, please."

"Marni, this is out of your hands. Where's your father?"

30

Jake: Fallout

It should be my week with the girls. I should have been pulling them out of bed this morning, playing sous-chef as they made their lunches, checking Charlie's backpack to make sure she had her homework, telling Elizabeth to get out of the shower immediately, toasting bagels for them to take in the car on the way to school. Instead, it is quiet—just me, getting ready for work, putting one foot in front of the other. It's like someone died, like that way you feel when you keep thinking it can't be real, and then it hits you in a wave that it is, that you're never going to see the person again. Not the same, obviously; I'm trying not to be overly dramatic, because my girls didn't die, and I will be seeing them this weekend. But the point is that it's a familiar sensation: disbelief at what just happened, your mind trying to adjust to a new reality, and you having trouble accepting it.

I am driving to work, alone in my personal metal container like all the other commuters—imagine the aerial view as we spread out across the city and suburbs like trails of ants in our little pods, busily heading out to our anthills—when my phone rings. I see it's Ellen, which is very impressive because usually I have to track her down. I realize she said we would talk later about the appeal, but I'm surprised she'd be seeking me out to have that conversation, at eight thirty on a Monday morning, no less.

"Jake, we need to talk," she says.

I thank her for calling and start to ask her about what's involved in an appeal, but she cuts me off.

"We've got a major problem. Marni disclosed to me this weekend that you came on to her sexually that night she babysat for you. I'm not using the words 'sexual assault' only because, at eighteen, she is technically an adult, but to me, what she described was absolutely an assault. I am shocked. And disgusted. I can't believe you would do that to any girl babysitting for your kids, much less my daughter. The daughter of your lawyer who, oh, by the way, is representing you in a custody case involving those same girls she was babysitting for. What were you thinking?"

I was totally not expecting this, and I am not prepared for this conversation. What did Marni tell her? Sexual assault? You've got to be kidding. "Woah," I say, "I did not sexually assault Marni. Or anyone, ever. That's absurd. Look, I don't know how else to say this, Ellen, but the fact is that she came on to me. She starting kissing me when I was letting her out the front door of my building. I didn't initiate anything, I stopped her as soon as I realized what she was doing, and believe me, that's all that happened. And no, I didn't say anything to you about it, because I didn't want to embarrass your daughter. But as you may have noticed, I never asked her to babysit again. I'm not sure what got into her that night, but whatever it was, I did not want to be put in that position again."

"*You* being put in that position? I can't believe you're blaming Marni," Ellen says. "She's basically still a child. You're supposed to be the responsible adult. And that is not at all how Marni described your behavior, and I believe my daughter over you, you can be sure. Both because she's my daughter, and I know she doesn't lie, and also because I happen to know from firsthand experience that you do. Your credibility with me is pretty much shot, Jake, after the other day in court."

"How did this come up?" I ask. "Is it just coincidental? Did she just happen to tell you this, six months after that night she babysat? Or were you talking to her about my case? And isn't that like a total violation of confidentiality? Did you talk to anyone else about it too?"

"Nobody, Jake. Don't be ridiculous. And don't deflect. Marni asked me how work was, and I mentioned something generic about having a custody trial involving two girls, and she asked me if it was your case. I said no, but she didn't believe me, and then she told me about what happened that night."

"Great, so now Marni knows all about my personal business. I can just imagine how long it will take for the rest of Greenwood to find out. Thanks a lot, Ellen."

"Don't get on some kind of ethical high horse with me, Jake. I didn't tell Marni anything; she just guessed that yours was the case I mentioned in passing. She knows no details, and I would never disclose a client's information. But all that is not really the point. The point is that I'm not comfortable representing you anymore. It's one thing to find out you didn't tell me the truth and apparently lied under oath—that's bad enough—but now I find out you tried to have sex with my teenage daughter. Which at the very least shows incredibly poor judgment and lack of impulse control, if not criminal behavior. So it's going to be impossible for me to stand up there and zealously advocate for you on appeal or back in front of Judge Jones, because now I have serious concerns, from my personal knowledge, about your parenting."

I can't believe my lawyer is firing me, and essentially calling me a sex offender. What more is going to happen to me? Am I going to lose my job too? Maybe when I get to work, Mario's going to accuse me of raping the receptionist and fire me on the spot. Lisa, Samara, Marni, Ellen—all these women out to get me. And it's so fucking unfair. I'm just a normal guy who loved his wife, really liked his polyamorous girlfriend, and had one awkward encounter with a teenage sexpot babysitter. So what? And I don't want to start over with a new lawyer. I saw Ellen in that courtroom, and she was really good; it wasn't her fault that Samara decided to rat me out. She may be mad at me now, but she'll get over it.

I tell Ellen I'm sorry that I didn't tell her about what happened with Marni at the time, but repeat that I didn't want to embarrass Marni. I say I'll think over what she was saying and call her tomorrow. She says okay and then hangs up. Maybe I really am a total piece of shit.

CHORUS #4

The Yogis

Savasana is drawing to a close, and Summer can feel the yoga serenity spiraling up into the ether as the weight of Saturday's to-do list, which had briefly floated up to the ceiling, drops back down with a thud. The instructor closes the class with a group om, which, if everyone is able to find the same pitch, usually does make Summer feel at least a little bit at one with the vibration of the universe. She rolls up her mat and heads for the studio door, thinking about how much she really does not want to make the trek out to PetSmart, even though the dog food there is so much cheaper. Miriam, releasing her ponytail while looking at her phone, reaches the door at the same time.

Hi, Summer, she says. Haven't seen you in forever.

I know, I know, says Summer. How are you? I'd give you a hug, but I'm all sweaty.

Oh, right, says Miriam, you're one of those women who look all sexy and glistening after they've been working out. Not like me, I just get red and blotchy.

Summer laughs and makes the obligatory denials, but really, Miriam is kind of blotchy, and Summer knows that she does look excellent in her black bralette with those tiny beads of sweat rolling slowly down from her collarbone and disappearing between her breasts.

I think last time I saw you was at the class potluck at Lisa Naudain's house, right? Summer asks.

Yup, I think so, says Miriam. Speaking of Lisa Naudain, did you hear that she went to court and took custody of the girls away from Jake?

No way, says Summer. He's like Mr. Mom. How could that happen?

Well, I don't know for sure, says Miriam, but based on what I heard, I'm thinking it's related to this polyamory thing he's gotten into with his twenty-year-old girlfriend.

Polyamory, says Summer. Wow, interesting. And is she really only twenty? But so what? I mean, what does his sex life have to do with anything? Taking the kids away? That seems extreme.

Yeah, says Miriam, I agree. Not sure what the whole story is there.

But I have to say, Summer says, locking eyes with Miriam, I always thought Lisa was sort of a bitch. I mean, she had this dreamy husband who worshipped the ground she walked on—right?—but she would make these offhand digs at him to people she didn't even know. Like me. Like, I remember the first time I met her, at Mariposa. We were chatting, and she saw Jake on the other side of the auditorium talking to that guy who used to be the music teacher for the lower school, I can't remember his name. And she pointed him out and said, "That's my husband" and then made some snide remark about how all Jake cared about was his band, and instead of paying attention to his kids at their concert, he was over there trying to impress the music teacher by talking up his band. I remember thinking, why are you telling me this when I don't know you, and I've never even met your husband?

Hmm, that's interesting, says Miriam, because I never saw that. I thought they were like the perfect couple—I was really surprised when I heard they were splitting up. But what you just said is consistent with what Lisa's friends told me at the time, that he just wanted to do his own thing, and Lisa had to take care of everything with the kids and the house. But I'm kind of shocked by this custody battle. I mean, I know they were doing joint custody, and the girls seem fine when I see them, and I agree with you—so what if he's into polyamory? What century is this, anyway?

Well, says Summer, pulling a white T-shirt over the bralette and taking her car keys out of her bag, it's a shame for those poor girls. That's who gets hurt.

Agreed, says Miriam. They get hurt. And the lawyers make money.

True, says Summer. Great to see you, Miriam, and thanks for catching me up. And if you find out any juicy details about the polyamory, I know you'll tell me.

For sure, says Miriam. Have a great weekend.

You too, says Summer, opening the door to the studio and stepping out into the parking lot as she beeps open her late-model Subaru.

31

*

Judge Jones:
What Century Is This, Anyway?

N ow that the snow has finally melted off the stone path leading
from her front door to the sidewalk, and the sun is shining,
the judge has decided to do her Saturday errands on foot. She
knows some judges complain that one of the drawbacks of life
on the bench is that you no longer feel free to go out and about
in leisure wear, or without your hair done or your makeup on.
But this has not been an issue for the judge, because she never
goes outside like that anyway. There are clothes for work,
clothes for church, clothes for evening events, and clothes for
Saturdays. And yes, of course they are all different, but Saturdays
still have a style to them—a low-heeled boot, a silk scarf tucked
inside the neck of a fitted down coat—and anywhere, anytime,
lipstick. Checking her image approvingly in the mirror by the
front door—isn't that why everyone has a mirror by the front
door, in recognition of the fact that you need to present a public
face once you step through it?—she walks out into the bright
morning air.

First on the list is picking up her dry cleaning, a four-block
walk to the little commercial center of Greenwood. Right next
to the dry cleaners is the Green Life Café, and her plan—not on

her list, because it isn't technically an errand, but a firm part of her plan, nonetheless—is to stop at the café to get a tea. She does not particularly like the Green Life Café, as she has received dirty plates and silverware there on more than one occasion, and it is often crowded with sweaty people in exercise clothing who really should have showered before they came to a restaurant, if you could call it that. And the staff all seem to have those horrible round plugs in their earlobes, which makes it hard to even look at them when you finally do get through the long line. Nonetheless, one can get hibiscus tea there, which she happens to adore, and so long as she gets it to go, she is assured of a clean cup and minimal time spent in the company of the unwashed exercisers and the earlobe mutilators.

Arriving at her destination, she stoops to pat a charming poodle tied up outside: so soft and curly and well-behaved, so unlike many of the scruffy, unattractive dogs she often sees parked there while their owners chat their way through the coffee line. As she stands up and turns toward the front door, she sees through the café windows a man she recognizes, a man whose custody case she is certain she recently presided over. It takes her a moment to recall that it is Mr. Naudain, the attractive gentleman with the naked, polyamorous girlfriend sleeping in bed with him and his young child, the man who lied about it on the stand. The judge hesitates, thinking how good that cup of hibiscus tea would taste. She decides it would be uncomfortable to see Mr. Naudain in this context, and there would be no way to avoid an encounter, even if neither of them acknowledged it, given the small size of the café. It also brings her back to a conversation, which she'd had the previous weekend with her niece, that had given her pause about her decision in the *Naudain* case.

Jacey works for a health care advocacy organization and has a ten-year-old son. She is like a daughter to the judge. They frequently get together on Saturdays for lunch and shopping, just the two of them, talking about everything from the return of the stiletto heel to the politics of the Black clergy. It was Jacey who helped the judge prepare her speech for her judicial swearing-in ceremony and buy a new dress for the occasion. Although, immediately after the oath was taken, she donned the black robe and thus covered it up entirely, but still—such a momentous event required finery, even if cloaked in black. And it was Jacey to whom she had confided her dismay about her assignment to family court. Sometimes during their lunches, the judge tells Jacey about interesting cases from the previous week, and Jacey invariably has strong opinions about who is right, who is wrong, and what is best for the children.

Last Saturday, sitting in a neighborhood brunch spot favored by groups of women, perhaps due to its location in a converted greenhouse full of feathery hanging plants and Victorian bird cages, she told Jacey—without mentioning any names, of course —about the Naudain trial. She told Jacey that she was conflicted about how serious a parenting infraction the father had committed by having his seven-year-old daughter in bed with him and his new girlfriend, who was naked and was cuddling up with the girl. She explained that the initial allegation, made by the mother, that the father and his girlfriend engaged in some kind of explicit sexual activity while the child was in bed with them, had not been established. And it was in fact clear from the girlfriend's testimony that no such activity occurred. Had that been proven, there would be nothing further to discuss. But it wasn't, which made the case more complicated, with more shades of gray, so to speak. She also told Jacey about her conversation with Melinda, who had such a strong reaction, that it had tipped the balance of her thinking that day, but now she was having second thoughts.

The issue, she explained to her niece, was not that she had

any doubts that this incident was entirely inappropriate and should not be repeated. The issue that was bothering her was whether her drastic reduction of the children's time with their father was the appropriate remedy to the problem. Suppose this was just a one-time lapse in judgment, she asked Jacey. Suppose a stern lecture from the bench and an order prohibiting the specific conduct—no sleeping with either child—while keeping the custodial schedule intact, would have been better tailored to the circumstances? And was it appropriate to consider the girlfriend's unconventional lifestyle, and the father participating in polyamorous activities with her, as reasons to reduce his custodial time? And if the problem was really the girlfriend, she could have even entered an order prohibiting the girlfriend from sleeping there on nights he had the children, period. Invasive and insulting to the father, perhaps. But from the children's point of view, she believed, thinking back to her interviews with them in chambers, it probably would have been preferable to severely restricting their father's role in their lives.

What she did not admit to Jacey, but what was bothering her the most, was that she knew her ruling was at least partially based on her anger with Mr. Naudain for perjuring himself in her courtroom, for flouting her authority, and for thinking he was going to get away with it. Which he certainly would have, had Attorney Boyle not pulled off such a coup with the girlfriend's testimony. She had used her power to punish Mr. Naudain. Which he deserved and which, she had to acknowledge to herself, felt good at the time. And had this been commercial litigation, had Mr. Naudain been looking for the court to award him money, denying his request because he perjured himself might be entirely appropriate. However, this was a custody case, and she was mandated to act in the best interest of the children.

Jacey's reaction to the facts of the case was considerably

more measured and tolerant than Melinda's. "Aunt Andi," she had said, "a lot of people sleep with their children. All over the world. And throughout history. And it's popular with my generation, especially with all my friends from art school. You know," she smiled, "co-sleeping. Attachment parenting and all that."

She did agree that a father bringing his daughter into bed with him and a new girlfriend who does not have an established relationship with the child and, moreover, is naked, was problematic. But it seemed to her that reducing the father's time with the children to every other weekend was a bit like attacking a fly with a sledgehammer, or whatever that expression was.

"Aunt Andi," she had asked, "if you change your mind after you make your ruling, is there anything you can do to fix it?"

Jacey's question had been periodically popping into the judge's mind all week, where she kept pushing it back down, telling herself she would think about it later when she had time —as in, the weekend, which is now. But the fact of the matter is, there is no solution, and no amount of time spent contemplating the case is going to change that. She cannot just spontaneously change an order three weeks after she entered it. Certainly she could if she were correcting a typo or making a minor change jointly requested by counsel. But that is not the situation here— here, there is no request to change the order pending before her, no procedural vehicle which permits her to enter a new one just because she feels like it, just because she happens to have misgivings about her prior decision. It would be procedurally improper and, more importantly, it could seriously undermine the court's authority. In her short tenure on the family court bench—just over a year, at this point—she had learned that it is so important to be decisive, to take responsibility for delivering what may be bad medicine. People coming into family court are seeking a higher authority to tell them what to do, and they need to believe in the wisdom of the decision maker. However, if Mr. Naudain petitioned for reconsideration of her order, even if he did so based on improper grounds—because, really, there is no basis for claiming she made an error in the application of the law—well, then she could take that as an opportunity to soften her order. She could agree to reconsider, and then restore at least some, if not all, of his custody time, with appropriate safeguards in place to protect the children against exposure to their father's carryings-on.

But all of that is hypothetical. At this moment, on this sunny Saturday morning in Greenwood, there is nothing whatsoever the judge can do about the *Naudain* case, so really there is no point in further rumination. However, she is going to have to forego her hibiscus tea, one of those small prices to be paid for the honor and prestige of a seat on the bench.

The judge walks past the café and turns right into the dry cleaners on the corner. The Korean proprietress, whom the judge has known for at least a decade, if not two, greets her warmly and sends her son to fetch the judge's clothes—two jackets, three blouses, and a skirt. As the women stand there chatting about their respective Christmases, a somewhat younger woman, maybe fifty, wearing jeans and a peacoat-type jacket, opened to reveal a Connecticut College sweatshirt underneath, comes into the shop. "Your Honor!" she says, smiling at the judge, who immediately realizes who she is.

"Ms. Ackerman," the judge says, smiling. "Nice to see you. Do you live out this way?"

"Yes, just up on Litman Street. I had no idea we were neighbors."

"Well, apparently we both have excellent taste in neighborhoods," says the judge, smiling. "I'm Greenwood born and raised."

"You've got me beat, then," says Ellen. "I'm a more recent

convert. Like for the past twenty years." Pleasantries over, the women stand awkwardly close, each waiting for her clothing to be brought up to the register.

"Ms. Ackerman," the judge says, "I just happened to see your client, the one from the trial we had a few weeks ago, next door in the café. Needless to say, I decided not to go in. Should I be expecting an appeal from you in that matter?" Of course, the judge knows she is not supposed to engage in *ex parte* conversations with counsel about a case, but this seems like such a neutral question—after all, it is merely about procedure, not substance—that she deemed it acceptable to ask.

"I don't know, Your Honor. We have, I believe, ten more days left to decide before the thirty-day period runs. Not sure what the decision will be on that."

"Well, if your client decides to, I'll be looking for your petition for reconsideration first," says the judge.

Ms. Ackerman, eyes wide, takes a small step back, a fleeting acknowledgment of the valuable but entirely inappropriate tip she's just been given. "Of course," she says. "That's exactly the procedure I would follow."

"That's if you decide to appeal, of course," says the judge, taking the hangers of plastic-sheathed clothing and handing the proprietress her credit card. "That's all I meant."

"Of course," says Ms. Ackerman again, as she moves away from the counter to clear a path for the judge to leave. "Enjoy the rest of your weekend, Your Honor."

"You as well," says the judge, heading for the door of the tiny shop. "And Mrs. Kim, lovely to see you, as always."

"You too, Judge," says a smiling Mrs. Kim.

After the glass door closes behind her, the judge can see Ellen Ackerman standing there, appearing to be lost in thought. *Perhaps*, the judge thinks, *she will take the hint so deftly handed to her.*

32

Jake: Breaking Up

It's been almost three weeks now, and I haven't heard anything from Samara. Nothing. I can't believe she hasn't even called me to find out what happened, although my guess is she knows. She's probably hooked into that same grapevine where Lisa found out about the polyamory—there's got to be some connection, somewhere. But at this point, I really don't care. I don't care that someone told Lisa about Samara's lifestyle. What I care about is that Lisa didn't talk to me about it first before running to her fucking lawyer, and that Samara didn't talk to me about getting a subpoena to testify in Lisa's ridiculous case.

But in terms of Lisa, our relationship is already over. We're not supposed to like each other anymore. Unlike Samara who, last time I saw her alone, was lying on my living room couch giggling as I pulled off her jeans. The next time I saw her was when she walked into that courtroom. She and I really need to talk. Apparently she's not going to initiate it, so I will. She needs to answer for what she did to me.

So I text her, we need to talk ASAP. She writes me right back: can I come over Tuesday night? I say: yes, 8 pm. She says: k. So we have a date—like, the worst kind of date.

When she rings my buzzer on Tuesday, I go downstairs to let her in, and she tries to give me a sort of half-hearted hug. Hugging her is the last thing I feel like doing, so I sidestep the hug, turn around, and go up the stairs to my apartment. She follows me, not saying anything. When we get inside, I close the door, and we both sit down in the living room, looking at each other, me on the couch and her on the beanbag chair that Elizabeth insisted I buy. "So," I say, "you've been avoiding me."

"Not really," she says. "I didn't call you because I figured you were upset about what that judge did and needed time to yourself. I knew you'd call me when you were ready."

"Well, let's start with 'what that judge did.' How do you even know what that judge did? Who's your source? Lisa?"

"No, Jake, of course not. I've never spoken to Lisa in my life. The only time I saw her was in court that day."

"Well, who are you speaking with? Who told you about the outcome of the hearing? And is that the same person who told Lisa about you being polyamorous and all that?"

"I heard about what the judge did from Tilly. Tilly Epstein, the professor I work for as a TA, who's Lisa's friend. And she knows you too. And it's really fucked up what the judge did, taking your kids away like that."

"Yeah, it's totally fucked up, and it's completely due to your testimony about being naked and the polyamory and everything. What were you thinking, Samara?"

I hear my voice getting louder and louder. She is staring at me, sitting really still, big dark eyes, immobile. I continue. "And why didn't you tell me when you got the subpoena? Don't you understand how serious this is? Well, how serious it was, because now it's done, and I can't undo it. Don't you understand that?"

I realize I'm sounding panicked, like I'm desperate to get through to her, but really, what difference does it make? Rationally, I know that the only thing I can get out of this conversation is to make her feel bad. Which she should, which I desperately want, but it's not bringing my girls home, that's for sure.

Samara just keeps staring at me. Then she says, "I didn't tell you about it at first when I got it because I really wasn't sure what it meant or what I was going to do about it. But then the night before court, I did call you—you didn't pick up."

One attempt to reach me at the last minute? That's her excuse? Yeah, I do remember seeing a missed call from her that night, but so what? I was totally distracted, thinking about the trial, and she couldn't even leave a fucking voicemail letting me know she was about to ruin my life?

"I figured you'd call me back if you wanted to talk, and anyway, I didn't think it was necessary, because I just assumed I'd be able to talk to you when I got there. Jake, I've never been in court before. I didn't know you were already going to be in the courtroom. I had no idea what was going to happen or what they'd ask me."

"That is such bullshit. I can't believe you're saying that. You knew about the case, I told you about it when I got the papers. You knew it was all about what happened that night. And you knew I didn't want to tell anyone about it."

"Yeah, I know you said that. But, Jake, it's crazy that me being polyamorous, and you being involved with me and with Owen and the others in our circle, has anything to do with you as a parent. That's what's bullshit. The fact that we reject monogamy is something I'm proud of. I'm not going to lie about it, and I'm not going to pretend to conform to some archaic bourgeois ideal."

This is a lecture I cannot tolerate. I stand up and start pacing. "I don't *care* that you're proud of it. There was nothing at stake for you, so you could say whatever you felt like saying. Don't you get it? You can feel all good about yourself because you're all pure, and meanwhile, what you said cost me my kids."

"I'm really, really sorry about that, Jake, but what I said was true, and you know it. I guess you expected me to lie under oath."

"Right. I did. And you did lie. You just didn't lie enough. Tell me, just how did you decide where to draw the line? How come you didn't go all the way and tell the judge what really happened that night? I guess I should thank you for that because if you'd told her the whole story, I probably wouldn't even have them on weekends."

Samara shifts in her chair and starts playing with her hair, wrapping a long dark strand around her index finger, that familiar gesture that continues to remind me so much of Elizabeth. She speaks again, slowly. "I don't know. I guess it was just that I felt bad about us having sex when Charlie was in the bed with us. I knew that wasn't a good idea. We talked about it afterward, remember? We both said, wow, that was risky, we shouldn't let that happen again. I mean, it seemed like she was asleep, but maybe she woke up at some point. But anyway, the other questions that lawyer asked me were about stuff I feel like there was nothing to be ashamed about. What's wrong with sleeping naked and cuddling up with a child? I mean, it's all so unbelievably puritanical. But when the lawyer asked me about whether we had sex, I kind of wanted to tell the truth, but I knew it would be a bad idea. Like, that's the part of it I thought could be a real problem for you. So I lied, Jake. Even though it made me uncomfortable, I lied to protect you. I guess I didn't lie enough. But I really can't say that I regret not lying about the rest of it, because those questions were about who I am, and I'm not going to pretend to be somebody else to satisfy some old judge's outdated notions about sexuality—"

"You're so fucking smug!" Now I am full-on yelling. "And I'm so glad you got through this with your moral compass intact. You can feel good about yourself, and I lost my kids. I lost my kids, basically because I got caught up in your world, which is a world without kids or responsibilities, a world where anything goes. And you knew my kids are my life, and you encouraged me to have sex that night—"

"That's enough," Samara says, jumping up and starting to button up her jacket. "You can't pin this on me. You're the parent. If you thought it was such a problem to be fucking me when your daughter was sleeping in the bed next to you, you shouldn't have done it. It's your fault, Jake, not mine. So take responsibility for it. And I'm really sorry about what happened, but I'm not going to sit here and let you verbally abuse me anymore. I'm done."

She doesn't slam the door. She actually closes it carefully behind her. And when she is gone, I slump down onto the couch and curl up in a ball—a big feeling-sorry-for-myself man ball.

33

Owen: Kicking the Dog

Samara is out for the evening, and Owen has nothing pressing to do, which means it's a perfect time to watch *Game of Thrones*. Samara hates it, and hates that Owen doesn't hate it, and gets mad whenever he watches it, because it's so violent and sexist. She says it is, that is, and he agrees. But what he doesn't tell Samara is that those are actually major reasons he likes the show so much—he can immerse himself in a total fantasy world, which provides relief from all the complicated political and moral issues that seem to constantly crop up in adult life. And even though he talked shit about it when it first came out and everyone was obsessed with it, now he gets what all the excitement was about. Clearly, Owen knows that beheadings are gross, but when they are happening in a mythical kingdom two thousand years ago, so what? And some of the sex scenes are hot—like, superhot. Settling down on the couch with a beer and the remote, Owen is ready to be transported.

Just as the intro comes on and the titles appear, Owen hears the familiar click of the front door unlocking, immediately followed by the sound of Samara blowing into the living room like a tornado, her agitation palpable before she says a word. "What's wrong?" Owen asks, not looking up from the screen.

"I can't believe you're watching that shit again," Samara says, pulling off her boots and throwing them back toward the door.

The titles are still rolling, but Owen realizes that his evening plans have abruptly come to an end.

"Owen, please turn it off. I need to talk to you," Samara says, as she paces around the room, unpacking her backpack and flinging its contents onto various surfaces.

Knowing that this probably won't do it but hoping against hope that it might, Owen presses the mute button.

"Owen!" Samara yells. "Not just the sound! Turn it off. Like, all the way. This is serious."

Owen sighs, silently wishing the rulers and subjects of Westeros a good night, and hits the off button.

"What happened?" he asks.

"Jake's an asshole," Samara says. "He wanted to talk to me about what happened that day I went to court. Remember I told you that Tilly told me the judge took away his joint custody after the trial?"

Owen nods. He remembers.

"So obviously I know he wouldn't have been happy that I testified about being polyamorous, and him bringing his daughter into bed with us, and all that stuff I told you that Jake's ex-wife's lawyer asked me about, right?"

Owen nods again. Samara had described the scene to him in detail—Jake and his ex sitting on opposite sides of the courtroom while their lawyers fought it out, and some random judge told everybody what to do. The whole thing, everything about it, sounded horrendous.

"So Jake totally blames me for what happened with his kids. He thinks I should have lied about who I am—who we are—in order to protect him. But why would I do that, Owen? Why should I? Like I told him, we don't buy into his lifestyle—the monogamous, nuclear family thing. And I don't think it's wrong to sleep naked or for him to bring his kid into the bed, so why would I lie about it? Why would I compromise myself for something I don't believe in? Who does he think I am?"

Samara is getting more and more animated as she talks, and Owen, only half listening, is feeling very happy that he is her primary relationship. Him, and not Jake, that aging sort-of hipster who thinks he's so cool because he plays in a band on the weekends, while the rest of the week he's slaving away for some corporation, probably sitting in a cubicle with pictures of his kids and wife and dog—well, probably not his wife anymore, but he's pretty sure Samara said Jake has a dog—in little frames next to his computer screen. And also, he is distracted by the sight of Samara's petite feet, in their mismatched socks, stomping back and forth in front of him as she delivers this tirade.

With no answer required, or offered, Samara continues. "And then," she says, "he started screaming at me. He got really abusive."

Owen jolts upright. "Abusive? What do you mean? Did he hit you?"

"No, no, he didn't hit me," says Samara, lowering her voice, sitting down on the couch, and leaning against Owen, breathing hard. Owen puts his arm around her, and she snuggles up tighter. "Jake's not like that," she says, and starts to cry.

Owen strokes a curl of dark hair back from her forehead. Samara keeps talking. "But he was yelling and cursing, and he was just really mean. Like, he said very nasty things to me. And it was so unfair because none of it is my fault. I didn't make any decisions about his kids, obviously. He made them. And I didn't want to testify at that trial—his ex-wife made me. If anyone's to blame, it's her. And him. Both of them, really." Samara stands up, walks into the kitchen, and comes back with a tissue.

Appearing unexpectedly from somewhere out of his prepolyamorous past, possibly triggered by the briefly viewed intro to *Game of Thrones*, Owen feels a faint wave of machismo start to creep up his body. *You can't let that dude talk to your wife that way*, whispers a little voice inside his head, as the wave crests and crashes down over him. He definitely needs to take charge. "This is totally unacceptable," Owen says, standing up and reaching for his phone. "That guy is a total dick, and he owes you a major apology. I'm going to call him right now."

"Owen," says Samara, tears now dried, "that's really not necessary. You don't need to get all husband possessive-y on me. I already told him how I felt and that I was done with him. I appreciate you wanting to back me up, but there's no need to."

"Well, I don't see it that way," Owen responds, putting on his jacket.

Samara raises her eyebrows. "Where are you going?" she asks.

"I actually think it would be better to have this conversation in person," Owen says. "I'm going over to Jake's. I assume he's home, because you were just there."

"Owen, you are way overreacting," Samara says. "You do not need to go marching over there. I already took care of this. Please, Owen. Don't make it worse."

Owen picks up his car keys and turns toward Samara. "Look, he's insulted me too. It's not just about you. We invited him into a relationship. We introduced him to our circle. We trusted him. Both of us trusted him. I'm going over to his place. I'll just say what I need to say, and then I'll leave. What's his address?"

The GPS in Owen's phone says he'll arrive at Jake's in thirteen minutes. Owen drives fast through the dark Greenwood streets, some houses and trees still sparkling with Christmas lights but most quiet and dark, a bleak January night. *How many times,*

Owen wonders, *has Samara made this drive? And what was she thinking about when she did?* About sex, for sure, but also about the kick of it—he was familiar with that thrill of the meetup, the newness of it, the sense of danger, even though you had permission, you were not lying, you were not hurting your primary person. Owen often wondered, if polyamory were more widely practiced and accepted, would that kill the excitement? Does the thrill really come from defying the monogamy culture, knowing that you were doing something shocking to most people you interact with on a daily basis, rather than the novelty of the new person? There would be no way to know so long as polyamory remained outside the mainstream, and if he was honest with himself, even though he loved to tout the benefits of the lifestyle to anyone who was interested, he sort of wanted to keep it that way—a private club. He liked feeling like a rebel.

Owen finds a parking space right in front of Jake's building. There are lights on in the second-floor apartment, which, Samara had reluctantly told him when he insisted on making this surprise visit, is Jake's. Sitting there in the dark, Owen feels a little queasy thinking of Samara getting out of the car just like he is about to do, ringing Jake's bell, and disappearing into Jake's home and his bed. Of course, these thoughts are something everyone in their community has to deal with in their own way. He usually lets himself think about Samara having sex with another partner, because ultimately it turns into an erotic fantasy that he enjoys and can call up later. This time, however, he wants to banish images of Samara and Jake from his head. He does not want to eroticize Jake—he doesn't deserve a place in Owen's sexual fantasies—and anyway, Samara's relationship with Jake is over. Owen has a job to do, and it has nothing to do with sex. He can't let Jake get away with treating Samara and him with such disrespect.

After ringing the bell twice, Owen hears footsteps coming quickly down the stairs and a dog barking. A deep bark, like the kind from the type of dog who might bite you.

"Who is it?" a voice unmistakably Jake's calls out, from behind the door.

Owen answers, and the door opens a sliver. Owen can see Jake standing there, holding a lunging dog by its collar and telling it to calm down. "Owen! What're you doing here?" Jake asks. "It's eleven o'clock. Is everything okay?"

Owen stays outside the door. "Yeah, I mean, not really, but no one's hurt or anything, if that's what you mean. I just need to talk to you. Could you do something about your dog so I can come in?"

"Okay. I guess," Jake says, opening the door and letting Owen into the vestibule. "Pinky, calm down," he says, and releases the dog's collar. The dog, which appears to be some kind of pit bullish creature, but black, definitely does not look calm. He rushes toward Owen and jumps up. Owen backs up against the wall. "Pinky's fine." Jake says. "He's totally friendly. He wouldn't hurt anyone."

"Yeah, well, he's making it kind of hard to have a conversation." Owen says. "Could you take him back upstairs? We can talk here. This isn't going to take long."

"Well, I really don't know what's so urgent that you would show up at my door this late at night," Jake says, "but whatever it is, I'm not going to discuss it with you down here, where my neighbors can hear everything. If you want to talk, we need to go upstairs."

Realizing that there was an undeniable logic to this and feeling a little bit wimpy about letting Jake know that he's scared of his dog, Owen acquiesces and follows Jake and the barking dog upstairs.

"So what is it?" Jake asks, as he closes the door behind them and sternly tells the dog, who has finally stopped barking, to go lie down.

Owen takes a deep breath. "I think you know," he says. "You really upset Samara, and you had no right to. She has nothing to do with your whole divorce thing. That's your trip. It has nothing to do with us at all. You owe her an apology. Your wife, or ex-wife, I guess—I don't even know, and I really don't care—is the one who made her come to court. Samara had zero interest in being involved with that shit, and you knew that. After she got the subpoena—which was given to me, by the way, not even to her—I told her she shouldn't go, but she was afraid about what might happen if she didn't. Look at the fucked-up position you put her in! And so she went, because she felt like she didn't have a choice. And she told the truth. About herself and us and about whatever stupid thing you did with your kid when Samara was sleeping over here. And some old-school judge didn't like it and slammed you. What did you expect? How is that her fault? And what right do you have to blame her for your own mistakes?"

Jake, who had been standing in the middle of the living room when Owen started talking, starts to move toward him. "Whoa, man, wait a minute," he says, stopping about three feet from Owen and glaring at him. "Do you know that she didn't even do me the courtesy of calling to let me know she got that subpoena? She actually had the balls to tell me she tried calling me—once—but I didn't pick up. Really? That's it? The night before my *custody* trial! Not a text? A voicemail? Nothing! She didn't even try to find me in the courthouse before the trial started, which wouldn't have been too tough, since I was sitting in the waiting room outside the courtroom she was subpoenaed to come to! I had no fucking idea. I was totally blindsided when she walked into that courtroom, and so was my lawyer. We had no time to prepare. And if I'd known about it the night before, I would have told her not to come. She knew what was at stake. These are my *kids* we're talking about here, not that you would understand, but maybe you could try, just try, to see past your self-involved, self-satisfied polyamorous *lifestyle*," Jake says mockingly, "and instead of thinking about how superior you are to the rest of the world, maybe you could focus on other people for a minute, and the things that are really important. Like children—"

"Oh, get over yourself," Owen says, feeling increasingly alarmed that Jake seems to have taken control of this encounter and he isn't quite sure how to get it back. His plan to show up, deliver a devastating speech in defense of Samara—which would make Jake fear and admire him—and drive off into the night is not really working out. "None of this is her problem. She didn't ask to be involved. And all she did was tell the truth, because that's the kind of person she is. It's your fault if the truth about what you did wasn't good for you."

"Well," Jake says, with a weird sort of sneer on his face, "I wasn't going to say anything about this, but given that you're so insistent about Samara being such a Girl Scout here, you obviously don't know the whole story. I guess she didn't fill you in on the details. She only told the truth up to a point, and then she didn't. She was perfectly willing to lie in court when it got to the details of what actually happened that night. So she could have either decided not to come or, since she isn't really so concerned as you seem to think about lying in court, she could have skipped the whole speech she gave to the judge and Lisa and Lisa's lawyer about the joys of polyamory and the beauty of sleeping naked even when there's a kid in bed with you."

"What are you talking about?" Owen sputters, aware that the dynamic has now completely flipped, and Jake totally has the upper hand.

"Not sure you really want the details," Jake says. "Maybe you should ask Samara."

"Samara and I don't have any secrets," Owen says.

"Okay, then I guess you already know that we had sex while my daughter was in bed sleeping with us. I mean, she was asleep —she had no idea. I wouldn't have made that choice, but Samara wanted to and—"

"Shut up!" yells Owen, stepping closer to Jake. "You are such a dick! Do not blame Samara for whatever happened. I don't care what it was. It's your problem, because it involves your daughter, and you decided to do whatever you decided. Don't try to push that responsibility onto my wife!"

"Your *wife*?" Jake yells back. "I mean, I know you guys are technically married, but isn't it a little late to go all macho on me about your *wife* when I was fucking her with your blessing for all those months?"

"I told you to shut the fuck up!" Owen yells, which unfortunately comes out sounding slightly high-pitched and desperate. And suddenly, without thinking about it, he reaches out with both arms, puts his hands on Jake's chest, and pushes. Jake stumbles backward. Surprised by his own reaction, and trying to figure out how to extricate himself from the situation, Owen sees Jake's dog jump up from his bed in the corner of the room and start running in Owen's direction, barking and snarling. As he gets close, Owen sticks out his foot and kicks the dog.

"You are a fucking asshole!" Jake says. "It's bad enough you assaulted me—"

"I did *not* assault you—" says Owen.

"But to kick my dog? Really? You attack animals too? I thought Samara told me you were a vegan, because you didn't want to support the inhumane treatment of animals. What a fucking joke. So you won't eat eggs because the chickens are kept in crates that are too small, but you come barging into my house and assault me and kick my dog? Unbelievable."

The dog, meanwhile, had run back to Jake and was cowering beside him.

"Man, you are way out of line," Jake says, shaking his head. "I should call the cops, really."

Right at that moment, Jake's buzzer rings. Jake glances sideways at Owen. "I need to go see who that is. But I think we're done here. You should leave."

Owen is rocking from one foot to the other, nervously watching the whimpering dog. "I'm not leaving until you apologize for what you did to Samara," he says. "And I didn't barge into your house. You invited me up here."

"You've got to be kidding," Jake says, as he starts down the stairs. "And you need to come down with me. I want you out of here. Now."

Owen hesitates. This whole encounter is taking him back to fifth grade, when Johnnie Minicucci stole his anime lunchbox and called him a faggot. Owen had desperately wanted to stand up to Johnnie, but he couldn't think of an effective response fast enough, so what ended up coming out of his mouth was, "I am not a faggot!" It had sounded so pathetic. Then he turned around and walked away, trying to cut his losses, but Johnnie, who by that time was swinging Owen's lunchbox back and forth like a purse, followed him down the hallway from the lunchroom, calling after him in a fake, girly singsong voice, "My name is Owen Butterfield, and I am not a faggot." This feeling of not being enough of a guy, of not knowing quite how to assert his "guy-ness," was so familiar. *But I'm a grown man now*, Owen tells himself. *I'm the one married to Samara. Jake is the loser here.* But really, he should leave the apartment and go downstairs with Jake before it gets a lot worse.

As Owen heads down the stairs, he sees that the door of the downstairs apartment is open, and an older woman, with gray hair in a ponytail, wearing pink scrubs, is standing in the vestibule with Jake and a very large police officer. "Officer, I'm sorry about the noise," he hears Jake say. "My friend"—he gestures up the staircase toward Owen—"was just leaving. He got a little upset, and I guess he raised his voice. Sorry, Marie," Jake says, turning toward the woman in scrubs. "It won't happen again."

"Well, I heard lots of yelling up there, Officer," says Marie, "and carrying on, and that dog of his was barking. I worked a double today, left the house at six this morning, and just got home. I shouldn't have to deal with this. I need my sleep."

"Ma'am, I understand," says the police officer. "And your name, sir?" he asks, turning toward Owen, who is standing on the stairs.

"I'm not the one who was yelling. He was," Owen says to the officer, pointing to Jake. "It's his apartment, and it's his dog that was barking. I'm leaving."

"Excuse me, sir," says the officer, moving further into the vestibule, his bulky body blocking the doorway as Owen reaches the bottom of the stairway. "I asked you your name."

"I really don't see why you need it," says Owen. "I'm leaving, like I said."

"Not until you tell me your name, you're not," says the officer.

Jake turns toward Owen, glares at him, and makes a hand gesture like he is dismissing him.

Owen is so tired of being pushed around—Johnnie Minicucci, Jake, and a long string of relatives, teachers, coaches, and bosses in the two decades in between. And now this big, swaggering cop, who is clearly on a power trip, with his uniform and his badge and his gun. "Officer, I really don't think that's necessary," says Owen, now standing directly in front of the cop, who is still blocking the doorway. "My car's right outside. If you could just move, please, I could leave. That's all I'm trying to do."

The police officer looks at Jake. "You said this guy is a friend of yours?"

"Yeah, sort of," Jake replies. "Or he was. And his name is Owen Butterfield."

Owen jerks his head around to look at Jake. "Oh great. Thanks, man. Really appreciate you backing me up here." Jake rolls his eyes.

The officer turns toward Jake. "Your friend here better watch his mouth," he says.

"Yeah, well, like I said, not really my friend anymore. Actually, he assaulted me and kicked my dog. I wasn't going to say anything about it, but since he's giving you such a hard time, I thought you'd want to know."

Owen opens his mouth as if to say something and then closes it.

"You want to press charges?" asks the officer.

"Not really," Jake says. "I just want him to leave."

The officer turns back toward Owen and takes a step toward him. "Okay, wise guy. Let's try this one more time. Is that your name, what he said? Owen what-was-it?"

"Butterfield," says Jake.

"Butterfield," repeats the officer. "Owen Butterfield. Is that you?"

"Yeah, maybe," Owen says. "Could you please move, so I can just go home?"

"Okay, that's it," says the officer. "We're going down to the station. Put your hands behind your back."

"But I didn't do anything!" Owen says, voice rising with indignation.

"Want me to add resisting arrest to the other charges?" the officer asks Owen, as he takes the handcuffs off his belt, steps around Owen, pulls Owen's arms behind his back, and clicks on the cuffs.

"What other charges?" Owen asks, now starting to panic.

"Sounds like a simple assault charge on Mr. Naudain here, and you say he kicked your dog?" the officer asks Jake as he reaches around Owen to open up the door.

"Yeah, he did," Jake answers.

"So there you've got animal cruelty too," the officer says. "Good night, ma'am," he says to Marie, who is still standing in her doorway, arms folded, watching the scene play out.

"Mr. Naudain," the officer says, "you'll need to come down to the station tomorrow to give a statement. I've got your number." And with that farewell, he takes Owen by the arm and walks him out the front door through the dark Greenwood night and into the idling cruiser.

34

Jake: Real Housewife

Pinky is still all riled up, pacing around the apartment and panting, when my phone rings. It's Samara—no surprise. "Hey," I say.

"What happened, Jake?" she says. "Owen got arrested? And you're pressing charges against him for assault? What is wrong with you?"

Apparently, everything is my fault. And all the players in this ridiculous drama hate me. Fortunately, my kids still love me, but they barely get to see me anymore. Which leaves Pinky.

"What happened," I say slowly, "is that your husband was beating down my door at eleven o'clock, demanding to speak to me about how it's somehow my fault that my ex-wife's lawyer subpoenaed you, about how I upset you so much, and about how I owe you an apology. Which is bullshit, and you know it. I had nothing to do with you being subpoenaed, and you blew any opportunity to try to avoid you having to testify by not telling me about it in advance, when my lawyer maybe could've done something about it. I can't believe you sent him over here to defend your honor, or whatever. Very un-feminist and un-polyamoryish of you."

"Jake," she says, "I did not send him over to your house. I actually tried to stop him, but he was really upset about how I was feeling after I met with you, and he felt like he had to discuss it with you."

Knowing Samara, I can imagine that's probably true. But so what? "'Discuss' is not how I would describe what he had in mind," I say. "He was yelling at me, and then he shoved me backward really hard, and then he kicked Pinky. He kicked my dog! Jesus, Samara, what's his problem? He's lucky Pinky's such a wimp. And then, after my downstairs neighbor called the cops because Owen was making so much noise, he talks back to the cop! Like, who does that? If he were Black, he probably would've gotten shot. But because he's a skinny white boy with a man bun, the cop gave him multiple chances to cooperate by repeatedly asking him his name—his name, Samara! The dude just wanted to know his name so he could write up his little report or whatever and go back to the station, but Owen kept on refusing to answer that one simple question, so the cop took him into custody. I hadn't even planned on pressing charges, but—"

"Pressing charges!" Samara is now yelling. "Jake, do not go there. You know Owen was upset, just like you would have been if you'd been in his position, and he just lost his temper. He didn't hurt you or Pinky, right? I mean, come on, I can't believe you'd want to get involved with the courts over this. Haven't you had enough of that yet? Can't you fix your own problems without running to the cops?"

"Samara, none of this is my fault. I didn't start yelling at him, I didn't lay a hand on him, and I didn't call the cops, and I wouldn't have. I just told him to leave, and when we went downstairs, the officer was already here, and then your husband decided to refuse to give up his name. I have no idea what point he was trying to prove, but it totally backfired. And I already got a call from the detective, who asked me to come down to the station tomorrow morning to give a statement."

Samara pauses, then speaks. "You don't have to do that, Jake. That would be your choice, and you know it's not the right thing to do."

"Hmm, maybe," I say, sort of enjoying this in a perverse way. Which I realize is sad, but I feel so powerless about this whole custody thing, maybe it's turning me into a different person.

"Jake," Samara says, now quietly, "you need to get a grip here. You do not want me to tell Lisa what really happened that night, do you? I lied for you, Jake, which went against my conscience, but I did it for you, to protect you, because I cared about you. I'm not asking you to lie about anything, I'm just asking you not to pursue this crazy idea of pressing charges against Owen for a silly argument. I'm just asking you to do the right thing."

Stupid as it sounds, this had not occurred to me. It had literally not crossed my mind that Samara could effectively blackmail me, and now that she is suggesting it, it is totally surprising to me that she would even think that way. But then again, I really don't know her that well, it seems. All that self-righteousness about the polyamorous ethic and the rejection of mainstream monogamy culture and all its bourgeois trappings, all that stuff she says she believes in, and now she's acting like some character on a soap opera, the wife who is threatening her lover that she'll tell his wife something bad about him to extract a benefit for her husband. Yuck. But maybe she would. She and Owen are pretty tight, and she hates me now, and what difference would it make to her?

"Wow, I can't believe you're trying to blackmail me, Samara," I say. I say this despite knowing instantly that I am not going to risk her telling Lisa what she didn't say in court, even though it seems highly unlikely that she would actually do that, given that she'd be admitting she committed perjury, but whatever. I'm not risking it, and I don't really want to press charges against Owen anyway. I had already been thinking of telling the detective I didn't want to pursue it, and this clinches it. But Samara doesn't know that, and I am not going to let her off the hook for being so sleazy about this. "That is really something. Sounds like an episode of *Real Housewives of New Jersey*."

"I am not trying to blackmail you, Jake," Samara says indignantly, totally ignoring what was, I have to admit to myself, a pretty clever insult. "I'm just pointing out that I did you a huge favor, at the expense of my personal moral code, which you don't seem to appreciate. All I'm asking here is for some consideration for that. There is nothing to be gained by you pressing charges against Owen. This should all be a private thing—you, me, Owen, what happened with Charlie, and what you and Lisa decide to do about your kids—we don't need authority figures telling us what to do with our lives. And I know you agree with me, because you said so when Lisa filed that petition to change the custody. You said, 'Why didn't she just ask me about this?' You said, 'These are our kids. We should be working this stuff out. We don't need a judge to make these decisions.' Remember that? Well, same here. If there's anything left for you and Owen to talk about—"

"There's not," I interject.

"Then the two of you can sit down and discuss it. And if there's not anything left to talk about, then that's it. Everything is over, and you guys never have to see each other again. Which you probably won't, because clearly you and I are completely finished."

"Right," I say. "Completely."

Samara is silent. I wait. "So," she says, "you're gonna do the right thing, right?"

I am, but not to help her. I am because it's a waste of time. I'm not really that mad at Owen—well, I am mad about him kicking Pinky, but he didn't actually kick him very hard—and there's absolutely no reason to torture him by pressing charges, which probably wouldn't go anywhere anyway, except that he did piss off that cop, so who knows? But there's no reason to, because I am pretty sure that encounter didn't go the way he planned it. He stormed over here like the wronged husband, which is pretty funny when you think about the fact that he's a husband who says sure, have sex with my wife, it's fine with me. But whatever, I think he thought I was going to be scared of him or impressed with him, or something. Whatever it was, he was planning to leave here feeling powerful and good about himself. He thought he would go back home, and Samara would be all admiring and grateful. I could tell that he did not expect me to push back, and he certainly didn't expect to hear that Samara lied for me in court about having sex while Charlie was in bed with us. He did not expect me to tell him something about his wife he didn't know. And he was totally humiliated by that. And then he got hauled down to the police station. What an idiot.

"I'll seriously think about it," I say. "I heard what you said. Bye." And I hang up without giving her a chance to respond. Let her stew a little. Let her worry about her family life. Although trying to beat a super lame assault charge is nothing compared to losing your kids. Nothing.

CHORUS #5

The Co-Op Shoppers

The slim bunches of broccolini are glistening in their rustic crate—just the thing to go with the cute little package of mushroom agnolotti Kara grabs from the freezer on her way to the organic produce aisle of the Greenwood Food Co-op.

Kara, what's up? a low voice calls from the other side of the deli counter.

Nathan! Kara says. Since when are you the family shopper? Or did Pablo finally put his foot down and make you do your co-op hours?

How wrong you are, says Nathan, smiling while he pulls at the side of his well-sculpted reddish beard. In fact, I always do my co-op hours, and I usually do his too.

Right, says Kara. Sure you do.

And today, Nathan says, we're shopping together—a little family outing. As if on cue, a breathless Pablo comes flying around the corner to join Nathan, a box of Israeli clementines cradled in his arms.

Kara, Pablo says, come over here right now. I got something impor-tant to tell you. It's private.

Looking around to make sure no one she knew was close by, Kara steps toward Pablo and Nathan, looking concerned. Pablo leans toward her. Did you hear about Owen?

What about him? Kara asks.

He got arrested last night after getting into a fight with that guy who was seeing Samara. You know the one I mean?

You mean Jake, says Kara, that straight married guy, older?

Yeah, that guy, says Pablo.

Yes, I definitely know him, she says.

Well, it sounds like something went down between Samara and Jake, and Samara was upset, so Owen tried to talk to him about it, and Jake got real aggressive. And then someone called the cops, and then—get this—Jake told them that Owen assaulted him and his dog, and Owen ended up getting arrested. Like, handcuffs, police station, the whole nine.

No! says Kara. Owen assaulting someone? C'mon, guys. The hydroponic lettuce guru? No way. He got arrested? Oh, wow. Is he in jail?

No, says Nathan. What we heard is that the cops let him go after they took him to the station because, after all that, Jake told them he didn't want to press charges. After Samara found out and lit into him, is what I think. I mean, you know how she is. That girl is all about truth telling, right? Whatever happened between her and Jake, it must have gotten a thousand times worse when she found out he lied to the cops about Owen attacking him. What a joke.

Unbelievable, says Kara, shaking her head and reaching around Nathan to pick up a jar of wildflower honey. Poor Owen. You know, I feel like this is the kind of stuff that happens when one of us has a relationship with an outsider. Like someone who is just in it as a sexual thing, but doesn't really embrace the lifestyle or the values. You know what I mean? Like us, she says, gesturing toward Nathan and Pablo, we understand the rules. And we're careful. This guy Jake, we spent one night with him, me and Grady and Samara and Owen, and he was all into that, but afterward he pretended like it didn't happen. He just wanted a relationship with Samara. From what she told me, it was like he wanted to ignore Owen's existence, ignore that she had a primary relationship. Basically, he had no interest in our community.

Yeah, says Pablo, I agree. We should stick with our own.

Poor Owen, says Kara again. I'm going to make some soup or something and take it over there. Sounds like he and Samara could both use a little TLC. Maybe this Brazilian chicken soup I make with coconut and cashews. It's very comforting. Do you know where the cashews are?

Upstairs, says Pablo. And that sounds delicious. While you're at it, make some for us? I'm practically Brazilian.

Nope, says Kara. Not this time. And anyway, you're Mexican. But I love you both. Come here, and let me give you both a kiss.

35

Lisa: Boston

My cuticles are ragged, and my nails are brittle and cracked from the winter cold. At work today, every time I pulled a pair of gloves over my broken nails to examine a patient, I fantasized about getting a manicure before the next appointment. Nothing special, nothing expensive, nothing time-consuming. Just the same manicure I've had, many times, at the little salon right across the street from the clinic, which is teeming with highly competent Cambodian women who massage your hands and rub your arms with hot stones after they've trimmed your cuticles away into lovely, smooth nothingness and oiled your thirsty nail beds. I have been having this fantasy now for over a week, and I literally cannot find the forty-five minutes to make it a reality.

This new schedule is a bear. I don't get a break. At the beginning, right after Jake moved out, I missed the girls so much during his weeks, and I remember telling my girlfriends how tough it was. But I got used to it, fast. Having whole weeks to myself was a total luxury. In what now seems like a fleeting period in my life, the idea of having trouble finding time to get a manicure would have been ludicrous—everything like that I scheduled during my no-kids week. Going to the gym, getting my hair colored, paying bills, catching up on personal emails, drinking wine with Tilly—all of it fit. And on top of that, I actually read books. And even watched TV sometimes.

I know I wanted the judge to punish Jake. I wanted him to understand he just can't get away with impulsive, reckless, psychologically damaging behavior when the girls are with him. I would never act that way. I always put the girls first, so I know it's better for them to be with me, and that's the most important thing. But now I feel like I'm being punished too. Like this is just one more way I'm paying for Jake's inadequacies. Now I have no life at all, and he gets to skate; he gets total freedom. Before, he had to at least try to be the adult in the room every other week, even if he royally screwed up when it came to Samara. But he did manage to feed them, and get them to school relatively on time, and make sure they got their homework done. He even did their laundry. I wish we could turn the clock back to before Samara, or before Samara started sleeping over. But you can't turn clocks back, you can't unknow what you know, and I am just so tired.

My favorite item of clothing when it comes to complete comfort is an ancient pair of Jake's plaid green pajama pants, which I appropriated years ago. After the girls are in bed, I put them on. A sense of relief instantly floods over me in a wave that marks the end of the long day, the end of the time I have to be some woman's health care provider, some child's mother, some dog's human, some person who's in charge, who makes decisions, who has to be on every single minute. Instead, I become just me, Lisa Naudain, unencumbered and alone in my bedroom with the door closed. Alone with the wrinkles in my pale pink sheets still smoothed out from when I made the bed in the morning the way I like to make it, alone with my phone and my books and my unread mail. I sit cross-legged on my bed, and I breathe, in and out, in and out, until my parasympathetic nervous system finally kicks in. Calmed, I pick up my phone. Talk? I type. 2 min is the answer. The answer that went zinging up to outer space from a large white suburban house with a basketball hoop in the driveway and a pool in the backyard, a house I've only seen online while stalking the real estate sites. The answer that landed on the tiny device in my un-manicured hand, in my small Greenwood three-bedroom twin with the rotten floorboards on the front porch and the holly tree in back—steadfast, ever green, and constantly shedding berries.

Hey. Don't have long. Did you decide about the Boston conference? Boston. A hotel room. A king-size bed and blackout curtains. Room service. I can see Andrew standing at the sink, naked, shaving his head. I never saw a man shave his head, before him. I never knew how often you have to do it. I can feel his hands, large, capable, doctor soft, running down my body, tracing the contours of my face, opening my thighs. I still haven't decided.

Yes, I type. I'll figure out how to make it work. How can I make it work? It means switching weekends with Jake or getting someone else to take the girls. Jake is not going to do me any favors. He probably won't switch with me, but he probably will say he'll take my weekend, and then he would have them three weekends in a row. Which really isn't so bad, because he is not having Samara—or anyone else—stay there on the weekends he has the girls, as far as I can tell. Now he's trying to be Dad of the Year. Like, all of a sudden he's super interested in helping Elizabeth with her local-history research project, and he took Charlie to the art museum, just the two of them, last weekend when Elizabeth was at a friend's house.

So glad. I'll make sure you don't regret it:) Gotta run see you at clinic. Who am I? Sneaking around with another woman's husband? With a man who is no doubt deleting our texts after every time we talk? It's all so tacky. And I know it's considered wrong.

The younger me would have condemned this conduct as a moral transgression without giving it a second thought. But at this point, I'm not so sure. On some level, it feels oddly okay because I know it doesn't really mean anything. I don't want a new husband, and Andrew doesn't appear to want a new wife. My work and my girls are 95 percent of my life; I have no time. Right now, the shot of excitement that he is providing is exactly what I want. I want to have a secret. I want new sexual fantasies. I don't want someone to sync calendars with and plan who's taking which kid to which activity and figure out what we're making for dinner. I can handle that myself. I want to wear a thong and a tight black dress. I want the tall cocktail in the hotel bar. I want the long ride up in the elevator to that pristine, anonymous room. I want sex that electrifies me, that obliterates everything else. Andrew is perfect for this moment in time, this slot in my life.

But, Angela. Suppose she finds out, and his relationship with me ends up ruining their marriage? Would that be my fault? I don't think so. Look at Samara and her husband. They agreed to have other relationships. She didn't have to engage in any of this clandestine stuff to hide her relationship with Jake. Isn't that way better? Couldn't Andrew have done that? I've thought about this a lot, and I'm pretty clear that it's not my responsibility to stop something I enjoy in order to protect Andrew's wife. That's his call, and their marriage is their relationship, however they want to do it. So the moral lapse is his, not mine.

For now, with this new custody schedule, this is all I can do, and it's all I want. It has no bearing on Elizabeth and Charlie. Unlike Jake, I've kept it completely separate from them; this part of my life is tied up in a private box, and they have no clue. But even if my relationship with Andrew didn't need to be kept secret, even if it were completely out in the open, I have no intention of

introducing them to anyone I date anytime soon. Jake really
jumped the gun on that, because he has no impulse control, and
look what it led to. But at some point, won't he have learned his
lesson? Won't he have paid enough?

I know, and I have known from the minute Judge Jones is-
sued this custody order, that it's unlikely to be sustainable long-
term. I can imagine that at some time in the future, I will want a
real partner, not just a hookup, as Tilly would dismissively, and
at the same time enviously, call my relationship with Andrew if
she knew about it. And it would be so much easier for that to
happen with the old custody schedule, where I would have time
to get to know someone, time to develop a real relationship before introducing him to the girls. And then there's the girls. They
are not happy. They don't realize I did this for them. They miss
their dad. And they blame me, which he probably encourages,
but that doesn't change the sting of their reproach. No wonder I
find refuge in my tiny but wildly pleasurable doses of Andrew.

Exhausted, I get under the duvet, turn out the light, grab my
phone, and lie in the dark, glowing device cupped in my hand,
scrolling through girls' snow boots on Zappos, seeing them fly
by like so many sheep as my eyelids keep closing, until I drop the
phone on my pillow and succumb.

36

Ellen: Mom versus Lawyer

"Ellen, I forgot to tell you that Jake Naudain called while you were in your consultation this morning. He asked if you could call him back before the end of the day—said it's important."

Ellen stops on her way to the printer to pick up the first draft of a prenuptial agreement she had just finished writing—and which she really had done an excellent job on, considering the complexity of the situation with the family business and all—and glares at her assistant. "Jake Naudain," she says, "can go fuck himself."

"Wow," says Tiffany. "You still mad at him about that thing with your daughter?"

"I will always be mad at him," says Ellen. "Not forgivable."

"Okay, mama bear. So does that mean you're not going to call him back? And what exactly do you want me to tell him if he calls again? 'Ellen won't be calling you back and said you can go fuck yourself'? Also, I saw a reminder in the calendar that the appeal period in his case runs this week."

"No, I'll call him. I don't really have a choice. Thanks, Tiffany."

Ellen picks up the prenup, walks back into her office, closes the door, stares at her phone for a minute, looks up Jake's number, and calls it. Jake answers right away.

"Ellen, thanks for calling me back. I wanted to follow up on our conversation right after the hearing, about filing an appeal. I know you said we have thirty days to do it, and I'm pretty sure that's Friday, so I need to decide, right?"

"Right."

"Well, what do you think? Do you think I could win an appeal? And could I afford it?"

After a long pause, Ellen breathes in. "Jake, as I told you, I'm really not comfortable continuing to represent you, given what happened with Marni, and also you lying to me about the incident with Samara, which put me in a very compromised position with Judge Jones. However, because the appeal deadline is Friday, if you do want to go that route, I'll file the notice of appeal in order to preserve your rights, and then you can find another lawyer to take it from there. I can give you names of some lawyers who do lots of appellate work."

"Okay, if you really think that's necessary. I don't get it, but I understand that's your choice to make. But talk to me about an appeal. What's involved?"

"So it's not a new trial. The Superior Court won't hear any new evidence. They review the transcript from the trial before Judge Jones, and they decide if she made any errors in her application of the law. And given that the legal standard is best interest of the children, I think it would be tough to show that. Basically they'd have to find that she had no reason for reducing your custody time based on the incident with Charlie and Samara, and I think that would be hard to establish—the Superior Court doesn't have to think she made the best decision, or that they would have made the same decision, they just have to find that there was some legal basis for it. And appeals are expensive. You'd probably spend three or four times what you spent on the trial. And they take a long time. You wouldn't have a final decision for close to a year."

Ellen had painted this discouraging picture for clients many times before. One detail she was leaving out this time, though, is her customary practice of filing a petition for reconsideration prior to filing an appeal, essentially giving the trial judge a chance to rectify her mistake and change the order before hitting her with an appeal. Which Ellen knows judges don't like. They don't like appeals in general because they're a lot of work —they have to write detailed opinions justifying their orders. And they especially don't like them when the appellate court overrules them, giving rise to published opinions, to be read by lawyers and judges for decades to come, which find fault with their reasoning, sometimes even containing scathing criticisms of them. A well-written reconsideration petition occasionally does the trick.

Ellen's encounter with Judge Jones the other weekend is replaying itself in her head. It seems pretty clear that the judge had actually been encouraging her to file for reconsideration. Which could only mean that she wanted to send Ellen a message that she was regretting the harshness of her decision and was looking for an opportunity to remediate it. Even though it is possible that Ellen is wrong, and that Judge Jones is just prone to inappropriate *ex parte* chatter with counsel during chance encounters at the dry cleaners, Ellen is almost positive that she isn't. And if this were a different case, Ellen would be jumping on this opening. She would have already told her client what the judge said to her, and, in all likelihood, she would already have already started writing the reconsideration petition.

But Jake Naudain does not deserve anything from her other than to make sure he doesn't lose his right to appeal. No matter how disgusted she is with him, she has a professional obligation to file that notice of appeal before Friday. And then she's done; she can send him on his way. He will have no trouble finding another lawyer to take the appeal as long as he can pay for it, and that is not her problem. And as a general matter, reconsideration petitions are rarely granted—although, this of course is not a general matter, as she had essentially been invited to file one by the presiding judge—so why should she go out on a limb and spend her next three days working on his? She'd be working on behalf of a client who sexually assaulted her daughter and then lied to her about the critical issue in his case, and who currently owes her money, to boot. Really, there are limits.

"Is that my only option?" asks Jake, "because even if I wanted to do that, I can't afford it. I'm tapped out. I still owe you money."

"No, it's not," says Ellen. "Custody orders can always be modified down the road if you can show that a change would be in the girls' best interests. So your other option is to just wait a while, and if the girls don't adjust well to the new schedule and are asking for more time with you, your new lawyer can file a petition to modify Judge Jones's order and request that the court give you more time. But I'll say this—the new arrangement is going to become the status quo, and if the girls are doing well in school and seem happy, it could be hard to change it back to living half time with you. Especially if you continue to do things like bringing them in bed with you and your girlfriends."

"Ellen, Jesus, you don't need to say that. I got it, a thousand times, I got it. But in terms of right now, are you telling me there's nothing else we can do? Nothing right now, other than the appeal?"

Ellen hesitates for a moment. "No," she says. "There isn't. Let me know your decision. If you want to appeal, we'll prepare the notice of appeal and get it filed with the court before Friday, and I'll get your file ready to transfer to whoever you hire to handle it. And you'll need to pay off your bill with us."

"Okay. I understand. Thanks, Ellen. I'm sorry for the misunderstanding about Marni and the stuff that happened at the trial. It certainly wasn't my intention to put you in a difficult position. I think you're a really good lawyer, and you've always been straight with me. So thanks, and I'll be in touch."

Ellen hangs up the phone and stares at the picture on her bookshelf of Dan and Marni on Marni's first day of kindergarten, Marni smiling so proudly at the camera in her little denim jacket and brand-new backpack, Dan looking fondly down at their daughter. She gets up and opens the door. "Tiffany," she says, "I've taken care of Jake Naudain. Did anyone else call this morning who you forgot to tell me about?"

37

Marni: Field Research

Christmas had come and gone, a curious mixture of childlike wonder and embarrassment that her heart still jumped at the sight of a fully loaded Christmas stocking. Laundry had long since been done, refrigerator contents inventoried and eaten, high school friends home from college visited, large quantities of alcohol and weed drunk and smoked, and through it all, sleep had been administered like a drug. Sleep, twelve hours of it at a stretch, in her full-size bed, in her own bedroom, alone, with no roommate. Marni feels rejuvenated but also restless, navigating that space between child and adult, wanting to be back in her college life where parents don't exist while at the same time insisting that her mother make a dentist appointment for her. But there is no denying that break is coming to a close, and she cannot wait any longer to do her field research.

Within thirty seconds of typing polyamory and Philadelphia into Google, Marni locates a polyamory Meetup group in Greenwood and comes across a blog post from some film student at Temple, SamaraB, who is making a documentary about the polyamorous community in Philadelphia and looking for people to interview. Marni is hopeful that SamaraB might have some interviews scheduled before she has to go back to school that she could tag along on, thus saving her the job of setting up and conducting interviews herself. She now realizes, after finally paying attention to the project, it is a daunting task that she has no idea how to perform and seems highly unlikely to be accomplished in the week before she has to go back to New London. Marni emails SamaraB immediately, closes her computer, grabs her down jacket, and heads for the front door.

She's in luck. Within the hour, while sitting in her friend Emma's living room comparing notes on the mandatory campus programs about consent that freshmen have to take at their respective colleges, SamaraB, who is really just Samara, responds. She tells Marni that she has already filmed several interviews and is in the process of editing them. If Marni wants to watch them, she can, and it would be helpful to Samara to get Marni's perspective, as a college freshman, about which topics covered in the interviews resonate most with her. "Damn," Marni says to Emma, "looks like I'll actually be able to hand in my soc paper on time."

Samara's office at Temple, which turns out to be more like a cubby, is located smack in the middle of the film department. It's a place teeming with incredibly cool-looking people, mostly in their late twenties or older, many shades of Black and brown, a hijab or two, a group speaking Spanish. Marni feels conspicuously young and white and collegiate and boring with her long, straight, light brown hair, her un-ripped jeans, and her gray down jacket. This is so not Connecticut College, she thinks as she looks around the room, waiting for Samara; this is so great.

"Marni?" asks the delicate young woman walking toward the doorway where Marni is standing. She's wearing black leather boots and a fuzzy red poncho sort of thing, one of those items of clothing Marni would never have the nerve to wear because she'd be afraid of looking weird, but it looks amazing on the pixie-like Samara, who clearly has the confidence to pull it off.

"Hi, Samara," she says, holding out her hand, "thanks so much for inviting me down here."

"I'm really glad you contacted me," says Samara, taking Marni's hand. "The timing is perfect. There are two interviews I'm editing now that I want to show you and ask you some questions about, and you can feel free to take notes while you watch them too. Here, follow me. My office is right down this hallway."

Settling down at Samara's desk while Samara fusses with the settings on a large desktop computer, Marni gets out her laptop and asks Samara why she decided to make the documentary.

"The main reason," Samara says, "is because I want to educate the wider community about the lifestyle. There are a lot of misconceptions out there about who we are and what we believe, and I want to address those misconceptions by having people in our community tell their stories."

Oh God, what an idiot I am, thinks Marni. *Why didn't it occur to me that she might be polyamorous herself?*

"Oh, right, right," Marni says, trying not to sound flustered. "That's really cool. I mean, that makes total sense. So would you mind if I ask you a few questions then, before we watch the interviews? Since you're, like, someone I could interview live for my paper? But it's fine if you don't want to. I would totally understand."

"Sure," says Samara. "Ask away."

Wow, Marni thinks, *how perfect is this*? "Okay, awesome. So when did you start practicing—is that how you describe it— polyamory?"

Half an hour later, Marni has the full story safely saved on her hard drive. She learned that Samara started having sexual relationships with women as well as men when she was in college and initially identified just as bisexual. Samara also met the man she's now married to, Owen, when they were in college. This had really surprised Marni, because Samara seemed so young and sort of nontraditional that Marni wouldn't have expected her to be married, and she didn't even wear a wedding ring. Even though she had fallen in love with Owen, she had this close girlfriend whom she had a sexual relationship with, on and off, never like a couple, just casual, as part of their friendship. And Samara found that she still wanted to keep up the sexual part of that relationship, even though she and Owen had become a couple. She didn't feel that having sex with her girlfriend took anything away from that commitment to Owen. And the girlfriend had no problem with it, either. Samara wanted to be honest with Owen, and she thought that maybe because it had to do with a girl and not another guy that he wouldn't feel threatened by it, but she wasn't sure.

So she told him. And it turned out that he had been doing a lot of reading about monogamy and how it's not sustainable, and learning about polyamory as an alternative, and actually wanting to talk to *her* about it, but he was afraid to, because she might think he was just looking for permission to cheat on her, which was not it at all. He was interested in having an open relationship sexually, for both of them, and not hiding anything from each other. And Owen was bisexual too, like her.

"That's the thing," she told Marni. "Both of us were already very open sexually, before we officially identified as polyamorous."

So she and Owen talked about it a lot, and at the same time, there was a small student group forming on their campus for people interested in polyamory, or already living it, who wanted support, so they started hanging out with that group.

"How," Marni had asked, "did you start doing it? Were there rules you agreed to follow?"

Samara explained that there were not so many rules as commitments. They agreed that their relationship was primary, but each of them could have other secondary relationships, which they would tell the other partner about before anything happened. And sometimes they would have sexual relationships together with another partner or another couple. The point is that everyone involved would know, would agree, and would be comfortable.

"And it makes so much sense," Samara had said, "because monogamy is not the natural state of human sexuality. Just look at all the so-called cheating that happens. But when expectations are clear, and people are willing to share their partners and are secure that their feelings for one partner don't take away from their feelings toward another partner, then there's no such thing as cheating. There's nothing to cheat about. It's really a more highly evolved way to live, to be bonded with someone you love just because you love being with them, not because you are not allowed by the mainstream culture to have sex or intimacy with anyone else."

As Samara delivered this speech, Marni had typed furiously so as to record every word. But something else had also happened. There was the high clarity of Samara's voice; the way she moved her small hands, a little grubby and ragged around the cuticles like a child's or an artist's, as she spoke; her frequent smiles, which revealed precise, little sparkly teeth; and the long curls of dark hair spread out and down over the crazy red poncho. All of it, the whole essence of this lovely, self-assured girl-woman talking so openly about her multiple sexual partners, was utterly entrancing. And so sexy, to the point where Marni started to feel slightly dizzy.

She thought of Michaela, the friend at school she slept with that one night before they all went home for Thanksgiving, her obligatory freshman foray into bisexuality. She had wanted to try it; lots of her girlfriends had already. She definitely responded to Michaela, to her tongue, to the soft feel of another woman's body. It was pleasurable, for sure, but it was not anything like what she had with her high school boyfriend, not the raw, insanely powerful draw she felt when they had sex. But this feeling was different. Her skin felt hot. She shifted in her seat. She tucked her hair behind her ears and untucked it again.

"So," Samara had said, clearly unaware of the intoxicating effect she was having on her young interviewer, "that's my story. Let's get to the interviews. I have to cut them to five minutes each, so why don't you let me know which parts of each person's story are most interesting to you. I'll play Joey's first. He's a character. He was this straight business man who became polyamorous when he was like fifty, and it totally transformed his life."

Between her impromptu interview of Samara and the two filmed ones she watched, Marni is pretty sure she'll have enough material to write her paper. But academic pursuits are most definitely not her focus as she packs up her bag and puts on her jacket. She is still whirling in the orbit of Samara. Fortunately, so fortunately, when Marni tells Samara she lives in Greenwood, Samara offers her a ride home, because she lives there too.

Even riding in Samara's car is captivating. Marni takes in everything about it: empty coffee cups from the Green Life Café rolling on the floor, a Hawaiian hula dancer swaying on the dashboard, piles of books and magazines strewn about in the back seat. And it's a stick shift. Marni has no idea how to drive one, and neither do most of her friends, especially her female friends. She watches Samara's little right hand on the gear shift, revealing a cluster of tiny stars tattooed on the inside of her wrist, moving through the gears as the car speeds up and shifting again to slow it down with that loud whirring sound of the drag as they go into a curve, a competency both tomboyish and wildly glamorous at the same time.

"Let's stop at my apartment before I drop you off," says Samara. "It's right on the way, and I just realized I have a book you could borrow that would be perfect for your paper. It looks at polyamory from a cross-cultural perspective, which might help you with the 'contemporary social movement in the U.S.' angle."

Murmuring the obligatory, "Thank you, if you're sure it's not too much trouble," Marni continues to ride high on her good fortune. Samara turns a corner past two boarded-up houses and a church with a sign out front that says COME ON IN—JESUS IS EXPECTING YOU! She pulls up in front of a huge, old gray house with a pile of firewood stacked on the side porch next to two bicycles locked to the railing, turns to Marni, and says, "Are you in a hurry? If not, do you want to come up for a few minutes? I may have some other books for you too."

Marni, who is most definitely not in a hurry to say goodbye to Samara, tells Samara that would be great, gets out of the car and follows her up the steps onto the main porch, into a dark front hallway, and up two flights of dusty stairs. Samara unlocks the door at the top, and Marni goes inside.

Despite having lived her entire life in Greenwood, Marni has never been in an apartment like this, or really any Greenwood apartment at all, except maybe when she babysat for that creepy but sexy older dude, Jake whatever his last name was, that her mom is so pissed at. He lives in one. But her friends, and her parents' friends, all live in houses pretty much like hers, with multiple bedrooms and bathrooms, renovated kitchens with stainless steel stoves and refrigerators that make ice and dispense water, private yards with trees and flower beds and firepits. Some are bigger or messier or prettier than others, some have oriental rugs and dark wooden furniture, and some have recessed lighting and mid-century modern couches, but all are clustered into one demographic pool at the upper end of some graph, somewhere. Samara's apartment is thrillingly not in that pool.

"Have a seat," says Samara, pointing to a beat-up, navy-blue couch and throwing her coat on top of a fully loaded coatrack by the front door, causing it to tilt precariously under the added weight. "I'll grab the book I was telling you about and look to see if there are others." She disappears into what looks like a bedroom. "Do you want some tea?" she calls out to Marni. "I'm going to put some water on."

"Sure," says Marni as she sits down on one end of the couch, not sure whether she should also take off her jacket or if that would be presumptuous. "Thanks."

Samara emerges from the maybe bedroom carrying several books, which she puts down on top of a fake-antique-looking trunk, which serves as a coffee table, in front of the couch. "You can put your jacket over there," she says, pointing to the listing coat rack as she walks across the living room and into the kitchen. "I have black tea or peppermint. Which do you want?"

"Peppermint, please," Marni answers, as she starts rummaging through the stack of books in front of her. *The Contemporary American Family: The Role of Utopian Communities in Shifting Twentieth-Century Cultural Norms* is on top. It is fat. The type is small. There is no way she is going to read it.

"Wow, these look great," she calls to Samara, who comes back into the living room carrying two mugs and sits down on the couch next to Marni, the red fuzzy poncho spreading out around her like a flower. Marni's heartbeat vibrates through her body.

"There's something I meant to ask you when we were watching the interviews," Marni says, acutely aware that she has to say something to prolong this moment, where she is sitting close enough to Samara to see the faint smudge of mascara under her lower lashes, a smudge that on Marni would have just looked unkempt and trashy, but on Samara evokes mystery and seduction, the waking-up face of a lazy morning after the wild night before.

"What's that?" asks Samara, sipping from a purple mug.

"It's about jealousy," Marni answers. "How do you deal with jealousy? I mean, Joey and the woman you interviewed both talked about how they realized polyamory fit them so much better than monogamy, and how it was a big relief to discover that. And you told me about that too. You said how when you were in college, you didn't feel a conflict between your relationship with Owen and the relationship you had with your girlfriend. And when you talked to Owen about it, he was already thinking about polyamory, which was great for you. But what about relationships you've had, or maybe not you but other polyamorous people you know, with someone who does feel jealous—who can't, like, turn that off. How do you deal with it?"

"That totally does happen," Samara says, nodding as she speaks. "It's happened to me. And it is hard to deal with. Because it's incompatible with our beliefs. I was just in a relationship like that, a relationship that ended very recently. And really badly. It was with a guy who said he accepted that I was polyamorous, and he met Owen and everything, and we actually had sex with him together once, right at the beginning. But after that he only wanted to see me, and I realized he wasn't really interested in polyamory at all. He was an older guy who had just gotten divorced, and he wasn't looking for a serious relationship, just a dating, have-fun type one. That part was fine with me. But at a certain point, I realized it was like he wanted to pretend I wasn't married and wasn't polyamorous. He really did not want to hear anything about Owen. And after it was over, I realized that his acting that way had sort of changed the way I treated the relationship too. Like, I didn't talk to Owen about this guy much either, even though we were spending a lot of time together. And as a result, I think Owen did become jealous of him. Not jealous because I was having sex with him—we're not that way—but jealous because he knew this guy wasn't interested in polyamory at all and basically just wanted to have an exclusive relationship with me. He wasn't one of us, and the whole thing wasn't healthy for me and Owen. Fortunately, I realized that and got out of the relationship."

"So why did you start seeing this guy if you knew he wasn't really into polyamory?" asks Marni. "Because you define yourself as polyamorous, right? So wasn't it sort of like a rejection of who you are?"

"Yes, exactly. It was a rejection," says Samara. "But I just didn't see it at first. Look," she says, leaning toward Marni, smiling, and putting a hand on her arm, "we're all human. This guy was a lot of fun. And I was really attracted to him. The sex was amazing."

Marni, thrilled by the trajectory of the conversation, intoxicated by the seductive heat of Samara's touch, and ready to sign up for the polyamory club yesterday, turns her face toward Samara, brings her hand up to Samara's cheek, and kisses her. As they kiss, Samara moves toward her, so close that Marni can feel the pressure of Samara's breasts against hers. With the slightest encouragement from Samara, Marni would have immediately divested herself of all clothing, but instead, Samara gently breaks away. She takes Marni's face in her hands, looks her in the eyes, and says, "Marni. You're beautiful. And smart. But you're very young, you've just started college, and you're going back to school in less than two weeks. If you want to explore polyamory, that's great. But I don't really do hookups, I do relationships, and I would want you to meet Owen, and there's not really any time for that. Maybe if you're home for the summer, we can all get together then."

Simultaneously ecstatic and embarrassed, Marni hugs Samara awkwardly and stands up. "Okay. I get it. I'm sorry. I guess I just got a little carried away. But do you mean it about the summer? Could we get together then? I'd really like to meet Owen." Which she definitely does, not only because he's Samara's polyamorous husband, but also because there's a picture of a guy with long hair and a sexy grin on the bookshelf who must be him, and *oh my God.*

"Don't apologize. You didn't do anything wrong. You're adorable, but like I said, the timing just isn't right," Samara says, getting up and kissing Marni on the cheek. "But yes, the summer sounds good. I actually need to go meet a friend for drinks, so can I give you a ride home now? Feel free to take any of those books. Just return them before you go back to Connecticut, because I may need them this semester while I'm working on the film."

"Samara, thank you *so* much," says Marni, still panting internally. "For everything."

"My pleasure," says Samara, grabbing her car keys off the trunk coffee table. "Hope the paper comes out well. Guess you should leave out that last part of our meeting. Just saying."

Marni laughs. "Guess so," she says. "Although, it's supposed to be about my field research."

"Given that I work with undergrads," Samara says, as she ushers Marni and the stack of books Marni isn't planning to read out the front door and down the stairway, "I can guarantee that is not the type of field research your prof had in mind."

"Mom, can you edit my paper on polyamory?" Marni yells upstairs from the living room. "I think it turned out pretty good, but I'd really like your take on it."

"Turned out pretty *well*," comes the response from the second floor.

"Oh, Jesus, Mom. Could you please stop it with the grammar police thing? I know it's 'well.' I would always write it that way. But it's normal to say 'good.' Calm down. Are you going to read it, or what? I think you'll be really interested. Seems like a family law sort of thing you should know about. And this woman Samara I told you about is unbelievably cool. You'd really like her."

38

Elizabeth: Daddy

Sofia's dad is having a big party tonight for his fortieth birthday at the rec center in the park next to Mariposa, and Man With a Dog is playing. It's one of those parties with grown-ups and kids, which are admittedly getting sort of lame, but Elizabeth hadn't wanted to miss this one. Lots of her friends from Mariposa are going to be there, and they would get to run around in the dark. Leo would be there, and there might be an opportunity to hook up, and some of the eighth graders would probably be smoking weed. And it was considered somewhat cool that her dad was going to play guitar and sing—a little embarrassing but mostly cool.

Anyway, Sofia invited her, and her dad told her about it too. It isn't his weekend, but he told her to ask her mom if she could go anyway. Which Elizabeth did, but her mom said no, because she had planned some "girl time" just for her and Elizabeth because Charlie was sleeping over at her friend Nicki's. Her mom said she was thinking they could go to the movies and out to dinner, maybe at the new Mexican restaurant that just opened in Greenwood, where they had all different kinds of guacamole that they make fresh at your table.

But the thing was, her mom hadn't even told her about this, much less asked her if she wanted to have "girl time" that night—

she just went ahead and planned it. When Elizabeth said she wanted to go to Sofia's dad's party and hear Daddy's band play, her mom acted all hurt and said how she and Elizabeth never have time alone, and she'd been looking forward to this. Which seemed kind of crazy to Elizabeth because ever since the custody order changed, she's constantly with her mom—they practically always have dinner together. And it feels like she hardly ever sees her dad.

Elizabeth begged her mom to let her go, but her mom was such a bitch and just kept saying no, telling Elizabeth there would be plenty of other opportunities to see Daddy's band play. Which was so obviously not true, because they didn't actually perform very often, and when they did, they usually played at clubs where kids aren't allowed. So Elizabeth texted her dad and asked him if he could talk to her mom about it. He said he would, and then he texted her later and told her he did, but her mom had said no.

Under these circumstances, Elizabeth felt she really had no choice but to refuse to go along with "girl time." If it had been handled in a different way—like if she and her mom had planned it together, on a night when she didn't have something to do with her friends—Elizabeth would have liked going out to eat and to the movies with her mom. But the way this was imposed on her, like she was a four-year-old whose whole life revolved around her mom, it just sucked.

So now Elizabeth is spending Saturday night in her room, door closed, headphones on, texting with her friends who are going to the party about how much she hates her mom and how she misses her dad. Her mom had given up trying to get her to go to the movies after Elizabeth refused to leave her room. Knowing her, Elizabeth figures she's probably alone in the living room watching television and drinking wine, and probably talking to that doctor—gross. She's such a hypocrite, being all mad at Daddy about Samara, while she's basically sexting with that guy every night and pretending like she's the perfect mom.

The next morning, Elizabeth wakes up early when Pinky jumps off her bed and starts whining at her bedroom door. When she gets up and opens the door to let him out, she hears her mom talking on the phone, saying "How long was she up for? Was she crying a lot?" Deeming this a conversation that seems worth listening to if she can hear it from her room, Elizabeth leaves her door open and gets back in bed. There is silence for a while, and then her mom starts speaking again.

"Thanks for letting me know about this, Sandy. I know she does miss her dad. Both girls have been telling me that since our custody schedule changed, but all I'm comfortable saying is that he made some very bad decisions, and the judge felt that it would be better for the girls to live with me and visit with him on weekends." Another silence. Elizabeth can picture Charlie, waking up in her friend Nicki's room, and crying for Daddy. Ever since the court thing, when they're with their dad, she's noticed that Charlie's all over him, like she wants to sit in his lap all the time and hold his hand when they walk anywhere. She even follows him around the apartment, just like Pinky.

Her mom starts talking again.

"Yes, sure we could agree to change the schedule. We don't have to do what the judge said, obviously, but at this point I'm going to stick with it."

Silence.

"Sandy, I know they need us both, and I know you're a family therapist, but what Jake did is really over the top, and he needs to grow up and take some responsibility for his actions."

Silence.

"I appreciate your concerns, Sandy, and I'm really sorry that Charlie woke you and Rob up last night. I'm on my way to pick her up. Be there in fifteen minutes."

Elizabeth can hear her mom walking up the stairs. She puts the covers over her head. She hears her mom come into her room and ask if she is awake. Elizabeth doesn't answer. Her mom says she knows Elizabeth is awake because she heard her get up to let Pinky out. She wants her to know she has to go pick up Charlie, and she'll be back soon.

Elizabeth pulls the covers off her head and sits up. "Why are you picking her up now?" she asks. "It's so early."

Her mom says that Charlie woke up crying during the night and was homesick, so she is going to get her.

"Homesick?" says Elizabeth. "You mean for your home or for Dad's home?"

"Elizabeth, you know it's not my home or Dad's home. We've talked about this. They're both your homes. You and Charlie have two homes."

"Well, we used to," says Elizabeth, "but not anymore we don't. We're hardly ever at Dad's. And it sucks, Mom. I know why Charlie was crying. You should see her with Dad. She practically asks him to carry her like a baby. This whole thing about Samara is just so, so stupid. Were you, like, jealous or something? And he broke up with her anyway. That's, like, so over. I can't believe you did this to him. And to me and Charlie."

Elizabeth starts to cry. "It's bad enough that you got divorced. And I know you're the one who decided that. It wasn't Daddy. But anyway, the joint custody thing was working okay. I mean, we didn't love it or anything, but it was okay. But to do this to us, to make us go to court and talk to that old judge, and now it's like Daddy's a criminal or something, like he's being punished. And me and Charlie are being punished too. You're ruining three people's lives now."

Elizabeth's mom just stands there in the doorway, listening. Then she starts walking toward Elizabeth.

"Get away from me!" shouts Elizabeth. "I hate you. I want to live with Daddy. And so does Charlie. Just ask her. I dare you."

Elizabeth's mom stops in the middle of the room. "Honey," she says, "I'm so sorry. But sometimes adults have to make decisions about what's best for their kids."

"Adults making decisions!" Elizabeth yells, wiping her nose. "This is not that, as in two adults making a decision. This is just *you*! This was *your* decision. Don't make it seem like Daddy had anything to do with this. Daddy didn't make this decision. He doesn't think this is what's good for us. And he's our *father*!"

And with that, Elizabeth throws herself back down on the bed and pulls the covers back up over her head. "Get out of my room," she says. "Now."

39

Ellen: Reconsideration

For the past three mornings, whenever Ellen has sat down at her desk to boot up her computer, the tickler system in the firm's calendar has tormented her with a cheery blue pop-up reminder that the Naudain notice of appeal will be due in three, two, and now one, day. Meaning that tomorrow, she could be filing a one-line form with the court saying that Jake is appealing Judge Jones's decision to the Superior Court, which appeal could be handled by different counsel, thus fulfilling Ellen's obligation while simultaneously washing her hands of Jake Naudain forever. She could be doing that, but she won't be. She won't because after her last phone call with Jake, he emailed her saying that, based on her description of his poor chances of winning and the fact that he clearly couldn't afford it, he does not want to pursue an appeal. So that should be that. No more Jake.

But it isn't. Despite Herculean attempts to banish the subject from her mind, the conversation Ellen had with Judge Jones at the dry cleaners keeps creeping back in whenever there is an opening—like when she is sitting in traffic at a red light, or blow-drying her hair, or on hold waiting for opposing counsel to pick up the phone. Instead of only telling Jake about the lengthy, expensive, and unlikely-to-succeed appeal route, which she pretty much knew he wouldn't have the emotional or financial stamina to sustain, she should have told him about reconsideration. Instead of now just standing back and doing nothing, knowing that Jake gave up because he believed there were no further actions he could take, she should be furiously writing a petition asking Judge Jones to reconsider her decision in *Naudain v. Naudain*. She should be doing it right now, because it has to be filed before the appeal period runs out. And the only reason Jake didn't ask her to write and file such a petition is because Ellen did not tell him about it. And this was no minor omission. How often has a judge literally *invited* her to ask for a second pass at an earlier decision? Exactly once—this time, in this case, in which she had the horrible misfortune to represent a man who had sexually assaulted her daughter.

How did she ever get to this place? Ellen asks herself. She, who prides herself on her fierce commitment to her clients and her strict adherence to the *Rules of Professional Conduct*. She, who is morbidly obsessed with disciplinary board opinions and their litany of ethical violations, which never cease to shock and surprise her: the estate lawyer who takes his elderly client's life savings out of the firm's escrow account to pay his gambling debts, the personal injury lawyer who blows the statute of limitations on a wrongful-death claim worth millions because she forgets to calendar the date. Ellen devours these gruesome tales of woe, racing to the end of the opinions where the hammer slams down, and the errant lawyer, by then thoroughly disgraced, is publicly censured, or suspended from practice, or actually disbarred. Is she really a member of this sleazy club? She does not belong in it, she knows for sure, and yet she cannot bring herself to act. The day ticks by, and her fingers neither tap Jake's number nor type a petition for reconsideration.

"What's the matter?" asks Dan, strolling into the kitchen while Ellen is pulling dirty plates out of the sink and slamming them into the dishwasher with such force that Chester, who usually trembles with excitement at the smell of a load of unwashed dishes, is huddled in the corner by his water bowl.

"Oh, nothing," Ellen says, banging the dishwasher shut. "I just had a shitty day. Would you walk Chester? I need to go change. And there's nothing for dinner."

"Okay," says Dan, moving out of Ellen's way as she brushes by him. "But don't we have that leftover chicken with the lemons? And stuff to make a salad?"

"I don't want that chicken again," says Ellen, as she runs up the stairs. "And it's too old. Why didn't you throw it out? And why is it so cold in here? Did you turn the heat down?"

When Dan comes back in the house with Chester, Ellen is sitting at their faux granite kitchen island, contact lenses out, tortoise shell glasses on, shoulder-length gray-brown hair falling around her face as she silently flips through a yoga wear catalogue. She doesn't look up. "Before we figure out dinner," says Dan, putting Chester's leash away in the closet and sitting down in the other chair at the island, "why don't you tell me what's bugging you. Maybe I can help."

Ellen looks up from the catalogue and takes off her glasses. "I doubt it," she says. "I already know what you're going to say."

"Really?" says Dan, turning to face her. "I don't. Because I have no fucking idea what's going on or what you think I'm going to say about whatever it is. Or why you're mad at me about it."

Ellen sighs. "It's Jake Naudain," she says. "The appeal period runs tomorrow."

"Not that asshole again," Dan says. "So, what? You told me you were done with him. I'm sure you told him what he needs to do to appeal, right?"

"Yeah, of course," says Ellen, looking down at a particularly drapey and expensive jacket which is part of a collection titled Apres Yoga Wear. She wants it—in heather gray. She looks up at Dan. "Of course I did. And he's not going to do it, because he doesn't have the money—he still owes me for the trial—and because I told him his chances of winning an appeal are terrible."

"Which all sound like good reasons," says Dan. "So what's the problem?"

"The problem is," Ellen says, sitting up straight, and looking at her husband, "that I saw Judge Jones in the dry-cleaning place down the street the other weekend, and she started talking to me about his case."

"No way," says Dan, shaking his head. "How weird and inappropriate. What'd she say?"

"She said that if I were planning to appeal, she hoped I would file for reconsideration first. And she then gave me this sort of conspiratorial look. She was basically telling me she would change the order, Dan. Without actually saying it, that's what she was communicating."

"Okay, odd and unethical of her, but what does it matter? You're not doing any more work for that child molester, right?"

Ellen turns back to the catalogue and flips another page. Who needs a flowy scarf to wear to yoga? "No," she says. "I can't. I mean I wasn't going to. But Dan, here's the thing. I didn't tell him about what the judge said to me. I didn't even explain about reconsideration being an option. And when I was talking to him and giving him the rundown on filing for an appeal, which was after that conversation with the judge, he actually asked me point-blank, 'Is there anything more we can do?' And you know what I said? I said no." Ellen stands up. "I lied. And I could still file it. I have until five tomorrow. But I don't want to. I am so furious at him. I feel totally used. He lied on the stand like a pro, he lied about Marni, and then when I confronted him about what she told me, he had the nerve to blame it on her. She's a child, and he's old enough to be her father. It's disgusting."

Dan shifts in his seat. "Was anybody else at the dry cleaners when this thing allegedly happened with the judge?"

"No. And 'allegedly'? Really, Dan? It happened. That lady who runs the dry cleaners, I forget her name, she was there. That's it. What difference does it make?"

"It means no one else heard what you thought the judge said to you."

"What do you mean what I *thought*? I know what she said."

"Well, she didn't come right out and say, 'I want to change my custody order in that case of yours,' did she?"

"No, of course not."

"So it's all your interpretation. You could be way off base."

"Dan, this is not a matter of interpretation. It was clear exactly what she meant, both from what she said and how she looked at me when she said it. And aside from all that, even if the judge didn't tip me off that she was having second thoughts, Jake specifically asked me if there was anything else we could do, and I said no! I gave him deliberately false legal advice, which is preventing him from pursuing a strategy that would most likely benefit him. That's totally unethical! I could be disbarred!"

Dan stands up, walks over to Ellen, and stands in front of her. "Sweetheart," he says, smoothing her hair behind her ears, "you are *way* overthinking this. Listen to me. The guy is a scumbag. You went over and above for him. He dug his own grave. He lied to the court and did creepy shit with his daughter. And then you find out he tried to sexually assault our daughter! While you were working your ass off on his behalf, he's preying on our teenage child! Ellen, are you crazy? You don't owe him anything. And you are not going to be disbarred; don't be ridiculous. First, it's not even that big a deal—reconsideration is always a long shot anyway. And second, this whole encounter with the judge is just your interpretation of something no one else will ever know about. Remember that time you were convinced my sister wasn't going to invite us for Thanksgiving because of something you thought she said, or some look she gave you or something, and you got all twisted up about it, and then she invited us? And when I broached the subject with her, she had no idea what you were talking about? Remember that? This could be another one of those things—perceived by Ellen Ackerman only."

"Dan! That's a ridiculous analogy. And don't patronize me. The thing with your sister was a family misunderstanding. This involves my license to practice law! Suppose it was your license on the line?"

Dan kisses Ellen on the forehead, walks over to the refrigerator, and takes out the leftover chicken. "Calm down, and cut the drama. Here's the summary: You might have imagined this. Even if you didn't, you have no idea if what you think you heard and saw would even help your client. No one else heard or saw it. Your client has no expectation that you will continue to represent him given that he tried to fuck our teenage daughter—"

"Dan!"

"And there are hundreds, if not thousands, of other family lawyers in Philadelphia he could have consulted with to discuss his posttrial options. And you told him the deadline for filing an appeal, and he told you he did not wish to appeal, which you undoubtedly documented in his file. You're done. You have no further obligation to him. Don't overthink this. You owe that piece of shit nothing."

"Do not tell me what to do!" Ellen yells. "And do not patronize me! Just because all your clients are criminals, and the public defender's office is run by a bunch of yahoos, and this might seem like a minor thing to you in the context of that zoo where you work, it's not minor to me. This is my career we're talking about! And my ability to earn a living. I *knew* I wouldn't get any support from you."

Before Dan can reply, Ellen snatches the yoga-wear catalogue off the counter, turns around, and runs up the stairs.

"Do you want any dinner?" he calls after her.

"No!" Ellen shouts from the second floor. "I'm not hungry."

Whereupon Dan turns his attention to the leftover chicken, as the sound of their bedroom door slamming shut reverberates through the house.

CHORUS #6

The Boys in the Band

Hey, Earl. Good to see you, man. Lee's here already; we're just waiting on Jake. Earl follows Petie downstairs to the basement, where Lee is already plugged in, practicing that complicated line from "Papa's Got a Brand New Bag."

How's he doing? asks Earl.

Not good, says Petie, *as he gets three beers out of the basement fridge and passes them around. Craft IPA, guys. Local. Made by some new brewery in Fishtown.*

Damn, says Earl. *Forgot my six of Bud again. You guys still trying to turn me into a hipster, but it ain't working. Anyway, is Jake's ex still keeping his kids away from him?*

Yup, says Petie. *And he decided not to appeal what that crazy judge did, because he doesn't have the money. He said he owes his lawyer big-time already.*

Lee stops playing and looks up. From what I've heard, that whole system is rigged against men. And he got stuck with a woman judge, too. You know she sided with Lisa when she heard about Jakie carrying on with what's-her-name. They stick together. Like a tribe.

Petie and Earl nod as they sip their beers. And the thing is, Petie *says, it's fucking up the kids. His older girl, the one who's in Dylan's class, is acting out, according to my son. Who may not be the most accurate relayer of information, but then again, he usually doesn't tell us about anything that happens at school, so the fact that he mentioned Elizabeth Naudain getting in trouble means it must be pretty bad.*

What'd she do? asks Lee.

He said she was bullying other girls, says Petie, like posting mean shit about them and trying to turn other girls against them.

Sounds like she's taking after her mother, says Earl. As in turning that judge against Jake. Am I right? There are nods and more swigs of craft IPA.

You might have a point, says Petie. Anyway, it was a big thing in their class, and the school counselor is doing all this anti-bullying stuff with the kids, and they scheduled a parents meeting specifically on the topic of kids bullying other kids through social media. They're not saying why, of course, but according to Dylan, it's all because of shit Elizabeth Naudain did.

Poor Jakie, says Lee. Those girls just need their dad. I don't understand why that isn't obvious to Lisa. Maybe she'll come to her senses at some point. Hopefully, before Elizabeth starts doing drugs and having sex with random guys.

Lee, says Petie, she's in seventh grade.

Right, Lee says. Remember, I teach middle school.

Before anyone can respond with the predictable "things are different from when we were coming up" remark, the chime of the doorbell intervenes. That must be Jake, says Petie, starting up the stairs. Everyone go easy on him during practice, okay? If he fucks up that solo in "Badge," just let it go.

40

Jake: Parents

I see the Mariposa number come up on my phone, and it makes my heart stop, just a little, like it always does. It's Evelyn from the front office, who prefaces the call with the obligatory, "This is not an emergency; the girls are fine" but then says Lisa and I need to come in to meet with the head of school as soon as possible, preferably today. Of course I ask why, and she says it involves Elizabeth and an incident with another child in the class, and William—that's the head—will explain the details. She says she has a call in to Lisa and will get back to me to firm up a meeting time.

In what seems like another life I lived, light years ago, I would have immediately called Lisa, and we would have worried together, speculated together, about what it could be. We would have compared notes about our beautiful, smart, kind daughter—what could she possibly have done?—and we would have strategized about how to handle our meeting with William. We were each other's sounding board, co-conspirators, and allies. And it had felt good, when bad things happened, to have that. And now, not only don't I have that, I have the opposite. I can't trust Lisa at all; in fact, now I have to assume anything I say to her can be used against me. It makes me think of the Miranda warnings from every cop show you've ever seen: "Anything you say can and will be used against you in a court of law." Lisa is that court of law, to me, now.

So I worry, alone in my office, staring at the rain spitting down outside my window, about what happened to Elizabeth, or way more likely, given Evelyn's vibe on the phone, what Elizabeth did wrong. I feel weirdly out of touch with her, and especially out of touch with what's going on at Mariposa, since I hardly ever see her during the week anymore. I'm like a grandparent or a babysitter; that's how much time I spend with her.

Lisa is waiting in the hallway outside William's office when I get there. She's cut her hair shorter since the trial, shoulder-length and more groomed somehow, more sleek, not that luxurious mass of blonde that I used to tangle myself up in. But she still looks great. It's unbelievable how I can be so angry at her—so ragingly, scorchingly angry—and still, at some basic, primal level, want to fuck her. I can't help it; I'm still attracted to her, reminding me that I am, clearly, very shallow. In any event, that's not going to happen ever again, so I can just deep-six that thought, along with all the other "inappropriate" thoughts, which apparently make me a bad parent and for which I could get crucified in court.

I ask her if she knows what happened, and she says no, and then William opens his door. "Hi, Lisa. Hi, Jake. Thanks for coming in on such short notice. Come on in, and have a seat." He's smiling like we're there for tea or something.

Lisa and I go in and sit down in two shabby wingback chairs that look like old money, with that kind of slightly moth-eaten quality that certain furniture has—furniture, for example, that is stored over the winter in a big old barn in Maine, waiting to be taken out and dusted off when the summer compound on the Penobscot comes to life.

So it turns out, according to the extremely well-mannered

William, that Elizabeth has been doing some really mean stuff to another girl, Amy Decker, who is apparently sort of quiet and not very popular. She has trouble fitting in well with the other girls in the class, is the way William describes it. But recently, Amy had started to come out of her shell, and she was beginning to be included by the group that Elizabeth hangs with, Anya and Billie, her crew since around second grade. And that's when it started. William tells us that Teacher Caroline got a call from Amy's mother saying that Amy was very upset and had finally showed her a series of text messages from Elizabeth. They said we thought u would like this or some variation on that, which contained links to all kinds of insulting or inappropriate sites, like a store that specializes in clothing for "larger" girls, a blog post about how to talk to your friend who has body odor, and the one that really appalled me, a site with step-by-step instructions on how to give a blow job. And in conjunction with these text messages, Elizabeth has been leading the charge among her crew to not include Amy in anything they do together, like a skit they're working on for the school talent show. They said there was no room for her, and then they asked another girl to be in it with them. Stuff like that. Why Amy's mother called the teacher instead of Lisa or me, I have no idea, but I guess she wanted the school to deal with it.

William says he wanted to talk to us first about it and then bring Elizabeth into the meeting. Of course Lisa and I are both horrified and I, at least, am really surprised. I have never thought of Elizabeth as one of those mean girls. She has always been so nice to younger children and pets and old people—I find it hard to believe that she is capable of this. I ask William if another girl could be the orchestrator, if there might be a behind-the-scenes ringleader and Elizabeth just got caught up in some other girl's scheme, a girl who really is mean. But he says no, as far as they can tell from talking to Elizabeth and the other girls involved, Elizabeth was the instigator. She is the ringleader.

"Elizabeth knows I'm talking to you," William tells us, "and I told her after the three of us had a chance to meet, I would ask Teacher Caroline and her to join us so we can discuss it together."

Lisa asks William if Elizabeth will be suspended, and he says they hope not, not if we can come up with a plan for her to rectify the situation and if she adheres to it.

Elizabeth comes in with Teacher Caroline. She has clearly been crying, and her red-nosed, teary-eyed face, so familiar, so childlike, breaks my heart. Not because I am upset about the bullying, which I am, but the really devastating part of this for me is that my child is out there in the world, fucking things up, without her father really being there for her.

"Hi, Daddy," she says, as she sits down on William's sofa, another item that looks like it summered in Maine, on the side next to my chair. She doesn't even look at Lisa.

"Elizabeth," says William, "as Teacher Caroline told you, we asked your parents to come in so we could talk together about these incidents involving your classmate. I've explained to them what we know about the situation from talking to you and Amy and the other girls involved. I also explained to them that you've told Teacher Caroline that you are very sorry for what you did. Which I was glad to hear, because we've known each other a long time, haven't we, Elizabeth?" Elizabeth nods, looks up at William, and starts to cry. "And I don't think this behavior is representative of who you really are. The Elizabeth I've gotten so fond of over the years is a kind person, a person who would never intentionally hurt another child's feelings."

Elizabeth is now quietly sobbing. Really, this might be laying it on a little thick. Is all this guilt-inducing hand-wringing really necessary? If she were in public school, this meeting would never have happened. She would have just been punished. When I was in seventh grade, if I had done this, Mr. Hunneke would have stuck me in after-school detention and made me write on the board "I will not be a bully," like, a thousand times, and I would have had to clean the blackboard and sweep the classroom, or something like that. One thing I'm sure of: they never would have asked for input from my parents about what punishment to impose. And my parents would never have thought to question what the school did, so long as they weren't beating me. I know Lisa and I pay a lot of money for all this modern sensitivity, and probably in the long run it's good for Elizabeth to have to participate in this excruciating meeting. But sometimes I find myself seriously nostalgic for that time before adults cared so much about what children thought or felt and just told them what to do. Good thing Judge Jones doesn't have a portal into my brain, or she'd probably reduce me to supervised visits at the courthouse.

William drones on a bit more and then asks Elizabeth if there is anything she would like to say. Eight adult eyes focus on her. She looks at me and snuffles. Then she turns toward William and starts to talk.

"I'm really sorry about what I did to Amy. I don't really know what happened, but I won't do it again. It's just that I've been going through a hard time since my parents got divorced, and it got really bad recently when me and my sister had to go to court, and my mom made the judge change the schedule so we hardly ever see our dad."

Lisa's face is red, and she looks like she might cry too. Which is good—she needs to hear what she's doing to our kids.

"So it's just, like, I've been really upset, and I have trouble concentrating and stuff. I'm really sorry." Elizabeth starts to cry again.

Teacher Caroline, who is sitting next to her on the couch, puts her arm around Elizabeth's shoulders. Elizabeth, with her characteristic flair for the dramatic, jumps up and throws herself into my arms, sobbing. I stroke her hair. William and Teacher Caroline look at me approvingly. *Lisa must be so pissed,* I think, *but what can she say?* Nothing. Not here. After a few seconds, Elizabeth stops crying, and I tell her to go sit back on the shabby rich-person couch so we can finish the meeting. Teacher Caroline asks Elizabeth what she thinks she could do to make Amy feel better. A discussion ensues, the result of which is an agreement that Teacher Caroline will facilitate a meeting between Elizabeth and Amy, where Elizabeth will apologize to her in person. Also, Elizabeth will write Amy a letter, as in the kind on paper, which she will give to her at the meeting. And Elizabeth promises that she will tell her friends that it was wrong to exclude Amy, and they will make an effort to include her. I have my doubts about whether that part will happen, but the in-person and written apology seems fine. Although frankly, throughout this whole thing, my mind is fixated on the fact that Elizabeth is looking at websites about giving blow jobs, rather than the mean-girl stuff. I don't know how I'm going to deal with this next phase.

41

Lisa: It's Not My Fault

Jake is silent as we walk out to the Mariposa parking lot. I'm parked closer to the school. He walks with me and stops next to my car, hands in pockets, while I fish the keys out of my bag.

"So," he says.

"So," I reply, turning to look at him. His eyebrows are slightly raised, and he's looking at me expectantly, tilting his head to one side, silently inviting me to talk. It's an expression I know so well that I am simultaneously comforted by the "we're in this together" feeling and infuriated by the implicit ask, once again, that I come up with a way to solve the problem. "That poor girl Amy," I say, looking for neutral territory. "But I don't understand why her mother didn't call us before contacting the school. Don't you think that's kind of weird?"

"Yeah," Jake says. "It is. But maybe she heard about the custody trial and all that and didn't want to talk to us because she was afraid she would get, like, subpoenaed to come to court or something. Like maybe she didn't want to get caught up in the middle of our issues."

I am not going to rise to this bait. "I guess that could be it," I say. "The Mariposa gossip mill. But seems like such a far-fetched thing to be concerned about."

Jake's eyebrows go up again, but this time he isn't giving me the "we're in this together" look. "Being concerned about your lawyer subpoenaing her to testify against me? That's hardly a far-fetched thing. It already happened. It could happen again. Apparently everyone is fair game."

Here we go. I take a breath. "That's ridiculous, Jake. You can't compare my lawyer subpoenaing Samara, who knew whether Charlie was in bed with you and whether you were having sex while she was—God, I still can't believe I'm even having to say those words—with Amy's mom. The trial wasn't about Elizabeth's behavior at all, and you know that."

"Well, it could have been," Jake says. "I can totally see your dick of a lawyer finding out about something like this and deciding that he's going to try to show that judge that I traumatized Elizabeth too, and now she's bullying other kids as a direct result and needs to be taken away from me. I can totally see that happening. But yeah, of course, it would be ridiculous, because it's the exact *opposite* of what's going on. You heard her in there. She's suffering because you got her taken away from *me*. That's what's stressing her out and making her act out. It's like a cry for attention, Lisa. You saw the way she practically jumped into my lap, like a baby. She's the one who's traumatized. The girls need me, and you know it. And you should be ashamed of yourself."

Deflect, deny, refuse to accept responsibility—typical Jake. And all the more infuriating because I know, in my heart, that while I'm definitely not ashamed of myself, he is right about the new schedule stressing Elizabeth, and Charlie too, because they are super attached to him, and they really do miss him. But I didn't have a choice. When your seven-year-old daughter comes home and tells you she was in bed with her father and her father's girlfriend, and the adults had no clothes on and then tells you she had "scary dreams" where her father and the naked girlfriend were rolling around in the bed and making noises—when your seven-year-old tells you that, just what exactly are you supposed to do? Just hope it isn't true? Guess it will never happen again? How could I live with myself if I stood by passively and it did happen again, and it was something worse, like if Charlie was expected to participate in some way? So yes, I hired that "dick of a lawyer," and I paid him a ridiculous amount of money I didn't have and which I'm still paying back, because Tilly's sister had used him in her divorce and told me he was a litigator, not a negotiator. She told me he took no prisoners in court, and that's what I needed. I was done playing nice, because look where it got my girls. I needed to stand up and give it my best shot, and I'd do the same thing again.

"I'm not ashamed of anything, Jake," I say. "I did what I had to do to protect my children. Our children, actually, because you seemed to have completely fallen down on the job."

Jake starts pacing back and forth in front of my car. The tip of my nose feels like an icicle. I do not want to have this conversation, inevitable as it may be, standing outside in the freezing cold in the Mariposa parking lot. But apparently, Jake does.

He stops pacing and looks at me. "That's bullshit, and you know it, Lisa. Our children were never in any danger. This entire fucked-up situation is your fault. You're the one who put us all through this. And you know what really kills me? Still, more than a year later, I have no fucking idea why. I've racked my brain. What made you wake up one day and decide to hurt us this way? Because I brought the girls to band practice? Really? Because I haven't memorized the details of their schedules six months in advance? Because I'm not like your doctor buddies, because I don't care that much about money and status? That's the kind of shit that people go to counselling for, Lisa—they don't just throw away a marriage. Our family was everything to me, and you destroyed it."

Jake's cluelessness continues to blow my mind. "You are so

incredibly wrong," I say. "I tried so hard to make it work. Would it have made our lives easier if you were more organized? If you'd been more serious about supporting our family so I wasn't carrying most of that weight? Yes, of course it would have. But it wasn't those things, and you know that. It was the lying."

"Don't tell me we're going to talk about my guitar purchases again," said Jake.

"Guitars? Jake, no. Are you kidding? I can't believe you would even say that. I'm talking about the big lies. The stuff you never even really apologized for, which always made me think you couldn't see how completely terrible it was. I'm talking Steve's bachelor party in Vegas, and the shit show that followed."

Jake rolls his eyes. "Lisa, this is old territory. Just like the guitar. I apologized a million times."

This is blatantly untrue, and I still can't believe he's managed to completely rewrite our personal history to justify his narrative of being the poor wounded spouse. I simultaneously recognize there's no point to talking about this, again, all these years later, when we're already divorced, and refuse to give him the satisfaction of letting it go.

"No, you didn't, Jake. That is such a lie. Maybe you've selectively chosen not to remember what actually happened. But I haven't. I remember it all. I remember when I asked you how we were possibly going to pay for you to go to Vegas for a four-day bachelor party, and you got really indignant and told me you had to do this for Steve because he was your oldest friend, and I didn't need to worry about the money because all the other guys worked in Silicon Valley and made bank and were going to pitch in and cover your expenses when you were there, and all you had to do was pay for the ticket. And I *believed* you, Jake. I believed you, despite all the stuff that happened before. I wanted to believe you because you were my husband. And you had promised you'd never to lie to me again about money. Or anything else."

Jake is glaring at me. But I can't stop. "So think what a fool I felt like when it all came out later how you made up that whole story. Remember, Jake? Remember how not only did you have to pay for yourself, but you decided to impress those guys by picking up the tab for an entire evening at that ridiculously pricey restaurant with tickets to that show and all those drinks? Drinks all night? In Vegas? That was *thousands*, Jake. Remember? And why? Because you wanted them to think you were a big shot when we were still basically living on my paycheck. And you hid that from me for *months*. And remember how I finally found out? I *know* you haven't forgotten that. Remember when I asked you about the college funds your parents set up? And how you acted all weird about it and kept putting me off, so finally I asked your mom directly and found out they had set one up for Elizabeth which had $15,000 in it? And you were the custodian, so you were the only one who got the statements? And then when I asked you about that, you acted like you couldn't remember, and then you changed your story and said you got the statements electronically but never looked at them so you didn't remember your password, and then you miraculously remembered the password after I kept bugging you about it? And then I looked at the account, Jake, remember? And found out that you'd made all those withdrawals right after the Vegas trip, that you literally stole ten grand of our daughter's money! That *your* parents had given to *her*. That you were supposed to be the *custodian* of! And remember what you told me when I found out?"

I finally pause to catch my breath.

"Lisa, I've heard all this before," Jake says in the exasperated tone of someone talking to an annoying child. "And it's really cold out here. What exactly does this have to do with Elizabeth being mean to that girl?"

He really is a master of deflection. "I'm responding to your question to me two minutes ago," I say. "Your question! You're the one who just said you had quote, 'no fucking idea why,' unquote, I wanted out of our marriage. And in case you don't, I remember exactly what you said when you were busted. You said it was no big deal, and you just needed a little extra cash, so you took it from there and were going to pay it back as soon as you got a raise. Or a bonus. Or some bullshit like that. And then you basically blamed me! You said you hadn't told me about it because you knew I would worry, since we have different attitudes about money, and really there was no reason to, because you were going to pay it right back. So to protect me from myself, you decided it was best not to say anything about it. 'Pay it back'! What kind of father raids his kid's college account! And I felt so incredibly betrayed. I had tried so hard to convince myself that all the stuff that happened when Charlie was a baby was just because you were under so much money pressure, and I really wanted to believe that was in the past. But it wasn't. That was the final blow. It just hit home to me that you were going to keep doing whatever you felt like in the moment, no matter what the long-term consequences were, no matter how your actions affected me or the girls. And for you to now act like I just got out of bed one morning and randomly decided I wanted a divorce is so untrue. And so insulting. How can you forget all of this stuff?"

Jake opens his mouth to say something, but his phone rings. "It's the school," he says. "Hold on. Unless maybe you're done?" He gives me the eyebrow-up, head-tilted look again. God, he is infuriating. He puts the phone to his ear. "Casey, hi. No, actually Lisa and I are both still here, in the parking lot. What's up? Is Elizabeth okay? Charlie? What do you mean you can't find her?"

The fight with Jake instantly evaporates into the gray afternoon light. "What is it?" I say, suppressing an impulse to grab the phone out of his hand. "What's Casey saying?"

Jake is quiet, listening, ignoring me. Then he starts to talk to Casey. "Okay. Maybe she knew we were here for the meeting with William, and she's looking for us. Like, maybe she tried to find our car in the parking lot?"

"Jake!" Now my voice comes out really loud. "What's going on? Where's Charlie?"

He turns toward me and says, "They don't know. She wasn't in the playground when they were rounding the kids up at the end of recess."

"What do you mean, she wasn't in the playground?" I say, panic rising. "Where did she go? Do you mean the recess teacher *lost* her? Jake, let me talk to Casey."

Jake turns back to his phone. "Casey, go ahead and do the building lockdown in case she's hiding somewhere. Lisa and I will search the parking lot and the playground. I'm sure she'll turn up soon."

I don't wait for Jake to finish the call. I start running up and down the aisles of parked cars, calling Charlie's name, looking for her purple jacket, her curly little head. Maybe she crossed the street from the playground because she saw us in the parking lot, maybe she got close and heard us fighting, maybe she hid because she thought she wasn't supposed to hear us, or maybe she's still hiding so we won't find out what she did. *Please let that be it,* I think, *let her be behind that black Jeep, let her be crouched down beside that red Mazda. Let her be hesitant to answer me because she thinks I'll be mad that she was spying on us; let her be hiding in plain sight.* And when I do find her, that flood of relief will be so sweet, and it will all be over, and we can hug and talk about never leaving Mariposa without an adult.

I get to the end of the row and start down another one. I

scan the rest of the lot. I don't see her. I'm shivering. It's getting colder. Does she have her mittens? Jake is walking really fast toward the playground. But I can see from here it's empty. No one is on the swings or the climbing structure, no one is kicking a ball or drawing with chalk. Just some little kid's left-behind jacket, discarded on a bench next to a crumpled up Dunkin' Donuts bag, under the quickly darkening sky.

42

Charlie: Lost

After-school always starts with recess, which Teacher Casey calls free play, even though during the school day it's called recess. But it's the same thing. Lately, Charlie has been playing hand-clapping games with Leah, which are really hard to learn at first. But once you get them, it's like your hands just do what they are supposed to without having to think, and you can go really fast, so fast that your fingers are blurry. She and Leah know they're the best girls in their class at Miss Mary Mack, and now they've learned Down Baby and Slide, which they've been practicing at free play. But today, Leah didn't stay for after-school, so Charlie has no one to clap with, and she doesn't feel like playing with Mae or Bridgette or any of the boys.

As they all go out the door into the playground, an older boy in a puffy blue jacket pushes past her and then turns around and says, "Hey, Charlie, your sister's in big trouble. I just saw her going into William's office with Teacher Caroline, and she was crying. She's probably gonna get suspended!" Charlie doesn't have time to say anything before the boy turns back around and runs across the playground to the basketball court.

Charlie is confused. What kind of trouble? Suspended? Would Elizabeth have to leave Mariposa? There is so much happening to everyone in her family, and no one tells her anything.

Like, she thinks her mom might have a boyfriend. She picked up her mom's phone when she heard a text buzz, because she thought maybe it was her dad, since he and her mom always text now instead of talking on the phone. She wanted to see what they were texting about because she misses her dad, and she doesn't understand why she isn't allowed to live at both houses anymore, and no one will explain it to her. But when she picked up the phone, it wasn't from Dad, because it didn't say Jake, it said A, and the text said, Hey sexy see you Saturday xxoo. And then her mom ran over and grabbed the phone away from her and was really mad at Charlie, so Charlie didn't even ask who A was. But she has a bad feeling. Maybe A is her mom's secret boyfriend, and maybe Mom is going to marry him, and then she and Elizabeth will have to live with him instead of their dad, which would be awful and terrible and so unfair.

And when they do get to see Dad, he tells them he's sad because he only gets to see them for the weekend, and then they have to go back to Mom's. And also, Dad told them Samara isn't his girlfriend anymore, and that probably makes him sad too. Charlie could tell he really liked Samara, by the way he laughed when she was at his house with them, and also, he used to hug her a lot.

Maybe she can at least find out what Elizabeth did. Charlie runs across the playground to the basketball court where the boy with the puffy blue jacket is standing with his friend, who is holding the ball. She doesn't know his name, so at first she just stands there, hoping he will say something to her. But he doesn't, which is really embarrassing. Finally, she says, "Why's my sister in trouble? What'd she do?"

The boy turns toward her. "You don't know?" he says. "She was bullying this girl Amy. I think she, like, tried to get her to kill herself or something."

"Shit," says his friend, looking at Charlie. "Your big sister did *that*?"

He turns back toward the basket and shoots the ball, which misses the hoop. The boy in the puffy blue jacket catches it, and they start laughing. Charlie's face feels hot, and she starts to cry. The boys act like she isn't even there. Elizabeth? How could she do that? Charlie walks over to the bench at the side of the playground farthest away from the school, where no kids are. She sits down. This is the worst thing, worse than her parents. Will Elizabeth go to jail? Charlie can't stop crying. It's cold, and she can't find her mittens. She puts up her hood. She hears Teacher Casey, from across the playground, calling everyone to come back because it's time to go inside. She doesn't want to go inside, because everyone will know her sister is going to have to leave Mariposa and maybe go to jail.

The kids are all running back to the school door. No one is looking at her. Charlie stands up, turns away from the school, and walks out of the playground. She walks to the corner by the pizza shop where Elizabeth and her friends sometimes go after school, waits for the light to turn green like she is supposed to, crosses the street, and keeps walking.

43

Jake: Our Baby

It's obvious that she's not in the playground, because I can see all of it from the parking lot, but I run over there anyway, doing useless things like walking around the trash cans and looking behind benches. Lisa's checking the parking lot, but I know she's not going to find her there, either, because we were standing in the middle of it arguing that whole time. We would have seen Charlie if she crossed the street from the playground to come into the lot. What a fucking disaster—first Elizabeth and now Charlie. I can see Lisa finishing up her reconnaissance of the parking lot and turning to walk really fast toward me in the playground.

"Nothing," I say, shaking my head as she approaches.

Lisa is breathing hard and has that locked-down look of resolve I recognize from times of pain or danger. It's like she needs to conserve energy. Initially, she registers shock, like when we had that car accident when Elizabeth lost consciousness for a few minutes, or when we thought Lisa's dad was having a heart attack at Thanksgiving. But then, instead of flailing around like some people do in those situations, she gets quiet and steely. I remember being blown away by her focus and concentration when she was in labor with Elizabeth, which went on forever. I knew she must have been in excruciating pain—she definitely said so afterward—but it was like she turned everything inward and just did what had to be done. There are still plenty of things I admire about my ex-wife, and this is one of them. In a crisis, she's awesome. Plus, she can't blame this one on me.

Without saying anything, we both turn and head toward the Mariposa entrance, which is locked because they're all inside, presumably trying to locate Charlie. Someone buzzes us in, and the first person we see in the lobby is Casey, who runs the after-school program and who is apparently the person responsible for losing our child. Lisa approaches her first, and I can tell Casey is terrified, but locked-down Lisa is wasting no time berating her; she is just focused on getting information.

Casey is describing all the places they looked in the building. Lisa cuts her off, saying she just wants to know where they haven't looked yet, because she and I will go there. Casey says they've covered it all, and I hear Lisa say, "Jake and I are going to look again." Lisa dispatches me to the third floor to recheck the art room, because she knows it has storage closets and a separate pottery space, and it's Charlie's favorite place, while she goes down to the basement where the after-school program is located.

I can tell, as we part at the stairwell and go in different directions, that we're both thinking the same thing: that Charlie would have already turned up if she was in the building. And if we can't find her in the next few minutes, we need to go outside and start combing the neighborhood. Because if she's not in the building, the playground, or the parking lot, that's where she is. And it's January, and it's freezing, and it's already getting dark.

As this last scenario is fast emerging as the one to focus on, I am frantically trying to push away thoughts of her being kidnapped by some guy in a van, or some pedophile with a puppy or candy luring her into an alley and raping her. It is unthinkable, but I can't control the images. I open every door on the third floor, calling for Charlie. As I rush through the art room, I see last year's first-grade self-portraits hanging on the far wall. Looking out at me is the smiling face of my daughter, instantly recognizable by virtue of the fact that the entire background of the portrait is painted in different shades of purple. Next to her in the portrait, painted with considerable accuracy for a seven-year-old, is a dog who looks remarkably like Pinky, except he's lavender.

I run down the stairs and practically collide with Lisa coming up from the basement. Lisa tells me Billie's mom picked Elizabeth up and took her to their house. I realize I had completely forgotten about all the stuff with Elizabeth, about the whole reason we were at Mariposa this afternoon. Fortunately, Lisa did not.

Casey and William are in the lobby, organizing a search party to go outside.

"You have our cells," Lisa says to them. "Jake and I are going out now."

We go back to the playground's exit to the sidewalk, where Charlie must have walked out. We talk quickly about places she knows in the neighborhood and might have thought to go to: the pizza shop on the corner, the library four blocks away, the little hippie boutique that had that sort of Indian jewelry and lotions and stuff that Elizabeth and her friends like.

The streetlights have all come on, and rush hour traffic is starting to clog the intersections. We divide the territory and set out into the evening in opposite directions, cell phones clutched in hands, searching for our baby.

44

Charlie: It's My Fault

Sometimes when her parents can't pick her up from after-school, Charlie's mom's friend Tilly does. Tilly lives really close to Mariposa, so she can walk there and pick up Charlie, and they just walk back to her house. Sometimes they go to the library first, because Charlie likes taking books out. Tilly lets her take out as many as she wants, because Tilly's house is right across the street from the library, so it's easy for her to return them. And there is this handle near the library door that you can pull, and it opens. You put the books in the slot, then you close it, and you hear the books fall down into the library, so you don't even have to go inside if you don't want to or if the library is closed.

Charlie likes going to Tilly's house. It always smells good there, and Tilly has lots of plants and a really cute, fat yellow cat and good snacks, like English muffins with lots of butter, which are delicious. She sits with Charlie in the kitchen and asks Charlie about her day, and they just talk—"girl talk," Tilly calls it. Charlie is sure Tilly will know what Elizabeth did and what will happen to her, and Tilly will also know if her mom has a boyfriend and if she is going to marry him.

So this time, she'll walk to Tilly's herself, and her parents can pick her up there, like they do whenever Tilly gets her from school. Actually, it will be her mom, because now her mom picks her up almost every day. She'll talk to Tilly about that too, because maybe Tilly can tell her mom that she and Elizabeth need to go to their dad's house more, like they used to.

Charlie keeps walking to the next corner. There's a really big street with lots of cars on it going in both directions. To cross it, you have to wait for the green light; go across one street; stand in the middle on, like, a platform; wait for another green light; and then cross to the sidewalk. Tilly always holds her hand when they cross. Charlie feels a little scared, but there are lots of grown-ups waiting to cross, so she follows them to the platform and then follows them to the other side. She keeps walking. She knows to look for the library, but now she is next to a big supermarket, which she doesn't remember, and she doesn't see the library. Everyone is rushing around her.

Everything is starting to look the same—buildings, cars, grown-ups walking fast, talking on their phones. Charlie gets to the next corner and isn't sure if she should keep walking in that direction or go back, or turn on another street. She stands at the curb, shifting from one foot to another, not wanting to cross but not knowing where to go next. An older woman with long gray dreads, who is carrying a big shopping bag, comes up behind Charlie and stands next her. At first she thinks it's Teacher Mona who runs story hour at Mariposa. But when Charlie looks up at her face, she realized it isn't Teacher Mona, and Charlie actually doesn't know her at all. She is just another stranger.

The woman looks down at Charlie and asks, "Honey, are you okay?"

Charlie nods and tells the woman that she is supposed to meet her mom at the library but isn't sure where the library is. Then she starts to cry.

The woman says, "Don't cry, honey. I'm walking that way, so you can come with me. We can cross now."

Charlie follows her across the street, and the woman waits for her. "Do you want to hold my hand?" she asks.

Charlie shakes her head no, because she is not a baby, and she doesn't know the woman, and it would be embarrassing to be holding her hand.

"Okay," the woman says, "but come with me. I'm sure your mama will be there waiting for you. Do you want a tissue?"

Charlie shakes her head again but walks next to the woman, and then all of a sudden they are standing in front of the big red door into the library. Charlie runs into the building, not even saying goodbye. She is afraid the woman will come in behind her and see that her mom isn't there, and then she'll be in trouble, and maybe the woman will call the police. Charlie stops by the desk where the person sits who lets you into the room where all the books are. She waits a minute, drying her tears with her jacket sleeve.

A man comes out of the room where the books are and sits down at the desk. "Can I help you?" he asks. "Are you waiting for someone?" Charlie says no and then quickly walks back outside so she doesn't have to answer any more questions. She looks across the street. It is kind of dark, but she thinks she can see Tilly's house, except not really. There are three houses in a row next to each other that all look the same. One must be Tilly's, but she doesn't know which one.

As she's thinking about how to cross the street, Charlie hears the high-pitched wail of sirens in the distance, which are quickly getting louder and louder. Cars with flashing red-and-blue lights come roaring up toward her and screech to a halt right across the street from where she is standing. Two police officers get out of one of the cars. Charlie starts to shake. How did they find out where she went? Where are they going to take her? Is it because of what Elizabeth did and because she's Elizabeth's sister? She's afraid to run back into the library because she might see the man who asked if he could help her, and then he will know she's lost and lied to him.

The police officers are quickly walking across the street, right toward her. They have guns and handcuffs attached to their belts, just like on TV. They're talking to each other but looking right at her. The officers step up on the curb in front of her. Charlie is frozen in place, silent. Tears run down her cheeks. But the officers act like they don't even see her; they brush right by her and head toward the entrance to the library. Charlie turns around and sees the man from inside come out of the big red door to meet them.

"Which way'd he go?" she hears one of the policemen ask. "Was the other guy hurt?"

The man from the library starts talking to them. Charlie realizes that the police officers are looking for someone who did something bad in the library. But maybe when they turn back around, they'll see her. Maybe they're looking for her too, just not as much as the bad man in the library, and they'll come to her next. She has to get to Tilly's house.

Charlie knows you're not supposed to cross a street in the middle of the block, but her dad does it all the time. There are no cars coming from either direction, so she runs across the street and goes around the back of the two parked police cars to the sidewalk. Their lights are still flashing, red to blue, back and forth, so bright. She walks up the steps to the door of the middle house, and a dog barks really loudly. It sounds like he is right on the other side of the door, and it sounds like he would bite her if he could get out. Tilly doesn't have a dog, so Charlie goes down those stairs and up the stairs to the next door. There is a door-bell on the side, and she rings it. She hears the sound of footsteps coming toward the door and Tilly's voice calling out, "Who is it?"

"It's me," she says, tears still streaming. "Charlie."

The door opens, and Tilly is standing there. "Charlie!" she says. "What are you doing here? Come in, come in—you just surprised me. Is your mom or dad outside in the car? Or did you get a ride here in one of those police cars?"

Charlie shakes her head and wipes at her eyes.

"Aww, sweetie, I was just joking about the police car. What's the matter?" Tilly asks, crouching down so she is eye level with Charlie and giving her a big hug. Charlie starts to sob.

Tilly gives Charlie a tissue to blow her nose, takes her coat off, and reassures her that the police are not looking for her. She calls Charlie's mom and dad, and sets her up at the kitchen table with a cup of cocoa, then sits down across from her and asks why she came there. Charlie tells her about Elizabeth and how she might be suspended or go to jail; how she thinks her mom may have a boyfriend and might get married to him; how she's not seeing her dad anymore; and how she had to go to court and talk to the judge, and it was scary, and then later, the judge took her and Elizabeth away from their dad. And she tells Tilly how all of it is her fault.

"Charlie," says Tilly, leaning forward across the table, "why do you think it's your fault?"

"Because," Charlie says, "when I talked to the judge, I told her I would tell the truth. And then she asked me about Samara sleeping at Dad's house when Elizabeth and I were there and if I ever slept in bed with them. And I said I couldn't remember."

"And?" Tilly says.

"And that wasn't really true, because I did sort of remember. I sort of remembered Daddy carrying me into his room one night when Samara was sleeping in his bed, and she was talking to me, and I was lying in between them. And I had dreams about kittens. And later, like a few days later, I remembered more of it. But I didn't tell that to the judge. I just said I couldn't remember."

"Why?" Tilly asks.

"Because I knew Mommy was mad at Daddy about it. Because after it happened, Mommy asked me if Samara was still sleeping over at Daddy's, and I said yes and that I didn't care if she was. And Mommy asked me, 'Well, what about if you wake up at night and want Daddy?' and I told her that had already happened when Samara was there, and I just got into the bed with both of them. And Mommy got really mad and told me that was wrong, and Daddy was bad to do that. And I asked her why, because when she and Daddy weren't divorced, I used to get in bed with them all the time."

Charlie starts to sob again. "And she said it's not the same thing, and Samara's not your family, and your dad should never put you in that position, and I'm going to make sure he doesn't do it again. So then we had to go to court, and I didn't tell the judge what I remembered about it because I didn't want Daddy to get in trouble. But the judge said I had to tell the truth, and I told the judge I was telling the truth, but it wasn't really the truth, and she must have found that out, and that's why she took us away from our dad. But if I had told her what I remembered, maybe she would have agreed with my mom that Dad was bad and taken us away anyway, so that's why I didn't know what to do. But maybe if I had explained it to her, she would have known it wasn't bad, and she wouldn't have taken us away. And then Elizabeth wouldn't have told that girl she was going to kill her, and Mommy wouldn't be getting married to someone else."

"Charlie," Tilly says reaching her hands across the table, "come give me a hug." Charlie gets up, and Tilly pulls her onto her lap and rocks her like a baby. Tears are running down Charlie's face. "Charlie," she says, "first of all, Elizabeth is not going to jail, and your mom is not about to get married to someone else. And second of all, and listen to me, Charlie—are you listening?"

Charlie nods.

"Charlie, none of this is your fault. And it's not Elizabeth's fault or your mom's fault or your dad's fault. Sometimes grown-ups don't agree about things, and sometimes they ask judges to help them make decisions. I know your parents, and I know they both want what's best for you and Elizabeth. No one is trying to punish you for anything you said or didn't say."

The doorbell rings. "That must be them," Tilly says. "I know they'll be so happy to see you. And, Charlie, remember—not your fault. Got it?"

Charlie nods, silently.

Tilly picks Charlie up off her lap, gives her a kiss, walks down the hallway, and opens the front door.

"She's fine," Charlie hears Tilly say. "But she's blaming herself for everything that's happened. You two need to get it together. Here's advice that you didn't ask for: Jake, keep it in your pants when your kids are around. Lisa, you're my best friend, and you know I love you to pieces. But you need to lighten up about all this. And keep your phone away from your kids."

"What do you mean?" Charlie hears her dad ask.

"Never mind," Tilly says. "None of your business and not important. Now both of you go in there and get your girl."

45

Judge Jones: Reconsidered

"Judge!" Melinda calls out from her desk. "Guess what just arrived? And on the thirtieth day, of course." Not waiting for an answer, she continues. "Remember the *Naudain* case? That one where the dad had his poor little daughter sleeping in bed with him and the naked girlfriend? That hippie chick, who Cowboy Boyle subpoenaed on rebuttal, and she ratted out the dad?"

"I remember the case," says Judge Jones, walking out of her chambers and hanging her robe up on the hook by Melinda's desk in the anteroom. "Quite well, in fact. I ran into the father's lawyer the other weekend in my neighborhood—Ms. Ackerman. She mentioned in passing that she might be filing for reconsideration. Is that what we received?"

"She mentioned that to you when you saw her? So much for the rule against *ex parte* communications. But yeah, that's what she did. It's a Petition for Reconsideration, time-stamped at 4:30 p.m. today. She squeaked it in just under the wire. Seeking . . . lemme see . . . reinstatement of shared custody. Says you made a mistake in changing the custodial schedule based on an incident the child had no recollection of, and she cites some case from 2010 I never heard of that supposedly supports that. Says your order is not in the best interests of the children because the rem-

edy should be to prohibit the conduct, not change the entire custody schedule. She's asking . . . um . . . here it is. She's asking for a
reinstatement of the previous order for alternating custodial
weeks with a restriction on any paramours—oh my God, she's
actually using that word, Judge! What century is this, anyway?
—a restriction on any paramours sleeping at Dad's house, then
re-list the case for status in six months to evaluate if there's a
continuing need for the restriction. Well, I'll tell you this, Judge
—you didn't make any mistake. You did the right thing in that
case. You're going to deny the petition, right?"

Well, didn't this work out just perfectly? thinks the judge. This
is exactly what she had discussed with Jacey and what she now
believed to be the right outcome. Maybe it had been a little unusual to give Ms. Ackerman a gentle nudge the other day, but
there was nothing wrong with it, really. She didn't mention the
substance of the case, after all, just a quick passing reference to
the procedure. Attorney Boyle would have to be afforded the
opportunity to respond, but unless there was some new bomb-
shell, this was the order she would put in place.

"Melinda," she says, "I know you had strong feelings about
this case, and you were very persuasive on the day of the trial,
but I have been thinking about it since, and I have to say that I
am inclined to agree with the position being advanced by Ms.
Ackerman. Upon further reflection, I do think that a drastic
change in custody was too extreme when the conduct in question—which, as far as I could tell, the little girl did not even remember—can just be prohibited."

"Judge, how do you know she didn't remember it?" asks
Melinda. "You couldn't get her to talk about anything. She wasn't
able to testify one way or the other."

Oh, for heaven's sake, thinks Judge Jones, *this is a court of law,
and rules of evidence do apply.*

"Exactly," she says to her agitated law clerk. "There was no admissible evidence presented by anyone that she remembered the incident at all. The Court can't just decide that she did. But no matter what, I now believe it makes more sense to take a surgical approach here, to remove the source of the problem by prohibiting the father from having girlfriends stay at his home overnight when the children are with him, rather than overhaul the custody schedule. Because, as I recall, Melinda, the parties had agreed to a joint custody arrangement, and there was no evidence that there had been any problems with it before this happened. And, if you're about to remind me," the judge says, as Melinda is opening her mouth to speak, "that Dad missed a ballet recital or some such event, which I believe Mom testified to, don't bother. I do not care about that at all. The only reason I changed the schedule to every other weekend was because of Dad's extremely poor decision to bring the child in bed to sleep with him and his girlfriend when at least one, if not both of them, were naked."

"And don't forget that he lied about that, under oath, Judge!" says Melinda. "One thing you gotta give hippie chick—she had no problem telling the truth. But he lied, remember? He said he never took the kid in bed with them. He perjured himself, Judge. C'mon. And now you're going to reward him for that?"

"I don't see it as rewarding him, Melinda. How he feels about it is not my concern. We need to determine what's best for the Naudain children, and I do believe the approach proposed by Mr. Naudain's lawyer is better tailored to their needs."

And also, the judge thinks but does not choose to share with her law clerk, if she were to deny the petition, the father might appeal that decision. She could end up being overturned, which she really does not want on her record so early in what will hopefully be a long and successful tenure on the bench.

She dreads the thought of becoming the subject of one of those Superior Court opinions that describe, in disapproving or condescending terms, what the trial judge did wrong. Opinions that are published, that are read by lawyers who will be appearing before her, that might be perused by journalists in search of a juicy story. Suppose, for example, the same judge who wrote the opinion in the 2010 case cited by Ms. Ackerman was assigned to the appeal and took personal offense that his or her ruling had not been followed? The thought makes her shudder. No, she does not want that kind of reputation. She needs to be careful and strategic about her career. Changing the order is right for the children and right for her professionally, and now she has the perfect opportunity to do it.

Melinda sighs. "Okay, okay, Your Honor, I got it. That's why you wear the robe. But I think you're way off base on this one. That guy's a sleazebag, and those little girls are better off living with their mom."

"Understood," says the judge. "We shall agree to disagree. It won't be the first time, dear. Monday morning, please contact both counsel, let them know that Mr. Boyle has twenty days to respond, if he chooses to do so. If he does not respond, I will be granting the petition and entering the order requested by Ms. Ackerman. If he does respond, I will schedule oral argument on the request for reconsideration. But, Melinda, please keep in mind that even if Attorney Boyle does file a response opposing the petition, I am very likely to grant the relief requested by Attorney Ackerman. I am certainly not suggesting you say that directly to Attorney Boyle, as that would be inappropriate, but if there is a subtle way to communicate that to him, I trust you'll do so."

Subtlety not being Melinda's strong suit, the judge is nevertheless satisfied with her instructions to her law clerk and heads out the door looking forward to a pleasant weekend.

46

Ellen: Call of Duty

Jake answers his phone on the first ring. "Ellen! Hi. I was just going to call you. I got a copy today of that petition you sent to Judge Jones asking her to give me back the girls. I was blown away. It was awesome. What made you do that? I thought the only thing I could do was appeal to the other court."

"I decided to do this at the last minute," Ellen says. "It was a long shot, but I happened to come across a case I was not previously familiar with, which I thought helped your position, and I felt professionally obligated to file this petition for you. Even though I absolutely do not plan to represent you going forward—for obvious reasons. And even though you owe me money. I thought this case could possibly be a basis for Judge Jones to change her order, and I am still your counsel of record, so I felt I didn't have a choice in the matter. I wrote the petition the night before the appeal deadline and filed it."

This narrative, carefully crafted during Ellen's drive to work and rehearsed out loud during the breaks in *Morning Edition*, satisfies her goal of portraying herself as both the martyr and the hero, which is her consolation prize for staying up until 2:00 a.m. researching and writing the request for reconsideration the night before it was due. She is a martyr and a hero, as far as Jake is concerned, and a shining light of professional ethics to her

husband. Let Dan be the one to engage in moral relativism, not
her. She had struggled with the conflict and taken the path of
righteousness. She did what she was required to do by the rules
she must follow as a licensed member of the bar. She envisions
herself as a character in a television law show, the lawyer who is
uncompromising in her ethical duties even to her most odious
client.

"Wow, Ellen, I don't know how to thank you enough. Even if
nothing comes of it, I really appreciate you sticking up for me
like this."

"To be clear, Jake, I did this because it was my duty as your
lawyer. Not because I personally felt like sticking up for you. As
you know, I don't."

"Okay, right. But whatever, I really appreciate it."

"You're going to appreciate it even more when I tell you
what I just learned from Judge Jones's law clerk. Yesterday she
notified me and Boyle that the judge would give him twenty
days to respond, and if he didn't, she would be changing her order to the one I proposed in the petition without any kind of a
hearing. This morning, I get a call from Boyle—which is so unlike him, I have no idea why he contacted me about this instead
of keeping me hanging—telling me that, against his advice, Lisa
has decided that she doesn't want to fight you on this, and she's
okay with the order I proposed. Which means you go back to
the same week-on, week-off custody schedule, the only difference being it will now include a restriction that you can't have
any girlfriends, or boyfriends, I guess—I actually used the term
"paramours" since Boyle has such a fondness for it—sleep over
during your custodial time. And the case will be re-listed for status, which essentially means a check-in type hearing, six months
from now. At that time, Judge Jones will evaluate whether the
no-sleepover restriction needs to remain in place."

"What? Are you serious, Ellen? Are you telling me Lisa agrees to this? After everything she put me and the girls through, now she's decided it was all a mistake? I mean, it's so great that I get them back, that's amazing, but I can't believe how she just did a complete one-eighty, like it was nothing. And this restriction thing, on the sleepovers, for six months, that applies to both of us, right?

"No, it doesn't. It just applies to you. And from what I gathered from Boyle, Lisa had already been thinking about backing away from the every-other-weekend schedule because your daughters were not happy with it." And, according to Boyle, Lisa had also told him that maybe this would turn out to be the quote, unquote, "wake-up call" Jake needed in order to get his act together. But there was no reason to share this tidbit with Jake. It would make him mad, and therefore make the phone call longer.

"No shit. They were totally unhappy with it, and we've been dealing with this whole mess at school with Elizabeth where she was bullying another girl and stuff. And then Charlie literally ran away from school and was missing for hours. It's been a total shit show. Which I completely blame Lisa for, because she caused this entire thing—she blew something she heard, or maybe she didn't even hear, way out of proportion. And in terms of the new custody order, Ellen, why should Lisa be allowed to have a boyfriend or whatever sleep over, if I can't? Shouldn't it be mutual? It doesn't seem fair."

This man's lack of insight is truly stunning, Ellen thinks. "Let me spell this out for you, Jake. It's fair because Lisa didn't have Charlie in bed with her naked polyamorous boyfriend. And I really cannot believe you're even asking me this question."

"Okay, okay, sorry," Jake says. "I'm not going to argue with you. I'm so grateful to you, Ellen. I can't even begin to tell you how much this means to me."

"Understood. But as I said before, I filed the petition solely out of professional obligation. I expect you to find other counsel to represent you at the status hearing in six months, and I expect you to pay my bill as soon as you can. I'll send you a copy of the new custody order as soon as I receive it from chambers. Good-bye, Jake."

After hanging up the call, Ellen immediately dials Dan's cell. She can't wait to tell him about the outcome of the case. She did her duty in the face of adversity and was totally vindicated by the judge's response. She can practically feel the halo hovering over her head. And the icing on the cake is that, while she has no further obligation to the immoral Jake Naudain, he will be forever grateful to her and will undoubtedly sing her praises far and wide to anyone in need of a family lawyer. It really could not be a more perfect ending.

47

Pinky: Car Ride

My couch is on the sunporch. It's soft and fluffy. I sleep on it during the day when no one's home. I'm not supposed to sleep on it, but when any of my humans come home, I'm not on that couch anyway. I'm waiting at the door. I'm waiting there because I love them so much! When Lisa comes home, she feeds me, and then she puts on my leash and takes me for a walk. Sometimes we go to the park, and she takes the leash off so I can run. When I smell her outside, I get so excited.

But today when she comes home, she doesn't go into the kitchen where my bowls are, and she doesn't take me for a walk. Elizabeth and Charlie are with her, and they are all talking to each other. Only Charlie pets me. They all keep talking, standing in the living room, and then Elizabeth and Charlie run upstairs. Lisa sits down on the other couch. She is very quiet, and she doesn't move. I try to show her that she should go into the kitchen to feed me because it is time to do that, but she isn't looking at me or touching me. She is just sitting, not doing anything.

Elizabeth and Charlie come down the stairs with the bags they wear on their backs and the ones they hold in their hands. Lisa stands up, gets my leash out of the closet, and attaches it to my collar. She opens the front door, and Elizabeth and Charlie go running to the car. I love the car! Elizabeth gets in the front. Lisa puts me in the back with Charlie, and then she gets in, and the car starts to move. I put my head in Charlie's lap like I always do, and Charlie strokes my ears like she always does.

When the car stops, Lisa doesn't get out, but Elizabeth and Charlie do. Elizabeth takes my leash and helps me jump out of the car. I know where we are. We're at Jake's house. The door opens, and Jake comes out. He puts his arms around Elizabeth and Charlie for a long time, and then he bends down, put his hands on both sides of my head, and kisses me on my nose. I love Jake's kisses!

Jake walks over to the car and leans his head in the window. He and Lisa are talking and talking. Elizabeth and Charlie are trying to get his attention. They didn't get to eat, either. Then he stands up and says, "Thank you so much, Lisa." The car starts to move, and then Lisa is gone. He walks over to us and kisses Charlie and Elizabeth and says, "Girls, I'm so happy you're back."

And Charlie says, "Me too, Daddy, and we get to stay for the whole week."

And he says, "Yes, yes," and then we all go upstairs to his house. I go right to the bowls Jake keeps for me on his kitchen floor. They're dry and empty, but they still smell so good! I sit down next to them and bark and bark and bark so Jake will know to feed me.

Epilogue:
June, Three Years After

The sun is shining, and the azaleas are resplendent in their shocking shades of pink as Judge Jones approaches the Green Life Café, dressed appropriately for a summer Saturday morning in tan pants, black flats, and a matching shell and cardigan. A younger woman, sitting in the back of the café with a book and a cup of something, smiles and waves at her.

"Jacey! There you are! I didn't see you at first," says the judge, making her way past the coffee line.

"Aunt Andi!" the younger woman says, standing up and giving the judge a hug. "You look fantastic! I guess the move out of family court has really agreed with you." The judge puts her handbag on the table, tugs her cardigan down over her hips, and smiles at her niece.

"It certainly has," she says. "Honey, I do not miss the fist-fights, or the cursing in the waiting room, or all those tears and drama in my courtroom. And I don't miss feeling like I was expected to be judge and lawyer and social worker all rolled into one. Civil is so different. My hours are shorter, and my cases are so much less stressful. The parties all have lawyers, and most of my list is jury trials, so I don't even have to make the final call, which is just fine with me. Believe me, Jacey, I struggled with enough hard decisions in my four years in family to last me a lifetime. Let the jury deliberate over the amount an insurance company is going to have to pay. And guess what? I actually get to take a lunch hour every day!"

Both women smile. "Auntie, that's great. You deserve it! Sit down, and let me get you a cup of tea. Hibiscus?"

"That would be lovely," says the judge, as she takes a tissue out of her handbag and wipes the crumbs off the seat behind her before slowly sitting down.

In the front of the café, next to the windows, a blonde woman in a pale pink tank top sits alone at a table, nursing a tall iced coffee, and intently writing on a laptop. After a flurry of typing she looks up, drains her glass, and closes her computer. Taking a flyer out of a floppy black leather bag, she stands up and walks toward a crowded bulletin board in the back of the café.

"Lisa!" calls Jacey, rising to greet the woman with the flyer. "Great to see you! Do you live in Greenwood?"

"I do," says Lisa Naudain. "Right down the street. I don't think we've seen each other since that last community relations meeting at Turner. How are you? And what brings you over here?"

"All good with me," says Jacey. "And I'm here visiting with my aunt Andi. She lives near here too."

"Nice to meet you, Andi," she says. "I'm a big fan of your niece's. She knows how to make a roomful of doctors who think they're the most important people in the world shut up and listen."

Judge Jones shifts uncomfortably in her seat and smiles at Lisa. "I'm sure she does," she says. "She's been that way since she was a little girl."

"Jacey," Lisa says, turning back to the younger woman, "so glad we ran into each other. I've been meaning to get in touch with you about this community health project I'm involved with in Haiti. I've been going down there for the last three years with a doctor colleague and some other nurses from the hospital. We work with a Haitian medical team and do vaccinations and other primary care for moms and kids out in the countryside. We just got a grant to build a clinic, and we're looking for people to come down and help with the construction. Here, take a copy of this flyer. We're having an info session at Greenwood Unitarian next Sunday."

"Wow," says Jacey. "You go, girl. That's great. Will circulate."

"Thanks," says Lisa. "Really appreciate it. We need all the help we can get, and there's only so much I can do personally. I got divorced a few years ago—did you know that? Anyway, it's tough juggling stuff like this with everything I need to do to take care of my girls."

"I can only imagine," says Jacey. "No new Mr. Wonderful in your life?"

"No," says Lisa. "I mean, not really."

"Hmm," says Jacey. "Better work on that. And also make sure that ex-husband of yours is pulling his weight."

"Yeah, well, if you figure out how I can make Jake do that, please let me know."

Jacey laughs. "You know all about that stuff, don't you, Aunt Andi?" she says, turning toward the judge. Murmuring something noncommittal and looking intently down at her tea, the judge smiles and nods her head.

Lisa gives Jacey a quick hug and pins her flyer in a prominent place on the bulletin board, crowded up against an offer of ukulele lessons and a seeker of roommates for a pet-free, vegan household. She heads out into the summer day.

Outside, three middle-aged women are sitting at a café table, all dressed for various athletic endeavors they may or may not have partaken of earlier in the morning. Lying at the feet of one of the women is an elderly, curly-haired, spanielly sort of a dog, napping soundly in the morning sun.

"So, Ellen, what's Marni doing this summer?" one of the women, wearing a baseball cap, asks her friend with the dog.

"Mostly she seems to be sleeping until noon," says Ellen Ackerman. "Which, given that she's now a college graduate, supposedly ready to live on her own and be self-supporting, is a bit concerning. She does have an internship at a startup doing something I don't understand, and I've hired her to do some office work at my firm, which she can barely hide her disdain for. You know, I'm happy to have her home, of course, but it's not that easy. She regresses the minute she walks in the door."

The woman in the baseball cap laughs, and the third woman, stretching out long legs encased in shimmery green running tights, nods, adding that her Emma is exactly the same way.

"How are things at your firm, Ellen?" asks Running Tights. "I know you were concerned after Marni left for college that you'd just end up working all the time. Has it turned out that way?"

"Yes and no," Ellen says, "I definitely work longer hours, but I've been trying to focus more on the types of cases I really like, so I actually feel better about work than I did a few years ago. The main thing that happened is that I made a decision, right around the time Marni started college, to stop taking custody cases. I never really liked them, but they started to bother me more and more. I just got so burnt out from dealing with the bad things parents do to their kids, and the arbitrary decisions judges make, and how I would get caught up in it all. I guess I finally came to the realization that I can turn down certain types of cases if I want; no one's making me take them."

Baseball Cap and Running Tights nod appreciatively, commenting on the perks of working for oneself. To which Ellen responds by pointing out the downside of not getting a regular paycheck, which, they all have to agree, is certainly a negative.

"Ladies," Ellen says, standing up from the table and startling the dog out of his blissful slumber, "it's been lovely getting to catch up with you both, but I have to get home. I have a date with Sleeping Beauty to go shopping, to get her a dress for my nephew's wedding. She wants me involved because she needs me to pay for it, and I want to be involved so she doesn't pick something totally inappropriate." Cheek kisses are exchanged, and the group disbands.

As Ellen coaxes her elderly dog up off the warm sidewalk, Jake Naudain comes into view, strolling down the sidewalk toward the café in shorts, flip-flops, and a Rolling Stones T-shirt. "Hi, Ellen," he says, bending down to greet the dog. "Chester, right?"

"Good memory," says Ellen. "I'm impressed. I can't say I remember your dog's name."

"Pinky," says Jake. "Unfortunately, he's no longer with us. We had to put him down last year. He had cancer."

"So sorry to hear that. Such a sad thing. How did your girls take it?"

"They were devastated—beside themselves. And now they're obsessed with the idea that we, meaning me, should get a puppy. So we'll see—I don't think I can deal with a puppy, but I do want to get another dog. I really miss Pinky."

"I know what you mean," Ellen said. "Chester's a nuisance to take care of at this point because he's so old and he has so many medicines and stuff, but I can't stand the thought of him not being around. I feel like he understands everything that's going on; he feels what everyone in the house is feeling. I realize that sounds like one of those annoying animal spirt-y things to say, so keep it to yourself, okay?"

Jake smiles. "My lips are sealed. I won't out you as my former lawyer turned crazy dog person. And I agree with you. That's definitely how I felt about Pinky. He was kind of like the family glue, especially after Lisa and I split."

The safe territory of dog conversation exhausted, Jake and Ellen shuffle awkwardly from foot to foot until Jake takes his leave, pleading a dire and immediate need for caffeine.

Jake walks in the open door of the café and takes his place in the coffee line. Two fortyish women sitting at a table look up at him, put their heads close, and giggle. Outside, a very attractive young mother with long dark hair and a short skirt walks toward the café door, holding the hand of a charming little boy wearing tiny Converse sneakers and clutching a stuffed walrus. As they come through the door, Jake freezes.

"Samara!" he says. "I thought you moved to West Philly. How are you? And is this—"

"Hi, Jake," says the lovely mom, with a wide smile. "This is my son, Cedar. He'll be three in July. And we did move to West Philly, but we missed Greenwood a lot, so we're moving back here. We're looking at some houses to rent today, actually. Hey, how old is Elizabeth now?"

Jake is staring intently at little Cedar. He looks up at Samara, down at Cedar again, and then up at Samara.

"Fifteen," he finally says. "Elizabeth is fifteen."

"That's what I thought," says Samara. "Does she ever baby-sit?"

Acknowledgments

My first book, a work of non-fiction about my daily life as a family lawyer, was published a decade ago. Soon afterwards I decided to start working on a second book because I had so much fun the first time around. I figured I would make the task easier for myself, and therefore even more enjoyable, by writing a novel because I could just make everything up and not have to worry about the accuracy of the stories I was telling or changing facts to protect clients' identities.

My ignorance of what it would actually take to create a novel was breathtaking. Fortunately, it was immediately apparent to me, some thirty pages in. Even though I didn't have a clue how to write fiction, I did know how to ask for help, and I received it, in spades. The thank you list starts with my good friend, the terrific novelist Jon McGoran, who patiently explained basic concepts to me like point of view and tense, and edited the first version of *Every Other Weekend*; my previous editor at Algonquin Books, Amy Gash, who was an early reader and connected me with my lovely and tenacious agent, Stacey Glick; the fantastic developmental editor Sarah Branham, who really got this project and improved it so significantly with her excellent editorial work; and Brooke Warner and the team at She Writes Press who made it all come together with their expert guidance, professionalism, and stunning cover design. Thank you all, so very much.

I also want to give a special thanks to my colleague Sandy Ford and the Bookends, a wonderful book group of astute women readers, together since 2003 and now expanded to two generations, who enthusiastically read an early version of the book and gave me detailed and extremely helpful feedback. Their reactions and suggestions really helped shape the story it is today.

And, my family. To my daughters, Zoe Metcalfe-Klaw and Robin Metcalfe-Klaw, thank you for being my consistent champions and helpful readers from the beginning. To my husband, Alan Metcalfe, there are really no words to express my love and gratitude for your constant encouragement since you read the earliest draft of the manuscript and the multiple iterations which followed. Thank you for your unwavering support and sincere enthusiasm about this book, and for your relentless one-man public relations campaign among our friends and neighbors.

Finally, the setting of *Every Other Weekend*, the Philadelphia neighborhood I call "Greenwood," which is in fact my beloved West Mount Airy, is the source of my inspiration and amusement. The scenes set in the neighborhood cafe, school, yoga studio, food co-op, band practice, and basketball court, as well as a gritty courtroom in Center City, while fictitious, are intended to reflect the fabric and texture of the lives we—my family, my friends, my kids' friends, my clients, my forever bonded COVID pod—live in this community, and the lives of so many others in communities like it all around the country.

About the Author

MARGARET KLAW is a writer, a lawyer, and a founding partner of BKW Family Law, an all-women law firm in Philadelphia. Named a Preeminent Woman Lawyer by Martindale-Hubbell, she has been recognized by *Best Lawyers in America* and designated a Pennsylvania "Super Lawyer" in the area of family law. Starting with day-in-the-life vignettes about practicing family law published in *HuffPost*, she has written for *The Wall Street Journal, The Washington Post, Time,* and *Salon* and is the author of *Keeping it Civil: The Case of the Pre-Nup and the Porsche & Other True Accounts from the Files of a Family Lawyer* (Algonquin Books, 2013). *Every Other Weekend* is her first work of fiction.

SELECTED TITLES FROM SHE WRITES PRESS

She Writes Press is an independent publishing company founded to serve women writers everywhere. Visit us at www.shewritespress.com.

Wishful Thinking by Kamy Wicoff. $16.95, 978-1-63152-976-4. A divorced mother of two gets an app on her phone that lets her be in more than one place at the same time, and quickly goes from zero to hero in her personal and professional life—but at what cost?

A Marriage in Four Seasons: A Novel by Kathryn K. Abdul-baki. $16.95, 978-1-63152-427-1. When New York couple Joy and Richard experience a devastating stillbirth, the must navigate the repercussions of their loss—including infidelity, divorce, and an illegitimate child—before finally reconciling.

Other Fires by Lenore H. Gay. $16.95, 978-1-63152-773-9. Joss and Phil's already rocky marriage is fragmented when, after being injured in a devastating fire, Phil begins to call Joss an imposter. Faced with a husband who no longer recognizes her, Joss struggles to find motivation to save their marriage, even as family secrets start to emerge that challenge everything she thought she knew.

So Happy Together by Deborah K. Shepherd. $16.95, 978-1-64742-026-0. In Tucson in the 1960s, drama students Caro and Peter are inseparable, but Caro ends up marrying someone else. Twenty years and three children later, with her marriage failing, Caro drops the kids off at summer camp and sets out on a road trip to find Peter, her creative spirit, and her true self.

Our Love Could Light the World by Anne Leigh Parrish. $15.95, 978-1-93831-444-5. Twelve stories depicting a dysfunctional and chaotic—yet lovable—family that has to band together in order to survive.

Peregrine Island by Diane B. Saxton. $16.95, 978-1-63152-151-5. The Peregrine family's lives are turned upside-down one summer when so-called "art experts" appear on the doorstep of their Connecticut island home to appraise a favorite heirloom painting—and incriminating papers are discovered behind the painting in question.